Beyond These Woods

MARK ROGER BAILEY

A NOVEL

ISBN-10: 0989940667
ISBN-13: 978-0-9899406-6-5

www.markrogerbailey.com

To Lenore

ACKNOWLEDGMENTS

Special thanks to the molecular biology sciences communities in La Jolla, CA, Woods Hole Research Center in Falmouth, MA and the Centers for Disease Control in Atlanta, GA for their tireless dedication to the life sciences. And to the U.S. National Park Service staff of Sequoia and Kings Canyon National Parks for preserving and protecting one of the most extraordinary high elevation forest ecosystems on earth.

Beyond These Woods

1

THUNDER PEAK, CA

The night was bone cold with just enough moonlight for Sara Hart to see enormous tree trunks rise into the star-filled sky.

As she moved, massive old-growth trees materialized into view briefly and then melted into shadow again. They had outlived fire, ice and, until now, man. Unlike Melville's white whale, these natural wonders had nowhere to hide. Rooted in place, they could not defend themselves, so she and Gabriel would defend them.

She breathed in shallow, measured inhalations of the thinning Thunder Peak air. Remembering how Gabriel looked three hours earlier, his red hair rimmed in firelight, she rededicated herself to be brave and pure like him. During their months together, she had learned to walk quietly in the forest, read the winds, and seek vantage points. Unlike so many men before him, Gabriel had looked past her green eyes, her beauty, and her wealth. He looked beyond these aspects and into her soul. He filled every void left by her privileged past and showed her the true nature of life. Gabriel's purity of purpose was the antithesis of her father's corporate whirl.

Moonlight burned through the drifting mist and revealed a vast, silent world. Dark forms melted into distant gloom. A glare on the ground revealed the bend of a small stream. Condensation dripped from a high branch and splashed impact on the forest floor. Sara adjusted her backpack and deftly crossed to the opposite bank.

The earth was deep, rich, and fragrant. Small hay-colored puffball mushrooms dotted the ground.

"*Who--?*" a voice came from behind her.

She stifled an involuntary gasp and spun around to face the sound.

Hhooo-hoo, *hooo!* A Great Horned Owl's shadow lifted into the night.

She shivered and wished Gabriel was with her. She wanted to do this right. Yet he had convinced her that she was ready to help mother earth. *Get moving.* Go, *GO!*

Ponderosas gave way to a stand of Douglas Firs. And finally, at about 7,000 feet elevation she found the small stand of giant sequoia, sentries from millennia past standing watch over the southwestern slope of the Sierras. She hadn't seen trees this large since California's Humboldt stand of coastal redwoods. This was the place. *It had to be.* Starlight glimmered through the canopy 300 feet over her head and glinted in her eyes.

She stopped in a clearing among the cathedral of giants and eased out of her backpack, set it against a tree and opened it. Inside was a honeycomb of five-inch cardboard cylinders.

You can do this – one every ten feet around the largest trees. Remember, Sara, in wildness is the preservation of the world, he had quoted Thoreau. Such a statement would have been pretentious in another context, yet coming as it did in Gabriel's clear, rising tone, it was as right as a breath of wind.

She extracted a jug from her shoulder bag and poured a stream of tea-colored hormonal slurry in a circle around the largest giant sequoia, and over the forest floor, mushrooms, needles and sprouts of diverse plants trying for their place in these high woods. Next she troweled a shallow depression in the damp, aromatic soil among a patch of mushrooms with star-patterned outer fruit body tissue extending from the base of their puffballs. Into the depression she poured more of the brownish liquid over the delicate web of subsurface mycelium mushroom root structure. She pulled one of the cylinders from the honeycomb in the backpack, carefully twisted off the cap, and inverted the cylinder over the hole she had dug, pressed it down and lifted it straight up in one unbroken motion, revealing a puffball similar to, yet sharing little in common with, the native variety. After recapping the empty cylinder, she put it back in the tray, bottom up. She pushed soil into the hole around the fungi and tamped it precisely.

What you do tonight, Sara, will save the world.

She repeated the action every ten feet in a wide circle around the largest tree, a 2,000-year-old matriarch born the year that Caesar led his army across the Rubicon. Working quickly, silently, she moved on to other trees until her pack was empty.

The final planting was more mature than the others; its sporophore - the earthstar's distinctive cap, or *pileus* - was large and swollen. She took a moment to admire it. Seeping cold and a growing sense of relief were making her clumsy. She slowed to be careful, warming at the thought of Gabriel, and tamped down the loose earth around the last mushroom.

Hhooo-*HOOOT!*

Looking up, she saw the owl on a high branch.

Her glove brushed the puffball, which trembled and ejected a small puff of microscopic spores a few feet into the moonlight. She leapt back, lost her footing and stumbled amid shadows. She tried to rise again and flee but it was too late. She was running in a dream, growing stiff, her limbs unresponsive.

Her vision irised down to a narrow tunnel. The mist from her final breath dissipated before her unbelieving stare. Soon, the silvered night darkened around that, too.

2

GREENWICH, CT

The vibration in Lotte Keene's coat pocket distracted her again.

Standing on a crest in St. Michael's cemetery overlooking the city, she was distantly aware of early snow slipping between the pines. Large flakes melted into her tears while a soft blanket formed on the cold bronze casket in the grave below.

She lifted her face, grateful for the sensation on her skin. Charley would have appreciated the sensuality of it.

Grayness rose from the pit, flat as the light above. She discovered that her right hand was bleeding where it had squeezed the *Bullata's* stem. Her blood dripped onto the snow. She released the rose and watched it slide off the rounded casket lid, down to the root-tangled wall of freshly excavated earth.

Nature always wins, Charley used to say when the mystery of disease, an unexpected death, an undiagnosable outbreak defied their science. *Always,* she'd say quietly to Lotte even as her mind worked on the problem, *no exceptions.*

After a respectful interval, two laborers filled the grave and left Lotte alone at the earthen mound.

Lotte had never been susceptible to such poetic notions of hope's abandonment. Nature was all encompassing. Hell, Nature was everything, including science. She could never see disease as a problem of nature; it was merely a symptom, a characteristic, a behavior. A necessary process resulting from imbalance of one kind or another. Her mission was to learn enough about it to recalibrate the elements and restore a semblance of balance. When Charley was stricken, Lotte had not been perceptive enough, smart enough, or sufficiently quick to tip the scales in Charley's favor in time to save her. Lotte's chest tightened and tears flooded her freckled cheeks. A moan escaped her throat and she tried to breathe.

Her cell phone vibrated and stopped again.

A breeze whispered through the branches overhead and dropped a pinecone that rolled to a rest over Charley's heart six feet below. The world was suddenly an empty place now that that heart no longer beat.

The vibration started again. She pulled the phone from her pocket and recognized the number: the office on the third floor of the Centers For Disease Control in Atlanta. Three weeks since Itamarati and not a word.

"Lotte?"

"Where the hell are you?" she asked angrily. Her voice rang impotently in the wintry silence.

"Atlanta. Listen—"

"No, *you* listen, Professor! You should be here!"

"I couldn't, Lotte."

"Work can wait!" It was one of the things that separated them. She could never be a CDC functionary. A loose, on-call arrangement was as much of a commitment as she could make. They didn't pay her benefits and she didn't have to censor good science for career advancement. "This is Charley, for God's sake."

There was a pause on the line. "I'm sorry. I really am," he began to explain. His precise male timbre still had the power to touch her.

"What do you want?" she began to pace.

"There's been an event on the Kamchatka Peninsula near Dalni. CIA and NSA suspect the worst. I need your take on the imagery."

"No," she answered firmly, "and screw you for asking."

"The Joint Chiefs are rattling my cage. Lotte, —"

"You're the one who traded in the academy for the government teat." She ended the call, and refocused on Charley.

It vibrated again.

She walked to the foot of the grave. The phone persisted. Ignoring it was useless. She answered, "No way, Vin."

"Lotte, I need you--"

"And we needed YOU! How could you not come to Charley's funeral, you heartless bastard?"

"Because *I* don't have the luxury of choosing which crises I respond to."

"There's always a situation somewhere."

"It's different this time."

"Why?!"

"Because this outbreak is headed straight for us. Washington has its finger up its nose and YOU'RE the only one who can tell me what the hell it is!"

"You're damn right, I'm the only one and I am not going to play this game right now!"

She hung up the phone again.

They had been the 'Crickets.' Lotte the crusader for whom life was a passion and a struggle. Charlotte Goodwin, the beautiful, high-spirited daughter of Greenwich privilege. Best friends since college, they had shared their hopes, dreams, victories and failures in a tiny off-campus walk-up. Professor Vin der Root, the gangly Texan with the southern polish, was their mentor and had knighted his two student protégés in honor of Sir Francis Crick, the manic scientist who, with Dr. Francis Watson, unlocked the secret of life itself in the discovery of DNA's double helix structure. Lotte and Charley shared internships on the biotech frontiers at Chembotan and parallel career tracks in epidemiology and biochemistry. Now, Charley was six feet under Greenwich and Lotte stood on the edge of nowhere.

The phone vibrated and she raised it again to her ear. "Dammit, I just watched Charley being put in the ground."

"You answered."

The truth stung like a slap in the face.

"Come down here. I'll get you into NSA at Ft. Meade."

She bristled at the thought of being back in Maryland under the spooks' observation. She belonged in Boulder. She could either jump to his request or risk losing access to CDC resources.

Checking her watch, she saw that she had just enough time to catch United's 3:00 pm flight to Denver. If she left now, she could be back by early evening.

"You should have been here. She deserved better from you."

"I know."

"I can't talk to you right now. I'm going home." She hung up and turned back to Charlotte.

"He's moving up, getting what he wants, as usual," she said to her dead friend. "You're home. I hope it's what you wanted," she sighed. She and Charlotte had been so close; not as close as rumors hinted, but close enough to finish each other's sentences and entrust life's secrets. "I know," she echoed Charley's signature parting line, "'don't miss me too much.'"

She turned toward Boulder as the afternoon light slid to a deathly hue and walked toward her car. Every step was a fresh ache.

3

BOULDER, CO

At her home above town on the border of Rocky Mountain National Park, Lotte found three messages from der Root on the answering machine. She ignored them, caught a few hours of sleep and went to her laboratory to regain a sense of control. Science never let her down.

At her office in the Centers for Disease Control (CDC) - Division of Global Disease Detection and Emergency Response (GDDER) Satellite Monitoring & Analysis Facility at the University of Colorado - Boulder, it was his message on her voice mail that persuaded her to call him back. Space-based American strategic assets had detected a pattern of toxicity spreading east from Dalni on Russia's Kamchatkan Peninsula. CIA, NSA, DOD, and now the White House were clamoring for an accurate reading on the source and a forecast about its arrival in North America. der Root was on the hunt for glory and Lotte was the scout who knew how to read the clues. He was tied in knots with anticipation of the moment when he could declare from his personal Mount Sinai his authentic revelation.

During the Cold War, the Russians had a chilling interest in the Machupo virus, the virus that causes Bolivian hemorrhagic fever.

They obtained strains in Bolivia, brought them back to Russia to cultivate as biological weapons and suffered numerous laboratory problems. It had been seven years since the last disaster. This outbreak could signal a dangerous escalation of Russia's biological research.

After reviewing the data from NASA's newest satellite, BIOSAT-7, which was currently jointly assigned to CDC and DARPA, she dialed his number. "I've looked at BIOSAT-7's Kamchatka overflight. Where did you get your information?" she asked.

"DOD, CIA," answered der Root. "Why, what have you got for me?"

"Dalni is a mess, all right. However, it's not what the Generals think it is. Foul air, yes. Environmental abuse on a criminal scale, definitely. I'm seeing the limits of human tolerance being pushed far beyond anything we're accustomed to."

"Sudden spike in mortality rates extending east from Dalni in a plume," der Root said deliberately, as if repeating the clues could make his theory a fact. "That coincides with winds that eventually carry all the way to Seattle."

"True," she spun a dial on her console and the image on two of her monitors zoomed in by a factor of 50x. A black line extending west to east took on twists, turns, and various shades of green. She glanced at another monitor, which displayed a 3-D image of winds over the area, from ground induced thermals all the way up to the jet stream, which circled the earth, and eventually swept over Washington State. She pushed a button to display the Dalni and Bystraja River image on a fourth monitor; typed in a series of file names that plotted the deaths over the satellite imagery. They hugged the gradually expanding contours of the river's course across the peninsula. Finally, she pulled the console fader halfway to superimpose the wind pattern over the satellite image and it was only a 45% match. "But the deaths don't match up precisely with the winds," she continued. "I'm sending you the data now."

"Got it. Damn, you're right. That's not airborne or biological. Aren't the warriors supposed to have the best satellites and technology? How could they have botched this? It's the river."

"Has to be. Somebody in Dalni released some very nasty stuff into the Bystraja and everyone downstream is paying with their lives. Sarony, Milkovo, Scapino — it's a mess."

"So it's contamination of the watershed, not an airborne bio agent. That's your analysis?" asked der Root, the stress draining from his voice.

"It's as clear as can be and now you've got the files to prove it."

"Good," he said without much enthusiasm, his disappointment was unmistakable.

"Sorry, this won't exactly get you the corner office with the view," she teased. "Now go stop those cowboys from dropping warheads on Kamchatka's peasants and let me get back to work."

"Thanks, Lotte," he said, chafing at her characteristic lack of respect for his standing.

She hung up as the Aleutian Islands slid west on the monitor like a necklace around a smooth black neck.

4

LONGWOOD, CA

Oren Pocknett's body was as stiff as bronze, yet strangely *ad vivum*, lifelike. Same as the Hart girl a week ago.

When Sheriff Nate Stimson informed the young woman's parents of the California state law requiring a medical examination of all deaths from unnatural causes, Mrs. Hart screamed and Mr. Hart held himself together long enough to extract a commitment from Stimson that he would keep them informed about when the state of California would release Sara's body and how they could retrieve their daughter.

Unfortunately, Miss Sara Todd Hart's beautiful remains had disappeared mysteriously four nights ago. A midnight break-in that wasn't professional, yet efficient. Shattered window glass was found by the back door. Nothing else was disturbed, except for the lock on the door to the refrigerator unit, the missing body and the Longwood Coroner's Office heretofore spotless record for stewarding the human remains in its keeping.

Again Sheriff Stimson had the difficult responsibility of informing the parents when her body went missing. That call was testimony to Stimson's people skills. He somehow found a way to communicate both human sympathy and a veteran cop's strength and commitment to serving their interest during their time of need.

The theft of Sara pre-empted Ben McCandle's autopsy before he could perform it. He had opened a file, made preliminary observations and set up his basement morgue for the procedure the following morning.

At one a.m. last Tuesday, Ben McCandle had a stiff victim. By dawn two days later, she was gone and there was no body to examine.

Until today.

Oren Pocknett still gripped his mountain rifle, index finger on the trigger, right eye intent on the scope. A hunter poised for the kill.

What did that eye see? wondered Ben as he yawned. *Nothing . . . get this over with, McCandle . . . you might get another half hour sleep before the real day begins.*

"Whatever it was got him before he could react," he said in a sleep husky voice as he sprayed Dis-spray disinfectant into all of the body's orifices, his mouth, ears, all his dim openings. "Look at his face - all concentration, no fear."

Nate moved around to the other side of the autopsy table, looked the body over and scratched his jaw. His open jacket revealed a holstered .45 Colt and gleaming silver handcuffs. "Can't let you do it, Ben."

"Look how stiff those arms are." Ben attempted to pry the left hand off the rifle stock. It wouldn't budge.

"No."

"It's *my* name going on the certificate."

"No." Nate studied the corpse from Oren's expression to his thick neck and barrel chest. There was no sign of struggle, nothing foreign on the clothes. "He's full blood, Ben."

"He's a victim."

"Of what?"

"That's what I have to find out."

"You want to be the one to condemn his spirit to wander?"

"'Course not. But if they find out I shined on a rudimentary autopsy, the state will lift my license. I'm finished."

"You're finished with the Ahwahnee Nation if you offend this body."

Ben sighed wearily.

"Can you close his eyes?"

Ben brushed his fingers over Oren's startled, wooden eyelids. He pressed down harder, but they still wouldn't close.

"Dang, that's creepy." Nate stepped back. "Just clean him up . . . see if you can get those arms down to his side or folded over his chest. No casket built can hold him the way he is." Nate moved for the door. "I'll tell Helen and send his boy down to pick him up later this morning."

"Take his long gun."

Ben gripped the wrist while Nate pulled on the rifle barrel from the other side. It took a screwdriver to pry the fingers free. The trigger finger took more time.

"What're you going to put on the wire?" asked Nate as he wedged the screwdriver between Oren's finger and the trigger.

Since the Hantavirus scares in the southwest in '82 and '93, all deaths had to be reported to the State Medical Examiner's office in Fresno or Tulare County, depending on where the disease was detected within 24 hours. This was in Tulare County, but that office had recently been shuttered by the CA state legislature for budgetary reasons. So he would report to Fresno. Regardless, Sacramento and L.A. County would know about it soon enough and then Ben's life would get interesting.

For now, he had to come to decisions and make his report, which required an official opinion about three things: the apparent cause, the mechanism, and the manner of death.

This was to be followed by a detailed autopsy report, but health officials wanted early data to help them spot infectious diseases before they could spread out of control.

Medical and law enforcement opinions about cause of death frequently changed. What first appeared to be an accident turned out to be a murder. What first looked like spontaneous heart failure was actually caused by a new viral strain that *resulted* in heart failure.

"I don't know, heart attack maybe. Infarction, blood poisoning . . . not sure yet."

"What do I say to Helen?" asked Nate, already halfway up the stairs.

"Tell her it's too soon to know."

The Sheriff accepted that and left. His boot steps faded down the gravel walk.

Evidence of injury: *none.*

Central nervous system: *impossible to remove the brain without offending the Ahwahnee's spirit.*

Internal examination of his chest, abdomen, and pelvis: *ditto.*

Toxicology: *negative.*

Ben picked up his digital recorder, pressed the record button, and began, "Case Number 01-003, Oren 'Half Moon' Pocknett. Body is that of a fit and healthy 52-year-old Native American – Ahwahnee – male. Hair is black, and eye, correction, eyes are brown. The body is 72 inches long and weighs 185 pounds." He paused the recorder, set it down on the table, and checked the fingers, hands, elbows, neck, and the knees again. Restarting the recorder, he continued into the microphone, "Rigor mortis is abnormally present throughout the body. Skin is normal; no apparent scars."

He put down the recorder and leaned against his instrument bench.

Nate had said that Oren's son reported him missing the day before yesterday. Kerri Lightfoot didn't see anything unusual in the area when she found him while out running in the woods.

Oren's body exhibited no symptoms of shock, heart disease, or the purple skin associated with lividity.

No signs of stress from strained breathing after his heart stopped.

No sign of relaxed sphincters. Damn near instant rigor mortis; not progressive as should be expected. It was all over within seconds.

Flies had laid eggs in the mouth, nose, and eyes. They would have done so within ten minutes of death. However, none had hatched. There were no maggots feeding on the tissue yet. That meant he had been dead longer than ten minutes but less than 12 hours.

He took the corpse's temperature. 82.1 degrees. Judging loss of body heat at the rate of 1.5 degrees F per hour, Ben estimated he had died eleven hours ago.

What *happened* up there?

If ever an autopsy was needed, now was the time. But Nate was right, Oren Pocknett was full-blooded Ahwahnee. Whether or not he personally cared about his immortal soul, it was a matter of the gravest spiritual significance for the Ahwahnee.

Ben leaned down and sniffed Oren's open mouth. He smelled tobacco. No alcohol.

Raising the recorder, he pressed the red button and continued: "It's my opinion that Oren Pocknett, a 52 year-old male, died as a result of -" He pressed the pause button. How could he provide an opinion that could answer his questions, let alone the questions of the family *and* the state medical examiner in Fresno? He couldn't.

Yet, he had to record something.

What if the death certificate surfaced and caught some bureaucrat's eye?

He released the pause button. "...massive cardiac arrest. Mechanism of death was shock secondary to cardio electrical failure. Manner of death was -" he paused again. This was obscene. Had he slipped so far from his former ideals? Had he sold out to the rural expedient to protect his simple life here? The answer to both was yes, he had to admit. But that's what its all about, right? After Hannah died, he toughened up and became what he had to be: a survivor. So be it. He rewound the last few seconds and finished the sentence, "The manner of death was . . . natural."

He felt the small hairs stir on the back of his neck. Time for a smoke. He ascended the stairs into the chilly night and lit up.

Mars glowed red overhead. Without the glare of city light to haze the sky, he could see the inner workings of the heavens. Life *is* good here beside the National Forest.

He inhaled and visualized the smoke curling into his lungs, migrating into his bloodstream. Above, a satellite glinted as it crossed the Little Dipper.

The stir became an itch and the chill night air burned when he rubbed his neck. *The stout peg on the second vertebra allows the skull to move freely up and down, side to side,* he recalled Dr. Friedman's gross anatomy lecture his first semester at the University of Chicago. Looking at his watch, he saw he needed to get home if he was going to be there before Mary Margaret awakened. She'd expect breakfast with her dad and a ride to school.

High overhead, the satellite observed his movement and registered his body temperature as $-5°C/73°F$, a $+15°C/41°F$ differential from the ambient air temperature.

He crushed out his cigarette and returned downstairs to get Oren's body ready for his son.

5

BOULDER

BIOSAT-7 » »»SPCT ZULU: 10:07 LIMA: 01:07 14-10-13 17891
N 36°27'52.0014" W −118°45'56"

The spectrometer orbiting at 17,286 miles per hour 155 miles
above California commenced its scheduled 01:07 HR spectral
analysis of the area between Merced and Lone Pine.

"The spectrometer was BIOSAT's charter. If anything in nature
generates or reflects heat, we can measure it, track it, and,
ultimately predict it," explained Lotte in the CDC-DARPA-NSF
monitoring station in Marmion Hall.

"The black is cold earth, like rocks, right, Dr. Keene?" asked
Lieutenant Ed Rensberger. His civilian jeans and canvas shirt fit in
on the CU-Boulder campus but they couldn't disguise his
profession. His posture, regulation haircut, and manner shouted
career military. This was his first shift of a two-week Air Force
rotation here during which time he was to get actual mission
experience with federal intelligence assets at Boulder. He was
fascinated.

"Right," answered Lotte "intrusive granite and metamorphic
schists and gneisses, 200-plus million years old. It heats up in high

summer, but by this time of year, it is a steady 46 degrees. The blue areas are also rock and soil, but radiating retentive heat from yesterday's sunlight."

"Sure you're a forestry biologist and not an E-7 rockhound? You sound like you know your geology," observed the intelligence officer. Lotte smiled at last. Her usual expression of distracted puzzlement - the outward reflection of chronic curiosity - dissolved into something resembling feminine warmth. She brushed a soft tangle of hair back from her forehead. Illumination from the monitor screens gave her face a faint glow.

Maybe this guy isn't such a military wonk after all.

She raised her lukewarm coffee to her lips and considered him. He couldn't be more than 22 years old; all potential, no proof.

She looked back to the screen and continued, "BIOSAT-7 is the newest high-definition digital analysis satellite designed to monitor geological change, ground thermal retentivity, wildlife migration, forest and grassland health, even take the crop and livestock census."

Variegated blacks and browns replaced color bars on the monitor. Red and pink spots appeared in clusters on the right side of the screen and migrated left as the spectrometer instrument package aboard BIOSAT-7 soared eastward.

Lotte's doctorate in epidemiology scarcely qualified her for a position that required post-graduate degrees in forestry, geophysics, or geology, but her innate curiosity had made her a fair specialist in those arcane fields. Besides, CU-Boulder was a casual university environment and encouraged interdisciplinary research. No one thought twice when they saw the intense biologist at BIOSAT-7's control console, spinning dials, playing the $43 million satellite like a video game. She was brilliant. It was she who coached members of the GDDER team to help them identify new or emerging pathogens. A star in the international high-stakes disease derby; the one at viral ground zero ready to defeat the world's deadliest pathogens. The University was lucky to have her.

She taught just one seminar per semester, and seating for that was reserved a year in advance, mostly by out of state and overseas specialists. The chancellor did not understand or appreciate her appeal and several of the more ambitious faculty were jealous of her autonomy, but the NIH funding that she attracted bought tolerance of her eccentricities.

She kept odd hours and often refused to answer the telephone. Cashmere sweaters softened her youthful features. She favored Birkenstocks for most of the year; trekkers in the heart of Boulder's bright, fair winter. Her scent was a rare combination of rose water and pine needles, which seemed foreign, almost antiquated in an age of provocative musks.

"The green?" he asked.

"Water features - rivers and lakes."

"This river here is black before it turns green."

"Good eye, Lieutenant. That's the Kaweah River, black at the higher elevations near Horkett Lakes and warmer below. Amber, orange and yellow are various shades of organic life – trees, scrub, and so on. Except for this straight line? That's Route 198."

"So the reds must be animals--"

"Warm-blooded mammals: deer, bear, bighorn sheep, mountain lions, bobcats, goats. The more active the animal heat source, the more intense the red. Mountain lions are a brilliant scarlet when they hunt, humans less so. Then again, it's rare to see humans here."

"Why?"

"The Sequoia National Park and National Forest are rugged, sparsely settled, and protected, yet still threatened. Industry and government have mismanaged much of the surrounding land, so the Ahwahnee like other tribes have put their Thunder Peak Wilderness off limits, especially to loggers and hunters.

"Those faint pinpricks that come and go – those are sheep, bighorn, mostly. Well-insulated. Most feral animals are pink, well-adapted to the rugged environment and usually curled up warm in their dens at this hour, conserving body heat."

She pointed to a cluster of bright red lights. "This here? A town. It's a clear night so we're getting clean data. We don't see much more than lights against darkness and have to interpret from color and movement. These lights moving against black? Automobile headlights. Bright pink dots here? Street lamps.

"Now, if I boost sensitivity in this spectrum and magnify this mammal . . ." A pinpoint glow appeared beside it and grew. It moved ever so slightly, brightened, then moved back the way it came. "Can you guess what that is?"

The lieutenant thought for a moment. "A firefly?"

"Cigarette. Somebody is having a smoke in --" she clicked the cursor, and up came data about: "Longwood, California. Classic small town America tucked right up against the Thunder Peak Wilderness."

He whistled softly. "My instructor at Langley told me that the newest environmental surveillance satellite had more sophisticated instrumentation, but I had no idea it was this powerful. This is like Keyhole!"

"Keyhole?"

"Oh, sorry, that's classified. So, what's that pool of dark green? Old growth?" he quickly changed the subject.

"Right. Virgin wilderness. And those lighter areas around it are clear-cut. Case-Kaiser Industries has taken every toothpick they can haul out of there. It will take centuries to recover, IF it ever recovers."

She watched the screen, her eyes prisms of concentration open to the minutest detail. Perhaps someday, satellites would detect disease. Flashing colors for viral mutations spreading like weather systems. Epidemiologists would see vulnerabilities open like low-pressure areas, viruses build strength and start to fill the vacuum. CDC could alert NIH and the government could act to preempt diseases before they caused epidemics. If only she'd had BIOSAT-7 over Itamarati. "This is real-time data. Amazing, isn't it?"

"Can you magnify it for even more precise coordinates?" asked Rensberger.

"Sure," she rotated through 1800 degrees of magnification.

The image on the monitor suddenly broke up into video static and shards of digital color. BIOSAT's spectrometer and transmitter attempted to recapture a coherent image, but it was in the grip of a force greater than its delicate instruments.

"Dammit." Lotte toggled the navigational uplink and reset the spectrometer stabilizer. The image assembled fuzzily, enough to see Longwood drift down and out of frame.

"What's happening?" asked Rensberger, sensing disaster but keeping his emotions in check.

"What time is it?"

"Oh-two-oh-seven."

"Sun spots. Right on schedule. The ion storm generated by last night's solar flares just blind-sided BIOSAT. Its brain is scrambled and it's tumbling out of control."

"Out of orbit?"

"We've got :90 seconds before it's unrecoverable," Lotte said calmly as she reached into her shoulder bag and pulled out a flash drive, read the handwritten label and inserted it in the master control console.

"What are you doing!?" his voice climbed as streaming code filled the screen in a hyper flow of zeroes, ones and jargon too complex to register.

"Reprogramming its driver."

"You can't do that. BIOSAT-7 is a key national intelligence asset, Doctor!

"It's about to be key national toast."

"But you're not authorized! You can't just interfere with a classified asset file!" Rensberger was incredulous.

"I just did," Lotte said as she retrieved her flash drive and tossed it back into her shoulder bag.

The image on the monitor settled back into spots of pink, red, and green on a dense black background.

They sat watching the slowly moving image as BIOSAT soared eastward, Rensberger regaining his composure as Lotte resumed her routine.

"So you're a programmer, too?"

"A girl's got to have a backup plan, Lieutenant," she smiled. "Sometimes with technology, you need to get under the hood and tune up the engine. Seriously, there's no such thing as pure science. To be effective at anything today, you have to be proficient in multiple disciplines. I also write code. I need every available tool to combat disease."

"Does NSA know you do this kind of thing?"

"You'll have to ask them."

After a moment in which he considered that possibility, he asked, "What about this lens cursor with the crosshairs?"

She moved the crosshairs over one of the pinpricks of light pink and magnified. Then, with a touch of another button, GPS coordinates appeared along with relative thermal readings. It was a bighorn registering a body temperature of 70 degrees, plus or minus 3.5°.

"So, BIOSAT-7 is more than a geophysics and geological research tool."

"Much more. BIOSAT-7 is an unblinking fly on the wall that provides unprecedented quality data if you know how to read it.

It's up to you and your cabal of spooks what's done with all this information . . . AFTER I get my data, of course," she deadpanned.

"Of course," repeated Rensberger. Either he missed her slight on his profession or he chose to ignore it.

When she looked back to the monitor, a movement in the dark green pool caught her eye. It was moving steadily deeper into the Thunder Peak Wilderness.

"I've got to check in at the base," Lieutenant Rensberger said.

The pink form progressed steadily between great trees. She didn't look away from the monitor.

"Doctor? I have to shove off." He extended his hand.

"Right," she said, continuing to track the deep pink glow, which neared a red spot – a mammal - she had not noticed before.

Rensberger gave up and left.

Lotte leaned closer to the monitor and squinted. A human.

In the Thunder Peak Wilderness?

6

THUNDER PEAK WILDERNESS

Unspringing rabbits crossed the trail as Lars Broder made his way through Thunder Peak's cold moonlit shadows. He was a large, raw man with too much strength to lie quietly in bed while the Ahwahnee and Federal courts that protected them denied him the life he had worked for.

The animal in him had survived. When he tracked in the woods, he heard the life force. His thoughts made sense. Prey moving under branches and over leaves, unaware of danger, was music to this solitary stalker in a shrinking universe. He found healing dreams in night hunting.

Nearby, the red trunk of a massive Sequoia towered 290 feet into the star-filled night. It had been here for more than 800 years in 1805 when Lewis and Clark camped beneath other forest giants farther north with teenaged Shoshone guide and interpreter, Sacagawea, on their way to the Pacific coast.

Below this hollow of ancient timber, the mountain's shoulders dropped steeply into the town of Longwood, which glimmered against the darkness.

He slowed as he neared the great tree and listened, but all he could hear was the roar of his own bitterness.

"Jesus," he spat.

Business is hobbled by environmentalist rodents. Government is paralyzed by special interests. Hell, if those bureaucrats inside the beltway had to work for a living, we'd see how fast things would change. Between increased regulation and damned trade agreements, even Case-Kaiser Corporation couldn't turn a profit in the American West anymore. So, they up and went down to Honduras where folks were more reasonable about using natural resources the way God intended. Anymore, hard-working timber men like him couldn't find a fair day's wage for a day's work.

He sprinkled scent shield on his rubber-soled boots, then squeezed some Super Exciter Buck Lure on the scent pad pinned to his camouflage overalls. He couldn't afford Cabela's so he used doe urine harvested by his brother from a three-year-old he took in Utah last weekend.

A man couldn't hunt on his own land any more. That's right, *his* land. No federal proclamation declaring a place a national park can give away land. No treaty can make a place off limits to the people who had lived there since before memory. Not to the Ahwahnee, or Piute or Mowok. Lars knew good Ahwahnee men, but they were people, too; not special in any way that he could see. The federal forest could be harvested, now it was the Ahwahnee's turn. A forest belongs to the man ambitious enough to take it, strong enough to defend it and clever enough to make it pay. This was perfectly good timber. There was enough lumber in this one sequoia to build four homes and a church. We can always grow more. And it isn't as if the tree feels the saw or has a wife and children to feed. Keee-rist.

Reduced to hiring himself out to out-of-state-hunters, he'd sold half the secrets it took him 23 years to learn: where deer browsed, where the bears used to den and might again someday. At least it paid cash and the people he worked for got it. He took them on horseback up into the tree line where the deer were thick. Maybe saw a cat. Bear, too. Mostly blacks.

Sometimes a man has to break the law just to make a point. And if taking a buck from right under the Ahwahnee's noses is what it takes, then that's what it takes.

He grinned tightly. There's a killer inside waiting to get out. Government does a fair job of keeping the killer inside, but there ain't anything stronger than a man's basic nature. He's a predator at the top of the food chain. Only thing more dangerous than a man is another man. So you got to keep that sharp edge to defend what little you have: your rights, your plot of land that the rest of the killers want but haven't yet taken from you . . .

A wafting scent derailed his grinding thoughts. It was strong, maybe a tule elk, more likely mule deer stag, and it was close. Looking around for cover, he saw a way to cross the five feet between himself and the tree without making noise that would alert the deer. The ground was needle-strewn and mushrooms ringed the great sequoia. He stepped silently behind the tree and a tangle of branches.

Given a choice, deer move nose to wind. This is a smart buck. He knows the wind drifts uphill in the heat of day, downhill at night. So, he's out when the wind is light and steady from the north, nice and predictable. He thinks he's got Thunder Peak to himself.

Then Lars saw it. Sharp rack points rimmed in silver light.

In Marmion Hall, Lotte magnified the image until the pink glow occupied a quarter of the screen. The chaotic splash of pastel pixels on the phosphor was scarcely readable at 1500% magnification.

A man in thermals that were retaining his body heat. Had to be.

Lars remembered to breathe open-mouthed as he counted prongs on the deer's rack. 4 . . . 5 . . . it was a 6 x 6! A Royal stag with 12 points.

He raised his compact rangefinder in a slow, unbroken movement to avoid startling the buck. It was difficult to see much at night through the plastic optics, but he could just make out the faint rim of light on two points. Turning the dial with his left index finger, two images of the magnificent profile merged into one. He squinted to read the dial, still avoiding any sudden or unnatural movement. 21 yards. Longer than he liked, but hey, fortune was fortune. And it *never* smiled on *any* bow hunter the way it was now beaming on Lars Broder. A 6 x 6 out for a middle-of-the-night stroll right past him!

He waited for the buck to look away, then carefully reached for a 2219 shaft tipped with a Black Diamond broadhead. It was the strongest combination in his quiver. A bit light for this buck, but if he could get a clear sighting, he could center the heart.

The buck looked to the right, its eye glinting in the slanting light. Lars stilled.

The buck looked to its left.

Lars placed the aluminum shaft in the arrow rest and pulled. The 48-inch mountain mahogany bow multiplied force smoothly as he drew back. He'd tried the high-tech compound bows with their frictionless wheels and Fast-Flite cables, but they were soulless. The Shoshone crafted the best bow on the planet. 87 pounds of lethal physics, restrained only by Lars' curled fingertips, now rested against his right cheek.

The buck moved forward a half step. Its right shoulder appeared in an opening between branches less than a foot in diameter. Lars visualized the great heart beating beneath the buck's rippling coat, dead center in his line of sight. A small shoot projected into the target area: that was a concern - even small twigs could deflect his arrow. Blood pumped into his coiled arm. He would have to shoot soon or his straining bicep would begin to spasm.

Lotte watched the shape change as its mass moved up and outwards. His arm? She zoomed out for better resolution, then back in again. The squares of light on dark suddenly turned to snow and the color bars returned.

BIOSAT-7 had lost contact with Boulder's reception grid. The server switched Lotte's monitoring channel to standby mode, hence the bars. BIOSAT was somewhere over Kansas now, feeding another monitoring station its brilliant spectral imagery of the Red Hills or wheat fields.

Lotte typed in instructions for the satellite to target the same view on its next pass. She checked the clock. BIOSAT-7 would complete its orbit and be back in position in precisely 85 minutes and 22 seconds.

Lars' adrenaline flowed. It was now or never. He took a breath to calm himself and reset his right foot on the spongy ground. His boot thumped against a small mushroom.

Below and behind him, the puffball released its spores into the night.

Lars took another deep, calming breath.

The night darkened. His muscles grew heavier. Strength drained from his arms and shoulders. The bow's pressure pulled his right arm forward, overwhelming his will as he lost command of his body. The bow and his rapidly petrifying right arm tugged at one another until they were equal in strength, halfway to the arrow's release. Propped against the pine, bow half-drawn, Lars Broder was dead. A final synapse deep within his oxygen-deprived brain sparked feebly. Then it also surrendered and died.

Ben lost track of how much time had passed.

Shadows flew up the hood and windshield. The yellow centerline rose and fell hypnotically under the pickup's wheels. Up and down, up and down in sensuous waves. Ben shifted on the truck's bench seat. It was a hell of a time to be thinking about Grace.

He rolled down the window. The sharp-edged air brought him back around.

The truck surfed effortlessly down a long wave into a silent trough. He recognized the zero-G sense of free fall, the absence of the engine's roar. The only sound was the slap of tires on asphalt . . . he was coasting.

He pulled onto the shoulder. With his physician's penlight clenched between his teeth, he saw a rusted grit-and-grease tangle of parts under the hood that did not inspire confidence. The truck, which had instilled pride just moments before, now mocked him.

He tried the key again. The battery obligingly jolted the spark plugs deep in the engine block. The butterfly valve rocked and clicked uselessly inside the carburetor. The engine was flooded.

He stepped back out of the cab and leaned on the front fender, another citizen of the night like the unseen owl above. A breeze whispered in the high branches. If he was more imaginative, he would hear voices, he thought. In an owl hoot. A creaking branch. The push of air under a nighthawk's turning wings. The woods were alive and it would be a tragic loss if Case-Kaiser stole this land from the Ahwahnee.

Having the ranch and cash flow to service, the debt that grew meaner every year was still better than being foreclosed off your land in the flat wheat states or afraid in the city.

At least he was here for his mother if she needed him, although that was rare. Since her husband died, she had come into her own. After a time of adjustment, she had grown into an independent, capable, even happy woman. The new Alice McCandle took Ben and herself by surprise. She hadn't been unhappy in Arthur McCandle's shadow, just numb inside that cocoon. When he died, she emerged from her chrysalis determined not to let any of her remaining days pass unchallenged. She took up trekking and spent more of her time alone and with a few Ahwahnee friends. The woods that would have frightened her before now drew her to them. She would still be walking the wilderness along with Sacagawea's ghost when Ben was beyond these woods.

After ten minutes of enforced inactivity while waiting for gravity to drain the cylinders of excess fuel, the old engine achieved equilibrium. He poured pure alcohol down the carburetor's throat. The engine turned over with a wracking cough, gasped asthmatically, and eventually settled into a reliable, wheezing pace towards home.

On the Peak, Johnny Walker Black fueled Nelson Hatch's anger as he hiked purposefully into the Hollow. The sound of wind in the high branches was as lost on him as the metallic edge of the approaching winter.

He swung his old double-bit ax off his shoulder and leaned it against the tree trunk. Its cutting edges - honed over countless nights with too much time to think, too much energy left over from idle days - gleamed blue and white. No work for nine months. Broker than he had ever been and too much time with the bottle.

Look at all this perfectly good timber. What has the Ahwahnee Nation ever done for this place? Our grandfathers came and built roads, sluices, a mill, stores, and schools. We created jobs. What do these Ahwahnee do but sit around and watch the damn trees grow?

He dropped his rucksack and folded his shirtsleeves. Like a priest preparing for sacraments, he rolled and folded until they were out of the way just so.

After spitting into his palms, he gripped the white ash handle. The hardwood felt like an extension of his forearms. He lifted his eyes to the tree he was about to take down. The sky spun, vertigo overtook his scotch-soaked senses, and he fell to the ground. Climbing back to his feet, he rededicated himself to his crime.

He shook his head and sighed. The liquor on his breath smelled sweet and familiar. Crossing himself, he reset his grip on the axe handle.

A breeze whispered in the crown of the seventeen hundred-year-old sequoia. The high branches creaked. Movement carried down the length of the tree and vibrated in the earth under his feet. Deep within the trunk, red rings that recorded drought in 1767 and fire in 1892 stretched and compressed with the movement. From deep within the trunk, a muted groan sounded.

"It's time ol' boy," he said to the deeply ridged bark. "Jes' you 'n me. We have to show 'em . . ."

He hoisted the heavy axe, coiled, and began his swing. The eighteen-pound head gleamed as it traced an arc through the predawn darkness and orbited toward the trunk. He leaned back, countering the axe's desire to break free. Then in a practiced shift of his weight to the left, anger, skill, and experience combined to double the velocity of the blade. It raced hungrily for the 30-foot diameter trunk and taste of wood.

Thr-r-rrump.

Steel divined centuries of evolution, yet the mighty sequoia took the blow without flinching. This stirred more bitterness in Hatch. He loathed his weakness before government, Case-Kaiser, the Ahwahnee, and this great tree.

A glimmer traced across the sky. He looked up and noticed the telltale silhouette of a passing satellite.

He rocked the axe free and coiled again.

7

BOULDER

In Marmion Hall, Lotte noticed that the spot of pink on the screen had cooled by several degrees since BIOSAT-7's last pass.

Zooming out, another shape appeared not far from the cooling pink form. This one was a more intense red, larger than a mountain lion. Another human? Zooming in, she saw it swivel to the right and then come back quickly. Like it was swinging a bat. Like Brazilian peasants cutting vines and branches with their machetes. She couldn't shake thoughts of Brazil.

That nightmare grew heavier every hour. She had no idea how to deal with her failure. Compounding her distress was certainty of her theory: nature had evolved a mechanism to defend itself that was capable of eluding scientific method. How else to explain the unexplainable mini plagues? The viruses that carried reverse transcriptase enzymes like HIV and whatever it was that killed Charley?

The *earthstar* mushroom shook imperceptibly in the waves of sound vibrating from the tree as it absorbed Hatch's axe blows. Biochemical connections switched and a genetic program activated the next phase of its life.

Taking a deep breath, Hatch wound up for another swing. The cool air carried thousands of the tiny spores past his pharynx and trachea, down his two main bronchi all the way to the pink alveolar sacs and alveoli.

He flew into a dark tunnel. It wasn't the scotch. His limbs stiffened and he fell onto his axe handle. The last image to register on his retina was a shooting star. The last sound a bear's moans. Then all was numbness and darkness.

The red form on the phosphor screen twisted again and suddenly stopped.

When they arrived with der Root in Itamarati, Amazonas State, Brazil they'd met with a cluster of stiff peasant corpses. All males, struck down while clearing jungle land to grow food crops. Each with dazed children and distraught wives left to fend for themselves.

The alert from CDC had come two days earlier.

"We think trees have something to do with this outbreak, Lotte. You're the leading epidemiologist and biogeneticist in the country. We need your take on this," said Dr. Ed Peters, head of the Epidemic Intelligence Service (EIS), the functional hub of the Centers for Disease Control.

They had already served on seven other international missions for the CDC. Most were routine viral outbreaks of infectious disease and did not involve stressed forest ecosystems in any way.

With the help of two graduate assistants, she had her field lab packed and ready when the government Gulfstream-IV arrived for the flight to Itamarati.

After days of tense, frustrating work in Brazil with Charley and der Root, they came up empty. Charley's death was the last. The crisis ended but the mystery remained.

While reading a paper describing Ireland's deforestation in the twelfth century, the crucial link dawned on her: there had been a significant Irish die-out at the same time. Nearly two hundred thousand perished. On the farms mostly, but also in the expanding towns. Records were sketchy, yet there were too many clues for it to be regarded as coincidence. Why didn't anyone else see it?

She had researched logging and die-offs and found that small-scale clearing of trees emerged as human practice thousands of years before the beginnings of civilization. It began during the Mesolithic period as early as 7000 B.C. when foragers used fire to open parts of dense forest for red deer and wild boar. Had they experienced plagues or some other epidemic that coincided with their clearing of virgin forest? Maybe, maybe not.

Was there evidence of other epidemics that coincided with human assaults on forests? It wouldn't amount to much without some kind of proof.

The whole issue was complicated. There were too many social, cultural, economic, even religious dimensions to the problems of deforestation to ever get enough people of good will together to focus and collaborate on a balanced solution. From the perspective of the developing world, the benefits of preserving forests as carbon sinks or biodiversity reserves went primarily to the richer developed nations. The United States of America cut down its forests centuries ago. In the sixteenth century, so dense was the land with forest that a squirrel could travel from Plymouth Rock to the Mississippi River without once touching the ground. America had benefitted by cutting down its bountiful forests and becoming the world's richest, most advanced culture on the planet. Why shouldn't they do the same?

Still, circumstantial evidence suggested twenty or more deforestation-related die-offs throughout recorded human history.

The Itamarati incident was significant among these. How did so many die so quickly, so inexplicably? The medical authorities had been helpless to inform the world about the cause, manner, or mechanism of the deaths at the time. They didn't admit this publicly, of course. 'Virulent viral hemorrhagic fever' became the CDC line. Sufficiently impressive to sound authoritative, fuzzy enough to defy public memory, and arguably justifiable, however tortured that argument was to those who had been there to witness the deaths.

Except for Charley, the victims had been struck down while cutting trees. Now Lotte was seeing something similar on the high-definition video spectrometric scan of southern California.

She picked up her cell phone and dialed while keeping her eye on the monitor. Somewhere in the California night the phone at the other end was ringing.

"Stimson," a gruff male voice answered after five rings.

"Is this the Sheriff's office?" asked Lotte.

"It is."

"This is the NSF monitoring station in Colorado. I've just detected something strange on Ahwahnee land out there, in the Thunder Peak Wilderness."

"Yeah?" the voice came back, polite but skeptical. "Who is this?"

"Dr. Lotte Keene. Biosat monitoring in Boulder."

"You can see our forest from Boulder, Colorado, can you?" he asked, glancing out the window.

"Yes. I'm monitoring one of the Bureau of Land Management's terrain survey satellites for crop and forest census, that kind of thing. Epidemiology is my specialty, and there's some activity out there that caught my eye in your Thunder Peak Wilderness."

"S'not mine," the Sheriff corrected her.

"I just meant – Sheriff, I've just seen one large organism - human probably, mammal definitely – die. And another, I'm not sure, it could be injured and dying."

"More?"

"There have been others?"

"Yeah, some folks died up there."

"Where," asked Lotte? "Specifically where?"

"West mostly. Young woman not from around here. A second yesterday. Where are they?"

"Which?"

"Your mammals."

"About a mile in from the north boundary."

"You saw this from a satellite?"

"Yes."

He opened the window and waved to the sky, "Can you see me?"

Who was this clown? She played along. "Where are you - in Longwood?"

"Yes, Ma'am," he squinted upwards, scouring the stars.

She would have to prove herself. She zoomed out until

Longwood appeared, then panned and zoomed in toward the small town. "Are you in one of the buildings on the main street?"

"Ye-a-ah."

"There are three buildings on the south side of the street, one with the lights on and plenty of thermal radiance coming through the roof. That you?"

"Might be." The Sheriff leaned out the window, aimed his service revolver at the Little Dipper, and fired.

A scarlet flash blossomed on Lotte's screen.

"Hey! Did you just shoot at my satellite!?"

"I'll be damned," the Sheriff whispered, holstering his revolver.

"Cause of death?"

"What?"

"The victims!" *Calm down, Lotte.*

"Doc's figuring that out right now. The body was what we in law enforcement would call—"

"Stiff?"

"As stone. You say you were a doctor?"

"Ye-a-ah."

"Oh."

"Doctor Lotte Keene," she repeated defensively. "I need to know what's going on up there in the Thunder Peak Wilderness."

"I do, too."

"I'll fax you what to look for, what precautions to take, my number and how to reach me."

"You call me back in a while, Dr. Satellite."

The phone clicked and the connection cut off.

8

LONGWOOD

The 150 year-old live oak in the front yard stood gnarled, mute, all–knowing in Ben's truck headlights. He drove to the side door of his house, a low-slung timber and stone structure with a salad garden below the kitchen window. On the west side, a barn and fenced paddock nestled among white birches. A high-wheeled carriage loitered off to one side, shafts raised in surrender. Winter ice and summer heat had stripped its paint and warped one iron-rimmed wheel.

Leaves fell carelessly over glowing drive stones. The brisk, ringing autumn night had replaced warm, buzzing summer evenings.

Ben tried to clear his mind, yet it refused to assemble itself into any coherent order. His uneasiness about Hart and Pocknett persisted. Sudden death was unusual in this open country. People knew how to take care of themselves. There was the occasional death by mule kick or falling tree, but those were rare. Most deaths in Longwood he saw coming from a suitable coping distance. Folks slid from this life by disease, age, or loneliness. Now he had two dead discovered within one week, and no apparent connection between them. Same place. Same symptoms. What else did they have in common?

Mary Margaret was not in her bed. Her blanket and Pooh Bear were missing, too. After looking in the bathroom, he checked the kitchen. On the way, he found his mother, Alice, curled in his chair in the great room, her head tilted back, hair a silver-white halo, face glowing like porcelain in the television's reflected glare. She had Ben's WW-II Navy blanket pulled up around her chin, the one his dad willed to him. Beige with a wide blue stripe and "U.S. NAVY" in block letters, it was incongruous here in California, so far from the ocean.

'That blanket says everything I've got to say about the war, son. It kept me warm when I was cold and there were men trying to kill me,' he'd said on his sickbed before he died, push and pull to the end.

Ben was coming to understand Arthur McCandle's true legacy to his son. He had carved a modest, comfortable existence out of these mountains for his family as a ranch and farm equipment salesman. On the road six days out of seven calling on crusty ranchers and thrifty crop farmers, he earned their respect with straight talk, fair deals and a helping hand when a tractor engine gasket needed replacing, when a silo needed restrapping, or too many lambs needed birthing in the rain at 3 a.m. Sometimes it seemed he cared more about his customers than his wife and son, Ben remembered hearing his mother cry after lights went out. It was true that they weren't the best match ever made, but they weren't the worst either.

Arthur McCandle and Alice Strasser were married for 46 years, each one better than his so-called glory years as a deck gunner in the Pacific, he once told his son on a rare fishing trip up Pelican Creek. Ben doubted that was true. The call of the bounding deck and the twisting road was always there in his eye, just behind the straight look.

Snow fell on the screen of the somnolently hissing television. He found the remote control and turned it off.

He checked the sleeping porch. Mary Margaret was not there, either. Stepping down into the march of long moonlit shadows on the wood floor, he checked the couch, looked past the oval braided rug in the center of the room to Cookie's corner. She sometimes curled up with the Border Collie and Pooh Bear in the sheepskin bed. Now empty, it looked larger.

A chill passed through him. Before he could associate a word like fear with the sensation, he left the house and crossed in long strides to the barn.

The great door's dry hinges squealed. A snort sounded from the corner stall, followed by a rustle in the hay. Wings ruffled in the high raftered darkness and a hoarse wheeze carried from Beauty's stall on the right. He put his flashlight's beam on the heifer. She stared mutely back at him, her eyes deep black pools. No hay shoots hung from her lips. She still wasn't feeding.

Then he saw the flare of gold hair at Beauty's side. Mary Margaret was snuggled beside her heifer, wrapped tightly in a blanket.

"I didn't have the heart to move her, Ben," Alice's voice rose from the shadows as he reentered the house. "M needs to be there for Beauty."

"Not good her getting too attached to that heifer, Mom," Ben answered as he passed through to the kitchen. "You know how I feel about that."

He took plates from the cupboard and placed them on the table, "Staying for breakfast?"

A yawn sounded from the other room. "No, I should be off." Alice's joints cracked as she entered. "My granddaughter knows what's important to her and acts on it," she said with unmistakable pride. She handed him the silverware, looked him in the face and smiled, "You might take a page . . ." She shuffled down the hall.

"You two are so much alike it scares the hell out of me," he said after her.

"That's a compliment, right?"

"I just don't know how to handle her lately." He pulled a spatula from the drawer.

Alice stopped and turned. "Stop trying to handle her."

"What?"

"Love her. Just love my granddaughter."

"I do love her, she knows that!" his voice rose defensively.

"Tell her, Ben," she gazed across the dim shadows at her son. "Once in awhile a girl likes to hear the words." She turned and vanished in the darkened hall. The floor creaked once and a door closed quietly.

Ben dialed the phone.

"Missed you last night," Grace moaned into the receiver cradled on her pillow.

"Between your painting and my doctoring, we're missing the good parts, aren't we?" he whispered apologetically.

"I can come over now . . ."

His heart was willing, but he couldn't get his body in it. That twitch on the back of his neck was distracting him. The connection between his mind, which continued to ask ceaseless questions, and his gut, which was tied in knots, was an open line. His nerves were on four-plus alert. "'Fraid I'm not much company."

"What's up?"

"I'll explain when you come over."

"Alice still there?"

"Mmm. Found M sitting up in the barn with Beauty."

"She has heart."

"Too much maybe."

"Not now, Ben. She knows. Let her learn how to love. It's not easy being her age."

"Not easy being this age, either. You make it better."

A pause on the line stretched as their thoughts commingled somewhere between the ranch house and Grace's White Raven studio loft three miles away. Imagination was more potent than physics.

"So . . ." Grace sighed.

"Right, . . ."

"Mmmm, what's this down here . . .?" She broke through science with hypnotical sureness, drawing him in.

Alice's cracking joints sounded again. He turned to see her enter the kitchen, turn on the coffee, and find her car keys.

She took the receiver from Ben, "Morning, Grace. You're going to be around, right? I'm camping with Adrian, 'member?" She listened for a moment. "Shell Mountain and Jennie Lakes Wilderness to the south. Two days, three maybe, depending on weather."

"Let him build the fire, Alice," Grace quipped, "makes a man feel useful."

"And they say women are high maintenance!" Alice chuckled,

handed the receiver back to Ben, and bussed his cheek.

How many grown men had 70 year-old mothers camping with gentlemen friends? Ben had finally gotten over his irrational concern about her dating. There was still the issue of her safety so far from medical help.

"Take your cell phone."

"That thing never works when you need it and it's impossible to use. We'll be fine."

She would not tolerate being parented by her son.

"So when is Adrian going to make an honest woman of you?" he needled her.

"Oh Ben, grow up," she waved and was out the door. Her old car turned over on the second try and purred out the drive.

"How soon can you be here?" he asked Grace.

Lotte dialed the number associated with her life's most annoying mystery.

There was a click followed by a man's voice. "This is der Root at CDC EIS. Leave a mes--"

She dropped the receiver into its cradle.

Strict rules of protocol for interagency alerts mandated that she submit her suspicion to the NSF district director in Denver. It was up to him to judge the merits of her concern and either deny her request for an alert or push it up the chain of command to the Bureau of Land Management, Forestry, National Health and so on.

It would take the Sheriff several hours to find the bodies. What if she was wrong? What if the pink glows on the screen weren't human? She had cried wolf before; it hadn't helped her. On the other hand, what if she wasn't wrong? What if she could get there before it was too late this time?

She checked her watch. *Damn!* She remembered the 'Biology In The Balance' seminar that she had scheduled for this morning.

The image on the monitor broke up and switched to color bars on its programmed rotation. BIOSAT-7 passed out of range again. It would be another 85 minutes before she could confirm whether the second man had also died. *Men* - she already accepted that the pink glows were human - *dying suspiciously in the Thunder Peak Wilderness ancient forest 1,150 miles west southwest.*

Why should she care about the chain of command?

The second hand of her wristwatch swept time forward under the crystal. A voice within her urged her to risk everything. For what? A hunch that she had just seen Nature reveal one of her secrets. Was it the canary in the coal mine?

She felt dangerous. She reached for the phone and redialed.

9

LONGWOOD

Grace cracked fresh eggs into the fry pan and filled the kitchen with the savory buzz and sizzle of a country breakfast.

"M will be here in a minute," Ben said as he poured orange juice for Mary Margaret and settled back with his coffee. He was content to put the night aside for a little while.

Grace smiled at the sound of him at the table behind her. It was still early to trust the powerful physical and emotional attractions that gripped her, yet she had something with Ben and Mary Margaret she had been missing in her artist's life. In the three years since she came to Longwood, her paintings had found their 'voice' and she had come to rely on the familiar light and warmth of this single father's kitchen. She hadn't let that thought slip, of course. Although it rarely occurred anymore – the last time at Christmas when a northern lights display stirred fond memories of Bernina - the pull to familiar Dolomite villages and Aegean beaches occasionally returned. She knew she wasn't ideal wife material. She was coming to believe, however, that soon she wouldn't trade a minute in Ben's house for years in genius-filled Renaissance galleries.

He was not like the native ranchers who would never

understand a woman's needs beyond this valley, but he was a man. He viewed the world simply, occasionally sensing there was more but not trusting that awareness. She lived in multiple dimensions. It was part of her power as an artist; nothing was simply black and white, everything was gradated, multi-colored.

Outside the bay window, a gray squall moved east over the distant plain. The view was another result of Case-Kaiser's clear-cutting. Up until two years ago, 300 hundred year-old firs would have obstructed the view of storm clouds weeping over stumps.

"Thanks for coming over," Ben said to Grace's back as she watched the eggs turn white in the pan. Her riotous raven hair was tied back loosely with a satin ribbon. Faded jeans fit snugly around her long thighs and stacked casually over her boots. Her tailored white blouse accentuated her femininity. He visualized the European lace next to her skin that boosted her spirits and his. Such sophistication amid California's rough-edges fascinated him. Unlike the locals who were caught here by birth or circumstance, bound by inertia to narrow existences under California's vast skies, Grace *chose* Longwood to live and paint in the shadow of Thunder Peak. He couldn't take his eyes off her.

Grace read Ben's expression as she turned to fill Mary Margaret's plate and straightened. "How about you, cowboy? See anything you'd like?" Her green eyes slow-danced in the slanting morning light.

Ben smiled. At least he thought he smiled.

"You're off your game, Punch. I've seen better when you were half asleep. Where were you?"

He nodded. "Hard to explain. Oren Pocknett, from the reservation? Nate brought his body down."

"What happened?"

"I don't know. It's weird. Oren was frozen, no, mummified. No, not mummified either. He was stiff as a plank, petrified, but not."

Grace waited.

"Never seen anything like it. As coroner I'm supposed to identify the cause of death."

"Did you do an autopsy?"

"Oren's full-blooded Ahwahnee."

Grace nodded and sipped her coffee.

"Whatever it was happened fast. He was still holding his long gun, ready to pull the trigger. And his expression . . . eyes wide, surprised like . . ." Ben's voice trailed off.

Grace touched Ben's arm as she listened, partly to encourage, partly to calm the shiver that the image of Oren Pocknett generated within her.

"Maybe he was scared to death. It's happened before, hasn't it?"

"Fright doesn't petrify."

The back screen door slapped its frame. Mary Margaret came to the table and faced her father, hay tangled in her hair and defiance in her expression. "I'm not going to school today," she announced.

"Yes you are," growled Ben.

"Beauty needs me," she argued.

"Beauty will be fine and YOU need an education," Ben felt himself winding up. His patience was frayed at the edges and an irrational need to control his daughter came to a quick boil.

"Daddy!" M screamed, "If I'm not here, Beauty'll get worse. She's scared!"

"Beauty is just a calf," he roared. "Got it?!"

M's eyes went wide. Tears welled up and she ran from the room. Her bedroom door slammed loudly behind her.

"Well, that was dysfunctional."

"Don't start, Grace. You can't say anything to make me feel any worse than I do already."

"She's a little girl; frightened and holding on to fairy tales for all she's worth. Look at me. Look at me, Punch."

He did.

"Let her be a girl for a little longer. She needs to feel safe while she figures out what the world wants from her."

"I just don't know anymore."

Grace stared at him. "M is a child, not Hannah's ghost. She needs to believe in the Magic Kingdom and Prince Charming – which until a minute ago was you."

"I can't deal with this. Not this morning," he growled in exasperation.

"Well, you better. There's still time to enjoy your daughter. If you don't, you'll lose her."

A roar from the driveway filled the air and gravel tattooed the side of the house. Before Ben could get to the door, the Sheriff entered the kitchen without knocking.

"Glad I caught you, Ben. Got another report of bodies in the

'Peak."

Ben checked his watch, disbelieving. "Jeez, Nate, it hasn't been . . ."

"It's just a report."

"From who?"

"Some doctor in Boulder."

"What?"

"One of them science doctors. She saw something on her satellite and called me."

Grace touched Ben's shoulder. "I'll make sure M gets to school and call Alice."

"Might not be anything," suggested Nate unconvincingly.

Grace pushed them toward the door, "Go."

10

ATLANTA - BOULDER

In the CDC building at 1600 Clifton Road in Atlanta, a telephone rang against silence.

The hallways were vacant, the parking lot empty. Only the hiss of forced air heat and the muted chatter of fax machines conveyed life in the old building. Soundproofed labs containing macaque and rhesus monkeys, pink-eyed white mice and Norway rats dotted rambling stories on the campus. During the workday whenever the lab doors opened, the din of cage running wheels or the chatter of the gregarious monkeys migrated down long corridors. At the moment, the loudest sound was the hushed shuffle of Vin der Root's cross trainers on the freshly scrubbed composite floor.

Balancing his thermos, inkjet printer from his home office, and four metropolitan news dailies, he unlocked his office door and shot a scowl at the raucous telephone. He resented the interruption before he had an opportunity to calibrate his weary senses for another day. Hell with it.

He cursed the predictable symmetry of his office as he plugged in the printer. The square room's sterile banality depressed him. It had never fit like the worn plaster and wood sock of an office he had at the university. Not that he wanted to be back there; this

44

gleaming beaker might be soulless, but at least it reflected achievement. Tenure be damned. Those unctuous tweedbacks on the committee would never have granted it to a rogue biochemist from the Lone Star State.

There were fourteen messages in his e-mailbox, most from the usual correspondents. Two from the Bureau of Land Management (BLM), three from *lkeene* in Boulder. BLM - maybe there was another hantavirus outbreak in the southwest. Ever since the 1980s, civilians saw Hantavirus under their beds.

There was also one from NSA. Hearing from NSA was never good, like hearing from the IRS.

He opened Lotte's e-mail first.

Vin, call me.

He scrolled down, expecting more, but that was it. Odd. Wasn't like Lotte to be mysterious.

The second -- a resend of the first -- an hour old.

Lotte's third e-mail told him more.

Vin,
Aberrant deaths Thunder Peak Wilderness, CA. Will explain when we talk.
Lotte K.

He swallowed more coffee.

He had a long day ahead and was loathe to let a distraction get in the way. Two thirds of the inquiries turned out to be false alarms. But false alarms required the same time and attention that valid alerts required. He had become maniacally selective about what calls he accepted.

CDC was the lab of last resort. Disease eradication command and control.

For centuries, soldiers who fought in faraway swamps and marshes brought malaria home, American soldiers included. They brought fever, chills, sweats, lethargy, severe headaches, and violent shaking, frequently resulting in death. In 1942, Washington created a tiny bureau devoted to controlling malaria. It evolved into the Centers for Disease Control.

By mid 1995, when a series of lethal epidemics raged into world populations and decimated thousands, the CDC had grown to 7,000 employees and scores of buildings on eight campuses in

Atlanta. It had learned from each bacteriological crisis and developed superlative expertise in evaluating breakouts, interrupting their lethal progress and accumulating samples of every known virus on the planet.

Because viruses mutate and evolve more or less constantly, the CDC's future was assured.

Along the way, it became the sole superpower in the international war on disease. If a doctor, research scientist, or local health official needed help, CDC specialists provided knowledgeable assistance. It was not unusual for a team to show up in the center of an outbreak within 24 hours of a call to Atlanta for help.

He decided to call Lotte back after he charted the Macaques' morning vitals. He imagined her sitting with a fire in her gut out there in the Rockies and lost count of the monkey's pulse. He started R-1017's exam over, recorded nominal diastolic and systolic readings, returned to his office, and dialed the number in Boulder.

"Let's extend the biological metaphor," Lotte tapped the dais for emphasis.

Every seat in the Benson Earth Sciences building lecture amphitheater was filled for Dr. Lotte Keene's *Biology In The Balance* seminar. Even the aisles were filled. Students, visiting biologists, geologists, foresters, and toxicologists sat with open notepads or raised digital recorders.

"Try to eliminate morality from discussion for the purpose of understanding life. We don't know how far along the biological thread of life that morality exists. We humans like to think we are the only organism capable of principles, ethics, and integrity. That's not true. Primates have proven to be moral creatures with an ethos of community and fairness. Whales and dolphins are guided by principles of morality. Read the study from Dalhousie University in Halifax about selective breeding among sperm and killer whales for the genetic transmission of socially positive skills. We don't understand how far what we call morals extend throughout all living organisms, but they are there."

She paced the length of the lecturer's platform, hands deep in her jeans pockets. As she turned and paced back again, the microphone clipped to her sweater issued a soft rustle over the wall speakers.

"Do dogs or cats have a sense of morality? Does a spider? The praying mantis? How about liver cells?" She paused and faced the audience.

"How about fungus, lichens or cancer cells?" She waited for her listeners to confront the outrageous idea for themselves. After several seconds, she answered for them. "We really don't know."

"In fact, we don't even know what we don't know. The universe is so vast and complex that we may never know. We are learning - at a frustratingly glacial pace - but we *are* learning. What was science fiction just five years ago is now science. Doctors at Johns Hopkins are putting microchips in the brains of stroke victims. Formerly catatonic patients with healthy minds imprisoned within failed bodies are now able to communicate. Permanently lost stroke victims have regained their ability to express themselves."

"Think back to your childhood. Whether you grew up watching Buffalo Bob, Big Bird, or Transformers you grew up in a divided world. Between us and them, democracy and communism, between man and animals, earth and the rest of the cosmos.

"We have come to an almost universal awareness that we are all made of the same stuff. Every living thing here, there and everywhere is made of the same building blocks of life: DNA. Inside the nucleus of your cells, the strands of DNA that dictate what you are, who you are, how tall, heavy, strong or beautiful you will become also tell the leopard what color spots it should have, the elephant to accurately remember its past relationships, the Douglas Fir to grow 300 feet tall, the spruce to only 60.

"And each DNA chromosome is made of just four enzymes: adenine, thymine, guanine and cytosine. A, T, G and C. From those four letters arranged in an infinite variety of combinations come the hummingbird and Tyrannosaurus Rex; the Chihuahua and the wolf; minnow and blue whale; miniature bonsai and great ponderosa, mushroom and macadamia nut, and of course, man and woman.

"As we have digested this fundamental law of the universe, we've adopted biology as our new paradigm."

Pencils pushed against paper as she brought her audience along, creating for them the universe according to Keene.

A muted electronic ring sounded from her purse. Everyone including Lotte looked at the bag on the table. She pulled her smartphone out and held it up for all to see. It continued ringing like an infant asking to be fed.

"The cell phone. Most of you have them, right?"

Nods rippled across the audience. It rang again.

"Aren't you going to answer?" asked a young graduate student in the second row.

"They'll leave a message," Lotte continued as the electronic ring brayed on. "Cell phone. Any of us can reach or be reached from anywhere in the world digitally. The language of the technology reflects our biological arrogance: CELL Phone. Even our machinery has taken on biological meaning."

The phone stopped ringing.

Vin der Root frowned when he heard her recorded message again. Why did she ask him to call if she wasn't picking up? The distant possibility that something was wrong occurred to him briefly, and then he dismissed it.

"As a result of our new awareness of universal laws," Lotte continued, "we see ourselves as part of a larger whole. No matter how far out into the cosmos we probe, or how far inward we explore into cell, nucleus, DNA, molecule, atom, and so on, we now understand that all of it is one great, evolving organism."

"Has this humbled mankind? Apparently not. Too many think they've got it all figured out. Like the cardinals in 1633 who wanted to condemn Galileo to life in prison for suggesting that the popularly held belief that the sun orbited around earth might be misguided. Too many fundamentalists – at both extremes of faith or science, traditionalists or new age visionaries, loggers or conservationists - think they know the one and only absolute truth.

"Who today is so certain of what they know that they would kill for it -- aside from religious and political fundamentalists, that is?"

She paced again, allowing her listeners to absorb her meaning.

"Here is some of what we do know: the cell is the smallest unit of matter that can be considered to be alive. When a cell is attacked, it will not allow anything into itself without the correct chemical key. The intruder cannot get past the front door. Viruses, however, are clever, they mimic the key. Once inside, they commandeer the cell's machinery and impress it into duplicating for the virus' cause. If that happens, the affected cell is doomed and must rely upon other cells to carry on the battle.

"Balance is the goal. All life wants to live in balance. Just one too many chromosomes, Down's Syndrome. One extra oxygen molecule, toxic carbon dioxide.

"Cells respond to an out of balance condition just as we do: badly. When it rains for too many days in a row, we get depressed. When the arctic night persists all day every day for months in northern Sweden, the suicide rates climb. Landlocked for eleven months of the year? We escape to the beach. Not enough passion with our partner? Well, you get the picture."

Laughter filled the hall.

"We see the need for balance over and over again. When we are deprived of a balanced regimen of food or water or stimulation or education or business or work or liberty or whatever, we will respond by seeking that which we are denied. It's the genetic imperative. Also known as the life force.

"The Life Force — this is very powerful mojo, people. When one species or group abuses another, they may succeed for a time because they are better armed or more ruthless. But eventually, the oppressed will respond. Often with violence.

"In 1793, the long-suffering French had had enough, so they took off Marie Antoinette's elegantly coifed head.

"When nineteenth century settlers in the west slaughtered millions of bison, exterminated the wolf and leeched nutrients from the soil through abusive farming practices, the ground hog, rabbit and grasshopper multiplied out of control and damaged the fragile layer of grassland and topsoil. Later, the topsoil turned to dust and blew away, along with the farmers, the jobs and America's economy in the 1930's."

"Dr. Keene," interrupted a stale-looking academic in the third row.

"Yes," she looked for the source of the voice, pointed, and acknowledged him.

"By these examples do you mean to suggest that Nature is defending itself?"

"Is that so preposterous?"

Looking to others around him for confirmation that he wasn't alone in feeling troubled by Lotte's *Nature's Defense Theory*, he stammered, looked away, then found his tongue, "There's no scholarship, no evidence."

"Sure there is. The scholarship is young but robust; the evidence is empirical."

"What evidence?"

"Excessive intervention in Florida's Everglades now threatens the freshwater aquifers. Oxygen-depleting algae in waters that have been poisoned by pesticides and fertilizer runoffs. Vanishing life-sustaining coral reefs in over-fished sub-tropical waters. Closer to home, in our own bodies, overdependence on antibiotics has encouraged Nature to evolve super viruses that are resistant to medication. Nature is proving to be more clever and persistent than even the richest biotech and pharmaceutical firms.

"Nature evolves biological mechanisms to protect itself from humankind's excesses. It's one of the prices we pay for our privileged position at the top of the food chain. We've taken our atrocious behavior for granted for so long that we don't see it as hubris."

"Surely, not every disaster is man-made, Doctor," a woman in the eighth row offered.

"No, I agree that we can't trace all evil to ourselves. My recent experience of bizarre sudden deaths in Itamarati, Brazil, for example, defied all of our best scientific techniques and technology to identify a cause. Nature seemed to mock our science.

"There may well be discoveries that will alter our understanding. So far, however, we seem to bear the brunt of the responsibility for Nature's responses.

"We are scientists. We are passionate about learning, about understanding, about helping. And because of the exquisite mystery of life, our answer to every question is another question. When confronted by so much overwhelming evidence of the forces at work around us, how can any of us not dare to ask if Nature might not be defending herself?

"What if so-called acts of God are actually acts of self-defense?" she challenged everyone in the auditorium to consider.

"Earth, cells and human beings," she continued, "share this critically important trait: they require balance to survive. If forced out of equilibrium, they organize to reclaim it. Nature wins every time. There *will* be equilibrium . . . or else."

11

ATLANTA – BOULDER

der Root double-clicked the envelope on his screen labeled NSA. It was an AVI video file from an unidentified source.

NSA watched over the planet from its fleet of unblinking satellites and listened with computers that netted every radio wave and free electron, and eavesdropped on the Internet. Its charter expressly limited intelligence gathering activities to areas outside America's borders, so whatever this AVI file was, it was a foreign matter.

A window opened on the screen. Streaming numbers and text appeared at the bottom of the frame. They were unintelligible at first, but as Vin's eyes adjusted, he saw they were coordinates, a running frame count, and other technical data. The time and date indicated it was recorded just hours earlier this morning. When he identified the coordinates – 36° 27' 52.0014" N, −118° 40' 14.6382" W – he checked Asia on the map. It was the only continental landmass other than North America that was above the equator, except for the Arctic, of course, and that was 80+ degrees north. And Greenland. There had never been an outbreak in either of those places. All of Europe and Asia combined were EAST longitude.

He found 36° north latitude and followed it to the west, his finger brushing past Gibraltar, across the Atlantic to North Carolina, Memphis, Oklahoma City, Albuquerque, Flagstaff to the Sequoia National Forest, California. California? He double-checked his coordinates and retraced the 36th latitude across the United States international border and into America's southwest.

What was this? NSA spying on its own?

Looking more closely, some snow he thought was video noise enlarged. One spot moved and revealed greater detail. What was he looking at? He clicked outside the window to see if there was an accompanying text message.

There was not.

There was also no precedent. He had never heard from NSA before. Why now?

Reds and pinks brightened against the shifting blacks. Then the video ended with the last frame frozen on screen. Running time - :73 seconds.

He clicked the replay icon. Knowing better what to expect this time, he studied the image. It zoomed into the black field and enlarged the pink figure.

He had seen spectrometric scans once before. A series of color stills from a satellite scan of the Rwanda genocide. It all came back to him: the varying shades of reds and pinks of murdered victims – the murderers bright red, the victims in various shades of cooling pink.

The red figure swiveled back and forth, not unlike the Rwandans who murdered their victims one at a time with machetes.

The red figure twisted and repeated the swing, froze, fell and didn't move again. Just like the peasants described the sudden deaths in . . . Itamarati.

He reached for the phone.

We're all in this together," Lotte summarized to the sea of faces before her. "Each species belongs to a community. You and I are Homo sapiens; humans who can interbreed and produce fertile offspring naturally. We can exist when and where suitable conditions exist: ambient air temperature in the 0-to-110-degree range, humidity between 38% and 87%, and so on. Food, a certain amount of space, liberty, physical, and intellectual stimulation…

"There are other species, communities, hundreds of thousands of them, some going extinct every day, new ones being discovered. We live in a vibrant, often volatile environment in which species are all competing for their place in the universe.

"If an invertebrate species such as the common sand flea suddenly decides it wants a bigger piece of the pie and multiplies too fast, it starts a sequence of destruction that can be difficult if not impossible to stop.

"We are interdependent, not merely between nations, but also between the biological classifications of kingdoms, divisions, classes, orders, families, genera and species. Between plants and animals, cells and organisms, ALL of it. If just one of us decides he doesn't want to play by the rules of balance, then everyone pays, eventually with their lives." She paused for emphasis before coming around to the front of the dais.

"War and disease are not natural events in the sense that neither contributes to fertility, reproduction, or the healthy propagation of a species. War and disease are reactions to other events. Reactions to stress created by assaults on the balanced system. Somebody or something took more than its share and tipped the scale. The victims – be they an oppressed minority like Native Americans, oysters under assault by zebra clams in the Hudson, or immune systems thrown out of balance by decades of antibiotics and ever more rapid exposure to foreign viruses – eventually react. In violence at Wounded Knee, destruction of the Hudson fishery, or escalating mutations of lethal viruses that outpace our ability to identify and counter them.

"Ultimately, the outlaw species suffers, too. That is the beauty of the system: ultimate justice. The problem for us, however, isn't ultimate justice." She paused to remove her glasses and polish them with a tissue. "It is recognizing our interdependency." She looked into the eyes of her listeners, hoping to see an answer to the nettlesome conundrum she posed to them, "How do we get through today without further upsetting the ultimate balance?"

der Root bit his lip as he waited for Lotte to answer. "This is Keene," Lotte's voice came breathlessly through the phone.

"Did I catch you jogging?"

"No, I'm on my way back to my office. Something's come up. Might not be anything, but I wanted you to know."

"California."

"Yes, I have some Biosat video I want you to see."

"The BIOSAT-7 video - pink and red spots against black."

"You saw the AVI?"

"I did. It looks --"

Lotte stopped walking.

"Lotte?"

"What's going on, der Root? I did not send that video to you. I'm the only one who has it."

"You didn't send it to NSA?"

"Are you out of your mind? Holy--," Lotte hissed under her breath.

"—shit," Vin finished for her. "Maybe it's just some G-5 clerk in Fort Meade trying to be helpful."

"Big brother eavesdropping on scientific research?"

He didn't respond.

"I want to go out there."

He still didn't respond.

"I know what you're thinking: Keene's a nut."

He chuckled.

"It's all right to think it, Vin. Just don't let it influence your science. You don't have to decide anything, but this could be relevant."

"Call me – and me only – if you find anything."

"What? You're passing up epidemiological glory?"

"Call me." His voice sounded thinner, distracted.

"Alright. I'll call."

12

THUNDER PEAK

Interstate 198 serpentined over a high ridge and passed one steep valley of endangered Sierra Range land after another. The blur of terrain racing past Ben's window had been a forest primeval for millennia. Now it was a scarred, surreal landscape. Some of the destruction was legal, most of it was not.

Before long, the speeding pickup carried them into aromatic subalpine Lodgepole. The temperature dropped ten degrees as the truck entered filtered grove light. They were above 9,000 feet elevation now in the Thunder Peak Wilderness. Ahwahnee land.

The two-lane crossed skeletal stubble of what had been for uncountable centuries a stand of dense larch giants.

"Used to see woodland deer in there," Nate said quietly, gesturing out the pickup's windshield to the right. "Secretive animal, that one. Anymore, there's no habitat for the northern creatures. The ones I saw as a boy - twelve, maybe fourteen in all — must have wandered down from the north."

The deer were trophies on backwoods cabin walls now. Great curves of bone not seen anywhere south of the Arctic Circle.

The truck engine's steady thrum transported Ben across time. What must it have been like here 22,000 years ago, before dark-skinned explorers from Siberia. They would have seen dense old growth from sea to subalpine ridges. A New World untouched. Before the Spanish, the Finns, the Germans and English. Before land grants and chainsaws.

Forest management enjoyed a brief, idealistic adolescence here from the 1930's into the 1950's. The heavy cutting that devastated sections of the western slope from the banks of the Kaweah River to Alpine Meadow had yet to begin. Old growth was plentiful. Forestry professionals still logged selectively and enabled sustained yield. Those were the days.

Woodcutters went for the dense low-elevation conifers hugging the riverbanks because they were accessible; easy to extract. So they cut and cut some more. When these dense stands were gone, the land became real estate.

The less accessible old growth stands higher up then became desirable. Folks who bought that clear-cut cum real estate had to make a living, pay their mortgage.

Large conglomerates like Case-Kaiser saw the future and bought up the higher elevation woods as commercial forest. This kept it out of John Logger's reach for a time. But the drug had taken effect, regular folks were addicted to the jobs and needed ever more frequent fixes. More timber, more real estate, more taxes, more, more, more. Problem was, the woods couldn't keep pace. The drug supply was running out.

Now, all that was left was the Thunder Peak Wilderness, California's last stands of quality old growth timber. How long could the Ahwahnee hold out? Japan, California, and Florida had acres of subdivision home foundations poured and waiting for wood.

Soon Nate and Ben were in the subalpine firs above 10,000 feet. Ben glimpsed the Wilderness' gray granite citadel, Thunder Peak, through occasional breaks in the upswept branches of western yellow pines. It appeared wizened from a distance, streaked white at the crown and on the left side. Nate's father, Chief Adrian Stimson, occasionally prayed up there at sunrise. Sacred place, said the chief. Ben couldn't argue with him about that. It looked like a pulpit in the cathedral pines.

Nate coaxed the four-wheeler as high into the ponderosas as he could. The truck groaned and squealed as he powered over rocks and deadfall. When he could go no farther, he turned off the engine, reached behind the seat and handed Ben a face mask.

"What's this?"

"What's it look like? Put it on."

"No thanks."

"Ben, put the damned thing on."

"Why should I?"

"The satellite Doc in Boulder thinks it might be something airborne up here," he said evenly. He wasn't sure he believed her, but he sure as hell didn't want to end up like Oren. He'd decided he would play along, at least until they knew more.

"Well hell, Nate. If it's what the satellite Doc orders. How about gloves? Got any sterile gloves?"

Nate handed him a pair.

Ben rolled his eyes and slid out his side of the truck.

The walking was difficult, but they were soon deep into the open ground beneath the old growth giants.

Sunlight broke through dissipating clouds and glistened on fern, lichen, and bark. Rainbows appeared in mists rising from the spongy forest floor. And ahead, cold nectar air glimmered in the slanting light.

Nate led the way up, threading between massive pines.

The slope used to host million-acre stands that had co-evolved for millennia, since before man first stood upright in Africa. Old growth was the best example of biological process anywhere. From ragged, broken-topped, mossy crowns to the intricate subterranean web of mycelia, the fungus threads that carried nutrients from soil to plant root-tips.

There were 5,000 individual organisms in a single square foot of soil beneath the canopy. As many as 70 separate species. In 1988, Gordon Robinson documented how the total animal population in one square foot of old growth soil approached 10,000 animals!

Above ground in the Thunder Peak stand, the Spotted Owl hunted the Flying Squirrel. The Pine Marten dashed from treetop to treetop and ran down the Chickaree. The Red-backed Vole resided two hundred feet above ground where its ancestors had dwelled for hundreds of generations without ever touching earth. Any sense memory of the feel of soil under its pads was lost a century ago. The earth was as mysterious and forbidding to it as deep space is to man.

Three ravens crossed Nate and Ben's path. The last one, a glossy youngster, kraa-a-a-kked, blinked its silver eyes and brought up the rear. The three shadows continued down slope.

A winter wren moved to a low branch a few yards to Ben's right. He noiselessly fluffed his feathers on the slender shoot. Tilting his head first to one side and then the other, he evaluated Ben and Nate.

He was brown with precise dark reticulations and his beak and tail were cocked at energetic angles. He leaned forward and with two wing flaps disappeared into a thicket. The air filled with exuberant scales up, down and up again. It was the wren's song Ben recalled when he returned to the woods in his dreams. The wren flew on to another part of the forest, leaving the men to the crunch and shuffle of their boot steps and hoarse gasps of exertion as they climbed.

Nate checked his notes again for the coordinates Dr. Keene had given him, and then compared these with the department's handheld GPS readout. "Should be up ahead to the right," he pointed to an outcrop that projected like a giant's nose from between the skirts of centuries old matriarchs.

They had trudged ahead just twenty yards when Nate suddenly stopped and sniffed the air.

"What is it?" asked Ben.

Concerned, Nate pulled off his mask and sniffed again. His expression clouded over and he began to systematically scan every tree, scrub, and boulder ahead. "We've got company."

"Bear."

Ben spun around in place, seeing nothing.

"It's not too strong but it's there. Smell it? Musky, kinda musty."

"Damn," hissed Ben.

"Black." Nate clapped his hands and said in a loud voice, "Keep your eye on that grove just to the left and make noise."

"Okay," shouted Ben.

"Let's get on with it."

They moved forward.

They might have missed their man if they had come upon him from another angle. He blended into the red and gray bark of a colossal fir tree. His green/gray/black camouflage made him invisible if you didn't look closely.

He was a bow hunter. His right arm was raised and crooked for release of a mean-looking three bladed big game arrow. Could be any one of hundreds of locals. When Nate and Ben spotted him, they paused and observed for several moments, expecting him to move. He didn't.

Nate pointed to a spot 30 yards to the left. Ben looked and saw more tree trunks and undergrowth. Nate gestured emphatically to the same area. Then Ben saw it, six points. A six by six and the proud outline of a great buck's head. It didn't move either. They observed the eerie tableau – *Archer and Stag.*

Finally, Nate cleared his throat. Still, the hunter didn't react. After a quick glance at Ben, Nate cleared his throat again, more loudly this time. A hawk lifted off from a high branch and soared along the ridge to the north.

"Lars?" said Nate in a low voice. Then louder, "That you, Lars Broder?"

Still no movement.

Nate grimaced. "Step careful. Evidence."

Ben scanned the trees and shrubs for signs of airborne poison. Nate's warning reminded him to be equally observant about ground cover. All he saw were dew-covered boot prints, needles, cones, and some mushrooms.

Leaning against the great tree, half-heartedly aiming at the buck, Lars Broder appeared strangely comfortable, almost relaxed. Not like he was about to let that fierce arrow fly.

Ben and Nate made a wide circle and saw that he wasn't fully coiled for the kill. The arrow lay impotently on the bow's arrow rest. Ben noted that Broder's index and middle fingertips still gripped the arrow nock; the tips ruddy with the flush of blood. Maybe he wasn't dead. Gravity would have drawn blood earthwards, away from the extremities shortly after death and left the fingers ashen and colorless.

The itch returned on Ben's neck.

Up close, Broder's open eyes and ruddy color still mimicked life. Matted hair across his forehead reminded Ben of a rain-soaked goat. His facial expression looked as if a momentous thought had distracted him just as he was taking aim at his prey. Despite the lifelike mask, however, he was cold, stiff, and lacked a pulse.

Ben nodded 'no chance.' Broder was beyond anything they could do for him.

Nate bear-hugged him, shifted to a clear spot, and lowered him to the ground. He stepped back to survey the body. "Jes' like Oren," he muttered.

"Exactly," agreed Ben.

Nate looked around for another body. He'd be happy to be done with this for the morning. But the satellite Doc had predicted he would find two. She was batting 500 so far.

"What's that?" Ben asked.

Nate turned to see Ben pointing behind the tree, beyond it.

The evaporating mists were nearly gone by now. Visibility extended 100 yards before it was overwhelmed by shadows in the cool glen. Nate followed Ben's gaze past the tree trunk, over dense scrub and deep into a gathering of trunks that marched up the next ridge. He saw damp bark, tangled undergrowth, occasional flashing wing flaps, and dewdrops raining.

"What?" he snapped.

Nelson Hatch was slumped over his ax, which was set deep in the flesh of a giant tree. Whatever it was that got him stopped him cold after his second cut. He hung there like game on a hook.

No symptoms of shock, or heart disease or the purple skin associated with lividity.

No signs of the stress of strained breathing.

There *was* a faint pulse.

"Quick, let's get him down," Ben threaded his arms under Hatch and lifted. Nate helped lower him to the ground and Ben started compressing his chest. He tried lifting the arms to force blood flow but they were too stiff. He was concerned about breaking them. A dewdrop splashed on the pupil. Hatch didn't blink. There was something unmistakable going on inside his eye. Whatever it was, *something* lived inside Nelson Hatch's apparently dead body.

As they packed the bodies out of the clearing, Nate sniffed the air and frowned.

Ben caught a movement in his peripheral vision. They both saw the branch thirty feet upslope lower and snap back up into place.

"We've got to go . . . NOW," Nate shouted.

"Why did I have to hear from some outsider what's happening in my own backyard? Can you tell me that, Doc?" Nate paced as Ben fought the shadow spreading over his patient.

Hatch's symptoms were identical to those he observed in Oren Pocknett: the steady hardening, 'embalming' effect that had happened before Nate brought the body to him. Here Ben had a victim in the early stages yet he was helpless to stop it. Blood thinners were ineffectual. His training and skills utterly useless.

Ben administered lidocaine. That helped a bit. "What the hell was Nelson Hatch doing out there on private property, cutting a seven hundred year-old tree in the middle of the night? And why an axe and not a McCullough? Was he trying to steal the tree? There's no way he could have done anything with it even if he felled it."

"It's no secret that every lumberjack in Longwood is pissed off at the Ahwahnee for refusing to sell. Maybe ol' Nelson just wanted to show the Ahwahnee who's who..." Nate offered.

Ben went to the other room and considered Broder's corpse. There was no sign of anything to give them a clue. Even the rigor mortis was enigmatic. Not progressive. It was over in seconds, a minute tops.

He tested the neck muscles for rigidity. They were no more rigid than any other muscles.

No signs of sudden numbness in the face. No symptoms of sudden weakness on one side of the body.

There was no way of knowing if Lars Broder experienced dizziness or slurred speech or diminished comprehension of sounds.

Same rate of temperature loss as Oren Pocknett.

Same with Hatch. 82.1 degrees. Hatch had been hanging there like that for hours and still clung to life on Ben's table. Why did Broder die and Hatch live?

Positional asphyxia?

So what was the provisional cause of death? Asphyxia secondary to . . . what?

In Boulder, Lotte looked around her office at the computer

displaying BIOSAT-7's most recent pass over the Thunder Peak Wilderness . . . at the wall map with its bright green pushpins where she had plotted disease outbreaks . . . at the stubbornly silent fax.

She looked at a framed photo on the desk, the one in which she, Charley, and der Root appeared immortal. It had been taken in Termez on the Kazakh-Afghan border seven years and eight outbreaks ago. They were the three musketeers then, fearless whiz kids who turned epidemiology upside down with their exploits. What went wrong? Vin was AWOL. Charley was in a snow-covered grave. And she was here on the front line with the war still to be won. Alone.

She had to go to Thunder Peak. It wasn't rational, she knew. It could be nothing. There was no proof of anything. Going would violate basic interagency response procedure. But she wasn't feeling rational. She needed to fight back.

She picked up her go-pack shoulder bag from the corner. It contained a weeks' change of clothes, medical kit containing inoculation vials for all the usual fevers and viruses, toilet and beauty kit which consisted, in her sole concession to vanity, a tube of rose-pink lip gloss.

The clothes were lightweight jungle shirts and pants. Too light for autumn above the 41st parallel. Whatever she didn't have, she'd purchase in California. She grasped her field lab hard case and her briefcase. The old Sherpa feeling returned as the weight bowed her shoulders.

Mounted up and ready to close the door, she paused and looked at the AVI file cycle over and over on the monitor screen.

She turned off the computer, placed the photo in her backpack and locked the door behind her.

13

LONGWOOD

Boulder West to Grand Junction on the ribbon that reflected a dozen hues a day on BIOSAT-7's spectrometers, south on 15 through Vegas to Barstow, west on 40 to 395 north to Lone Pine, then left into the High Sierras.

By morning, she was among the largest trees she'd seen since California's coastal redwoods. 250-270 feet, she estimated. Their deeply creased trunks glowed red in the dawn light like pilings in a forested bay.

Lotte drove the last remaining Volkswagen Deluxe Microbus Type 2s in the western hemisphere. After eight Colorado winters, her tired, pre-owned, once-white classic microbus still gripped the narrow mountain road like a goat. Thanks to a bonus after the Rwanda trip, its rubber was fresh. The new sidewalls, which brandished the Goodyear logo, looked incongruous under the oxidized and rusting body. The air conditioner no longer worked and the engine sounded like a Cessna. She rolled down the window and adjusted her straw hat to hold her hair back in the wind. Road weary, she found a turnout and allowed herself a roadside nap. Then it was up, up, up, then down the western slope into some of the most spectacular forest south of the Coastal Redwoods, Buck

Peak, Kanawyers, Cedar Grove, past Lookout Peak and, the Generals Highway and Longwood.

Traffic was light on 180. The van huffed and rattled as it gasped for air at 10,600 feet - twice Boulder's elevation and with only half the oxygen. "You'll adapt," Lotte shouted encouragement above the transmission's wail and downshifted. "Liked Boulder? You're going to *love* the Sierras, darlin'!"

Across the two-lane, blast-channels glistened like battle scars in the stone. To the right, the mountain dropped steeply into clear-cut oblivion. How did logging trucks negotiate these narrow passes? Some of the scars in the stone looked like they were created by rigs that got too close.

The long drive alone with her thoughts had compressed time between today and the past. Itamarati cancelled out Boulder. Charley haunted her. The other peasants stoic in their mortal poses were part of the past, yet now they were alive again and asking, 'why?'"

Why?

Lotte braked for a large buck browsing on the outside shoulder, then accelerated into a sweeping left turn around a high outcropping. A movement in the rearview mirror caught her eye. A late-model Cadillac, gleaming pearl white, charged up behind her. Lotte braced for the impact, but the Caddy braked just short of the van's rear end, dipped like a boat in ponderous seas, drifted back, then accelerated again.

He leaned on his horn and flashed his high beams. Gray haired, tanned, in his mid-50's, he flipped her off and mouthed something. She wasn't sure, but it looked like he said: "Out of the fucking way!"

They were on a narrow stretch now that tunneled through a massive arbor of centuries-old pines. It would have been beautiful if she wasn't so pissed off by this Neanderthal in the DeVille. He accelerated into the inner lane and began to pass her.

"Oh no you don't, you son of a bitch." She turned towards the wall and forced him back again.

Banging on the horn, he leaned out the window of his land yacht and screamed into the wind.

"Cool off, Mario," she said to the red-faced image in her rearview mirror.

Apparently, he didn't hear her advice because he roared past and cut her off. Lotte braked and felt the tires lock up in a cloud of blue smoke. The van skidded to a stop three inches from his passenger side door. He was out of his car and walking towards her. She thought about throwing the van in reverse and escaping before things spun any farther out of control. But the command over his hair-trigger road rage was astonishing. He wasn't pounding at her like a Bronco defensive tackle. Short and stocky, he strolled up to her in a businesslike, almost genteel manner.

Lotte reached for the pepper spray canister she kept in the glove box just in case, and eased down from behind the wheel. It wasn't a gun, but it could get his attention if she had to use it.

Gawd, that walk! "What are you doing, Mister. You could have gotten us both killed!"

He looked her over. "You're not from around here, so I'll do you a favor and advise you that, number one: use the road up a little faster - you're in California now — and number two: keep driving. The people of Longwood are god-fearing, hard-working folks. There's no place for gypsies, hippies, or radicals. We've got a zero-tolerance for anyone without visible means of support." His lips curled into the semblance of a smile, but his eyes remained stony and cold.

Lotte held his gaze and answered. "You the Sheriff?"

"No, why?" he said menacingly.

"I'll find him, thanks. Seeing as you're in such a rush and need the entire road to accommodate your, ah, driving."

"You were doing 55!"

"Yes, I was, exactly."

"I'm in a hurry."

"I see you are. You this quick at everything?"

Something flashed in his eyes. He wasn't used to being challenged by a woman. Or anyone else, from the way his expression darkened. "I advise you to –"

"Didn't you say you had to be someplace?"

"Why you b—" he leaned toward her.

Lotte raised the pepper spray and was about to shoot when something caught her wrist and held it. She spun around to see a large, powerfully built Native American in a sheriff's uniform.

"That's all for now, folks. I'll make sure our visitor is well taken care of, Wilburn."

"Now see here, Nate." His pride had been dented and he wasn't ready to let this go.

"I said I'd take care of it," the Sheriff repeated.

The little man glared at Lotte again, returned to his car, and drove away.

14

LONGWOOD

The van wouldn't start.

"Whoever replaced the carburetor installed the new model without the adaptor," Nate Stimson explained as he wiped his hands. "Made the same mistake on my Dad's ol' van. Same year as yours here. The garage in town has some tools and can fix her right up."

He attached a tow bar to her van's front axle and told Lotte to get into the truck for the ride into Longwood.

As he eased the truck off the shoulder and on to road, he kept an eye on the vintage van in his rearview mirror and soon settled in to a steady 55 miles per hour pace. "Well, Dr. Keene, you do make an entrance," he grinned.

"Your timing's not bad either, Sheriff," she relaxed a little as her adrenalin receded.

"That *gentleman* you almost shot with pepper spray? That was our Mayor, Wilburn Spivey."

She should have known: the Cadillac, the attitude. Of course.

"He listens to you," she observed.

"Not really. Votes are scarce in this country," he quipped.

"Maybe. Or you might be underestimating your power of

persuasion, Sheriff."

He sniffed and checked the rearview mirror again. She had touched a nerve, but he wasn't the kind to take compliments easily. She took the moment to look him over again. He appeared more nimble and energetic behind the wheel of the truck than on foot.

A white Range Rover roared past, the driver honking and waving as he sped by. The logo on the side door read *Case-Kaiser – better living through resource management*. It must have been going eighty miles an hour.

Sheriff Stimson glanced over, nodded perfunctorily to the driver, and returned his eyes to the road ahead.

Lotte noted that Sheriff Nate Stimson had particular priorities. She had seen it in small towns all over the world. The corporations that controlled the jobs usually controlled everything else, too. Apparently, Case-Kaiser had a pass to ignore speed limits. She wondered what else they ignored.

"So when do I see the bodies?" she asked, seeking firmer ground.

"Doc McCandle's waiting for you."

The sky opened as verdant shadows of dense forest gave way to vast fields of stumps and trash timber, the detritus of clear-cut. Omaha Beach. All that was missing was bloated bodies of slain invaders.

The air changed, too. Gone were the aromas of damp bark and new growth. They were replaced by progress' dusty and abrasive air. She had experienced the jarring sensation of sudden destruction so many times: the Cascades in Washington State where Case-Kaiser had destroyed what Nature had taken countless centuries to create, paid the fines and left devastation in its wake. India. Nigeria. Brazil.

The temperature climbed as sunlight beat down on the truck. She focused on a dark line of trees across the dead valley floor and willed the truck to go faster. After several minutes of progress toward the forest ahead, a scent of evergreen wafted into the cab.

"Tell me Longwood is in there," she said with scarcely suppressed pleading in her voice.

He glanced over at her and warmed. "It is. And that tall peak off to the right?" Lotte spotted a dagger-like shard of granite towering above two other spectacular promontories. "That's Thunder Peak. All the forested land you see is protected - National

Park, National Forest and Treaty land - and threatened. Longwood is just ahead."

It was stunning. Her anger at the waste ebbed as gratitude built for the preserved old growth. It was magnificent.

The road wound steadily higher into an endless forest of firs. The truck rolled into the embrace of cool scented shadows again and they both relaxed.

Where the tall trees thinned, it was apparent why. The occasional ranch house gave way to a mercantile, an ACE Hardware, a John Deere dealer. A produce field with a weathered stand by the road separated the parking lot of green machines from a row of four cedar shingle-sided homes, wooden porches with well-used upholstered chairs, black wrought iron stair railings, old pickups in narrow drives.

Sheriff Stimson signaled left, looked both ways, and turned down Longwood's main street.

The centerline needed a fresh coat of yellow safety paint. There weren't many citizens to be seen. Three men talked in the shade of a weathered diner's sign that featured a large dot in flaking red paint and the words 'The Hut' in white letters. They turned to watch the Sheriff's truck and the van in tow move past. A small dusty station wagon backed into the street and braked. The driver, a woman, gave a small wave to Nate and waited for him to pass.

Another left turn onto Redding Street and a Victorian house that looked good for her age appeared on the right side.

"You'll be bunking upstairs," he pulled in to the gravel parking area and was halfway out the door before she noticed the sign on the front porch that read: *Longwood Medical Clinic* in plain black letters. Underneath: *Benjamin J. McCandle, M.D.* Below that: *Hours: 7:00 a.m. – 4:30 p.m. M-F.*

The Sheriff led her down a narrow walkway beside the cold-stone foundation to a weather door. She braced herself for the inevitable blast of foul air, formaldehyde, and disinfectant that characterized every morgue she had ever been in, but it did not come. She stepped through and followed the wooden stairs down into what had no doubt served at one time as a root cellar. The walls were well fitted stone, the floor was poured concrete painted light gray, the ceiling was raw timbers. Several fluorescent work lights with diffusion lenses provided general illumination. A large, homemade but serviceable examination table hovered like a stainless steel UFO in the center of the room under two surgical suite lights for close work. The body of a male in his mid-forties on the table lay hunched and poised like a dancer contemplating his feet. There were pillows under his shoulders and neck and he was covered to the waist by a blanket.

She noticed a doorway that led into another, more finished room. White walls glowed from within. There was a walk-in refrigeration unit. She also spied a sheet-covered form on a gurney. Whatever was under there wasn't prone like a corpse; one arm was fully extended and tented the sheet.

At the far side of the room, a man at a bench with his back turned was reading. He looked to be sprouted from this rugged country, wiry, with just enough meat on his bones to stand up to the wind, the sun, and solitude.

The Sheriff paused a few feet from the table and apparently had no intention of venturing farther. "Ben, the lady doc is here from Boulder," he said quietly.

The man in the white lab coat marked his place in the book, removed his glasses, and turned, "Dr. Keene?"

"Lotte, please. Doctor McCandle."

"Ben," he shook her hand. "So you're the alpha epidemiologist. Nate tells me you and your satellite observed what happened to Nelson here," he gestured to the body on the table.

"You found him in the Thunder Peak Wilderness?"

"How high is that bird anyways?" asked Nate.

"155 miles."

The Sheriff whistled softly.

Ben was looking at Hatch and didn't answer. Silence seemed to be his form of assent. Sheriff Stimson had filled her in as they passed through town: Doc McCandle brought his wife and daughter back home to Longwood nine years ago. He did his residency in ER on Chicago's south side. After a few years in that war zone, he said he and his family were ready for peace. His wife, Hannah, died four years back. The Sheriff paused. He'd said too much. "Anyway," he continued, "it's a good man you'll be working with."

She saw a man with the usual appetites, she guessed. His expression was open, yet his body was coiled as if in anticipation of the need to act. His denim shirt and the t-shirt underneath were fresh. He hadn't shaved this morning, his hair was uncombed, and his face was sun dark, older than his years. A man of contradictions, she thought. His jeans were worn, baggy at the knees and stacked over construction boots. He was fit, wore no wedding band, had broad shoulders, narrow hips, and a lean face.

"He's alive, but only technically," Ben's deep-set eyes seemed preoccupied as he took her in. "I've performed the A, B, C's, and every emergency medical protocol - airway, breathing, circulation. There's no response."

Lotte reached over and placed two fingers on Nelson Hatch's carotid artery. "Bradycardic."

"His heart is straining along at 59 beats per minute, every one defying the inevitable." He looked across at Lotte.

"Atropine?"

"I injected him, but it can't circulate." Atropine blocks the Vegas nerve, which could block conduction and stimulate circulation. In a reasonably healthy patient, that is.

"It looks like rigor mortis, but," she began.

"It's not," Ben finished for her.

"Couldn't be, of course. He's still alive. But from the looks of your other victim," she nodded in the direction of the outer room, "I'm assuming *that* is rigor mortis?"

"No. That's what's so strange. The body shows no signs of the primary muscular flaccidity and subsequent generalized muscular stiffening of rigor mortis you would expect."

"Is that why you're not refrigerating the body?" asked Lotte. "So room warmth will accelerate secondary muscular flaccidity?"

Ben nodded, grateful for Lotte's medical competence. "Pretty crude, I know, but I guess Lars shouldn't mind much."

"No," she repressed a smile, "he shouldn't mind. So, one somatic death, one legitimate cellular death and no identifiable cause."

Nate Stimson looked from Ben to Lotte and back again, following their conversation from a distance. They were the doctors with the jargon. He would leave this part of the investigation to them. He hoped Nelson couldn't hear what was being said.

"Today," agreed Ben.

"Today?" asked Lotte. Then she remembered Sheriff Stimson's ready acceptance of her bizarre report of deaths on her satellite monitor. He'd admitted that there had been other victims in the

Thunder Peak Wilderness. Two more hadn't surprised him.

"There was Oren Pocknett last night and another last week," continued Ben.

"With the same symptomologies?"

"Identical."

She stared at him, not expecting him to say more. After a moment, she turned again to the patient on the table. "Comprehensive Drug Screen?"

"Can't get urine, no."

"What do you mean? The urethra is blocked?"

"Totally obstructed," answered Ben patiently.

"CBC with differential?"

He handed her a blood vile partially filled with a dark red crystalline muck.

She grimaced as she held it up to the light. What should have been deep red blood looked more like something he'd cleaned out of a clogged kitchen drain.

"I'll try to do a blood count, of course. But I'm not expecting much. Not sure what to do at this point."

"The red count might tell us if he is bleeding. I'm more interested in the white count. My guess is it would be off the charts," she looked at Ben, then back to the vile, "if we can get a count, that is."

Lotte mentally checked off the protocol. Having a Chem 20 – a.k.a. SMAC 20 – would help explain what was going on inside Nelson Hatch's body, such as liver, kidney or electrolyte problems and if his blood sugar was out of norms. But she could no more run a Chem 20 on this sample than Ben could run a CBC.

She wanted to know what Hatch's fibrinogen levels were. That would tell her something about the blood's capacity to coagulate. It was a possibility with this sample, but a remote one. Besides, it would only confirm what she saw with her eyes – Nelson Hatch's blood was already coagulated.

"An Arterial Blood Gas workup is out of the question, too," she thought aloud. But that triggered another question.

"It's a good thought, but the nearest ABG analyzer is 115 miles from here, in Bakersfield."

"How did you draw this?" she asked as she held up the vile. An ABG draw should be either radial or brachial. "Elbow or wrist?"

"Brachial. His elbow artery was swollen from exertion. I cut and scooped," answered Ben flatly.

Lotte saw the bandage inside Hatch's left elbow. "How about an X-Ray? Do you have one?"

"A 1973 GE," Ben guided her to a bench she hadn't noticed and switched on a wall-mounted light box. "Read film, Doctor?"

"The basics - air pockets appear dark, fluid lighter. The more dense the tissue, the whiter the image," Lotte answered as she studied the film.

"That's about it, really. In this case, it's enough."

The film looked more like an X-ray of a sculpture than a typical X-ray of the human body. Everything was white. Organs, muscle, everything. Bones were visible, but just barely, like bones in a blizzard. The vertebral column showed as a white column in the white torso, apparent only after staring for several seconds at the film. Lotte had never seen anything like it.

"That's the fifth film," explained Ben without a trace of defensiveness. "I couldn't believe it the first four times."

Lotte understood what he meant. It would be tempting to jump to the conclusion that the operator overexposed the film. In the upper right corner the control strip appeared perfectly calibrated.

"Lumbar puncture, then?"

"That's what I'm thinking," agreed Ben. "But again, what good will it do us?"

"If there are white blood cells in the fluid, we know we're fighting an infection."

"Sure, but we can learn that from the sample we have."

"Maybe," she examined the vile again and shook it. The blood inside scarcely moved.

"Maybe," repeated Ben. "Nelson's somewhere in hell right now and he doesn't need a painful procedure to remind him."

"IF he feels anything at all," countered Lotte. *It was Itamarati all over again.*

15

LONGWOOD

The clock on the whitewashed cinderblock wall clicked ahead.

Nelson Hatch's stiffness, atypical blood crystallization, and absence of putrefaction gave her a familiar chill.

"You're supposed to be the expert," Ben interrupted her thoughts, frustration rattling his voice.

Here it comes, she thought. The time in every epidemic investigation when local authorities -- tribal chiefs, politicians, doctors, or whatever -- realized that the experts were human. First, they resented outside interference, then they welcomed the presence of someone to share their fear, then they resented the time required to perform the most basic scientific protocols, and then they felt let down when they realized that the experts were subject to the same self-doubts, fallibilities and frustrations. In this case, there had been no obvious sign of the first three stages. As a medical doctor, Ben McCandle surely experienced the same sequence of emotional reactions in his patients. Still, he was human and the recent spate of deaths in the Thunder Peak Wilderness was clearly getting under his skin.

"Both Broder and Hatch were found within yards of each other, stricken by the same symptoms. Broder is dead and Hatch is not. I don't know why, Doctor." She returned to Hatch's body, glanced at the heart rate monitor that was now chirping along at a thready 60 beats per minute, and, not trusting the monitor, felt again for a pulse in his carotid. "These symptoms are … intriguing."

Lotte's reaction to the stressful circumstances annoyed Ben: she was growing calmer, deliberate, almost relaxed. It was her way whenever people around her became tense or excited. She slowed to a plodding, deliberate pace. By removing herself from the gathering emotional noise of those around her, she remained objective.

"You seem to be enjoying this," Ben said irritably.

She looked directly at him. "I don't enjoy anything about disease or death, except defeating them."

"Can it be a variant of *Hantavirus*?" he suggested.

Everyone in the western U.S. knew about *Hantavirus* after the Four Corners event in 1993. The CDC had attacked its investigation with more than the usual resources; whether because the outbreak occurred within America's borders or because in the evolution of scientific skills, the CDC had a better understanding of the threat and the expertise to combat it, only history could judge. The death toll had been significant: 27 out of 48 cases that they know about. The epidemiologists' successful identification of the source enhanced the CDC's credibility. And it was a media-friendly virus with all the elements of a good story – colorful settings, horrific symptoms, and a mundane carrier: deer mouse droppings. A modern day echo of the Medieval Black Plague. Great television, a real ratings grabber.

"Sound suspicion, but I don't think that's the case here," she observed. "This killer's incubation period is practically non-existent. It seems to function more like a chemical nerve agent."

Ben winced. He knew enough about nerve agents to know that they destroyed the fragile balance of the human nervous system and reduced normally functioning persons to convulsing, tainted meat.

Nate unwrapped a stick of chewing gum and popped it into his mouth as he listened. More attuned to the mounting violence among unemployed loggers and angry environmentalists, he glanced at Doc McCandle for confirmation of his concern. He expected some sort of ugliness to develop eventually. *Earth Rebirth!*

radicals led by the shadowy Gabriel the Fox, as he was known to the media and law enforcement, had spiked trees, sabotaged half million dollar heavy haulers, and hacked into Case-Kaiser computers. Despite *Earth Rebirth's* efforts to slow the pace of logging, however, clear-cutting spread like a disease across the West's remaining old growth forestlands. He didn't see any reason why the bioterrorism that plagued the industrialized cities wouldn't soon be visited upon logging communities, perhaps even Longwood. He just hadn't expected it this soon.

"*Is* it a nerve agent?" asked Ben.

Nate stopped chewing and waited.

"I doubt it. But it's not a naturally occurring forest phenomenon, either." She held her chaotic hair away from her face and gazed at Hatch. "I want to file an alert. We need to get a team in here."

Ben and Nate looked uneasily at one another.

"No thanks," objected Ben. "Longwood's been to hell and back this last year. You bring in white coats, no offense, Federal investigators will follow. Then, media!"

"Doctor McCandle - Ben," she corrected herself, "I've seen these symptoms before, just once."

"Where?" Ben frowned. He was tired and short on patience. "Is there something you need to tell me, Dr. Keene?"

"It doesn't take long in this job to see that disease is a *reaction* to other events. Reaction to stress created by assaults on a balanced system. In escalating mutations of lethal viruses that outpace our ability to identify and counter them. In new symptoms, and new diseases that have been waiting since they were born in primordial soup, adapting through millennia until conditions were right for them to prosper."

Nate and Ben exchanged glances.

"Are you suggesting that something in the Thunder Peak has been stressed to the 'reaction point?'" asked Ben.

"I am."

"Doctor Keene, I know Nelson's symptoms are strange," Nate leaned on the table and spoke over Hatch's curled body, "but just what are you saying here? There's a monster in the woods?"

"That's one way of looking at it."

Nate and Ben traded glances again.

"I know I'm just a plain country boy, Doctor," Ben faced her,

76

hands in jeans pockets, boots planted shoulders width apart, "but what the hell are you talking about?"

Lotte took in Ben, amused at his effect on her. He was neither plain, nor a boy. She also questioned just how much country he was.

"Brazil. Same symptoms. We hadn't seen anything like it before."

After a pause, Nate asked, "How many died?"

"Twenty One."

"And you experts haven't found the cause?" asked Ben.

"No."

Ben and Nate waited in vain for something more.

"Sometimes Nature isn't ready to reveal her secrets. Sometimes, she's had enough and strikes back."

Their faces clouded over.

"Don't worry, gentlemen. I'm many things, but crazy isn't one of them. Despite what the scientific establishment thinks."

Ben paused. "Just what does the scientific establishment think?"

Nate stood arms folded across his deep chest. One eyebrow rose slightly.

"Are they right?" asked Ben.

"Well, they're not completely wrong," she forced a smile.

Silence descended on the cellar, punctuated by the muted electronic pulse of Nelson Hatch's heart monitor.

She took his vital signs again. "Enough of that for now." Lowering her voice to a caregiver's whisper, she said to Ben, "At the moment, gentlemen, Nelson's problem is our opportunity. If we learned anything from the Four Corners outbreak, it's the value of good postmortem information..."

"Nelson is still here, Doctor," Nate objected.

"Of course he is," agreed Lotte, "for a little while at least."

Nate frowned. Ben wasn't listening. He stared wide-eyed over her shoulder at the body on the table.

"What is it?" she asked.

"He just moved."

16

LONGWOOD

Two blocks west of Ben McCandle's medical clinic, at the Mayor's office in the vacant storefront five-and-dime, Wilburn Spivey and Case-Kaiser's CEO, Richard Jasperson, huddled at the large conference table.

"Can we do that?" Spivey's voice cracked.

He wasn't really the weakling that Jasperson thought he was. Loggers were no nonsense men. They wouldn't have elected him mayor if they didn't respect him. It was just that something about this man made him nervous.

The conference table was a massive pine slab four inches thick, twenty feet long and seven wide. The tree's pith ran straight down the middle and five branch traces – vascular bundles that supplied long absent limbs – orbited like planets in the deep honey gold top. The tree from which Longwood harvested its table had been alive in 1590, at the same time that Galilei Galileo was dropping various objects from the Tower of Pisa and Shakespeare was writing "Taming of the Shrew." The 410-year old giant had also supplied wood for thirteen of Longwood's homes, the foreman's shed at Case-Kaiser's field office, the church breezeway and half a dozen other projects.

Longwood's town meetings were held in the great room at The Hut Café. The county seat in Visalia conducted most of Longwood's municipal business including Board of Supervisors meetings, county bidding, public works, business licenses, taxes and so on. Law enforcement was handled by the Park County Sheriff's Department, of which Nate Stimson was the senior officer, State Troopers and even National Park Service Rangers by way of informal agreements between like-minded residents of this part of rural California. Mostly, folks took care of their own problems. It was easier than relying on an expensive police force. Conflict was clear-cut out here. Not to say that the solution to a problem was always easy, but at least the options were obvious. And the hard weather, scarcity of creature comforts and lack of money pretty much dictated how even the most drunken disputant viewed a thing. Survival, pride, and respect came before laws. If a man impugned his neighbor's manhood, there wasn't anything the law could do about it. Usually a wrastle and some punches settled it. A scar or two commemorated the event and it was put away.

The law was reserved for murders, livestock theft and property damage.

Jasperson was highly accomplished at working the system to his advantage. His mastery of the federal pork barrel had kept Case-Kaiser growing during years when Boise Cascade, Weyerhaeuser, and the other big players had scarcely managed to avoid hostile takeovers.

Ranchers pushed relentlessly to lower already artificially low, federally subsidized grazing fees on public lands. Mining companies worked the legislative angles to obtain 'Research' waivers to blast and mine Western deposits much as Japanese fisherman slaughtered hundreds of endangered Right Whales in the southern Pacific in the name of 'Research.' Just as the whale meat was sold in elite Tokyo restaurants for exorbitant profits, the West's coal, molybdenite, silver and uraninite was sold to the same government that was supposed to prevent its exploitation.

Loggers were also learning how to squeeze through esoteric loopholes to get at their timber. For every legislative attempt to control the worst abusers, men like Jasperson - the forerunner of a whole new class of white collar operators – pried open two more openings in the web of well-intentioned laws. He had made himself wealthy by blazing paths to profit through the federal and state labyrinth of codes, laws, and policies. Corruption flowed through the system like mercury on glass, transforming itself to evade capture, slipping from the grasp of career regulators. Smarter, quicker and less reflective than anyone in control of a major U.S. corporation, Jasperson was suited to his occupation. He was as dedicated to harvesting timber as the most ardent conservationist was to protecting trees.

"Of course, calm down. Government works for those willing to make it work. Sign here," Jasperson pointed to a highlighted line in the lower right corner of *Supplemental Emergency Request Form US589-G.*

Spivey leaned closer and read the small type.

"Now is no time for caution, Spivey. My assistant should be half way to L.A. Trust me. This form requests an emergency waiver of statutes protecting federal lands, and-" he flipped to another document filled with dense print, "this one gets a waiver of the state's responsibility to uphold antiquated federal treaties when confronted by severe natural disaster or civil unrest."

"It also says there's a penalty of up to five years in prison for perjury, Jasperson."

Jasperson paused, glared, and handed the Mayor his pen.

Nate drove out of Longwood alone on his late afternoon round.

The thirty-eight mile loop through the eastern part of the county would take ninety minutes if, like most days, nothing happened. He'd have time to think. He did some of his best thinking behind the wheel. Horseback was better, but the same loop would take a day and a half on Jesper, his eight-year-old Appaloosa. He scanned the foothills as he drove, one part of his mind registering that everything was routine in this part of the lower valley. Jim Byron's herd was growing; three new calves. Elsie Wilder's place was quiet, her shepherd mix Rex dozing on the front porch. Skies were clear. Looking ahead as he made the wide sweeping turn south, the Thunder Peak Wilderness loomed like a deep, dark medieval forest.

Three mule deer stepped into the road. Nate slowed to a stop and waited. After last winter's mild temperatures and light snowfalls, and spring's heavy rains, grass had been high and the deer were unusually strong. While he admired them, they warily eyed his truck. The big one with eight points seemed to see through the windshield's reflected glare directly at Nate. After the other two crossed the asphalt, the buck snorted and followed, jumping a fence and melting into wheat colored pasture.

Gabriel Fox. The name threaded through Nate's mind again. The notion that he was involved had a grip on Nate and wasn't letting go. As far as he knew, 'Gabriel the Fox' and his *Earth Rebirth!* associates had never killed anyone. Truth be told it was the loggers and company thugs who got carried away. People got hurt and some died.

Still . . .

He accelerated and resumed his beat, letting his instincts lead.

When Nate was a boy, his father had pointed out wild game and asked Nate to tell him where the animal was going. His senses and analytical powers grew stronger by this exercise. He learned to read a dozen clues in every situation. The raven flying into the north wind sought solitude and would return within 30 hours. Deer climbing the mountain's windward face were moving to the shelter of the protected leeward slope. When startled, the rabbit will run in a great arc and return to where it began. When a fox jumps a stream, don't wait for it to return, it almost never will.

Gabriel "The Fox" never repeated himself. Without a pattern, law enforcement was powerless to track him. So they simply watched for protests and hoped for a break. Gabriel was by all accounts a charismatic figure: handsome, passionate, and articulate. He once converted an entire town of loggers into environmental activists at an *Earth Rebirth!* rally. He climbed atop a truck cab and romanced the mob with appeals to goodness and empowerment, swept their fears away with visions of an old growth woodland where a man could feel the universal power of trees and perhaps touch the face of God in a shaded glen.

Loggers wanted to believe that there would always be giant trees and were ready to enlist after the Fox's transcendent sermon. They recovered after a few days and returned to their old ways, but by then the legend had taken root. Shortly after that, Gabriel Fox melted into the swirl of changing times, appearing at one protest as a distinguished elderly professor, another demonstration as a farm laborer, always with the mark of brilliance, a natural born jackal. He even posed as a nun in Idaho two years earlier and embarrassed Case-Kaiser in the national media when a foreman was captured on videotape beating 'her' with a chain.

He was a legend who had almost single-handedly altered the course of logging in North America. No longer was government complicity in building logging roads and subsidizing cheap lumber taken for granted. The regional controversy had taken its place on the nation's cultural agenda. And Gabriel the Fox was credited for putting it there. Consequently, he had joined the wolf and hippie on every rancher's and timber company's shoot-to-kill list. He was the symbol of everything folks eager to hold on to the old way of life hated about the New West. If they ever had him in their sights, they'd drop him like a mad dog.

Ben had left Nelson in Lotte's care while he went to get some rest. On the drive home, the notion of seeing Grace took over. M was spending the night at her friend Leeann's house so he headed for the White Raven.

Her studio was bright, the right side of her face glowed in naked detail: her direct, untamed eye, the Gallic angle of her jaw and slope of her neck into her shirt. She wore a rose-colored satin ribbon like a necklace. When she stood, its loose knot settled silently between her breasts.

Pleased by his interruption, she had put down her brush, wiped her paint-stained hands on a wet rag and went to him, hips swaying, eyes sparkling, a volatile sight for his volatile state. Light struck her hair and flared, adding fuel to his mounting need. If someone lit a match, the whole place would go up.

Silent purpose charged the air. Resting her moist palms on his waist, she looked at him directly. She kissed him, open-mouthed and deeply. His hands traced the rise of her breasts and removed the shirt in one unbroken motion. She rose under his touch while her hands quickly undid his belt.

He lifted her and spun around, seeking an altar on which to offer them both up to the flames. "Wait," she whispered, smiled, and turned on the bed. He raised himself and they began a strong, steady rhythm.

Later, when she awoke in Ben's arms, Grace saw him staring at the ceiling, deep in thought.

"*Is* she pretty?"

"What?"

"Your Doctor Lotte Keene. I hear she's pretty," Grace teased.

"I was thinking about my patients. Sara Hart, Oren Pocknett. Then Lars Broder. Soon, Nelson Hatch . . . he's not long."

She shivered involuntarily. "What's going on, Ben?"

"Don't worry."

"You are."

"It's just that I don't know where to start, how to approach this. Now I've got this Fed scientist with some theory about Nature defending itself . . ."

"Maybe she's right. Maybe it's the way Case-Kaiser's experts meddled with the natural balance up there. Maybe the dust from the clear cuts has a virus in it."

"Oh noooo," he groaned. "Not now, Grace."

"You build walls when you don't understand something. I hate that."

Ben stared at her.

"That forest has inspired my best painting. It's why I stayed here. It saved my life."

"Now it's killing folks."

"They're going to want to cut it down, you know," she said sadly.

"What if it's the only way to stop this thing, whatever it is?" Ben muttered as he headed for the shower.

"We can't let them!"

While Ben showered, Grace gathered events around her. When he returned, she declared, "I've decided that life is like a river."

"A river?" Ben tried not to grin.

"Don't laugh," she threw a pillow at him. "That's what I came up with."

"A river. This ought to be good."

"You can drift along and watch the passing sights," she continued, "or you can pick a patch of shore and make it your own. That's what I did when I came to Longwood. Now I see more of the world pass the White Raven than I saw anywhere in Europe. Clouds wrapped around Thunder Peak. Seasons whispering through. More interesting people than I ever imagined coming to this remote settlement on the shores of my life, bringing their dramas to me whether I'm ready for them or not."

"Maybe we should ask the trees what to do," Ben said sarcastically as he finished dressing. He knew it was best to let Grace go and not argue with her about certain subjects, Nature vs. Commerce near the top of the list. But he was wearing thin. "Seriously Grace, if we fought this thing your way, we'd love it into submission. Nature doesn't think, feel, or care. It reacts, adapts, and survives. That's all."

"Hah, you said reacts! How do you know Nature doesn't feel or care? Maybe she *is* reacting to all of Case-Kaiser's abuse."

"I don't have time for this. I'm a doctor. I use facts to understand cause and effect. When we find the clue – a chemical clue, most likely – we'll treat it. If it is viral, inoculate against it. It's biology, that's all it is."

"Something tells me you're not nearly as confident as you claim to be. Something new is happening up there. For once, open yourself up. Consider that the woods might have ways of defending itself."

"Look, we'll fix whatever's wrong. In the meantime, don't spend any more time outdoors than you need to. And don't even think about going into the woods."

"You're so arrogant! Pat Grace on the head, tell her to be a good girl and everything will be all right. Well, I may not have an M.D., but I have a mind, life experience, and an instinct for some things you can't even imagine. Grace rose from the bed, forced on her robe, returned to her easel, and resumed painting.

Ben watched her dip a brush into a white paint, mix it with purple and some red and pick up painting the fiery foliage of a rock maple in the foreground. She moved with precision and passion, her hand dancing across the watercolor paper confidently, beyond his doubts or power to control her. Back in her element. He loved that about her.

"I'm out of here," he said sadly and left.

17

LONGWOOD

Observation: life processes were absent from victim's cells.

Under magnification, the frozen section of heart tissue looked more like petrified wood – plated and granular – than recently living heart muscle. She adjusted the microscope's objective, lowered it and then raised the stage with its attached slide into focus. The minuscule spot of semi-transparent tissue was scarcely one cell layer thick – a result that required expensive technology in a well-equipped lab and that was nearly impossible to accomplish in the field, yet was a well-known Lotte Keene specialty – and hardly resembled anything at all to the naked eye. Under the microscope, however, it revealed organic tissue's magnificent pattern of ellipses, each shape a cell containing the machinery of life. In this tissue, however, the cell's interior mechanisms were barely recognizable.

Where were the microfilaments: the Golgi apparatus? The rough endoplasmic reticulum? She could make out the nucleus, yet it was reduced to something that looked like onyx. The chromatin substance within the nucleus of the cell that carried Lars Broder's DNA was no longer a recognizable network of fine crystals, but a compressed, dehydrated shale. The ordinary cellular process hardened to clay.

Analysis: Could this pathology be induced? An *exergonic* reaction, or a natural process?

She slowly twirled the fine focus looking for any telltale clues to the process by which Lars Broder's heart was robbed of its vitality. She expected to see flaked cells with sawtooth edges, lethal sickle-cell aberrations. But each cell's plasma membrane was as smooth as it had been in life. The cells were distributed as they had been when they mingled timelessly through phases of birth, reproduction, and eventual sloughing away. Yet they were hard as bone.

Hypothesis: Could it be the return of her nightmare?

She pulled a binder marked 'Itamarati' from her shoulder bag and turned quickly to a series of Polaroids. The title of the section was *Pathology: Heart - Binyacya, Geraldo.* Under each photo a caption identified the origin of the tissue shown in the microscope photographs: *Right ventricle … Left ventricle … Aortic arch … Pulmonary Artery - Left. …* She pulled the last one from the plastic sleeve and held it up in the light.

Peering into the microscope's eyepiece she compared what she saw with the photograph.

They were identical.

Conclusion: It was back. The mystery had reemerged.

She pushed back from the table, arms folded, squinting in concentration.

What now? Follow protocol in the hope that something would provide the clues she needed to comprehend the medical phenomenon that had struck Broder? Or take a hint from what she saw in the microscope and sound the alarm?

All the usual reasons came forward to object to taking any action in that direction.

Cry wolf again, it's exile for good, and it won't be back to the comforts of Boulder this time, missy. Let it GO! When will you grow up, get with the program and act like a responsible adult?

You mean shut up and don't rock the boat with what I know.

I mean can you prove your cockamamie theory? Is your truth better than the meticulously hypothesized, tested, and confirmed truth of hundreds of epidemiologists, biochemists, and pathologists? Are you above established and accepted truth?

At least it's based upon more than dogma. It's contextual, logical and . . . terrifying. I can't bury my head on this!

Charley! Why aren't you here? I need you.

Ben McCandle could be her ally if she explained what she was seeing on the table in his clinic. But that would take time. She couldn't expect him to understand the implications of these symptoms just because she laid it out for him. She would have to bring him along. Damn! There was *no* time for that!

The sharp knock on the clinic's back door startled her. "Doc?" a man's voice sounded from outside. "Ben?"

"Yes?" she called in a loud voice as she climbed the stairs. When she opened the door, she saw the Mad Mayor of Longwood and tried not to let her dislike for the little toad show. "What is it?"

Wilburn Spivey was equally disappointed at seeing Lotte Keene. They briefly faced each other cold-eyed and expressionless before he recovered from his surprise. "What are *you* doing here?"

"Good afternoon to you, too, Mayor. I'm assisting Doctor McCandle. Investigating the recent deaths on Thunder Peak and trying to keep your latest victim alive."

"Nelson Hatch?"

Lotte nodded yes.

"Nate told me. How is he?"

"Very critical."

"You're a doctor."

"Yes."

Mayor Spivey shifted his weight.

He pulled off his glove, extended a hand, and turned on his best hawking smile. "I hope you can find it in you to forgive me, Doctor."

Lotte warily shook his hand.

"I know you hold Nelson's life in your capable grasp and I won't distract you from your vital work any longer. Is Ben here, please?"

"No. He's gone for some rest. Should be back soon."

"Thank you, I'll catch up with him later." The Mayor smiled again and turned purposefully for his Cadillac.

"Do you want Doctor McCandle to call you, Mayor?" asked Lotte.

Without slowing, Mayor Spivey turned his head slightly, waved away the suggestion, opened the car door and settled behind the wheel.

"I'll tell him you —" her words were drowned by the roar of the Cadillac's engine, "-stopped by." She watched him drive away. Shaking her head in amusement, she returned downstairs to her patient.

The first spinal fluid results were ready to evaluate by now. The lumbar puncture was a difficult procedure under the best of circumstances and always required the assistance of a nurse to hold the patient in position and reassure them. Nelson Hatch was already in position: turned on his side, thighs flexed on his trunk, head lowered to his chest and back bowed. Just in case he might still register pain, Lotte explained what she was doing to reassure him.

Medical etiquette dictated that Ben McCandle perform the painful procedure, or at least approve its use. He would be irritated when she told him that she went ahead and did it. While he focused on Hatch's survival, she was concerned about the spread of a killer that, if left unchecked, might strike hundreds of thousands, perhaps millions of innocent people. He'd have to get over it.

The lumbar puncture could be worked up in Ben's clinic. Some results typically required 48 hours, but what she needed she could evaluate already. Spinal fluid provided insights into the human body's interior state unavailable from other tests. The presence of red blood cells in the fluid would indicate bleeding somewhere in the body. White cells would signal infection. Given the crystallized state of blood and other fluids in Hatch's system, she didn't expect to see red or white cells. His circulatory system was incapable of transporting cells in sufficient quantity to display symptoms of any kind, except this infernal hardening.

The spinal fluid sugar content was lower than Hatch's blood: 25 to 15mg. That was one indicator for meningitis. It was also suppurative – puslike – and turbid. That ruled out tuberculosis, encephalitis, and poliomyelitis.

She prepared a slide, no stain this time. She peered into the microscope's eyepiece and saw . . . nothing. Just the misty, hardened pus.

The cell count was 14 cells per ml., four above normal. This could mean a lot of things from a mild bout with the common cold or the beginning of some more serious disease. Increased cell count was a clear indication of disease, but it barely exceeded the normal 0-10 count; meningitis would produce cell counts in the hundreds and thousands.

She looked for cell shape aberration. Epidemic meningitis, for example, is indicated by gram-negative, intracellular diplococcus, biscuit-shaped microorganisms. Hatch's cells were normal, just hardened and dying quickly. A chill raced down her spine and the small hairs on her forearms stood on end.

Come on, Ben. Get back here.

What's the matter with me, thought Spivey? It was all he could do to remain still while Jasperson's factotum, Brad Wright, droned on. He wanted to pace, to vent his mounting concern that between the Ahwahnee and whatever was killing people on the Peak, he couldn't control the situation.

Perjury on the application for waivers of Federal environmental and treaty protections exposed him to certain legal liabilities. He knew it, so did Jasperson and he wouldn't put future blackmail past him.

Now the broad from Boulder. If the people of Longwood discovered that a Federal epidemiologist was in town, they would make his life a nightmare. Longwood was a tight knit community. She was a Fed. He had seen her kind before and they always brought trouble. He would have to keep tabs on her.

"Just tell your boss I need action. He owes me," he barked irritably at Wright. That last remark was going too far. He was getting carried away more often lately. Maybe Wright didn't catch it.

Wright caught it. It was one of the skills for which Jasperson had hired him away from his principal rival in Manhattan. He was a born chameleon, a bulldog on the facts and possessed a Zen-like ability to disappear without leaving the room. Invisible to the target who, forgetting his presence, grew overconfident and let slip some important revelation vital to Wright's boss.

"Mr. Jasperson knows who his friends are, Mayor."

"I sure hope so."

"The waivers are proceeding through committee in Washington, by the way."

"I'll believe it when the check clears the bank."

"Believe it. There is more at stake here than mill jobs. Mr. Jasperson is concerned that if the Thunder Peak remains outside our control, it will set a precedent for every radical environmentalist from here to Denali."

"It *is* protected land, you know," Mayor Spivey surprised himself by suddenly, inexplicably playing devil's advocate.

"Of course. That is a technicality. And the Ahwahnee will be compensated for their cooperation."

"Technicality," the Mayor repeated. "I hope you know what the hell you're doing," Spivey stood to escort this Praetorian Guard out of his office.

"One other item, Mayor. The Ahwahnee, could they be responsible for the deaths in Thunder Peak?"

"What!?" blurted Spivey.

"Desperate people do desperate things. Why not set traps to stop trespassers? Get the word out: Hunt or log in Thunder Peak and die. Gives new meaning to the term 'poison pill,' doesn't it?" he said with a faraway look in his eye, amused by his own cleverness. He pulled a dictaphone from his overcoat and spoke intensely into it as he left the Mayor without another glance, absorbed in a promising new scenario.

The knock on the door this time was perfunctory, followed by heavy boot steps on the stairs. Lotte looked up from her notes to see Nate Stimson looking road-tired.

"No news, Doc. Not another victim in sight."

"You checked Thunder Peak?"

"Best I could. I'm just one man and there's over 60 square miles of old growth. But, yeah, I checked where we found the other bodies and every path somebody would take up there. Nothing but ground fog, bear tracks, and owl scat. Not a thing out of the ordinary." He planted his feet and glanced at Nelson. "Maybe it's over?"

"That's a nice thought, Sheriff. Not realistic, but tempting to hope for."

"How is he?"

"No improvement. Judging from what's happened to these cells," she held up several sketches of what she had seen in the microscope, "it's a wonder he's survived this long."

"What're those?"

"Lars Broder's heart cells," she held up another sketch, "Nelson Hatch's epidermis – skin cells."

Nate cocked his head, then frowned. "Don't need to be a doctor to see something's wrong there."

"They're a mess, all right. Of course comparing heart cells to skin cells is apples and oranges," Lotte slipped easily into the role of teacher. "A skin cross section – from Nelson's finger - would feature layers of columnar, then spheroidal, then flat cells and finally scales at the surface. Not here. Hatch's skin looks like Broder's heart cells: scaly shards."

Nate checked his own fingers, suddenly appreciating his pliant skin and sense of touch.

"I made these sketches for Ben and a colleague back east," added Lotte.

"Back East? You mean law enforcement?" The suspicion in his voice was unmistakable.

She looked up. "No, a biogeneticist and, hopefully, a forensic pathologist at CDC."

"Medical types," said Nate with relief.

"Right. I have analyzed Hatch's spinal fluid – very unusual - and now I'm checking his skin sample. I need to biopsy some organ tissue to know for certain if his symptoms are the same as Mr. Broder's."

"That's pretty rough for a patient in critical condition, isn't it?" Nate leveled a concerned look at Lotte.

"Either I biopsy now or autopsy in an hour, Sheriff. Waiting gives the killer valuable time, time we need to prevent it from spreading."

18

LONGWOOD

Could he be wrong? Ben sat in the Jeep, his hand on the key, looking through the windshield at the scarred ridges on the horizon. Had his view of life so narrowed after losing Hannah? Had he become intolerant while raising Mary Margaret alone? Had he become the man he swore he would never become: his father?

"Ben?" Grace called from the front porch, her voice weary.

He went to her, eager for a chance to put the argument behind them.

She held up the cordless phone. "It's her."

"Hello?"

"Ben."

How'd you find me? "What's wrong?"

"The CBC, X-Ray, EKG, and now epidermal analysis show identical symptoms. I'm calling Vin der Root at CDC and want you in on the conversation."

"Calling in the cavalry is exactly the thing you DON'T want to do."

"Three – soon to be four - dead. That's an epidemic. I can't handle this alone. Pride and local sensitivities aside, Longwood is out of options. Vin der Root heads up CDC's Rapid Response division. He's a friend - well, not exactly a friend – but, we go back. This will be just a conversation between equals. He'll keep a low profile."

"I'm the doctor of record."

"Forgive me for being blunt, but you're out of your league, Ben."

There was silence on the line.

Lotte waited for several moments, then said, "I have a hunch this thing is airborne. It's the only mechanism that makes sense, unless each victim was injected."

Ben remained silent.

"I have more tests to do," she continued. "Since it's unlikely that the victims cooperated in their own deaths, I'm pursuing airborne agent. Is there some military experiment underway up here that I don't know about?" she asked.

Great. A paranoid Fed. "Longwood is a long way from anywhere, let alone a military installation," Ben said, his tone more irritated than he intended.

"Just the kind of set-up favored by the men in black, Doctor. The military prefers to perform its riskier tests as far from prying eyes as possible. That way they don't have to explain their failures. Unless you've been living in total isolation for the last twenty years, I don't have to tell you that."

She was right. The military was renowned for bumbling new technologies and then going through contortions to distance itself from responsibility. There was Agent Orange, the still unidentified source of Gulf War Syndrome, Anthrax vaccinations, and thousands of toxic sites across the country being revealed long after the men responsible retired with comfy pensions. *Jeez you sound bitter, McCandle.* He didn't know if it was fallout from his argument with Grace, Lotte rubbing him the wrong way, or the feeling of impotence this entire situation gave him.

"In the meantime, we need help. Forensics, pathology, biochemistry and the kind of lab resources only the government has."

"Wait until I get back there." He hung up, handed the receiver to Grace, and tried to come up with the right thing to say. He wanted to smooth things over with her but wasn't about to tell her that she was right, he was wrong and everything he believed in was false. No, he had some valid reasons for believing the way he did: experience, instincts and, yes, he had to admit it, pride. "I have to go, Grace," he said neutrally. "Nelson Hatch, Lotte Keene, and someone at CDC ... a teleconference."

"Call me," she said evenly.

"As soon as I know anything."

"Is he any better?"

"Worse." He wanted to say more, but he didn't trust himself. If he started to talk, he wouldn't be able to stop. He would fall into Grace's spell and confess to sins he'd never committed.

She straightened his collar. Warmth spread to his chest. He wanted to stay and let her overwhelm him, but he couldn't.

Reading his mind, she smiled. "Go."

He was halfway to the truck when he turned, "Do me a favor? Go to the ranch. Keep an eye on M and make sure both of you stay inside."

Grace's expression turned serious. Whatever Lotte Keene said on the phone got to him.

He looked at her strangely, as if he was memorizing her.

"Ben."

"Stay with M, okay? I'll be back."

'Pssssst! See the Sheriff wear'n that surgical mask? Ask me, he knows something.'

'I felt lightheaded when I woke up this morning. Bert and I are sending the boys to their grandparents in Stokely . . . Jimmy, don't let the dog lick your face like that anymore, hear?!'

Whispers buzzed like summer horseflies as Ben arrived at the clinic. Halfway to the basement door he saw Marge Ryerson waving to get his attention from the window of the waiting room above. He couldn't ignore her; she knew the doctor was in. With a scarcely concealed groan, he ascended the front stairs and pushed into his waiting room, which was crowded with concerned mothers, sniffling infants and two widows with pissed off sons-in-law.

"Doc, is it safe to let Lisa go to a slumber party at her friend's in Red Fork?"

"Why wouldn't it be?"

"Her girlfriend lives two miles closer to the Peak."

'Why isn't anybody telling us what's happening?'

"Folks," Ben shouted from the front of the room, "I know you've heard something's going round, but you can be sure I'll be the first one to tell you if you need to worry. In the meantime, take normal precautions: avoid feral animals in case they're carrying something, don't spend more time outdoors than you need to and call me if you're really sick."

"If nothing's wrong, what's that lady doctor from Colorado doing in Longwood, Doc?" Marge Ryerson shouted.

"Take it easy, Marge. Doctor Keene is doing some research s'all."

Lars Broder's widow, Raisa, still pale with grief, wrapped her coat tighter around herself and made her way to the front. "What kind of research?" she asked. "Mr. Colbert down to the funeral home said she was holding my husband's body."

Ben stepped forward and put an arm around her. "We need to do some tests, Raisa. Then you can have Lars back."

"When?"

"I promise I'll call you as soon as I know something."

"Please folks," he turned to the rest of the group. "Let me get back to work. There's nothing you can do here. Dr. Keene and I are moving as quickly as we can. In fact, we're about to consult with some experts as soon as I can get downstairs. Go home. Anything I learn I'll pass along to the Sheriff here to keep you informed."

The waiting room emptied quietly.

Downstairs, he found Nelson Hatch still curled, a question mark on the table, his EKG tape with its lethargic lines humming slowly to the floor, and his heart rate monitor chugging away at a not quite life-sustaining 56 beats per minute. Lotte remained at her microscope.

"Good thing you arrived when you did. Would have gotten ugly if they found me down here," she said, made a note on her chart, turned to face him, and did a mild double take. "If that's how you look after a rest, I recommend less rest," she quipped.

He was feeling defensive, and then shook it off. "What's up?"

"Not much. Nelson's leaving us and there's not a thing I can do about it." She dialed the phone, punched the speakerphone button. "It's time to call for some help."

"I told you I'm just not comfortable—"

"der Root here," a male voice burst from the speakerphone.

"It's Lotte. I'm in Longwood, California with Doctor Ben McCandle."

"What have you got?"

"Thirty-four year-old Caucasian male. Presents stiff yet not cyanotic, normal skin tone, just stiff. Bradycardic --"

"Conscious? Responsive in any way?"

"Negative. His pupils are dilated and fixed, so I figured he is brain dead," she explained. "But the EKG keeps chirping away with tantalizing little sparks of activity. Not enough to call it thought, but enough to verify that he's alive."

"He was struck while chopping down a tree during the night, time not yet known," Ben filled in. "He was slumped over the axe handle with a respiration rate so discreet I thought he was dead at first."

"He was chopping down a tree at night?"

"Don't ask," interrupted Lotte. "Anyway, his eyes along with every other organ seem to have frozen in place, including his low light dilated pupils."

At this point, she expected der Root to pick up on the bizarre clues and make the same association with Itamarati that she had, especially after their earlier conversation and the BIOSAT-7 video. She'd given him one of the principal hallmarks of the Brazilian deaths, but he didn't bite. Instead, he kept to medical protocol. It was maddening.

"ABG?"

"Impossible to know. His blood isn't really blood."

"What is it then?"

"Mud?" Lotte suggested, looking to Ben for confirmation.

"Healthy red . . . sand," he added.

"So hemoglobin isn't an issue," der Root thought aloud. "Hmmmm." They heard him opening a book and fingering through pages. "And you say your patient is alive?"

"Vin, no kidding. You have to see how eerily familiar these symptoms are."

"You've got a survivor. Sure the symptoms are similar, but a breather nixes the diagnosis."

"What are you two talking about?" Ben was tired of feeling left out of the conversation, which had shifted from medical jargon to some secret code.

Neither answered for a moment. Then they both spoke at once. der Root asked about urine output. Lotte touched Ben's arm and explained, "Brazil."

"Look," Lotte interrupted, her voice climbing impatiently, "More than a dozen otherwise healthy peasants turned to stone in the jungle. And here we go again: three dead in Sequoia National Forest so far."

"Lotte, we're a long way from finding any evidence that you've got the same situation," der Root's patience was wearing thin, too. He couldn't have sounded any more patronizing if he was speaking to a preschooler.

She lifted the receiver, "Go to hell, Vin!" and slammed it down in its cradle.

Stunned at first, Ben soon caught himself grinning. "Smooth, Doctor. Think the boys at CDC will still send us a Christmas card?"

She turned to face him, still furious. He was sure she was going to tear into him now, but when she moved to speak, recognition of the absurdity of the situation registered in her expression and she burst into laughter. "He really is an ass. Sorry you had to be a part of that."

"You two have issues?"

"You could say that. My science is better than his. His politics are better than mine."

The phone rang and Ben walked over to pick it up. "Sure, just a minute," he pushed the speakerphone button and replaced the receiver.

"Lotte?"

"Yes?"

"Where did you learn your phone etiquette?"

Lotte glanced at Ben and shook her head. "What do you expect? I know what I'm doing. Don't treat me like a first-year resident."

Ben interrupted, "Look, Doctor der Root, I don't know what happened to you two in Brazil but I'm grateful to have Dr. Keene here. If she sees a link with something CDC has responded to before, maybe you should trust her enough to take it seriously."

Lotte was stunned. She had felt barely tolerated since she arrived. Now Ben was defending her.

"That's why I called back, Doctor. Now, can we get back to work, class?"

"I know what you're going to ask," Lotte decided not to further the argument. "No, there is no significant difference between Broder and Hatch physiologically. They are equally fit.

"From what I've been able to determine so far, their diets were classic: rich in protein and carbohydrates. Disease: none. Medication: none. Hatch had a few shots – correction: several shots - of Johnny Walker Black. But that's it." Lotte settled against the table and waited for der Root's next volley.

"How about a CAT scan?"

Lotte looked at Ben. "No," he said, "The closest CAT Scan is a sixteen-year-old jalopy in Fresno. No federal grants for country medicine, Doctor."

"Let me do a little research at this end." der Root hung up.

Lotte shook her head in disgust. "He won't do anything. 'Research' is code for 'leave me alone.' What a bureaucrat!"

"Welcome to Longwood, Lotte. You're talking like a Californian already," he saluted her.

After a moment of silence in which they both considered the situation, Ben asked her if mysteries happened frequently in her line of work or just in Brazil and California.

"Every epidemic begins as a mystery. We can usually figure it out with a combination of science and cultural insight. But this one defies science, so I'll be needing your insight into local life and, together, we'll need some luck."

"What makes you think science can't solve this?"

She looked at him for a while trying to decide whether to answer. "There's a growing body of thought, call it pre-science, that suggests the world is more exquisitely complicated than we were taught. The old model of Man-as-the-supreme-sentient-creature at the top of the food chain doesn't fit so neatly with emerging science."

"Now *you're* going to tell me the Thunder Peak Wilderness is alive and thinking about things."

"Something like that," she answered simply.

"The trees stand around conspiring to get back at their hard-hatted persecutors?" Ben teased her. *She is pretty*. He hadn't noticed it before.

"Conspiring? No. But reacting in some as yet unknown

genetically triggered response to threat? Maybe."

Ben considered this for a few moments. Then he pulled up a chair and said, "Tell me about Brazil."

19

LONGWOOD

At The Hut Café, tempers were rising faster than the room temperature.

"Keep your head down, Lotte," Ben whispered. "This is not good. I've never seen so many folks in one place in all my time here. They must be coming from the surrounding counties, too."

Lotte nodded and continued to watch the meeting proceedings. She had mixed feelings about taking time away from Nelson Hatch, but with nothing more to be done for him, she decided to take a few minutes. She knew from long experience in places more primitive than Longwood the importance of awareness of local concerns and attitudes.

"As for the motion before District Judge Williams in Salt Lake City requesting that he lift his order banning sale of timber on Federal or Treaty lands, well, frankly that can go either way," the Mayor admitted to the crowd, trying to sound confident yet realistic.

A tanned, fit-looking young man with long hair tied back with a headscarf stood. "No court can overrule Nature!"

The Mayor frowned and clenched his jaw.

"What are we supposed to do in the meantime?" asked a sunburnt rancher. "Jeez, I'm tired of waiting for judges, bureaucrats and millionaire snow bunnies to decide what else they're going to do to my family and me. Case-Kaiser slicks – nothing personal Jasperson – leave these good ol' boys' pockets full of nothing but bills," he nodded at a cluster of loggers at the bar.

"Well, Jake, I'd prepare," the Mayor advised sympathetically.

"For what?" demanded a logger standing by the window.

"For more hard times," said the Mayor.

Groans rumbled across the café like a flood tide.

"Now I'm not saying that's going to happen," Spivey continued. "It's just that we've hit a bad patch, not much seems to be going our way and we've got to be tough. I have more irons in the fire than I can count – including consultations with our Senator and other lawmakers in Washington - but nothing has caught fire just yet. Now –"

Lotte couldn't help but admire the way that Spivey worked his constituents. By appearing to talk strong and straight with them he was establishing credibility, putting himself on their side of the hard times. Convince them that you're suffering as much as they are and when it comes time to prescribe bitter medicine, they'll swallow it because you're swallowing it, too. She watched and waited for the prescription pad to come out.

"Natural law always takes precedence over national law, Mayor," a young blond woman in a Macintosh said loudly from the front table.

The Mayor smiled tolerantly. He had expected one of the dozens of the *EARTH REBIRTH!* activists he suspected were in the room to disrupt the meeting and he was ready for her.

"As if there were safety in stupidity alone," he said a little too loudly, proud of himself for having expressed Thoreau's *bon mot* without tripping over it. The laughter and applause he had expected did not come.

"'How narrow we selfish, conceited creatures are in our sympathies,' said your hero John Muir!" Jasperson picked up the ball from his chair beside the dais, then settled back, pleased with himself.

"You didn't finish what he said, you fascist," blurted a slight young man in spectacles. "Muir continued, '...How blind to the rights of all the rest of creation!' If you fellas plan to turn literature's greatest voices to your cause, read their books, will you?"

That got a reluctant laugh from the worried ranchers and loggers.

"What are you city kids doing here in the real America, anyway," asked the Mayor, hoping to win back the group.

"As opposed to the faux America?" quipped the blond.

"This is a local problem with real local consequences. Folks' lives depend on timber jobs," the Mayor ignored her jibe.

"You've already cut 80% of the timber in the surrounding 300 square miles! Cut any more and your town will turn to dust like those clear-cut killing fields!" Spectacles argued. He was getting worked up.

"You don't know what you're talking about, son," the Mayor tried the tolerant fatherly approach.

"Now you've got a virus—"

"The Ahwahnee Stroke!" a woman in the back of the cafe shouted.

"—or something up there in the woods that's killing you and still you're in denial," Spectacles finished, having added fuel to the room's explosive atmosphere.

"Yeah, Mayor, what about Oren Pocknett, Lars Broder and Nelson Hatch. What's going on?"

"And that Fed lady doctor?" asked a middle-aged rancher's wife.

The Mayor looked around the room and when he spotted Ben, pointed to him, and said, "What can you tell us, Doc?"

Ben stood slowly, unsure exactly what he would say. All eyes turned to him and waited in silence for the first time of the evening.

"Well, it's true that there have been some deaths and while we haven't identified the precise cause just yet, we will. I'm not worried. Especially, now that we have the assistance of Dr. Lotte Keene from Boulder. She happened to be passing through and I asked her to lend a hand."

"She's not a Fed then?" asked one of the loggers.

"She's an epidemiologist and accomplished medical specialist, Frank. She studies disease and knows what to look for in situations like we have here."

"Fine, but that doesn't answer my question."

"Dr. Keene is a contract scientist working on studies that several Federal agencies utilize. If that makes her a Federal employee, then I guess that makes me one too, since Medicaid pays some of my patients' bills." It was a sleight of reasoning he hoped would change the subject. Grumbles rippled across the room.

"She just happened to be driving through?" someone asked from the doorway.

"That's right, Ridley," answered Nate. He understood Ben's strategy and was casting in beside him. "The Mayor can tell you how he happened to meet her this morning out on Route 11." He looked to Wilburn Spivey with a straight face.

"Anyway, the deaths seem to be over and although they're still a mystery to us, we'll figure them out," Ben finished. "Don't worry."

"The Fed from Boulder, she agree with you, Doc?"

Ben turned to tell Lotte to sit tight but he was too late. She was on her feet.

"Doctor McCandle is right, sir. The deaths seem to have ceased, for now at least. We have much work to do yet before we can positively identify a cause. I can tell you that conditions in this valley could provide at least a partial explanation for aberrant biological response."

"Partial, what?"

"Huh?"

"An unusual response by the ecosystem to stress on it," she explained helpfully.

"Oh geez, Spivey. What the hell is this all about," a rancher said with deliberate calm.

"Let her finish," the blonde at the front table encouraged her.

"If you all weren't speaking English I couldn't be sure I wasn't in a slash and burn moonscape in the Amazon basin. Let's face it, these slopes are damned ugly and close to dead. Overlogging may not be the only source of the problem, but it's a primary cause, I'd say."

Her listeners grumbled and shifted in their seats.

"I bet this valley was paradise before the cutting. I bet some of you can remember it, am I right? I just have to wonder then: rather than push against the best existence any one could ever hope for, why not push against the destroyers of that existence?"

Ben groaned and sank lower in his chair. "Lotte!" he hissed under his breath.

"The Stroke is in the forest still standing, not where it's been cut!" one of the loggers objected.

"You've pushed nature too far, and it is fighting back in some way we can't explain," argued Lotte.

"Oh Christ, another live one!"

"A damn hugger!" a logger shouted.

Spivey and Jasperson patiently observed all of this. A little too patiently, Ben thought.

"Let her speak!" shouted the blonde.

Jasperson leaned forward. He was enjoying this.

"It's a relatively new theory called Biological Defense and it suggests that any organism, when pushed too hard, fights back."

"Excuse me, Doctor," the blonde interrupted, "are you saying that the Stroke or whatever it is is the forest's way of fending off attackers?"

Lotte nodded excitedly. "Yes, something like that, except—"

"There ain't nothing out there," the logger growled at Lotte, then turned to address the rest of the loggers, "What do these book jockeys know about the Peak that we didn't learn our first week of cutting old growth!" A round of cheers went up.

That emboldened Spectacles. He jumped up on the Mayor's platform and shouted to the crowd: "'When we shut our eyes to cruelty and suffering, we shut out part of the spirit that made America stand apart in the world as a nation that puts moral principles and decency above sheer material value.'" He paused for effect before attributing the quote, "Hubert Humphrey."

Ranchers argued among themselves. Loggers argued with *EARTH REBIRTH!* activists. The meeting spun out of control.

A strikingly handsome man with a long gray ponytail and wearing an expensive Armani suit stepped calmly to the dais and held up his hands. Gradually the arguments quieted and folks settled back down.

"I'm Larson Black Kettle. As most of you know, I am Legal Counsel to the Ahwahnee Nation."

"I speak for the Ahwahnee people and our forebears who have been dedicated and responsible stewards of the Creator's Thunder Peak Wilderness for 9,000 years, since the glaciers retreated north. The Case-Kaiser machines have destroyed the once healthy forests. Now you all want what is not yours." He paused for that thought to sink in. "In the interest of fairness, I ask you to clean up and rebuild your own house before you destroy the Ahwahnee's house."

The loggers leapt to their feet as one and hurled bitter recriminations at the unflappable Ahwahnee attorney. He tried to listen politely but gave up after several moments, unable to make out a coherent phrase from the verbal assault.

The Mayor rose again and thanked Larson Black Kettle for his comments.

"Our concern, Mayor, is that you don't allow any dangerous notions to gain credence during this troubled time," Larson spoke firmly in his most neutral tone.

"Dangerous notions, Larson?" asked the Mayor.

"Attempting to get Federal authorities to waive the prohibitions against logging contained in the Thunder Peak Wilderness Treaty of 1908. Or worse, persuade Washington to declare Eminent Domain." Larson held Spivey in his unblinking gaze.

"Eminent Domain? Why no, Larson, of course not. We have been good neighbors going back to our fathers' fathers' time and I wouldn't do anything to jeopardize the good will we share." The Mayor turned to address the assembled, then turned back to the attorney and asked, "How *is* your father? Feeling better is he?"

Larson stepped down and returned to his seat.

Ben and Lotte looked at one another and waited for the other shoe to drop.

Returning his attention to the meeting, Mayor Spivey rubbed his chin thoughtfully, appeared to consider an idea, discard it, then, as if embarrassed to have been so rude to his listeners, reluctantly gave voice to his thought. "Now, Larson Black Kettle brings up an interesting notion. Eminent Domain IS one possible option here."

The entire room was on its feet. Loggers smelling opportunity, *EARTH REBIRTH!* activists outraged, Ben in shock that Spivey could so easily suggest the idea and Lotte screaming louder than anyone, "NOOOOOO!"

Nate whistled above the din and reigned in everyone to hear what the epidemiologist had to say.

"You can't do *anything* in the Thunder Peak Wilderness, not until we have identified exactly what is going on up there."

"The safety and well-being of our families is my foremost concern, I assure you, Dr. Keene," said the Mayor calmly.

"Good, then we have an understanding."

"How long do you think you need?"

"There's no way—"

"Just let us do our work, Mayor," Ben interrupted. He saw what Spivey was doing and, whether Lotte caught on or not, he needed to close down their discussion.

Jasperson stood. "There may be a middle ground here, ladies and gentlemen."

"Yes, Mr. Jasperson, I agree," beamed Spivey. "Perhaps now, with your permission, I could make an announcement?"

Jasperson smiled magnanimously, nodded, and approached the dais, surveying the audience like a prince reviewing his subjects.

"Well, I'm pleased to tell you that we have received word from Senator Prentice's office not an hour ago that the Bureau of the Interior will almost certainly grant Case-Kaiser a temporary waiver permitting limited salvage logging and a timber survey."

"The Federal Government has no authority!" objected Larson Black Kettle.

"Hot damn, THAT's more like it!" the burly logger by the window shouted.

"Unfortunately we can only afford to pay half your former wage for this study. It's a Federal grant and it's not much," Jasperson added apologetically.

"It's work, isn't it, Mr. Jasperson?" another logger asked.

"Yes sir, it is work," beamed the Mayor.

"HOLD IT!" Lotte screamed. "It's not safe for anyone to go into the Thunder Peak Wilderness right now!"

"It will be fine, Dr. Keene. I'm sure you, Ben and Sheriff Nate can figure this thing out. You've got a couple days before anything can get started, anyway." He was gleeful. The meeting had gone exactly as he had planned. The loggers and ranchers had hope and they had him to thank for it.

"You aren't listening, Mayor! It is NOT going to be fine!"

"Of course it will be, Doctor. You're not from around here—" he tried patronizing again.

"People are going to die, you moron! Are you prepared for the consequences?"

Mayor Spivey ignored her as he followed Jasperson out the door.

Lotte charged between chairs at him, but Ben caught her arm and held her back. "Lotte, he's baiting you. It's not decided yet.

Save your energy."

"He's an idiot! He can't ignore what's going on up there!"

"Let's go. We have a patient to check on." Ben was calm considering the tumult of the last hour.

"You can't let him get away with this," Lotte protested, pulling against Ben's firm grip.

"We won't. C'mon." He held out her coat.

"He's right, Dr. Keene," agreed Nate. "The Mayor is spooking the herd, s'all."

Lotte looked at the two men warily. She put on her coat and marched into the chilly night.

20

LONGWOOD

A sudden morning rain pummeled Ford Riley's pickup truck roof, roared down the slope and splashed in torrents. It came in sheets so heavy he could scarcely see twenty feet ahead of the truck as he leaned forward and squinted through the downpour.

His cattle usually sniffed fresh hay from a mile in any weather. If the sweet smell didn't attract their attention, the squeak of the Chevy's springs alerted them and they hemmed him in before he stopped the truck. This morning, they were nowhere in sight.

Peering ahead, he saw nothing but exploding prisms of Sierra Nevada storm rain. He had driven this route twice a day everyday for 32 years and was certain he was exactly where he planned to be: in the middle of his mixed herd of Herefords and horses on his fifty-acre section on the Thunder Peak Wilderness' south border.

He rolled down the window, poked his head out for a better look as rain hammered his wide-brimmed Stetson. There was nothing to see.

He mulled whether to get out and drop the dozen bales he'd brought along, one for every four head. Rain would soak it and end its usefulness as feed as soon as he lifted the tarp. If the cattle didn't eat it right up, bacteria would grow and fungus would form, if the flood wash didn't sweep it downslope first, that is. Either way he could write off another $2.50 per bale that he could fetch on the open market for his excess harvest.

He grumbled. The rain would move on, the constant tug of war between westerly and easterly winds would see to it.

He figured he had fourteen more hours of work to fit into the twelve hours of remaining daylight. That made up his mind. He opened the door and plunged into the deluge wondering if this is what it was like to be underwater. He had never gone swimming in his life and figured this was about as close as he would ever get.

Working quickly, he peeled back the tarp and hoisted the first bale onto the least flooded section of ground he could find nearby.

On his way back to the truck for the next bale, he looked up to the shelf of land where the herd often congregated in weather. Visibility increased dramatically between the blowing walls of rain. There they were! A dozen of his bigger doggies fifty yards up slope. Then the downpour hid everything from view again. He looked around in a quick sweep of the compass for more, yet saw nothing but sheets of rain over vacant range.

Puzzled by the cattle's reluctance to come to the hay, he carried the next bale toward them to see what had them acting so strange. The bale got heavier with each step as rain collected in it. Wave clouds curled across the furious sky and the indifferent wind bullied past him and his bale. Finally, the twine cut through the fingers of his gloves and he dropped the damned thing. He kept walking toward the last place he saw his cattle and soon they came into view, brown silhouettes against the clearing squall. Twenty head stood stoically enduring the downpour. Then he saw two geldings and a mare doing likewise off to the right. He couldn't blame them. The downpour had been one of the fiercest he could remember.

He moved to the yearling's side and patted her. She didn't move. Probably still braced against the weather. Riley walked across to two more, patting shoulders and necks as he walked. Rain or no, he loved this place, his life, these animals that he raised from newborns. He went to the chestnut gelding and stroked his neck. When he didn't get a nuzzle back, something in his distracted consciousness clicked. He looked into the gelding's eyes.

"Flash?" he said. The horse stared straight ahead, not blinking as the retreating shower dropped a few last raindrops into his gaze. A chill raced down Riley's spine.

"FLASH!"

He spun around and looked over the herd. They were all stone still, frozen in place.

Main Street looked like some bizarre rural California carnival. Half of the people scurrying here and there from the hardware store to the market to the feed store wore facemasks. Cowboys wore bandannas over their faces. Loggers made a show of bravado, marching tight-lipped, holding their breath, from store to truck, resolutely challenging the Stroke to try and get them.

At least some of his patients were heeding the warning, observed Ben as he drove back to the clinic after delivering the medical reports for Pocknett and Broder to the Sheriff's office. Longwood would be okay as long as the wind held steady from the north. He knew that if the disease was airborne and it spread, it would strike the area downwind to the south of the Thunder Peak Wilderness. That would be a significant escalation of the threat. So far, however, nothing had been reported on the news.

Three blocks up Main Street he noticed Nate Stimson turn suddenly south onto Route 16 and accelerate out of view. He wondered if that was significant, and then spotted the Mayor talking animatedly with Larson Black Kettle on the sidewalk outside the Hut. Mending fences, no doubt.

He pulled in beside the Cadillac just as the Mayor was pulling out his keys.

"Ben, let me tell you more about this waiver."

"You want to cut, right? You want to harvest the Thunder Peak Wilderness no matter how dangerous it is."

"Slow down. I love the Peak as much as anyone. But face it, Doctor, we have a situation here."

"What situation justifies risking more lives?" asked Ben.

The Mayor saw where this was going. "Must be nice living in a black and white world."

"Not black and white – right and wrong. Smart and crazy."

"The Stroke is going to kill this town if we don't get at it first," the Mayor's voice climbed. The balancing act of appearing to mediate between two extremes was wearing thin. "This is bigger than you or me, Ben. It involves the town, the West, the whole damn country!"

"We can handle it. Dr. Keene knows what she's doing and the folks at CDC—"

"—CDC!" shrieked the Mayor. He looked around quickly to make sure no one heard him. "Christ, Doc. Don't let anybody else hear you say that. You'll start a panic."

"The folks at CDC have a handle on what might be happening," he lied. "The head honcho down there is consulting and reviewing our findings."

"Do you know how to stop the Stroke?" the Mayor asked plainly.

Ben looked directly at Spivey. "Not yet."

"Well, there you go then," the Mayor concluded, "I have a compromise that'll answer some serious problems we have and give folks something to feel good about."

"Salvage logging, any logging is suicide, Wilburn."

"Hell, Ben, walking across the street is a risk! You grew up around here," the Mayor moved closer and took Ben into his confidence like an old comrade. "I don't have to tell you that these woodcutters don't function too well with subtleties and restrictions. And their math isn't like anything you or I were taught in school. They get to cut trees or they are victims of a great governmental or corporate conspiracy. You're their friend as long as you support their getting to cut trees. Anything short of your subsidizing cheap timber for the mills makes you their enemy. Having so many enemies keeps things simple. It's war, Doc."

Neither spoke.

"Times are hard right now and the choices are harder. So what else is new? California isn't for wimps, never has been. I'm doing what I have to for Longwood."

"So am I," growled Ben.

To the north of the Thunder Peak Wilderness, Willie Curtis was on his final pull eastbound to Longwood with just 27 miles to go. His load – a massive crawler – still rested securely in its restraints after 490 miles. He had hauled bigger loads, but none more finicky. It could shift at any moment and then he'd be screwed: cranes and winches would have to find him and readjust it, costing him thousands plus his bonus for getting it to Case-Kaiser in Longwood on schedule.

He downshifted to fifth gear as he entered a long sweeping turn, heard the big Cat under the long hood of his 377 Peterbilt hum agreeably and propped his left foot up on the dash in anticipation of an uneventful nine-mile stretch ahead. He flexed his stiff back muscles, rocked side to side, and yawned widely. Checking his watch, he nodded. Right on schedule. There would be time for three, maybe four hours of sleep in his walk-in sleeper before turning around for a load in Tahoe.

The dash-mounted teleprinter rang, then chattered quietly. Curtis glanced over and saw that it was from that dispatch biddy in Corvallis wanting confirmation of his position again. As if she didn't know. The GPS antenna behind the deflector above his cab gave her his exact position plus or minus 50 feet. The phone confirmation was just her brand of compulsive record-keeping that Case-Kaiser insisted upon. He'd respond when Case-Kaiser's foreman signed for the load.

A movement on the shoulder of the road a mile ahead caught his attention. It was a dark shape moving sluggishly in the tall grass off to the right. He grabbed the binoculars from the case hanging behind his head. If it was what he thought, he'd need the better part of the rapidly diminishing mile to bring the rig to a silent stop. Yep, it was a bear. A black.

In one familiar motion, he lifted the semi-automatic .308 Winchester off the rack and rested it on the passenger seat. Feeling his seat cushion's right side seam, he burrowed into the stuffing until his fingers found the lightly oiled four-round magazine loaded with 180-grain boat tail bonded deer slugs. Quietly satisfied with himself for being prepared for an opportunity such as this one, he flipped it around and expertly inserted the magazine, flicked off the scope's lens caps and repositioned the rifle within blind reach.

He scanned the horizon ahead and checked the side mirrors several times as he eased the heavy rig down through her gears. Each shift meshed gears smoothly and fought the rig's inertia. He also tapped the brakes to slow more quickly, but gave that up when he heard the percussive venting of the compressed air brakes. Fearful of scaring the bear, he sharpened his concentration on the downshifting to keep the engine's roar and backing twin stacks to a minimum. Eventually, all his efforts paid off with a smooth, not too raucous halt just 250 yards downwind of the bear.

He checked the mirrors again. There was nothing on the road behind him for miles. Nothing ahead either. No rancher in his pickup to take note of the supremely illegal act Curtis was intent upon. No tourists or civilians out for a drive. And no rangers or law anywhere in sight. Good.

He gripped the Winchester and brought it up to his chin, furtively glancing at the mirrors and the highway stretching east to the horizon. The bear loomed larger in the scope.

"Ooooweeeii-," Curtis whispered to himself. He wet his left index finger, put it out the window, and began to hum softly. He was directly downwind of the Grizzly. Today was going to be a very good day, he thought contentedly: a long haul successfully finished and paid, another haul waiting, clearing skies and a mature bear. He could already see the mounted head over his fireplace.

Four, five year-old . . . male in his prime. Lordy lordy, what a reward for my penance. I have hauled that tree killer up past 10,000 feet over the Divide, til this Peterbilt couldn't breathe and I'm about to deliver it safe and sound. *Thank you for the bounty we are about to receive.*

Checking the mirrors again and seeing only clear road in both directions, he scooted over to the passenger seat, poked the rifle barrel out and propped it on the mirror strut. He spotted the bear, put the crosshairs over the heart, and grinned. This was just too sweet.

He thought about checking the road again. No, that would mean he would have to shift position back to the driver's seat and look both ways again. Naw, if he acted quickly, he'd probably be okay. He steadied his breathing, nudged the stock squarely into his shoulder, flipped off the safety, and eased down ever so softly on the trigger. He calculated a one and three quarter inch drop over this distance, eased the crosshairs up a scosch, and remembered to open his left eye just before pulling.

A hum tickled the edge of his awareness. The bear started moving to the tree line, pawing and snorting as it searched for food.

Curtis kept the crosshairs on the bear's chest. It wouldn't be as clean a shot now that the bear had turned, but he could still drop it, he was sure.

Then the hum registered. It was a vehicle engine. He looked up quickly and saw the Sheriff's pickup less than a quarter of a mile from him and closing. He considered dropping the rifle on the ground, but the Sheriff might see it. No, be cool, Willie. He eased it back inside the cab and dropped it behind the seats. There was no way he could replace it in the rack; the Sheriff who was already slowing would see that.

Curtis slid back into place behind the wheel, ripping the teleprinter message off as he moved and began reading the communication intently.

"Howdy."

Curtis looked down at the Native American in uniform behind the wheel of the Sheriff's pickup. "Sheriff."

"Trouble?"

"Naw, just these dang teleprinters. Give me CB anyday, y'know?" he said in his most conspiratorial tone. "These things," he held up the printout, "an ol' trucker like me has to pull off – to be safe, don't ya know – read the paper, then call in to dispatch."

Nate Stimson wasn't buying the act. As long as the trucker wasn't drinking, however, and the rig looked to be up to code and there was no blatantly illegal activity underway, he was inclined to give him the benefit of the doubt. He studied the load for a moment.

"That for Case-Kaiser?"

"It is."

"Where you headed?"

Curtis made a show of checking his clipboard and read: "Mineral King Road at CA-198. Foreman up there is waiting. I guess they're getting some kinda waiver to get in there and cut timber."

Nate remained silent, gauging this new information and Curtis. Neither Jasperson's office nor Mayor Spivey informed him that the cutting was imminent. As far as he – and the rest of Longwood – knew, the waivers looked likely to go through and there would be some limited salvage logging sometime in a few weeks. Moving this expensive equipment into place was a sure sign Case-Kaiser was ready to cut. He didn't like surprises, especially this one.

"Get it moving. Not safe you're sitting here on the highway with that load," he said evenly.

Curtis was fine with that. Not even a registration and logbook check. He fired the engine, looked behind him, and eased up through the gears until he had the rig and its load rolling along at 35 miles per hour towards Longwood. As he passed the spot where he'd seen the bear, a branch bobbed just inside the tree line. That black was gone.

21

LONGWOOD

Ben stood in the doorway of his laboratory, Broder's shrouded corpse behind him in the tiled room. Lotte continued preparing tissue and blood samples, examining them under her high-powered binocular microscope and noting the observations in her notebook. Between them in the middle of the basement, Nelson Hatch spiraled slowly to certain death.

"There had to be other life near Broder, the buck, and Hatch" Ben said to Lotte's back. "Birds, rabbits, voles. But there were no corpses. Nate said there was a bear routing around while we were up there collecting the bodies. Then there is Riley's herd thirteen miles southwest. If whatever this thing is originated where Broder, the buck and Hatch were struck down, why not the bear? Why hasn't Nate found corpses across the intervening distance?"

"Go on," said Lotte without looking up.

"If it's a virus," he went on, "it kills some and leaves others alone. How is that possible?"

"It's not likely." She made another notation, swiveled in her chair, and faced him.

"Viruses are breakaway fragments of the genetic code – once

116

part of a living creature - that somehow find a new living organism," she deliberated, "they knock on the cell's front door and say, 'Can I come in?' The host cell doesn't let just anyone in. So it asks, 'Who are you?' The virus responds chemically, saying, 'I'm a friend, one of you.' Her thinking aloud meshed neatly with Ben's similar style of overt problem-solving.

"But DNA and RNA, they are fragile molecules. How would even a fragment survive the trip outside a cell to the next cell?"

"The genetic code is wrapped in a thin protein coat."

"A sheep . . ." interjected Ben.

"To the host cell, the virus looks and acts just like parts of another cell. The protein presses the right receptor 'doorbell' and the cell mistakenly takes in the virus."

"Once inside, the virus sheds its sheep's clothing and goes to work like the wolf it is," Ben finished the metaphor.

"And since a virus' sole purpose in life is to reproduce, it takes over the host cell's resources and clones itself wildly."

"Diabolical, isn't it," observed Lotte. "Almost human."

"You can be dark, can't you."

"But all that takes time," she ignored him and continued. "Broder and the others died almost instantly."

"Near as we can tell."

"I'm thinking Lars inhaled whatever it is."

"That's possible. And you're sure there was no external trauma? No open wounds?"

"Positive."

"All right, then. IF -- and at this point IF is as far as I'm willing to go – it is an airborne virus, what could possibly kill so quickly, impersonating contradictory symptoms?"

"A virus we don't know about?"

"Possibly. But Broder was asymptomatic for viral infection."

"No colony of the lethal virus still there in the body, hungover after the orgy that killed its host."

"Right."

"Very unviruslike. Usually, they leave plenty of clues," she held Hatch's chest x-ray film up to the light. "Aren't shy about leaving damage in their wake: concentrations of white blood cells, rotted liver cells, that kind of thing…"

"It has to be viral. What else could it be?"

"I don't know."

"What the hell do we do next, then?"

Lotte stood and paced, enjoying the familiar rhythm, the satisfying give and take of problem-solving she'd had with Charley. "Listen, you have something here in the Thunder Peak. It kills, apparently selectively. It walks like a virus, but it talks like a chemical toxin. And it's stealthy; it leaves no trace of its presence, except death."

Ben waited for more, and when Lotte did not say more, began reviewing Nelson Hatch's records for the hundredth time.

After several minutes, Lotte looked at Ben. "The process is slow, positively glacial. At least it always has been," she said aloud, as if a window had opened and permitted her thoughts to escape.

"What process," asked Ben?

"--but when man came along and started tinkering with the mechanism of evolution," she ignored his question, "the natural process of change and adaptation accelerated."

Ben stood with his arms folded, waiting patiently for her to finish.

"Man will succumb to his undisciplined nature to use Nature's processes to destroy Nature herself. Oh it's always perceived as a benefit, at first: interbreeding pigs to develop a larger hog, horses to make a faster, stronger Cup contender; cross-pollinating flowers to create a more spectacular rose. Problem is: man can't stop himself. Sooner or later, he turns from constructive to destructive purposes. First to control weeds in the garden, then to control encephalitis-carrying mosquitoes, then to vanquish his enemies."

"Your Nature's Defense Theory again," said Ben, his tone purposely neutral.

"Nature's and Man's relationship is more complicated than we ever thought. It's not always Nature vs. Man. At some level, it is Nature plus Man in a mutually destructive relationship."

Ben was listening closely now.

"Cells respond unpredictably to stress. We know that and yet we continue to add stress factors - chemicals, oxidants, and DNA-damaging agents - to our environment. What biologists are struggling to keep pace with is the altered uptake and efflux of chemical agents, intercellular detoxification and DNA damage responses."

Ben's mind raced. He was trying mightily to reconcile his scientific understanding with whatever metaphysical possibilities were forming in the air between them.

Lotte mistook his stare for resistance to what she was saying. "Biology *is* reacting to our accelerating experimentation."

"If over harvesting of the old growth were the culprit, why wouldn't we see it in other equally over harvested areas?"

I have, she thought. *In Brazil.* "Maybe we're on biology's front lines and don't even know it. Maybe cells are evolving faster here in the Thunder Peak than our knowledge. Whatever, our current knowledge of adaptive response systems is inadequate, woefully so."

"What you're saying, Doc, is we're in deep." It wasn't a question.

"This is what I'm saying."

Mary Margaret pulled down her pale blue facemask, bit into her candy bar, and replaced the mask. It was large for her small face and she was forced to continually adjust it to prevent it from covering her eyes.

The cashier in the grocery store who usually smiled and asked her about school was silent. Other adults that she and Grace encountered during their regular shopping morning looked preoccupied and unfriendly. Grace kept an arm around her and spoke in a solicitous tone.

"Why is Mr. Riley mad at Daddy?" M asked as they put the grocery bags in Grace's Explorer. The molded paper mask stripped personality from her voice. Grace paused, taken back momentarily by M's frontal assault on the tension that was straining nerves in Longwood. Grocery shopping was Grace's way to give Ben some time off and stay close to this young girl for whom she had come to feel increasingly protective. It hadn't gone well this morning. The awkwardness was palpable. Maybe insisting on keeping a normal schedule in this crisis was a mistake.

"He's angry at everyone right now, M. He lost his herd and your Dad isn't sure what caused it."

M handed Grace another bag. "Dr. Keene, too, right? Daddy says she is really smart, but I don't think she knows either."

"That's right. Not yet," Grace said, "But they'll find out what it is and make it better."

M fell silent as they loaded the last of the bags. Grace watched her put the empty cart with the others and return to the Explorer.

"What is it, sweetie?"

"I'm getting scared. Something terrible is happening and nobody knows what to do."

Grace pulled M close and hugged her. "Your Daddy is a great doctor. He cares about you more than anything in the world and won't let anything happen to you, ever. Nor will I. You're going to be fine. Everything's going to be fine."

They rode in silence for several moments. A bee bumped the windshield and brought Grace back from where her mind had been straying. "What else does your Daddy say about Dr. Lotte?"

M didn't respond. Her mind continued working on the threat.

"Somebody at school said it's the loggers' fault. Is it?"

Grace thought a moment. "It's impossible to know yet, M. Some people think that the clear-cutting may have stirred up a spore. They think that the wind carries it—"

"Like a dandelion?"

"Yes, something like that, only smaller."

"Do you think that?"

"I think that Nature is trying to tell us something, yes. But we haven't learned how to listen yet."

M watched the splintered terrain of harsh clear-cut pass by her window as they headed back to the ranch. "But everything grows back eventually, right?"

"Hopefully. Even when it does, it's different."

"How?"

Grace silently questioned how much to share with M. She was a child, already confused and off balance. It might not be fair to give her more to worry about. On the other hand, how fair could it be to deny her more of the story, another perspective?

"When they take a tree, a universe of life in and under that tree is suddenly stranded. Their home turns against them. Plants and animals shrivel and die. Without shade, the water in the nearby stream heats up. The crayfish, frogs, trout, and salmon can no longer live there, so they leave or die. So do the animals. The eagles have nothing to eat, so they leave. Carbon dioxide accumulates because the tree is no longer there to clean the air. The air gets worse and man leaves, too. Soon, there is no one and nothing left."

"Because someone cut down a tree?" M asked quietly.

Vin der Root heard his name.

"Hmmm?" he answered before the realization sank in that he was not alone. That was odd. The building at CDC should be empty of research scientists and administrators. Yet someone was in the halls calling out his name.

"Dr. der Root?"

The voice was a man's, a young man's and it was getting impatient.

He marked his place in the computer readout of results on a census of recent viral and bacterial outbreaks in the world's forested regions.

"Anybody here?"

Dammit, Gus, he muttered to himself. No one is allowed in here, anyhow, anytime! Gus worked weekends at the security desk and filled in as a substitute on weekdays. A retired cop from San Diego and a friendly enough fella, albeit a bit talkative, he was supposed to politely turn away anyone who happened into the lobby of his building. The CDC wasn't the CIA, but it housed some of the most lethal strains of disease known to mankind and posed a serious threat if released into the atmosphere. The remote location of the campus kept most people away. Still, if someone was determined, they could penetrate security measures and cause some trouble.

C'mon, Vin. Get a grip.

"Dr. der Root? Can anyone hear me?"

Vin stepped outside his office door just in time to see a teenager in baggy jeans, an oversized jacket, knit cap pulled low and headphones hanging around his neck turn from the adjoining hallway into his corridor. He was carrying a red vinyl bag on its side, the kind they use to deliver hot food. When he saw Vin, he approached directly.

"You the Doctor?"

"What do you want?" It was more a challenge than a question.

"Pizza," the deliveryman said impatiently.

"For who?"

He checked his order. "Dr. Vincent der Root," he emphasized the last syllable, and looked up.

Vin studied the deliveryman for a moment. "That's me, but I didn't order a pizza."

The teen sighed and copped an attitude. Like he hadn't heard that chestnut before. "Now don't waste my time. I got a pizza with your name on it. Paid for. You can do what you want with it, but I can't leave here with what's yours. Got it?" He pulled a pizza box from the *stay hot!* red vinyl envelope, handed it to der Root and waited.

When he didn't reach into his pocket for a tip, the deliveryman rolled his eyes and left, mumbling something about 'cheap motherfucker...'

Vin watched him disappear around the corner, and immediately called the front security desk to remind Gus that N-O O-N-E was permitted up to his floor without first getting phone authorization.

He set down the box and returned to his computer print out, determined to follow the outbreak to some kind of conclusion before he lost track of his train of analysis.

The aroma of the pizza inside the box soon filled the office and reminded him of the unexpected delivery when he looked up from his calculations.

His curiosity piqued, he lifted the box lid and saw a large mushroom pizza. Lots of mushrooms. There was no tomato sauce, no cheese, just . . . mushrooms. He checked the receipt for a clue to its origin. It had his name and the correct office address. The purchaser's name was nowhere on the receipt. On the signature line, someone had written 'cash.'

If it was coincidence that a mushroom pizza arrived at the same time he was following the hunch that brought him into the lab on Sunday, then it was an uncomfortable one. No one knew what he was thinking, much less fearing.

He swallowed hard. The chill that started in his gut crawled up his spine. His hair began to hurt as if a thousand needles were probing his skull.

There was nothing on the box but the mustachioed chef in the tall hat holding a steaming pizza high over his head with one hand, proudly carrying it to his appreciative customer. He picked up the box and looked underneath.

He looked inside again. There was nothing there but the pizza, sliced neatly into eighths. Nothing on the underside of the lid.

He lifted the wax paper under the pizza crust and saw it. A corner of paper. He lifted the pizza higher and pulled it out. A post-it. It had a paw print on it. A dog's. No, not a dog's, it was too small. A coyote's or fox's print about 2¼ inches long. He turned it over.

Stay out of Thunder Peak Wilderness.

He hadn't breathed since he saw the corner of paper. And he couldn't breathe now. The 'ea' of the word 'Peak' blurred and ran down the notepaper, a blue vein. Another bead of sweat dropped from his forehead onto the note and streamed to his desktop where it created a blue shape with a dark blue center.

It looked like a deadly malignant cancer cell.

He stared at the droplet for he didn't know how long, trapped, immobile. Lotte was right. Itamarati.

He thought for a long moment about what to do, then turned to his computer and logged onto the *New York Times* website. Clicking through to FORUMS, then HEALTH, then ALTERNATIVE, he opened a comment form, identified himself as *enigma* and quickly typed:

'Doing research on black phase. *Vulpes fulva*. Contact ASAP.'

'Black phase,' was the emergency phrase he hoped he would never have to use. He pressed the return key, sent the coded posting to the NYT Web Forum, and waited.

He looked at the paw print again and grew paler as minutes passed. He didn't expect an answer right away. The person who would recognize his message might not be on line or logged into the Forum. He had to give it some time.

Vulpes fulva. Red Fox.

Lotte knew she needed help. It was the wise next step. Yet, there was a part of her that procrastinated. If this killer was what she thought it was, she wanted to take it on, understand it, and vanquish it herself. Itamarati was personal. And it wasn't difficult to come up with reasons for keeping it to herself. While qualified assistance from the CDC would quicken the laborious and time-consuming testing required to build a comprehensive record of the disease's mechanism, it would also raise the 'Stroke's' profile. Once it showed on the media's radar, the situation would become a thousand times more complicated. Still, the professional in her knew to a certainty the importance of marshaling qualified help to contain this disease before it could gain ground and spawn more deaths.

That left friends or trusted colleagues. Professionals who could understand the situation's volatility and function discreetly. She didn't know many of those. Partly because she was a loner in a profession of loners. More significantly, because epidemiology was as vulnerable to the abundant temptations of the media age as law, politics and genetic science. No, the only person she trusted was Vin der Root. That trust wasn't absolute - he was a suit after all - yet she felt she knew him sufficiently well to predict his take in this situation.

He was evasive when she finally reached him on the telephone. Could be her own rising concern, thought Lotte, or her need for closure. No, there was something in his voice in multiples of his usual dodge and weave. The shy clip. The careful distance.

What was he into now? For as long as she had known him, he had heeled to the opinions of people more powerful than himself. He wasn't obsequious, just adept at the tactics of advancement. He could be influenced. No doubt that's all it was this time. Besides, she reminded herself, she was also distracted.

"Vin, listen to me, get your kit out here."

"I can't, Lotte. This influenza sweeping the Sunbelt-- "

"Republican fat cats in the Sunbelt catch a sniffle, Uncle Sam mortgages the treasury and nurses them. Yet he's busy when hard-working Ahwahnee, woodcutters, and ranchers in the Thunder Peak are dying. God bless America!"

"Lotte, I can't right now."

"I'm asking, Vin."

"Lotte."

"Please."

"You don't understand."

"No, I don't understand. Not this. I need your help."

There was a long pause on the line.

"I'll run the full regimen, complete protocols on anything you can send me as if it's a Level Four," his voice was stripped down, reaching out for her to understand that he was trying.

That was something. Not so much his commitment to throw resources and manpower at samples she might send; rather the overgenerous response, as if to compensate. She sensed she had reached his bottom line, for the moment at least.

It was not until she hung up and was taking Nelson Hatch's vitals again that something else occurred to her. He hadn't offered to dispatch even a low level team of graduate interns. That didn't sit right. It would have been the logical out for him. She couldn't have accepted them, of course. A platoon of white coats as Ben called them marching off the plane at the airport in Visalia was not discreet. Maybe der Root had the same thought. No, for all he knew, the situation could be worthy of media attention. He often used the media to alert the populace and, not coincidentally, boost his agency's profile. He specifically had withheld any offer of assistance.

Lotte stared disbelieving at the readout as the pressure cuff wilted on Hatch's stiff upper arm. Hatch's pressure was rising. Ribavarin had helped a little, but both his systolic and diastolic were climbing to unsurvivable levels. What was happening?

He's dying, Keene.

I know that! But why not immediately, like Broder. Why not yesterday. Why now?

22

LONGWOOD

"The genetic stuff shared by all five kingdoms of life – Animalia, Plantae, Fungi, Protista and Monera -- is identical, Lotte explained as she paced. Two purine bases: adenine and guanine. Two pyrimidine bases: cytosine and thymine. A, G, C and T. Adenine is always opposite thymine and binds to thymine. Guanine is always opposite cytosine and binds to cytosine. We know this. We also have mapped many of the nucleotides or DNA helixes of the plants, Protista and Monera. We find what's different, then we attack that."

"What about animals and, what'd you say the other one was?" asked Ben.

"Fungi."

"Mushrooms, right."

"And yeasts, molds and mildews," added Lotte.

"Plenty of that stuff up there all right," Ben observed. "At least there's one absolute amid all these variables: there's only one genetic code."

"That we know of," said Lotte. "There are millions of unexplored bodies in just the Milky Way galaxy. It's not unreasonable to expect that different life forms evolving from different DNA exist somewhere in all that. There are billions of objects flying through space carrying foreign matter we know nothing about. The Earth is impacted hundreds of times a day. Most objects burn up in the atmosphere, but not all. Occasionally one gets through. If it carries a single strand of different DNA, then . . ." her voice trailed off. "Even with the code we know about, there are millions of possible combinations, millions of ways to miss it. We need time.

"Add just one new enzyme, it changes the rules completely. Everything we thought we knew and understood would be instantly invalid. We'd be back in the Dark Ages."

"Then killing the forest would be the only way," concluded Ben, "That where you're going?"

"No. That's no cure."

"It *would* eradicate the disease," he argued.

"If we kill the killer by destroying Thunder Peak Wilderness we kill Longwood, too."

Losing patience with the direction the discussion had taken, she changed the subject. "I'm concerned about the sudden drop in platelets."

"Thrombocytopenia."

"Yes. Last night, Hatch had a slow and steady drop. That was of concern, but not too serious. In any other normal case, it could be infection, anaphylactic shock, hemorrhage, and anemia. Here? After several hours of rehydration, it's dropped like a stone."

"It's not a surprise," Ben said.

"No, listen, what's surprising is the pattern. It is producing effects similar to the *shigella*-like toxin *E. coli* bacteria. They cause intravascular platelet coagulation. That is one of the hallmarks. It also destroys red cells. The chain of destruction then progresses rapidly to multiple-organ failure. Kidneys from uremia. Liver, lungs… nasty, nasty business."

She paused.

"What are you thinking?"

"It's so fast. Even *E. coli* takes time to overwhelm internal organs and kill."

"Nelson's not gone yet."

They observed Hatch curled grotesquely on the table.

"I need samples," Lotte said suddenly.

"Samples?" He looked at the dressings on Hatch's arm and fingers where she had taken tissue samples. He looked over at her microscope with the rack of slides beside it "Samples of what?"

"Botanical samples."

"From the woods you mean?"

She nodded.

"What do we look for?"

"Everything I can find. And not 'we.' Me. It's too dangerous. I'll go for them alone."

"Are you out of your mind?"

"Out of alternatives. I'm an epidemiologist. I collect samples and test them," she explained as she ascended the stairs.

"Dammit Lotte, wait a minute. Where are you going?"

"To my van," her disembodied voice answered out of sight from the top landing. The door thudded closed behind her.

Ben took the stairs three at a time and emerged outside in time to see Lotte turning the van around.

"Wait!" he yelled.

"No time!" she shouted over the VW's engine. "Stay with Nelson."

Ben heard it the moment he opened the door: a shrill electronic tone from the lab.

The flat line trace on the ECG monitor hadn't yet crossed the screen. Hatch had coded just seconds before.

Ben turned the defibrillator to 300 joules, applied gel to the paddles and was about to apply a life-sustaining jolt to Hatch's heart when he paused, paddles high, frozen in indecision . . .

The high stands on a crisp October day gave Lotte a sense of well-being. Not even death stalking these ridges could dull the rebirth she experienced. Cobalt skies and pure sunlight illuminated subalpine lodgepoles. The bark on the ponderosas glowed like dusty roses, the needles brilliant green like clover. Higher up were dense, windless and silent stands of Douglas and white firs, their stillness broken only by the ubiquitous chickaree feasting on abundant fir cones. Still higher, the Engelmann's spruces' red and gray armor looked stronger than any virus that might threaten them. That wasn't the case, but the thought was satisfying in its way.

Approaching from the northeast, upwind, she followed the waypoints on her Magellan GPS receiver and found the place she was looking for. Tracks from the Sheriff's pickup left the road and threaded up the slope over scrub and undergrowth. The van's low ground clearance prevented her from going very far. She parked on the shoulder where she could get back onto the road quickly, just in case the unexpected happened.

After confirming that the twin filters on her rebreather mask were snugly fitted, she slipped the harness over her head and pulled the straps tight.

A pair of bighorn rams paused on a narrow ledge 50 yards away. There were also ravens in the high branches and squirrels below. She pulled one of the TyChem 9400 Level A Suits from its pouch, stepped quickly in, cinched the waist belt, and pulled up the gas-tight zipper. Next came slip-on disposable latex overboots. She taped the tops securely with duct tape.

Finally, she put on protective gloves. She probably should have worn Nitrile or Butyl gloves for maximum safety but they did not provide the tactile control she needed. Safeskin disposable latex gloves, .0006" thickness, and unpowdered were what she needed for dexterity. They were more difficult to put on, but posed less risk of contamination and consistently provided the lowest particle contamination from one sample to the next.

One eye on the Magellan, the other on the uneven terrain ahead, she trekked cautiously up slope. She wanted to move faster. Images of the Bear and the Sheriff's advice that she not spend any more time on the Peak than her professionalism required had her on edge. However, she also knew that haste made mistakes in her business, especially on unfamiliar ground.

The gawdawful rasping sound of her suit and the rush of her respiration inside the hood overpowered the sounds of the forest. If there was a bear within 400 yards, she was sure it could hear her coming. Every ten yards she stopped and listened. Reduced to relying mostly upon sight, she would walk, pause, turn 360° in place, and, when she was satisfied that there was no danger, she trekked forward another ten to twenty yards and repeated her slow, steady turn.

As she approached the coordinates the Sheriff gave her for the clearing represented by a flashing dot on the Magellan's screen she began to expertly register the botany of her surroundings. Her suspicion that the killer was airborne was just theory. Still, more than twenty years of experience in fields of invisible microscopic killers was worth something. That experience and the instincts it shaped were often the most reliable tools she carried with her into danger.

Looking around, she saw the forest floor covered with shrubs and non-woody plants. Broom huckleberry – a blueberry prized by bears – and Jacob's Ladder with its tiny pale-blue flowers. There were rare and endangered plants: kidney-leaved violet, maidenhair spleenwort, fringed onion. Lotte knew them all in both their dormant and flowering states. Populations of these holdouts were rarely seen alone, let alone in such abundant gatherings. They preferred the moist, shadowed depths of old growth. Many could be witnessed only in the aftermath of fire, when intense heat opened the cones and released seeds.

Still others sought high, windy promontories where they curled up in fissures and nurtured themselves on scant detritus and brief glistenings of dew. There, they grew slowly against ripping winds, and built strength until they became dense woods of a quality all but unknown in the contemporary world.

Underneath the shrubs that yielded to Lotte's yellow latex-clad legs, the ground was spongy. Her footsteps rebounded off the pine needle carpet. Two to three inches of dense compost, she estimated. Needles on top, seed casings, dust from flaking bark, deadfall, fungi. All that underlain by packed earth. Under that, granite ridge all the way to 65 degrees North in Yukon Territory. Classic old growth terrain.

A chipmunk dashed out in front of her. Keeping one eye open for predators and the other focused on the ground for morsels of food, it skittered in a zigzag blur across her path and behind a spruce trunk.

A nutcracker chased an interloping gray jay into the shadows.

A ruby-crowned kinglet sang boldly from a hidden branch and a Clark's nutcracker hovered briefly over Lotte, soaring away only after satisfying itself that she wasn't a great yellow blossom.

There was nothing out of the ordinary that she could see. She stilled and watched for the subtlest hint in the dew-muffled silence. Condensation tap-tapped crisply as it dripped from bough to ground. She waited for the smells to penetrate the filter in her mask; the smell of dew-damp grass relaxing, uncoiling, releasing its essential scents, of damp moss stretching out on warming stone. If she weren't so wary of the microbial or viral threat, she would take off the damned suit and join the living universe, Nature's authentic life as it is away from chainsaws, diesels, cheap aftershave, and tobacco smoke.

Swaying crowns whispered from high above. A raven *knock-kn-kn-kn-knoccck-ck-cked*. A groan sounded from deep within the heart of a giant Engelmann spruce nearby. Lotte resumed studying the clearing, organizing her plan for collecting samples.

There were no carcasses in sight. There were, however, numerous mushrooms; fruiting bodies of underground threadlike fungi. Nature's chief decomposers. Their presence was an indicator for organic decay. A fan of *phyllotopsis nidulans* growing from a deadfall limb glowed in the sunlight. There were half a dozen other types in view. She would need to get started collecting samples soon if she wanted to be back in the lab by early afternoon.

And there it was, the great mule deer with its great rack not five yards to her left, partially hidden by trunks and huckleberry. He was huge. Her head didn't reach his shoulder. His blood probably flowed through half the deer population within a hundred mile radius. Standing erect, unblinking, proud, a stone stoic . . . as dead as Lars Broder.

She spun around again to double check that she was alone.

She took samples of everything she could find in 20ml tall clear vials with Teflon® sealed screw-on caps and larger 60ml wide-mouth borosilicate glass jars for the bigger samples. She noted the type and location of the sample with an indelible marker on the plastic caps.

Working carefully with a scalpel and tweezers to cause as little disruption as possible, she meticulously collected at least three grams from each genus. There were few flowers in bloom this late in the year making it easy to gather pollen and petal samples of each. The lichens on the shaded sides of rocks where the sun never shone surrendered samples readily. The bark, needles, and seedlings of the spruces, whitebark firs required nine tubes. The huckleberry and scant ground cover another 13. Then there were the fungi and molds. Fans, caps, and little puffballs with curled back 'rays' that reminded her of stars. That's what they were called:

Earthstars. When she reached to cut one off at the base, a percussive blast split the air.

She reflexively dove to the ground. Whether the sound was gunfire spawned from tribal hatreds as she had experienced in Zaire or a rogue hunter, she had long since learned how to survive in hostile situations. When she looked up, she saw a dead branch collapsed to the ground.

Her heart racing, she climbed back to her knees to quickly collect the Earthstar. She hadn't realized how tense she was until the branch spiked her adrenalin. That was enough; she had to collect this last sample and get out of there.

She recalled Vin der Root's fascination for unusual spore disbursal mechanisms. An amateur mycologist, he mentioned earthstars when they were at Hopkins. While most mushrooms passively drop their spores from dried gills, the earthstar actively propels them through the small hole at the top of the puffball. Not actively, exactly. It relies on raindrops, hail, or some other external disturbance to tap the ball, compress the interior atmosphere, and 'puff' them into the air.

She tapped the side of the small puffball. *Pooof!* Tiny spores sprayed through the hole on top and filled the air like dust in the slanting sunlight . . .

The line jumped. A sharp peak pointed high on the screen then settled into a series of fitful, irregular bumps that Ben knew were lethal. There was no predicting how the life force would behave in a dying patient. If the patient was lucky, he would either go quietly or come back loudly. Ben had seen both extremes. He preferred loud, of course. It meant a better chance for recovery. But a quiet departure was at least merciful.

Nelson Hatch's heart responded to the 300-joule jumpstart with surprising energy. Taking his cue from the vigorous electrical spike, Ben injected another .30cc of Ribavarin. Hatch's circulation and vital functions were beyond repair at this point, yet who could say? If his blood could be thinned just a little, just enough to permit oxygen exchange, maybe, just maybe Nelson could hang on another minute, another hour.

The powerful burst from his heart was a phantom, the life force's last bloom. A final push to be rid of the 'Stroke.' It wasn't enough.

Ben said aloud, "Time of death: 10:58 a.m."

23

LONGWOOD

The old Victorian house on Redding Street was a welcome sight. Longwood's Medical Clinic had become a home away from home for Lotte, familiar scientific ground, a safe zone. Another reason, she had to admit, was Ben McCandle. He set up a resonance in her.

She found herself dwelling on the immense sorrow hiding in the shadows when she was alone with her grief for Charley, her frustration with the Itamarati mystery, and the dead.

She unloaded her sample case and confirmed that the airtight cooler containing the used protective suit was securely locked. She had used up only two and a half hours of its rated eight-hour usability. If whatever was killing these victims was still out there and she had walked through it, the suit was irreversibly contaminated. It could never be safely used again and must be destroyed. She would burn it in the first biohazard-safe incinerator she could find. For now, it was safely double-sealed in an airtight biohazard bag, chemical taped and locked in the cooler.

Inside, the lab was strangely quiet. There were no sounds of shuffling feet as Ben moved about, no rustle of paper as he turned medical journal pages, or clinks of medicine vials on countertops, no chirp from the heart rate monitor. He was sitting round-shouldered at his desk, drained and staring despondently at Hatch's body on the table in the middle of the room.

"He's dead," she said.

Ben roused to his feet when he saw Lotte holding the two full trays of sample tubes and jars. He helped shift the sample trays to the analysis bench and glanced at the time, "forty-five minutes ago."

"We have to examine him," she said as she retrieved a surgical setup tray from the cabinet. "Why haven't you begun?"

Ben looked at the body, then back at her. "He saved Mary Margaret's life."

Lotte waited for him to explain.

"M was thrown from her friend's horse when she was seven. She was knocked unconscious . . . some bubble gum lodged in her airway and she was turning cyanotic. Her friend didn't know what to do. She flagged down the first truck that came by. It was Nelson who stopped. He cleared the obstruction, performed CPR and brought her to me. You should've seen her, all bruised and muddy, but *alive* in his arms."

Lotte looked at Nelson Hatch as if for the first time. He was suddenly real to her.

"Ben," Lotte touched his arm.

Ben nodded.

"I'll do the procedure; I know what to look for." She turned her professionalism up to full power. "You assist."

They had already photographed Hatch dressed and naked. Lotte had scanned every square inch of Hatch's clothing and collected two dozen organic samples for testing, which she had yet to analyze. Her post mortem protocol called for additional photo documentation regardless of the extent of documentation of the patient while he was alive, so they quickly snapped off another 50 exposures of Hatch naked from every angle.

The room was cold and still. The thick stone foundation of the old house contained the cold like a cave.

They observed the lifeless form, both silently noting the surreal presence of lifelike skin tone captured by the absence of normal lividity. The eyes would have started to flatten from loss of fluid by now, but they remained spheroid, healthy in appearance.

"Ready?" asked Lotte, now gowned, masked, and gloved.

"As I'll ever be."

"You take his knees while I hold his shoulders," suggested Lotte.

It worked. There was a sickening pop as Hatch's abdominal musculature tore and rigid ligaments snapped. The body was now flat on its back with knees raised.

After noting the time and date, she began, "No case number. Decedent's name: Nelson Hatch. Lotte Keene performing modified medical examination. Ben McCandle, M.D., presiding.

"The body is of a well-developed, well-nourished 34 year old Caucasian male with black and gray hair, hazel eyes. Body is 74 inches long and weighs 203 pounds."

"Atypical stiffness is present throughout the body. Not rigor mortis. Repeat, stiffness present in 100% of total body mass.

"Evidence of injury: none. Skin: normally textured, notably. There is a scar in the upper left thoracic quadrant. Measures ... 7/8 inch."

"An arrow he took when hunting with his son in the oughts," interjected Ben. "2009, I think."

"A three-inch scar in the right lower quadrant of the abdomen," continued Lotte.

"Appendectomy," Ben interjected.

"Multiple scars on shins of both legs, work injuries. Forearms layered with past-healed scars. No other abnormalities."

Another hard-working Longwood logger, thought Ben.

They took several shortcuts. Ben followed Lotte's assured lead. She knew what she was looking for.

"I am making a 'Y' incision across the chest, shoulder to shoulder," she enunciated as she fingered the chest to find the sternum, made an assured incision from the left shoulder to the sternum, then another incision from the right shoulder. "And sternum to pubis." Just as assuredly, she guided the scalpel in a straight line.

Ben cut the ribs, removed the breastplate, and lifted the heart, lungs, esophagus, and trachea *en bloc*.

Lotte studied each one, deliberating whether to separate them for individual weighing and testing.

"Lungs are pink yet stiff. Liver: ruddy, yet stiff. These are to be separated for testing," she said for the benefit of the recording.

"Also the trachea." She then reached in, snipped the heart free, and held it up to observe it from various angles. Eerily, it did not drip blood. Rather, it held its vigorous shape and glistened like a damp plastic toy.

She looked at Ben for a long moment. Disappointment and bewilderment showed in his expression above their filtered breathing masks.

Finally, she made an intermastoid incision from Hatch's left ear, across the top of the skull to the right ear, and pulled the scalp down over the front of the face. She cut a wedge of the skull plate away with a small power saw, and placed that on a stainless steel tray. She then removed the entire brain through the craniotomy and placed that on the tray. She replaced the wedge of skull plate and recovered it with the flap of scalp.

"I've taken the brain – which looks normal in all respects for a man of his age – for further examination."

Lastly, she tried to aspirate urine from the bladder for testing. A tiny amount of amber jelly crept into the syringe, less than 5 mils. At least it was something that moved, although it couldn't be described as fluid, or even viscous.

"Urine is jellified," she said loudly, her frustration evident in her voice.

She turned and transected one of the lungs. "There is no discoloration in the lung.

"Pending microscopic analysis of lung, heart, and trachea tissue for residue, it is my opinion that Nelson Hatch perished from rapid, chemical petrifaction of all organic tissue."

"Never seen anything like--," Ben blurted.

"--Nelson Hatch," continued Lotte, "a 34 year-old male died as a result of sudden hardening reaction of all internal organs by an agent – possibly inhaled – that overwhelmed his system. The cause of death: sudden insult to body chemistry. Mechanism of death was asphyxiation and shock secondary to sudden loss of electrochemical conductivity and chemical reaction in blood. The manner of death was ..."

There were only four recognized legal categories of manner of death: natural, accident, suicide, and homicide.

As presiding medical examiner, Ben *could* rule that this was natural, despite the fact that Hatch's affliction was not like anything in the medical textbooks or journals.

He could determine that it was an accident, but to determine the source, nature and cause of the accident would require detective skills unavailable within a radius of 200 miles.

It did not appear to be suicide.

Homicide?

"Lotte?"

"Mmm?" she answered as she prepared a slide of alveolar sac tissue from Hatch's right lung.

"How about we call it 'natural' for the time being. Until we can get a better fix on just what's going on up there?"

"The manner of death was … natural," Lotte repeated, weighing the feel of it.

"That will keep the media from Myra Hatch's door during her grieving," he explained.

"Sure. That works," she answered as she adjusted the slide in her powerful microscope.

Ben liked that. The law, oh sure, fuck it.

"Aha," she blurted as she peered at the slide. "I thought so." She stepped back to allow him at the microscope.

He looked and saw an array of healthy-looking, albeit dead human lung cells. "Nothing but life in stop action."

"There's something else: the lung tissue is more rigidly fixed than his epidermal tissues."

"So," he thought for a moment, "it spread from his chest – his heart or lungs – to his extremities."

"Most likely."

"It's airborne."

"Yep, this is proof."

She bagged Hatch's organs, respectfully reinserted them into his gaping body cavity, and started sewing his chest closed again. Her fingers moved swiftly and expertly, creating an efficient and symmetrical web of sutures.

"That was impressive, Dr.," Ben complimented her. "We're lucky to have you."

"Amazing what hanging around sudden, inexplicable death does for technique," she quipped.

"Your technique's too good for a minor epidemic in a remote corner of the Sierras, so far out West that most Americans couldn't tell you where the Thunder Peak Wilderness is on the map, let alone Longwood. What is it about our crisis that's got you dug in, committing your world-class skills to . . . this place?"

"Fresh air?" she offered as she continued working.

"Yeah, right."

"Some high mountain exercise."

"Really."

She glanced at Ben, then back to her suturing. "Last month. I was a contract EIS officer."

"EIS?"

"Epidemic Intelligence Service. There was an outbreak in a town called Itamarati on the banks of the Amazon River. Peasants killed where they stood. It was unlike anything any of us had seen or even heard about. There was nothing in the journals about it. Still isn't. Probably won't be for years.

"As the CDC's go-to experts in evaluating causes of sudden catastrophic diseases and pathologies, we were accustomed to racing into danger zones. Charley and I were Vin der Root's best. He was okay at his job, but, despite his degrees, he was more an administrator than a scientist. Ambition edged out idealism somewhere along the way; he rose in the CDC to the point where he assigned the teams and controlled the distribution of grant funds. Charley and I cared about the science of disease and its effects. It drove us beyond der Root's control.

"The skies were clearing and there were gusting breezes between 4-12 knots, which meant the high pressure front we'd read about was on its way in.

"Charley and I were obsessed with . . . whatever it was. We worked around the clock."

"What did you find?"

"Nothing at first. The jungle is a forensic technician's nightmare: mammals, reptiles, insects and birds wander, track dirt, pollen, carrion through nature's great room. Open to the elements like the afternoon torrents that wash away any tracks, drippings, dust, fingerprints and artifacts deposited there since yesterday's downpour. Everything moves or is moved, except the trees." She chuckled. "Even they grow a millimeter taller each day."

"We followed the sunlight into the clearing and saw scores of trees – internationally protected mahogany trees – sprawled on the forest floor. Judging from their size, three to four meters in diameter, they were virgin, probably 200-300 years old.

"The cuts were clean. Whoever was cutting was using professional equipment. Yet it was quiet. No chain saws. No chivvying horses. No straining truck transmissions. No chains pulling at the dead timber. No voices of men at work.

"Outlaws," Ben said quietly.

Lotte nodded. "That far from anywhere, no witnesses."

"'Except the satellite...'" said Charley and tapped the waypoint button on her GPS unit to mark our location." Lotte remembered and smiled.

"We arrived on site before the others. What we saw then defied explanation. Seventeen men in various states of work stealing protected mahogany trees – cutting, trimming, refilling chain saw gas tanks, and leaning on control ropes – frozen in place. One man had his hand to his mouth in the act of shouting to a man in the fall zone. Probably a foreman, if poachers had foremen."

"Charley saw movement on the far edge of the clearing and walked right into the center of the kill zone to find out what was what." Her right hand descended to Hatch's chest, her fingers pushed the needle expertly through the flesh, out the other side and then rose in a practiced and graceful movement, down and through, an arc of the wrist and back up. She did this three times without speaking.

"She did it to help us," she said finally.

She continued sewing in silence, remembering.

"A breeze scudded through the clearing. Even though I was wearing a facemask, I covered my mouth with a scarf. I'd been in deadly hot zones in Africa, Bangladesh, and Sri Lanka. I memorized every tree stump, every fallen tree, every frozen body. Then, as I rounded a tall tree stump, I spotted Charley. Her arm was extended, pulling the scarf to her face. But she was still. Only her scarf moved as it fluttered in that breeze. I was just seconds behind her, but when I got to her, she was gone."

Lotte tied off the first sutures at Nelson's right shoulder.

"The mask she was wearing turned out to be defective. She didn't have a chance. Vin and I argued for days about what to do to gather more evidence, learn more about what killed Charley and the loggers. On site analysis with basic biochemical tools was inefficient, we needed more samples."

"What happened?"

"The deaths stopped. We came home. And I buried my friend."

She continued working silently, her hands stitching and knotting expertly as her mind sought connections with the present crisis.

"Now you have an outbreak that is disquietingly similar. The difference this time is that I'm going to find the killer and stop it. It's a debt," Lotte said between clenched teeth as she cut the thread with scissors and tied a square knot.

"We'll beat it," agreed Ben and put his hand on her shoulder and regarded the dissected Nelson Hatch who looked almost whole again. He had been dealt an unnaturally disastrous hand and now it was up to them to play it out. Yet one question hung in the air between them.

How?

24

CORVALLIS

"Sir?" Richard Jasperson's executive secretary's voice sounded from his intercom, "it's Brad Wright for you."

Jasperson frowned and answered, "Yes?"

In the penthouse suite at Case-Kaiser Industries' Corvallis, Oregon headquarters, he welcomed the interruption as he read the last two pages of a business plan he had received 90 minutes earlier. He had agreed to review it for a friend in Seattle who was prospecting for investors in a new start-up. A proposal to use the Worldwide Web to 'educate' public opinion under the guise of a green approach to environmentalism. In fact, it was another attempt to get the big six logging and mining concerns to pay for a thinly disguised advertising and media arm. He saw it for what it was: a too late attempt to protect a rapidly vanishing way of life. Two years earlier, he might have thrown the entrepreneur a few hundred thousand dollars in return for a majority equity stake, but Jasperson had moved on. He hadn't survived in the competitive business of resource management by neglecting his golden rule: *If it doesn't make dollars, it doesn't make sense.*

"How do you want to handle the *Journal* story?" Wright had

learned early in his time with Jasperson to cut to the bottom line reason for interrupting his boss.

"What story? I haven't gotten to the papers this morning."

"The *Wall Street Journal* reprinted a late-breaking story on our suit before Judge Williams."

"What about it?"

"It's not good, sir."

Jasperson hung up the phone, plucked the *Journal* from the stack of newspapers on his desk, and immediately spotted the boxed story on Page 1: *Judge Uproots Loggers' Suit*, reprinted from the *Salt Lake Tribune*. He braced himself for what the article might say. At least they would go easy on Case-Kaiser, he thought. Case-Kaiser spent $8.3 million in advertising in the Salt Lake Tribune last year. It was a significant customer. They wouldn't offend their biggest client, no way.

Jasperson rubbed his jaw, sat back, and read the story.

Federal Judge D. Williams of the Ninth Federal Circuit Court, has dismissed a lawsuit filed by Case-Kaiser Industries, Inc. which claimed the U.S. Forest Service was promoting the 'religion' of environmentalism by restricting timber cutting in national forests and failing to negotiate logging on protected lands.

The suit turned on the novel legal claim that the Federal Government was advocating the spiritual values of the environmental movement by demurring to anti-logging pressure. District Judge D. Williams threw out the lawsuit as 'unseemly and baseless.'

Ruling that environmentalists have as much right as anyone to press their cause — even if they are motivated by a religious reverence for trees — the judge called the loggers' lawsuit "stunning" in its disregard for democratic principles.

Jasperson growled menacingly. What happened? He was certain he had Williams in the bag. Sure, the lawsuit was a stretch, but that's what lawyers were for, dammit, to push the envelope and work the will of their client. Undemocratic, hah! At least he still had the waiver on its way from Washington.

Judge Williams then ordered the loggers to prove they did not file the suit solely to "harass and delay" their foes.

"Miss Holden!" he ignored the intercom and shouted at the open doorway.

"Those cruise arrangements you've been working on for Judge Williams."

"Yes sir?"

"Scuttle 'em," he barked bitterly. "Get the attorneys in here and tell them to be prepared to camp out on the Ninth District Court's doorstep. Then get Senator Prentice on the line."

25

LONGWOOD

At the ranch, Ben and Grace held Mary Margaret close as the vet examined Beauty, who stoically endured the vet's probing.

"She has a temperature. Homeopathic Belladonna will push that down. Fluid in her lungs, Ben," Doctor Callahan said quietly as he replaced his stethoscope around his neck.

"Pneumonia?"

Callahan tilted his head and looked at Ben and Grace. It was clear that the calf was seriously ill. How much trouble did they want to go to save it was the implied question.

"Hoof and mouth in Hot Springs County," he observed.

"Oh no," Grace pulled M closer. "Are you sure?"

"Two days ago. Who knows where it came from or if Beauty here caught it. There's no other stock been through here, has there?" asked the vet.

"No," answered Ben firmly.

"What about feed? Where do you get Beauty's?"

"We graze her as much as we can," responded Ben.

"That's good for her. She's a ruminant and fares better on high protein grasses. You balance that with corn silage for energy?"

"I do," Mary Margaret assured him.

"Well that's fine. When you put her outside, does she graze?"

M nodded no.

The vet handed Ben a jar. "Lactobacillus cultures. Mix some of that into a paste. It'll help stimulate her appetite."

"Try to coax her outside into fresh grass, if you have it. The exercise can't hurt and the sunlight will produce Vitamin D."

"Not a good time to be outside," Ben objected.

"Right. Well, she doesn't look too interested in going anywhere right now, anyway. Increase her hay, reduce grain. Where do you get her grain?"

"Checkerboard in Piru, same as everybody else," Ben said defensively.

The Vet nodded. "Deer can carry it. Any deer come through here?"

M looked at her father, afraid to answer.

"When was the last time you saw Bucky, M?"

She hesitated for a moment before mumbling, "Three days ago, he took two apples."

"There's a stag who eats apples from M's hand, gentle as can be," explained Grace.

Callahan looked at Ben and Grace. He scratched his jaw and reluctantly concluded, "He'll have to go."

"You don't know, Gene. Hot Springs County is a long ways. Our feed comes from the south. There is no good grass to speak of this time of year."

"Ben," Callahan cautioned firmly. "Okay, I'll inject antibiotics to give her system a boost. The rest is up to her and you folks."

"Rupert Maxfield on line three from Hong Kong, sir," Miss Holden's voice insinuated itself into William Jasperson's thoughts yet again.

He picked it up right away. Maxfield, the northern hemisphere's premier broker of everything from boron diamonds used in new integrated microchip circuits to military fighter jets, was Jasperson's sole entrée into the incredibly lucrative – up to $32.5 million for a single tree - yet closed Asian market for sacred timber used in Buddhist temples from Japan to Kashmir. Closed, because to sell the perfect specimen required for a thousand year temple, the tree must have a pedigree as pure as its destiny. It must have sprouted in the wild, free from human corruption, and grown undisturbed by any human influence. Further, the logging executive had to be without taint of the slightest infraction of sacred law or be a descendant of Gautama Buddha himself. Without these credentials, one was powerless to gain an audience with the monk who searched the world for the perfect, unblemished tree that could support the roof of the next temple.

Maxfield had somehow succeeded in brokering the sale of two trees from North America, both harvested by Weyerhaeuser. Jasperson had spent a king's fortune cultivating Maxfield's favor to make Case-Kaiser his preferred timber source. A sale to him now would show Weyerhaeuser that Case-Kaiser was their better, swell its cash reserves, and diversify his market beyond forests like Thunder Peak, which were rapidly dwindling. It would also multiply Jasperson's personal power within his industry.

"Rupert, good to hear from you," he greeted his most desired customer. "I was just going to ring you up. I've discovered a stand of virgin old growth, some of the finest, straightest timber my foreman has ever seen. Your clients could build a hundred sacred temples with this find!"

"Jasperson, what's this I hear about a lethal virus in the Thunder Peak Wilderness?" Maxfield's Hampshire accent did little to warm the chill in his voice. "Is it spreading? What are you doing about it?"

"Don't pay attention to the media, my friend. There's nothing to worry about."

"Bollocks!" Maxfield's voice and color grew darker as he paced on the balcony of his penthouse overlooking Victoria Harbor. He was fifty-five years of age, balding, of medium height, with a body softened by too many perquisites of power. Even the Savile Row tailored Barathea suit could not disguise his excess weight. "You sell me on your timber for years. I have a client who needs six, repeat SIX perfect virgins measuring 80 meters or more. NOW my sources tell me that your trees in the Thunder Peak Wilderness are corrupted! Tell me they are wrong!"

"Nonsense, Rupert. Utter nonsense!" Jasperson soothed his quarry, even as the stain of perspiration spread down his shirt collar.

In the back of Jasperson's highly disciplined mind, another

dialogue continued even as he used every tool in his entrepreneur's kit to cajole Maxfield to stay in the Case-Kaiser fold.

Back in the 1860s through 1890s, when logging of the Sequoias peaked, most logging companies operated in the red and ultimately went out of business. The terrain in these mountains was just too damn rugged to harvest the forest giants efficiently or profitably. Better men than me have tried to provide these Sierra giant trees to the outside world and failed. Hell, logging in the 1980s caused such a fury that these lands were formally protected by new National Monument status. Thirty years later, memories of the fury faded and old forces of ignorance and the profit motive were at it again. The virgin timber was still plentiful here — Lodgepole Pine, Engelmann Spruce and even the endangered Sequoia giants.

So here the natural resource management industry goes again, namely yours truly. Case-Kaiser needs to secure new markets. Besides the monk who will pay a king's ransom for a virgin tree, ever-increasing numbers of multi-billionaires from Moscow to Beijing will pay anything to have an entire office suite built — furniture, built-in cabinets and wall paneling — from a single ancient tree. An energetic entrepreneur such as myself could capitalize on this demand for these 1,000 to 3,000 year old giants. Their beauty, longevity and California High Sierra prestige were priceless, literally. Jasperson hadn't figured out quite yet what the market would bear, yet he was certain that it would be enough to fund Case-Kaiser's future.

I'm pushing this massive project up a steep mountain against overwhelming odds, don't know if I can make it happen or not, and now the woods themselves are turning against me.

Despite his personal doubts, Jasperson's professional instincts and mastery of 'the close' succeeded in assuaging Maxfield's worries. By the time Jasperson bid him a good day and hung up the phone, Maxfield could smell the yen, rubles, and greenbacks awaiting him in the High Sierras.

At the clinic, Lotte cleaned and dressed Nelson Hatch's remains. She then carefully combed his hair to cover the intermastoid incision in his scalp. He appeared to be resting on the drawer in the cooler, waiting for a lift to the funeral home.

After assembling and pressure-testing her portable isolation chamber and battery-powered laminar flow booth, she wasted no time in her analysis of the samples she had taken from Hatch's clothing. The organic material on his shirt, jeans and boots was what she expected: pollens, bark dust, grass, old blood – his own blood in addition to deer and bear blood – traces of various decomposed scat of untraceable origin, and dirt, lots of dirt.

Then it was on to her Thunder Peak Wilderness botanical samples.

She thrust her hands through the isolation chamber's glove ports and aliquoted the already small samples out, dividing them into even smaller portions.

She first scanned them to verify they were organic and not mineral or chemical. Then she confirmed her field identifications: pine nut sheath, grass seed, flower pollen, etc. Everything checked out.

By the time she came to the mushroom sample vials, she had been working steadily for three and a half hours at maximum concentration. It was taking too long. In Atlanta with a proper epidemiological response team, the same work-ups could have been accomplished in one-third the time.

She stood to stretch her stiff shoulder and back muscles and considered going out for some air, then decided against it. She was determined to disqualify every sample she had. It was as important to know what the killer was not as it was to actually find and identify it. At this rate, she wouldn't be finished with this first batch until the early hours of the morning. She had to organize her time and efforts more efficiently. Then it occurred to her. Of course.

The steer's blood she had Ben obtain from Dr. Callahan. She had planned to use it to test the most promising samples - those samples that presented with unusual chemical makeup - as a final test on local blood; to see how it reacted with blood containing the complex blend of electrolytes, hormones, vitamins, antibodies, and oxygen, rather than more pure chemical reactions of traditional chemical analysis. She could use the blood first. If the sample didn't react with the blood then it probably wasn't her killer.

She sat down again and thrust her hands into the work gloves. Eleven of the twelve vials and jars contained mushroom sample tissues and spores. One contained a surprise: a truffle. Of all the things she expected to find growing in the Sierras, a truffle was not one of them. The harsh seasons, low humidity and temperature extremes limited what could live here. A truffle is a fungi, yes, but it is unheard of in this part of North America. She would never believe even one of France's famous truffle-hunting pigs could find one in so hostile a place and at that elevation. She returned that to its sealed jar and put it aside. A subterranean fungi with no exposure to open atmosphere and physically incapable of disbursing anything toxic or benign, she dismissed it.

One by one, she added tissue samples to blood droplets. *Amanita hemibapha, Amanita virosa,* and *Gyromitra esculenta* – she tested three samples from every mushroom genus she had found. The blood droplets were indifferent. They remained liquid. All results were negative.

Hydnum repandum: negative

Phyllotopsis nidulans – the colorful fan she found on the deadfall log: negative.

Astraeus hygrometricus sample 1: negative.

Steer's blood. Doubt crept into her disciplined thoughts as sample after sample had no effect upon it. *It's either brilliant or a bumbling waste of time.* It's too simple. *What was I thinking?* Blood is a complex compound of water and solids, of proteins, glucose, and lipids. There are red and white blood cells, platelets, water, gases like oxygen, carbon dioxide and nitrogen; nutrients, the proteins serum albumin, serum globulin and fibrinogen; salts, antibodies, opsonins, agglutinin, bateriolysins; and hormones. And excretory products: urea, uric acid, creatinine, and xanthine!

The killer could be associated with any of these blood constituents. She would have to disqualify every one of them.

Astraeus hygrometricus sample 2: negative.

Astraeus hygrometricus sample 3 . . .

. . . POSITIVE . . .

Lotte leaned in to look closer as the reflection of the overhead fluorescent lighting on the blood droplet cracked and bifurcated hundreds of times in seconds before her eyes. It contracted into a small clump of glistening dark red-black crystals.

She reached for the jar of steer blood to make sure it was still viable. Shaking it, she saw it slosh freely inside the glass container. It was normal in all respects, still oxygenated and healthy red.

She repeated the test and obtained the same hardening and crystallization reaction.

Again, she tried it and got the same result.

She shivered involuntarily. It was the fungi she had watched 'puff' spores when she tapped its side. It filled the air with spores – and dusted her face screen and protective suit! She visualized it in her arteries speeding crystalline death through her circulatory system.

She had found the killer. It was the *earthstar* mushroom.

No, she fought what she saw, this is impossible. The earthstar occurs most frequently in mixed woodlands, the kind that result from deliberate management by humans. The Thunder Peak Wilderness was untamed, beyond management.

The earthstar was an edible mushroom when cooked.

Its spores have medicinal properties; Native Americans have used its spores to treat nosebleeds and stanch minor wound bleeding for centuries! Arguments against the testimony of the steer's blood stampeded through her mind.

More confusing yet, two out of three earthstars were normal, only sample number three was a killer. How was this possible? Was her experiment compromised?

She cleaned and sterilized her equipment, then repeated the tests. Again. Again. And again. The results were the same each time.

Even the most toxic mushroom – the *Amanita* – rarely kills. It merely makes the victim ill and, if left untreated, sometimes forces doctors to transplant the victim's liver. Less than a dozen people are severely poisoned in the United States each year; so few that the Centers for Disease Control do not keep records of mushroom poisonings. They are scarcer than the number of deaths caused by bee stings and lightning strikes.

She picked up the phone and dialed Ben's cell phone, then quickly hung up. He was with Mary Margaret. It was a family crisis. She wanted to share her findings with him, but if she was honest with herself, Ben wasn't the most critical person to notify, scientifically speaking. That would be Vin.

She had to persuade him to take this seriously. A breakthrough like this could put extra shine on his ever-rising star, after all.

Assuming he pursued his interest in mycology, he must be some kind of authority by now. That was the leverage she needed. He wouldn't be able to refuse her. How could he resist getting in on the newest sensation in epidemiology: killer mushrooms!

He was better qualified than anyone she knew to explain why an innocuous mushroom would suddenly turn deadly. If he had lost interest since graduate school, he would at least know who the leading mycologists were.

No answer. Just that damn message again. She left a terse summary of the lab results and a message to call her back.

She dialed Ben.

26

LONGWOOD

Ben stretched and took in the chilly autumn air as he walked Dr. Callahan back outside. "Sorry to add any more misery to the home front," said Doc as he opened his truck door.

"You only see the big picture, the end view for ranching in the valley."

"It could be bad, Ben."

"I know. A real can of worms IF it's what you say. But it's not."

"How do you know?"

Ben didn't respond. The determined set of his jaw spoke for him.

"Alright, it's not the Stroke, or Beauty'd be dead. Assuming it's not initial stage foot and mouth, it's either A) simple pneumonia, that can be knocked down with antibiotics," Callahan ticked off the possibilities on his fingers, "or B) a new virus. The state folks are in now, I don't know if I'm brave enough to face down the California authorities, Longwood's edgy ranchers and, sooner or later, the Feds."

Ben considered Callahan carefully.

"I know, I know - you can't disappoint Mary Margaret. All

right," he unlocked the medicine bin, reached in, and pulled out a sealed vial. He checked the label and expiration date, then held it out to Ben. "This is the belladonna. Let's give her some more time. Just don't let any other cattle near. If she takes a turn, call me."

"Thanks, Doc."

Dr. Callahan started the engine and rolled out the drive, onto his next ranch call.

Grace gave Ben a little smile and mouthed 'thanks' as he returned to Beauty's stall.

He joined her in the hay and put his arm around her.

"She hasn't taken any food or water, Daddy," Mary Margaret said quietly.

Ben reached over and checked Beauty's pulse.

"It's not the 'Stroke' is it?" asked Grace.

"No. It looks like simple pneumonia. Though there's nothing simple about pneumonia." He paused, stroking Beauty's haunches. "Husbandry exploits a breed just so far and then Nature says, 'enough.' The genes falter and atrophy."

"Inbreeding, you mean?"

"Hard to say, but Beauty's mother was a free grazing cow. Beauty's sire could have been any bull. It happens." He was trying to keep himself up for M, for Grace, but images of Oren Pocknett, Lars Broder, Nelson Hatch and the Hart girl kept pulling him down into the outbreak's particular brand of hell. "Maybe this valley is playing itself out."

Ben listened to Beauty's heart and lungs. Beauty lifted her head, nudged M and lowed softly. She inhaled and wheezed.

"Remember the night she came bounding into this world? Bright, open-faced, stars in her eyes. Like M."

"My first midnight calving. The last, too. Beauty's mother had a horrible labor," recalled Grace.

"She hung on longer than I thought possible." He placed his hand on M's shoulder and silently repeated his vow to protect his daughter. Who was he kidding. He could no more protect her from the heartbreak of losing Beauty than he could stop the earth from orbiting the sun. He sighed tiredly. "Sometimes, . . ."

"What," asked Grace?

"Sometimes nature makes no sense at all to me," he finished his thought.

Grace looked long at him, certain that he was referring as much to Thunder Peak as he was to Mary Margaret and Beauty. She felt the uncomfortable drifting sensation again. The same feeling she had had when he left her studio yesterday after their argument. An alarm told her that the man she loved was off course and approaching danger.

Mary Margaret looked at her father for a moment, fear building in her eyes. She hugged Beauty closer.

"I can't take much more of this," Ben whispered to Grace.

"You're here, that's the important thing," she said softly and reached for him.

The harsh electronic tone of his cell phone suddenly broke her connection with him.

"McCandle here," he answered without hesitation. "Lotte. What's up?" He listened for several moments with a confused expression of intent concentration and mounting excitement. "You sure?" As he listened, Grace read the shift in his focus, a soldier responding to the sound of battle. "I'm on the way." He hung up and began to stand.

"Lotte thinks she's found the source of the outbreak," he said excitedly. "A mushroom, can you believe that!?"

"Ben—"

"Well, a mushroom spore to be precise." He was transformed, energized with renewed purpose. He almost smiled.

"Ben, that's great, but –"

"I have to get down to the clinic," he said.

"Can't she handle it? M and Beauty need you right now."

"M," he bent down and planted a kiss on her head. "This is important. You understand, don't you?" He paused and took in the three of them.

Grace saw her opportunity and took it. She rose, took Ben by the arm, and walked outside with him. "Ben, what are you *thinking*? I know whatever it is up there in the Peak is important, but your daughter is facing something more important. Her mother isn't here to help her through it, but YOU ARE! Call that woman and tell her you're busy."

"Lotte is trying to save Longwood. I can help."

"Is that really what's pulling you?"

"What?"

"I said is it the Hippocratic Oath pulling you away from your daughter and me? Or is Lotte Keene?" Grace couldn't believe she said it, but it was too late to take it back. She sounded like every suspicious schoolgirl brat she had ever despised.

"What!"

"Oh come on," she couldn't stop herself, "you haven't been here lately, really here. The Stroke is either a bad excuse to get away from us, or a good excuse to get closer to Lotte Keene!" It was like she was outside her body, watching her hack this wonderful relationship with Ben to pieces.

"Grace. It's my job."

"It's also your job to be the best father you can be for Mary Margaret. It's not easy. It's certainly not convenient. But it's damn well the most important job you will ever have."

That hit home. She saw a flash of self-doubt cross his eyes.

"This is how it happens. Fathers acting responsibly, answering the call of duty, and leaving the children they brought into the world alone and confused. Forcing them to grow up too fast." Grace paced in a tight pattern before him, straining to keep her voice down so Mary Margaret wouldn't hear her. "You have a chance to let somebody else heed the call this once. Stay here by your little girl's side and be here for her. She doesn't have the things that most little girls have – her mother, lots of girlfriends, Disney World – don't take this moment with you away, too."

What could he possibly say? It was cruel to leave Mary Margaret alone right now, he knew that. It was insensitive to leave M and Beauty's crisis on Grace's lap, he knew that, too. He had been feeling plenty guilty about the abysmal way he was treating them both for days now. He had spent more time with corpses in the last week than he had spent with the most important people in his life, yet in a strange way he'd never felt more alive. And what the hell was this about Lotte Keene! What was it about her that had him running. He looked down and kicked the ground. Could it be that he wanted to be with Lotte more right now than with M and Grace? He looked up at Grace and squinted thoughtfully. "I don't know whether this is the right thing to do right now or not. It's what I am. It's what I trained to be."

Grace shifted back on one leg, crossed her arms, and held herself.

"I can't do anything about that heifer dying in there, but I have a chance to prevent any more men and women from dying up there. That's something I can do."

"It's not about fixing everything, Ben."

They were at an impasse, both of them saw it.

"I have to go," Ben said finally. He got into his truck and left for the clinic, leaving Grace alone in the drive.

Ben found Lotte staring at her tightly crafted notes, glasses dangling from her left hand, pen suspended in mid sentence. The pages before her featured a step outline of her investigation, results, and analysis with occasional notations and meticulously printed footnotes. A good likeness for her mind, thought Ben. She may look like a hippie lost in time, but her mind was like a steel trap, a formidable intellect capable of Einsteinian connections.

"A mushroom that has provided folk remedies for centuries suddenly gets an attitude and kills," he said as he joined her at the lab bench. "What on earth made you look there?"

"I just cast a wide net where you found Broder and Hatch. Got lucky."

"Two out of the three were harmless. Just the one, right?"

She nodded, then smiled.

"What?"

"Hmm?"

"What? You smiled."

"Oh. It just hit me, I guess. It's good to actually find the culprit," she lied. She was happy to see Ben again.

"A mushroom."

"Yes."

"An earthstar mushroom."

"You want to see how it works?" she asked. "I have enough for another test."

"Hell, yes."

She grinned again. It was good to work with someone again who got it. Who saw the mystery in a toxic mushroom. Who was capable of appreciating the horrible power and majesty of disease and death. She positioned the magnifier over a generous puddle of steer's blood the size of a nickel. "Can you see?"

He leaned in over her shoulder and peered at the droplet, "Yep. 20-20."

"Alright then," she grasped a couple of spores from the earthstar vial #3 and held them over the blood. "Ready?"

"Ready," his voice came deeply just inches from her ear.

She felt his warmth on the side of her face. She inhaled his scent – aftershave, not cologne – and felt warmth spread throughout her.

She dropped the spores onto the droplet and it happened again, just as before. The blood shriveled, cracked and crystallized.

"My god," he whispered. "I don't believe it." He leaned in closer and watched in awe, his mouth partly open. "Son of a gun."

"A million times more deadly than any gun. It's almost chemical in its efficiency. Any organism that inhales this is finished."

"Can this be natural?" he asked. "I mean, I've never heard of anything like this occurring in nature. You've got carnivorous plants, sure, but even a Venus Fly Trap is slow and imperfect. This, why, it's --"

"Unbelievable," agreed Lotte. She fell silent and sat back, staring at the crystals. The tantalizing thread between the facts she knew and the elusive nature of the connection forming in her mind hovered just out of focus. She knew there was an answer to the conundrum before them, but what was it? She had sensed it minutes before Ben returned. It was in the room, darting out of view every time she got close. She closed her eyes and concentrated yet it retreated farther. She forced herself not to think, to just *be* and that helped. It tiptoed closer, but stayed just on the periphery of her consciousness. Damn!

"The killer is un-naturally toxic," she deliberated aloud.

"It's UN-natural," she stood and paced. "UNnatural. That could mean it is supernatural. Or it could mean literally UNnatural, as in man-made."

"Who would purposely make something like that?" Ben asked in disbelief.

"Who, indeed."

"I know we Californians are out of the mainstream up here, but biochemical mushroom grenades? Sounds like science fiction."

"The fear of the military, government and the virus hunters is that someone will engineer an organism that hasn't been on the planet before. A novel biological weapon. Any defense, let alone an effective defense, takes years and national fortunes to develop.

"There aren't many nations wealthy enough to combat the unknown biological super weapon. The U.S. has the Defense Advanced Research Projects Agency (DARPA), the research center of the U.S. Department of Defense."

Lotte poured herself a coffee. "The government hasn't dismissed the possibility that someone will create an entirely new biological weapon, but the finest minds in the field consider the likelihood to be remote. It's hard to imagine being able to improve on anthrax for the perfect weapon: it's lethal in minute doses . . ."

"Occurs naturally," Ben added.

"Like mushrooms," continued Lotte thoughtfully.

"But mushrooms aren't naturally lethal. A few are toxic but they require excessive doses or lack of proper medical treatment to kill."

Lotte sensed the connection forming nearby. It felt familiar. Then it came together like a thunderclap and the clouds parted for her. This is exactly what she had predicted in her thesis. Mankind would manipulate the genetic structure of some organism to make a better weapon.

"What is it?" asked Ben.

She looked at him without really seeing him. She was back before her Ph.D. oral argument committee judges twenty years ago. They were incredulous at her suggestion that man would turn the wonders of genetic science to weaponry and humiliated her with a withering wall of bitter accusations and derision. It was one of the worst experiences of her life.

Maybe she was biased in her entire approach to the Thunder Peak killer. Perhaps she was adapting the current facts to a past belief and wasn't seeing the problem clearly.

No, the earthstar was Nature's way of telling man that this time it had gone too far, logged too aggressively. Four were dead to date because of Case-Kaiser's arrogance. It was a logical reaction by an oppressed ecosystem. Yet her theory persisted. It fit here. Science evolved, after all. Human intellect insisted upon progress. It was one of mankind's finest traits.

"What is it, Lotte?" Ben asked again.

"What?" she asked. "Oh, right," she returned to the line of reasoning in their discussion. "So DARPA has been focusing on detection systems that will work in the field in 'real time.'"

"Real time. What does that mean exactly?"

"Soldiers, disease detectives, eventually even citizens, need ways to identify unknown bio-agents as they are encountered, when they don't have the weeks or months required to collect samples, send them to CDC, and wait for results. These new tools might utilize genetically altered human cells that trigger a taste or smell when they encounter threatening germs."

"A genetic smoke detector."

"Yes, but it doesn't exist as far as I know. I'm not saying our killer mushroom is a weapon, mind you. I'm just saying it is conceivable that someone will figure out how to do it. And it's important to remain open to possibility in this business. Answers are almost never in the expected places. Like our earthstar here: a mushroom! We now have a handle on what killed Sara, Oren, Lars, and Nelson. But now comes the hard part."

"What's that?"

"How to prevent it from killing again."

27

THUNDER PEAK

Alice McCandle noticed it first. A movement in the spruce.

They had been walking a high ridge for two hours and were less than a mile as the eagle flies from their campsite. They had spent more time climbing and descending unstable granite clefts than achieving linear distance. It was why Adrian Stimson was in such fine shape at his advanced age. Unlike many trekkers who measure time on a mountain by how many vertical feet of elevation they climb or kilometers of terrain they put behind them, Adrian found deep satisfaction in the qualities of the mountain. Sharp-edged granite pushed by millions of years of planetary pressure up under his soles. A thousand foot high cliff in the most unexpected place. The possibility of mountain life around the next tree trunk. He surrendered to a reality greater than his own and enlisted in the mountain's march across California.

A low branch on the opposite north-facing slope twitched and caught Alice's eye. She watched for more movement but there was none. She returned her concentration to the narrow ledge they walked. Several steps farther on she caught the motion again. An Engelmann's spruce near a giant Sequoia. Something at its base.

She paused and watched. It stopped again. She listened for sounds that would give her a clue: the cough of a deer, perhaps. Or the rustle of rip-stop nylon worn by a fellow hiker.

A growl sounded.

"Adrian," she said quietly. Adrian turned expectantly and when he saw her looking south to the opposite slope, followed her gaze.

A mournful whine followed the growl.

They stood motionless and waited.

Another branch bent and whipsawed. Out of the shadows, a massive brown shape emerged.

"A bear. Well, I'll be," whispered Adrian. "There's life in the Thunder Peak yet."

Alice watched in awe as the Bear lifted its nose in their direction and sniffed.

"Can he sense us?" she asked quietly.

Adrian noted the wind pushing softly on their backs. "Most likely," he answered. The Bear sniffed more urgently, its ears twitched toward the sound of their voices and he rose up to his full seven-foot height.

"My lord!" gasped Alice.

"Let's get over this ridge and leave him be."

"He's magnificent!"

"A bear that hungry is unpredictable. Let's get moving." Adrian took her arm and guided her directly up slope and over the crest of the ridge.

He led the way as they serpentined east, following ridges that grew increasingly thick with centuries-old pine and spruce stands. As they rounded a promontory, they were met by a gust of the north breeze and distant sounds quickly formed into coherent patterns. They were voices from nearly a mile below in the thick Ponderosa stands. The eerie hush of the woods was broken by the infestation of men's voices, cracking branches and scuffling boots. Adrian and Alice looked more closely and saw flashes of orange passing between giant old growth trees. Men in orange safety vests and yellow hard hats.

Case-Kaiser surveyors.

"What in the Creator's name are *they* doing here!?" Adrian's face darkened as he watched the loggers violate his tribe's protected land.

"Grace, listen, please. The source of the killer is a mushroom."

"Okay," answered Grace neutrally.

"I wanted you to know," explained Ben.

"You mean people die when they eat it?" she asked distantly. She was still angry.

"No. Its spores carry the killer. It is incredibly virulent, very dangerous."

"Oh." He pictured her standing in the barn's doorway, one hand thrust into her back jeans pocket, the other holding the phone to her ear. She was leaning on one hip, taking in his voice, but not giving in to him. Not yet anyway.

"Grace," he began to apologize. There was nothing to apologize for; he did what he had to do. "Is M all right?"

"Mmhmm."

"The spore kills anything that breathes it in. The ranch is safe. It's far enough away and upwind. But make sure M keeps her mask on, just in case."

"Of course."

"You, too. Put yours on, even when you're on the phone."

She did. "I'll close the barn." Her voice sounded muffled through the mask. "Are you coming back?"

"As soon as I can."

"Okay."

"Good."

"Ben?"

"Yes?"

"Just come home."

"I need more earthstar tissue."

"What?!"

Lotte needed evidence of the mushroom to continue her analyses, test reaction agents, and persuade authorities, if necessary, of the bizarre killer's identity. But going back to the hot zone in the Thunder Peak Wilderness and bringing more back was taking a big chance. Ben's response to that prospect surprised even himself.

"Look, we know what this whatever-it-is can do to blood. We know where it is originating," Ben moved closer. "Let's step back, find a strategy to deal with it rather than risk your life and possibly many more by bringing more of it to Longwood?"

"This isn't the time for caution, Ben. We have to move before Nature turns, before the wind shifts, or drought turns it to dust that will drift to the neighboring county, or rain carries it down valley," said Lotte as she added more vials and jars to her field kit, latched it and moved for the stairs. "I've got my cell phone if you need me. Keep yours turned on in case anything happens."

"Tell der Root when he calls, if he calls, that we need at least two complete teams here ASAP. Forensics and containment."

"Why not wait for backup?"

"I have to go." The door closed behind her.

He knew there was no sense in trying to stop her.

She stepped down hard on the van's accelerator. Knowing the identity of the killer should have given her a sense of accomplishment and calmed her down. It had the opposite effect. Her job was now more urgent than before. She had to track down the particular earthstar killers again and bring back enough samples for what might turn out to be an extended research, testing, and antigen development process. All the usual protocols for study, analysis, and strategy required the one thing Longwood, northwestern California and the cities in California's wind shadow did not have: time.

She pushed the accelerator to the floorboard. The six-cylinder engine opened wide with all the power it could muster and pushed the rear-engined van another ten miles per hour faster.

Alice shivered, zippered her anorak to her chin and trekked one hundred feet higher up Thunder Peak's alpine slope. While the temperature in Longwood was a comfortable shirtsleeves 71 degrees, here at 9,000 feet elevation the air was 52 degrees. Alice was invigorated and restless. The physical exertion of the hike left her with a satisfying weariness, but the Bear and the Case-Kaiser surveyors replaying through her thoughts wouldn't permit her to relax. After doing some housecleaning around their modest campsite, she decided to collect more wood for the fire. She and Adrian would need plenty to keep them warm through the chilly night. So, while Adrian napped in the tent, Alice gathered kindling.

There was scant fuel around the campsite: needles, cones. She worked her way upslope where she was rewarded with small deadfall branches.

Soon she entered a small clearing surrounded by gigantic Sequoia trees that were very, very old. A meandering freshet bisected the small opening in the forest. Their trunks seemed as big around as her house and rose straight into a canopy of strong branches and green needles where she lost sight of the crowns. The gray, brown and red bark grew in long deeply ridged plates, small piles of which lay like discarded armor at the feet of each giant. Scattered elsewhere around the clearing and between the trees were waif-like ground ferns and scrub, which, deprived as they were of sunlight by the dense canopy, strained to five feet in height. The ground was moist and spongy in places. Otherwise, it was bare earth with occasional protrusions of the underlying granite, and abundant untouched deadwood.

Faced with such plenty, Alice searched among the trees for the best candidates for their campfire. Preferably something about the size of a bedroll, easy to carry back to camp and longer burning than small kindling.

Then she saw them. Two five-foot logs about nine inches in diameter. Upon closer examination, she saw that they were part of the same branch, snapped in two when it crashed to earth. She lifted one end to test its weight. About twenty pounds, she estimated. She could manage it, but she'd have to be careful.

She cleared away the covering debris, tossing twigs and boughs to the side. One branch was wedged in place. She broke that, sent it skidding and the log came up easily. The branch she discarded decapitated two *earthstar* mushrooms, part of the ring that encircled the great tree. Spores rose into the shaded light and filled the clearing with a nearly invisible plume of lethal spores…

Huffing with exertion, Alice was halfway out of the clearing when she suddenly felt herself grow numb. The ground began to pitch and sway like the deck of a ship. She took a deep breath and began to pull again, but the stiffness overwhelmed her.

"Where are you?" asked Nate Stimson.

"I'm heading back to Longwood on Route 198. I have a man who tells me he's your father and a woman he says is Ben McCandle's mother. She's critical," Lotte shouted into her cell phone in the wind. Adrian had given her Nate's private cell number to dial. Her van roared and rattled down the road at 45 mph, as fast as she could manage the twisting mountainside road with its tortuous switchbacks. The engine noise was deafening.

"How's Dad?"

"Looks fine, Nate."

"I'll alert Doc."

"No, I'll call him."

"I'll meet you at the fork turnoff."

She hung up and dialed Ben. He picked up on the second ring.

At the same time Lotte's van skidded to a stop at the Longwood clinic's back door, Vin der Root's digital answering machine silently recorded the caller's message.

He had gone home to his townhouse. Events were gaining momentum in the West and instinct told him something more was about to happen. If his hunch was right, it would come to his home. The phone call confirmed that he was right.

"We won't be stopped this time, der Root." The voice was male, virile, but not macho. It was androgynous, alert, articulate, and calm as a vernal pool. Menacing in its controlled tone with a chilling undercurrent of certainty. It paused, expecting der Root to pick up. When he did not, the caller continued, "Not even Army Rangers or another Arnell Hill fire can prevent what is going to happen."

Garnet Hill was the site of a particularly nasty and still unidentified viral outbreak that devastated woodland wildlife in Arizona. It was stopped when an inferno transformed the 80 square miles of Northern Arizona forest into a moonscape of ash, hundreds of charred corpses – livestock, wildlife, and 18 smoke-jumping hot shot firefighters.

"I told you this day would come," the caller continued. The connection broke with a soft click.

Precisely 29 seconds after the machine began recording, noted der Root as he stared at the wall clock and listened. A bead of perspiration traced down his spine and absorbed into his shirt at the waist. It felt like an icy needle searing his flesh.

This time? Garnet Hill was an DOD operation?! No way the DOD was involved in one of the Southwest's worst disasters in thirty years? It couldn't be.

He paced to the sliding glass door and stared out over the city. Of course it could be. He had worked for the government too long to dismiss the possibility.

That voice. It was so familiar. der Root had heard it before in another lifetime. It was him. Had to be. The mushroom pizza yesterday. The Thunder Peak old growth forest. This was no coincidence. It was him.

He replayed the message. The chill returned. It was like he knew der Root was in the room, screening the call, listening like prey.

It was Gabriel.

28

LONGWOOD

At the clinic, Alice was unresponsive to all of Ben and Lotte's efforts. She was stiffened much as Nelson Hatch had been and, although Adrian found her quickly, her prognosis was worse than Hatch's. She was just barely hanging on to life. Her pulse was weak and thready. Her brain activity continued in a sluggish comatose fashion, autonomic synaptic activity that did not rise to the level of dream or thought. She lay wretched and abandoned by her own faculties, only the discreet hitch in her breath revealed any life at all in her.

Ben didn't know who he was more angry with: Adrian for not telling anyone about their change of plans and taking Alice to Thunder Peak or himself for not successfully warning them of the danger there. Normally self-contained, he stamped around the lab like a growling bully, passionate and intent on violence. Lotte helped in every way she could, but she knew Ben needed to be in charge of his mother's care and she stayed out of the way.

Adrian sat in the corner wrapped in a blanket, his hair still soaked from the disinfectant shower under Lotte and Nate's stern supervision. He now watched helplessly as Alice's son fought heroically to save her and Nate sat close by, ready to support him.

Ben touched the skin of her forehead, cheek, and forearm, looking for diaphoresis from exposure or the cold vasoconstriction that resulted from shock.

He had already palpated her head, looking for scalp hematomas, contusions or underlying fractures. Her trachea was not shifted from the midline. That was good.

He palpated the chest and listened for subcutaneous air, possible pnueumothorax, something to indicate internal injury. Nothing. Just solid mass.

As Ben went through the motions of the physician, steadily performing every medical examination in the emergency medicine and trauma manual, Lotte held herself back from the table.

If Alice were cold, clammy and gray, Ben could recognize the caso-vagal reaction to sudden, severe pain. Alice's color and tone were good. No heart attack, kidney stones, or even extreme fear. Nothing.

If Alice were cyanotic, they would know that Alice's blood was under oxygenated. Nor was she jaundiced or reddened. And there was no hint of lividity. That was the list. Damn. Just like Hatch.

Desperate attempts to revive her proved fruitless, even Ben was reconciled to her condition. They skipped the usual conservative emergency protocols and went to the only treatment that worked with Hatch: *Ribavarin*. This time, they injected it at several key points – carotid, elbows, chest, groin, knees, and feet - to distribute the effect in the absence of Alice's ability to carry it throughout her body via her circulatory system. It didn't make much of a difference.

His mother now slipped toward certain death.

"Ben," Lotte spoke softly but firmly, "was Alice taking any medications?"

"Heparin. She's been talking it for six weeks."

"Low doses? To prevent intercranial bleeding? Or more aggressive treatment?"

"Low. It was precautionary."

"So, Heparin added to what we're pushing into her blood is pretty much the limit, I'd say. Anything more would be fatal," concluded Lotte. She crossed her arms and studied Alice silently for several moments. "Acetaminophen, maybe. That could help."

"Recent studies show that taking acetaminophen with Warfarin is dangerous," Ben came instinctively to his mother's defense; the dutiful son responding to danger before the physician's training had a chance to intervene. "Taking it with Heparin may be just as unwise."

"Ben," Lotte paused. It was clear that Alice was dying, what could an experimental use hurt? She was inclined to go for broke.

Ben looked back at Alice. He had known that the day would come when her life would rest in his hands. He just hadn't expected it to arrive so soon.

"Why the difference," Lotte asked. "What is different in Alice from Nelson? What is in Nelson's blood that protected him, and, absent from Alice's blood, could not save *her*?"

"I don't know . . . the Johnny Walker," Ben offered impatiently.

"The Johnny Walker," Lotte's eyes widened. "Think about it: Hatch hung on. He was a drinker, which may have helped thin his blood just enough. Alice is hanging on. She is on a prescription blood thinner," Lotte's voice became more forceful as she spoke. She gripped Ben's arm, "It has to mean something."

"Alright, but I'll do it." He drew a small amount of acetaminophen in solution and injected it into Alice's IV line.

Alice didn't respond. Her agonal breathing continued. "C'mon, Mom. You can beat this," he murmured into her ear.

Lotte dialed her cell phone and tapped the desk impatiently as she waited for the recorded message at the other end to play.

"der Root, pick up the damn phone," Lotte hissed to the phone machine in Atlanta. She waited a moment. He didn't pick up. "Alright, listen to me, I've sent tissue and spore samples on prepared slides and in vials. Test them and tell me what you find. If you see what I think you're going to see, perform an electroscopic examination." She glanced up to see Ben standing beside his mother. "Dammit, der Root, this is important. If what we're dealing with here in the Thunder Peak is as bad as I think it is, it could spread in a dozen ways. A storm front is moving in from the northwest that could distribute spores to the Atlantic seaboard and beyond." She waited again. "Call me, der Root, goddammit!" She angrily slapped the cell phone down.

The life force is so strong, it always amazed Ben that it clung so tenaciously to the dying. There was no medical reason that explained why Alice was not already dead. Maybe she was holding on for Ben and Adrian. Some womanly instinct deep in her mind was staying with them, postponing her journey to settle accounts, reconciling her long life with them before moving on. Or some ancient inheritance in her brain commanded her to survive at any cost. Ben had seen enough death to wonder if the only purpose of life is to stay alive. What good, after all, did philosophy or religion do for the dying. Not a thing, he thought bitterly.

Alice's EEG was remarkable only in its lack of contour. Her brain activity was practically non-existent. The occasional minor spike due more to line interference than any significant improvement in her brain function.

The heart rate monitor was their only practical indication that life remained in any capacity. And when its alarm sounded, no one was surprised. Everyone in the lab knew that their's was a deathwatch.

"Keene," she answered the phone with scarcely disguised irritation. "der Root! It's about time! Where have you been?"

"What do you mean?"

"Why are you calling from a pay phone?"

"My cell phone battery died," he lied.

"I've been calling. I just left a voice mail," Lotte shouted. "You haven't gotten back to me since yesterday."

"What voice mail?"

"Dammit, der Root! I need your take on the findings I described in my e-mail."

"What e-mail?"

Lotte glared at Ben, her rage building to the bursting point.

"What's going on, der Root."

"Lotte—"

"I've got a situation up here and you're not doing your job!"

"Lot—"

"Do I have to fly down there and ramrod these samples through the lab myself!?! What's the matter with you?"

"LOTTE! There's nothing wrong with me. The world is a big place with bigger problems than yours. Excuse the rest of us if we have lives and crises of our own."

Neither spoke. They each stood back and waited.

"Send the samples," der Root said.

"They should be on your desk by now."

"Later." The line clicked off.

When der Root returned to his office, he saw the box on the chair by the door.

"NO!" Ben shook his head and slumped in the chair. He couldn't be expected to think clearly right now.

"I'm sorry," said Lotte, "but you know as well as I do how critical time is to discovery right now. Every second could be the difference between five deaths here and possibly hundreds, thousands of deaths tomorrow if that storm hits. It's not about Alice or you or me." She rested her hand on his arm. He looked up and glared at her. "It's a terrible choice, Ben, but it's necessary. The only responsible action now."

There were times he hated medicine, even the compassion that motivated his calling to it. Medicine prolonged the inevitable. Perhaps life was the unnatural state, after all. Maybe death was the authentic state to which all activity in the universe returned.

He looked into his mother's face for a clue to how she would feel about the decision to be made. Was her soul still behind those eyes? Was her spirit hovering above, observing his macabre dilemma? If she was in the company of angels now, did she care any longer for that mortal coil on the table?

Compassion pushed, always pushed him to make painful choices. Doctors had to struggle constantly to balance pain against life's mystery. Amputate a limb to save a body from gangrene. Blast the cancer patient's red blood cells with searing, life-annihilating radiation to make way for someone else's red blood cells.

"Are you out of your fucking mind!" he exploded. Then he turned cold and peered menacingly at Lotte. "You will not touch my mother's body. Damn you. Don't even look at her!"

Lotte wouldn't give an inch. She couldn't. It was their best chance to catch the killer before it vanished. Mankind needed what Alice's body could tell them now.

Ben sat down with Adrian. Speaking quietly, he explained as gently as he could what he and Lotte were about to do. Nate added his support, but it wasn't necessary. Adrian shook with grief as he listened. He struggled with mounting anger at his helplessness, but kept it in check. He nodded as Ben explained why Alice would want him to do his job: for Adrian, for Mary Margaret, and for the good of everyone in Longwood and beyond. When Ben finished, he asked Adrian if he understood. Adrian gazed at the remains of his friend on the table, then back to Ben. His open sorrow, faith in a greater power, and concern for Alice's son gave Ben his answer.

While Nate helped his father up the stairs and back home, Lotte began recording her initial observations.

"The body is of a healthy, well-nourished 74-year-old Caucasian female with gray hair and hazel eyes. Body is 64 inches long and weighs 128 lbs. . ."

Ben put on his gown, gloves and mask. He pressed his hands to his head, pushed against the bone and the brain inside, forcing his mind into position for the terrible task ahead. Finally, swallowing hard, he returned to his mother's side at the table.

The 'Y' incision was already made, the skin pulled aside and Lotte was about the cut the sternum. His mother's corpse seemed oddly serene, undisturbed by its dissection. The facial expression was composed and adapted to the circumstance in which it now found itself.

"Ben, do me a favor and check that we have at least a dozen sample vials ready. Ben?"

It took him almost two minutes to find the vials. By that time, the body on the table was laid open and no longer bore a resemblance to anything familiar. Lotte had purposely distracted him, spared him the dismemberment of his mother's body. He noticed that she had also turned off the audio recorder.

Moving quickly, Lotte lifted the heart, lungs, esophagus and trachea, placed them carefully on the tray and studied them.

"Same as Hatch," she muttered. "Same crystalline blood and petrifaction." She looked up at Ben. "Hand me a vial." She incised one stiff lung and expertly cut a series of strips, placing each in a vial and handing it back to him for sealing and labeling. Ben reacted, working as rapidly as Lotte, secretly grateful for her decisive action, not including him in the decision about where to section, how much to cut.

Once she had taken samples from each organ - three from the trachea, one from the esophagus, six from the lungs and two from the heart – Lotte bagged the organs and replaced them in the chest cavity.

"What about the rest," asked Ben?

"We have what we need. Could you pack five of the six lung tissue samples, one trachea and one heart in ice and box them for an immediate flight to Atlanta? Nate will be back to drive them to the airport. I'm hoping to get results as early as tonight, morning at the latest."

"You knew I would let you examine her."

"I know you're a good doctor."

They found in Alice's lung tissue what they had been unable to find in Hatch's: spores. Not complete spores, but the rapidly dissolving remains of spore cases. The lethally encoded genes formerly inside the spore were no longer visible, at least on the equipment Lotte had available. That's where CDC should be able to help. Now that she saw how rapidly the killer vanishes into the blood and tissue of its victims, she had little hope that the pathologists in Atlanta would make any significant finds. Besides, why should they believe Lotte's suspicions now?

She sighed, resigned to failure. All the rushing to get samples for der Root when he and his lapdogs couldn't see what they didn't want to see anyway. The assault on Alice in front of her only son. Suddenly, the whole situation seemed hopeless. She had made everything worse.

"There is definitely something there," Ben said coldly as he peered into the microscope eyepiece. "Look at how it stops cellular function." The scientist in him had reemerged. Just as Lotte was shutting down, he was functioning again.

Lotte looked again at the tissue sample.

He was right. In addition to the oval spore case fragments, she spotted a single tiny, nearly invisible zoospore with two cilia. It was wedged between two spent and hardened lung tissue alveolar cells.

The Zoospore is the sixth and final stage of development in the life process of myxomycetes, or slime-fungi. Myxomycetes are peculiar in passing through an Amoebid stage when they feed like animals. At this stage of their existence, at least, they are more animal than plant.

But it was an *earthstar* that devastated the steer's blood, not any of the slime-fungi she tested. Here was a Zoogonida from slime-fungi, however, in Alice's lungs.

How the spore could proceed through the six stages of its life in the time that its victims passed from life to death was a critical clue, she sensed.

"How long did you estimate Sara Hart and Lars Broder lived after inhaling the spore," she asked Ben.

"Impossible to be precise, but I estimated :40 seconds to :90 seconds max."

"Amoebid to Plasmodium to Encysted to Segmented to Rounded Spore to Zoospore in :45 seconds!?" she thought aloud. "Impossible," she whispered to herself.

29

LONGWOOD

"She never slept more than four hours a night. Didn't need it, she said. Now she'll rest." Ben spoke in a weary monotone. "Adrian wanted to marry her. She turned him down. Seven times. Just last Saturday, he took her to the most elegant restaurant in Three Rivers, thought that was what she wanted. She had done marriage; dating Adrian was more fun." A pause. "How do I tell M?"

He hung his head, his usual rock bed self-control ruptured beyond containment.

Lotte watched the quiet strength drain from Ben.

He turned away. "She deserved better," he said.

The sounds of a truck pulling up outside filtered through the high windows.

"I'd say she had the best," Lotte said quietly. Nate Stimson came halfway down the stairs and, seeing Alice McCandle at rest on the table, Lotte still in her bloodstained gown and Ben listless by his mother's side, paused.

"Sorry to bother you, Docs," he greeted them evenly, "A crowd is gathering downtown. Mayor Spivey's about to tell everybody what's what. I came to take you there."

"No!"

"Ben, you have to come. I'm an open sore, *persona non grata* to most of these folks. They need to see you there speaking up, being there for them now."

"Doctor Keene," Nate urged Lotte. "The Doc can come later."

"Ben," Lotte hesitated, reluctant to leave him.

"No."

"What's going on?" Lotte asked as Nate turned onto Main and she saw a great mass of people gathered in front of the Hut Café.

"'Fraid the word's out, Doc. Media's here from as far as New York," he growled as he looked for a place to park. He turned on the light array atop the cab and goosed the siren. The mob parted and he edged as near as he could to the café.

"What do they know? Or think they know?"

"Five are dead so far, all killed by something in the Thunder Peak."

"And the Mayor hopes to put a lid on any embarrassing public outcry," added Lotte sarcastically.

"Something like that."

"He's pissing on a brushfire."

Nate grinned.

"I wish Ben was here," she said quietly.

"Give him time."

"Time is running out," Lotte said evenly as she sized up the mood of the crowd.

"That television van from L.A. will speed things up," Nate observed.

The late model van bristling with state of the art microwave mast, onboard generator, lights, the works here in these foothills so far from the city looked incongruous. No place on earth was beyond the reach of a determined reporter anymore.

"Settle down folks, I don't have much time," Mayor Spivey began without preamble as he approached several microphones in the back of the café. "Let's get this over with, shall we?"

The crowd was too large. The hastily announced town meeting to update citizens on the status of the survey in the Thunder Peak Wilderness had mushroomed into a full-blown press conference.

He wanted to be anywhere but here and he wasn't doing a very good job of hiding his displeasure. His brusqueness spread tension like a foul odor.

In addition to the locals, most of whom were wearing surgical masks, there were now reporters from many of the regional and national media. Donna Cooper from KGO, the ABC affiliate in San Francisco, pushed her way to the front, directly before the Mayor. She was on the scent of a story that might be bigger than the 'Barbed Wire Strangler,' the horrific serial killer who burned the summer of '97 into California legend and simultaneously made Ms. Cooper something of a regional legend. She had tirelessly spun out coverage of the manhunt for the Strangler into a string of field reports that hooked evening news watchers. For a region where local news never could hold a candle to the glitzy New York and LA stories carried by local affiliates, Donna Cooper's search for the Strangler built a rare sense of local pride.

While she shouldered her way to the front, her cameraman collected B-roll footage of fear-filled eyes. Some people wore blue cloth surgical masks from the pharmacy, others wore disposable paper masks, others scarves or bandannas. He got seven seconds of a brown-eyed golden retriever wearing a homemade white cloth mask. That was the money shot. Americans from coast to coast would see that lovable and trusting expression repeated countless times over the next few days.

Also there were Ron Burns of KFSN in Fresno, numerous stringers representing the *Washington Post, New York Times, Chicago Tribune, L.A. Times,* Britain's *Guardian,* and the veteran CNN reporter-at-large, Tom Eberhart, who happened to be driving through Longwood on his way to Sequoia National Park with his 14 year old son.

The crowd overflowed the sidewalk into the street and blocked traffic. Nate Stimson kept them under control for about five minutes, but soon it proved hopeless.

The CBS van from Visalia was parked across the centerline in the middle of Main Street with its mast raised to its full 30-foot height. It wouldn't help KLAS's reporter or crew beam the story back to Las Vegas. The Sierras were an 11,000-foot high wall between them and their home station. It would, however, provide California stations with a high quality feed if they chose to pirate it.

"Here's the situation:" the Mayor announced, "Case-Kaiser

crews are about to complete their initial timber survey; all we need before cutting begins is a green light from the Ninth District Court."

"Mayor, are you telling us you still intend to send California's finest into the Thunder Peak Wilderness where they may be killed?" Donna Cooper held out her pocket recorder and cheated for the camera so that her cameraman could get a good two-shot. Mayor Spivey glanced at her and was about to scold her when he realized that he was on camera. Without blinking, he transformed from irascible to ingratiating.

"Why hello, Donna. Good to see you. I'm sure your viewers in San Francisco and the surrounding counties will want to know that the rumors of a contagion in the beautiful Thunder Peak Wilderness are just that, rumors. You and I deal in facts. The facts are these:

"California is still the home of the brave, the land of the free, and responsible steward of the richest resources in North America. I don't think it's an overstatement to say that all of us would rather be right here in California's Sierra Range than any other place on earth."

Donna had faced down more media savvy types than Mayor Wilburn Spivey. She wasn't about to let him off the hook. "What about California's fine young men?" she repeated.

"And women!" a woman in overalls shouted from the edge of the crowd.

Spivey ignored the reporter. "Next?"

"My editors in Atlanta want to know, Mayor, why you supported the so-called timber survey on protected land before its legality has been decided by the Ninth District," Tom Eberhart's familiar bass voice cut through the clamor of reporters trying to get the Mayor's attention.

The Mayor responded immediately to Eberhart's authoritative male tone, turning and listening as the other reporters quieted. "Happens all the time. If American business waited for government - and increasingly the wheels of justice – we'd be a third-rate economy instead of the free world's leading economy. Those surveyors aren't doing anything more than walking in the woods and taking notes--"

"Trespassing, you mean!" shouted Ahwahnee Nation counsel, Larson Black Kettle.

"Now, Larson, be reasonable. We're all neighbors here," the Mayor offered in his friendliest tone.

"Do you let your neighbors wander your property, Wilburn? Trample your garden, spray-paint big orange 'X's' on your shade trees?" asked the attorney angrily.

Silence descended over the crowd. No matter where anyone stood on the issue of logging and property rights, everyone saw that Larson Black Kettle had framed the issue perfectly for the news cameras. Now, Spivey had to perform the impossible: appear genuinely concerned for his constituents' fundamental rights as well as their ambitions, two intractably opposed extremes.

The Mayor looked out over the masked faces. The scene suddenly struck him as bizarre, right out of a Twilight Zone television rerun. He saw himself as the cameras now recorded him: an inept rural mayor caught with one hand on the Bible and the other in Case-Kaiser's wallet. He silently cursed himself for showing up at this damned press conference.

"Now, if the appropriate arrangements weren't made with the Ahwahnee tribal council, then I'm certain it was an oversight, unfortunate but understandable."

The crowd erupted. There was nothing he could have said that would defuse the mounting passions of Longwood's citizens and the media.

Incredulous ranchers demanded government action to stop the spread of the 'Stroke' that was threatening their families, livestock, and way of life. Frustrated farmers asked when the Federal authorities would arrive to sort things out. Irate loggers hoping for work with Case-Kaiser argued vehemently for a declaration of Eminent Domain or some equally aggressive action to circumvent the protections for the Ahwahnee. And where was Jasperson; shouldn't he be here?!

Mayor Spivey weathered the assault without letting his mounting intimidation show.

Lotte observed all this with a growing sense of disgust. Spivey was going to do what every other tinpot autocrat does when faced with a united opposition: run or dissemble.

"I'm sorry, ladies and gentlemen, but I have a previously scheduled teleconference with Senator Prentice," the Mayor lied.

"Tell him you're in a meeting! You'll call back!" suggested Larson Black Kettle loudly.

Lotte laughed bitterly. She wasn't alone in her disgust with Spivey. Resentment snaked from person to person like a thread uniting them in their helplessness and rage.

What mattered was what the ranchers and farmers and citizens did next. And there was no knowing what that was going to be.

Lotte considered what to do: warn them, or retreat to fight the spore. She couldn't take on Longwood and the Thunder Peak alone. Not and hope to win.

A wave of noise rose from nearby. A pack of loggers were lifting a new pickup truck and carrying it into the center of the street. Larson Black Kettle shouted at them to stop, but it was too late. Rage had the mob in its grasp and the loggers were giving vent to it. His Ford F-150 pickup truck was the object of their wrath and was consumed in flames before anyone could make sense of the situation.

Most of the mothers and children fled, leaving only enraged ranchers, farmers, and merchants in the thick of the violence. Haranguing them were *Earth Rebirth!* activists and sympathizers from atop vans and jeeps. There were significantly more of them now, at least 150 strong. Covering all this from the periphery were the reporters. Print journalists made notes and video crews shot the vehicle fire from every angle, mostly in tightly framed scenes. The rabble-rousers were relatively few in number, maybe 60 or so unemployed men. That was enough in tight shot to make compelling TV.

Lotte decided to retreat to the lab where she could do some good. On her way, she passed several dozen *Earth Rebirth!* activists who were watching the chaos. Seeing her jeans, sandals and wild hair, they at first welcomed her as one of their own. Until she warned them to stay out of the Thunder Peak Wilderness.

"That's where we're going!"

"Why?!"

"To show this town and Case-Kaiser that the old growth is worth defending," a lean firebrand in his late twenties answered loudly.

"Listen to me, I'm an epidemiologist. There is an airborne agent up there that kills. I've seen what it can do. You're too young to take such a risk."

"Age doesn't seem to have made those loggers or the Mayor any smarter, lady," another young man argued.

"They're killing beauty. They're torturing Mother Nature," a slender young woman chimed in.

"You're just another cog in the big wheel, epidemiologist," he spat out the word like a curse. "Who funds your research? Revlon? We're tired of trusting. We're closer to Nature than you'll ever be."

"We appreciate your concern, Dr., really we do." It was Spectacles, the activist who heard Lotte speak in yesterday's town meeting. "We have faith. Faith that the old growth forest will never harm us if we do it no harm. Case-Kaiser and those idiots are killing the land and all of us who need to live on it. God helps those who help themselves, right?" he smiled and flashed the peace sign.

30

LONGWOOD

The note tacked to the clinic door read: *Closed.* Lotte found the examination table vacant and clean.

Now what. She scanned the racks of slides and her notes. There wasn't much she could do until she had confirmation from der Root or someone at the CDC to take to authorities, stop Mayor Spivey, Case-Kaiser and cordon off the Thunder Peak Wilderness from everyone, including *Earth Rebirth!*

She bent down to the microscope to view the lung tissue sample again. Less than six hours ago, red blood cells were passing in single file through those capillaries. Oxygen from each alveolus entered the red blood cells and bound to the cell's hemoglobin. Carbon dioxide contained in the plasma and red blood cells entered the alveoli when Alice breathed, most of it as bicarbonate ions, about 25 percent bound loosely to the hemoglobin.

The nerves that controlled Alice's breathing were regulated by her blood's carbon dioxide concentration. High levels of carbon dioxide would have led to more nerve impulse activity and faster respiration rate.

Lotte stretched and inhaled, imagining the spore entering

through the nose or mouth, carrying down the trachea, through the bronchi, bronchioles, the alveoli, . . . into the blood and . . .

How did Alice react? Panic and gasp, try to take in more air to jump-start her failing lungs and heart? Or was the effect so immediate that there was no time for awareness, no time for the nerves to send a message back up to her brain: *oxygen, STAT!* Alice's relaxed expression supported that theory.

Lotte bent down to the microscope again. She had missed something. Otherwise, the same line of reasoning would have occurred to her the first time she looked at it. The sacs were still cup-shaped. The capillaries still red. The twin-cilia'd Zoospore—

She moved the slide carefully from side to side and up and down as she scrutinized the magnified image. There was no twin cilium Zoospore. She looked again.

It had been difficult enough to see the first time, partially degraded and decomposed as it was. But she had prepared the sample herself, fixed, and stained the section herself. It should be there nestled in the fold between two cells to the right of center. But it was not there. No spore case fragment. No cilia. And definitely no zoospore.

She rifled through the other slides. Perhaps Ben had moved them. She pulled the slide from the microscope stage clip and double-checked the notation written on the side. No, slide #AM-L-2 was the one she and Ben had examined and discussed before she left for the press conference.

She looked again. Nothing.

She squinted disbelieving into the eyepiece. It was impossible, but there it was. Or rather, *wasn't.*

The ring of her cell phone startled her.

"Lotte, it's me."

"It's about time, der Root."

"We have to talk." His voice was wound tightly as a drum.

"Fine, talk."

"In person."

"I can't leave! The situation here is too dangerous."

"I know."

"You know! How do you know? You aren't here. You don't have innocents dying on your watch, loggers burning vehicles on Main Street, *Earth Rebirth!* activists about to walk into the hot zone.

Dammit, der Root, what did you find in the samples?!"

"Meet me at the Hut. I'll tell you what I can."

"The Hut?!" It would take him six hours to get here from Atlanta, five if he made all his connections.

"Be there in ten minutes."

"You're in Longwood?" she started to pepper him with more questions. Better to accept what he was telling her and get back into town. "I'll be there."

He'd already hung up.

She spotted him in the rear booth by the hallway. It was the darkest spot in the Hut Café and offered both privacy and a clear line of sight to the front door. He was in his field outfit: bush jacket, jodhpurs, and felt safari hat, what he wore wherever he traveled. It was practical and didn't call too much attention to his nationality. In short, the uniform of the well-traveled virus hunter.

He remained seated as she approached, not rising to give her a hug, as was his custom after long absences. And, she noted, he kept his hat on. Vin der Root was in most ways a classic southern gentleman. No self-respecting gentleman east of the Mississippi or south of the Mason Dixon would be caught indoors with his head covered, especially in the company of a lady. In California, however, most cowboys would rather take off their pants before removing their Stetson.

He handed her a freshly poured cup of coffee.

She took a sip and asked, "What's going on?"

He leaned forward to speak and hesitated. der Root was usually facile, droll, ready with a line. Now he was thinking before speaking.

"It's the earthstar," he said solemnly.

"I know that, der Root. I told you it was the earthstar."

"You didn't have to."

"What?"

"I mean, until he called, I wasn't clear what was happening. After the poisonous pizza, at least it might have been poisonous, the phone threat, your quick work here and the results of the tests in Atlanta, I know it was the earthstar." His words rushed out of him like a cataract.

"Pizza? What are you talking about, pizza, phone message, he?

He who?" asked Lotte.

"Lotte, I know we haven't always been good to each other. We've gone our separate ways on most everything since Hopkins," he said plainly. She recognized his focused, unblinking manner reserved for moments of truth.

"But you're the one true scientist I know. Everyone else is tainted by one agenda or another, corporate sponsorship, junkets, foreign tributes, honorary degrees, book deals, you name it."

"Thanks. Isn't it grand here on the frontier of scientific truth," she gestured sardonically.

"Well, it's a fact. You stayed true."

"Where is this headed, Vin? You didn't come up here for a gestalt."

"No, I didn't."

"I'm waiting."

He glanced quickly over her shoulder and around the room. "The killer spore is not natural," he enunciated clearly. "It's engineered."

She held his gaze, absorbing what he'd said, interpreting the word 'engineered.' "It's man made," she fed back to him.

He nodded.

Lotte's face went pale.

He pulled three folded pages from his coat pocket and laid them out before her.

She recognized them as test result reports. The cover page summarized the results of all the standard tests that CDC and any other advanced laboratory would run under the circumstances. Hanging-drop preparation, darkfield illumination, differential stains, the usual. Except for cultures, animal inoculation, sterilization, of course; there wouldn't have been time for those.

Notably, their protocol showed nothing unusual in the three earthstar samples. Lotte looked up at der Root to see if he had an explanation. He reached over and lifted the cover to reveal a second page of results entitled:

ED-UAU
Astraeus hygrometricus (CAUSA0003071021-LK)

She froze. The ED-UAU heading was sufficient to give an epidemiologist nightmares. The 'Emerging Diseases – Unique

Aberrant Unknown' classification was a rare and dreaded occurrence in any virus hunter's experience. World Health Organization records contained fewer than a dozen such classification reports collected in its history. The reports were so rare, the threat of panic so explosive that many epidemiologists had never heard the acronym and it wasn't taught at any of the leading graduate schools.

'Astraeus hygrometricus' identified the source of the sample. The initials recorded the collection site, the proprietary CDC numbering identified coordinates, date and record number. The 'LK' identified the person who provided the sample.

It was a preliminary breakdown including botanical classification and chemistry. Missing was the molecular quantification of every identified element. Not enough time. She would have to do that herself. In the comments section at the bottom was a hastily scrawled notation:

'VdR eyes only. Do not record in IDR. Return samples, slides, all testing materials upon completion.'

Then, in another scrawled message in the same hand:
'dR – Comprehensive series urgent. Pls advise. –L'

She hesitated to turn to page three. If the ED-UAU was his second act, she couldn't imagine what he could have for a third.

Centers for Disease Control, Atlanta, GA

The game wasn't worthy of a Sunday. At the front desk of der Root's office building, Gus turned down the volume on the tiny television set under the counter at the front desk. He'd keep an eye on the action to see if Ryerson earned his fifteen million salary this afternoon. Man oh man - to be twenty-one, six-three, strong as Hercules, Guinness Book fast and good-looking, too. That Ryerson kid could make a franchise, even Detroit's. Who knew anymore? Kids made millions and grown-ups were put out to pasture by forty-five.

He decided to watch until the next commercial, and then make his rounds. With no one but him in the building, it shouldn't take more than fifteen to twenty minutes.

A reflection of sunlight traveled up the wall and stopped on the ceiling. Gus glanced up and saw a late model blue van parked at the curb. Two men emerged from the front and opened the side and back doors. Four more from the back. All in their twenties to thirties, all dressed in blue coveralls.

He watched them unload large wheeled trash barrels, a couple of housecleaning carts, and a large wood chest on wheels. It looked like the kind of tool crib you see on any construction site. They lifted it down to the sidewalk with ease. Either they were strong or the crib didn't have much in it.

They came in quietly. There was none of the idle chatter about the previous night's date or the bitching about working a Sunday shift, Gus noticed.

He stood and surveyed them as they approached the counter. "What can I do for you fellas?"

The compact one with the military haircut spoke first. "Just been rotated in from the Arkstone lab. Some lifer up in Admin doubled our workload. Got eight days of cleaning to do in a five-day week." He shrugged his shoulders as if to say, 'What're y'gonna do?' "Here to get a jump on it." He shared a long-suffering smile, the kind reserved for good friends.

Gus sniffed. "There's never been any work crews in on Sunday before."

"It's a first for us, too. Don't much care for it, tell the truth. But a job's a job, y'know?"

None of the other men spoke. It didn't strike Gus as anything out of the ordinary. He just figured it was a tight working detail. They let their foreman speak for them.

"Fresh uniforms for a fresh assignment, eh?" he noted.

All of the men looked down at their overalls, then at each other. Each wore new blue work shirts under new blue overalls. It confirmed Gus' judgment that working for the federal government must be a cush deal.

"Need to see some ID," he said as he came around the counter and straightened to his full five feet ten inch height.

"Sure," the foreman pulled an ID wallet from his work shirt pocket inside his overalls and flashed it. Gus saw a standard headshot, unsmiling, and the name: G. Hollingsworth. Embossed over the lower left corner was the official General Services Administration departmental seal. The others likewise pulled theirs' from inside pockets. All had GSA badges in single fold black leather ID wallets.

"Well, okay, boys. Go on then. Dial '00' if you need anything."

"Thanks, officer," said the foreman. "Let's go guys." They rolled their gear to the elevator and silently entered. Just as the doors were sliding closed, Gus heard one of the men whisper to his buddy, "The Lions will need more than Ryerson."

Lotte turned the page and saw an Interagency script, the lifeblood of government bureaucracy. The top third of the page was all boxed codes and acronyms, unbroken strings of consonants, prime numbers and symbols. The usual. Below, however, where a contact and number would normally be expected, there was only the word: 'Blackbird.'

Below that, the message: *Halt all testing. Seal lab. Await instructions.*

Lotte looked across the table at der Root, disbelieving.

He met her gaze evenly. There was perhaps even a flash of recognition of their past, she thought, a softening she took to be a momentary rush of brothers-in-arms camaraderie. Then it was gone again.

"This is Orwellian, der Root."

He didn't say anything.

"Isn't it? I mean, what! Does this idiot *Blackbird* care at all that there is a killer loose here in the Thunder Peak that could kill thousands, even millions by breakfast if this storm disturbs the earthstars up there!?!"

"*Blackbird* cares all right."

"Oh he does, does he-- Who the hell is *Blackbird*, anyway?"

"Not sure exactly, but I know enough about how things work to know that you don't want to know."

Lotte waited for him to explain further. He took a long, deliberate sip of his coffee instead. He had said as much as he intended for the moment.

The enemy was no longer the Thunder Peak Wilderness, the soil, or the trees. Funny, she thought, how her theory of Mother Earth's rational response to abuse had comforted her since Charley's unnecessary death. She could accept that Nature was so much more powerful and omniscient in its way than humankind would ever be. There had to be a reason for the deaths. The universal laws of cause and effect surely explained a rationale for the woods to fight for its life. The Amazon jungle. The Thunder Peak Wilderness. Somehow it made Charley's death comprehensible, a little less tragic. She was an accidental hero, caught in the line of a larger war, a martyr to humanity's best instincts.

Now all that fell away in the glare of what der Root had shown her. She had been fooling herself.

The earthstar spore was a killer. That was a fact. The steer's blood, the zoospore, and der Root's lab results proved it.

Fact: the spore's mechanism is complicated. Too complicated to have evolved naturally overnight. Its effect on living tissue is extraordinarily complex.

Fact: der Root who twelve hours ago couldn't be bothered to answer my phone calls is suddenly and as yet without any explanation here in Longwood sitting across the table from her with some very scary test results.

"So," she said thoughtfully. *What now?* Without a viable theory to explain what was happening, she had no idea who or what to fight. Or how to fight them.

She looked into her coffee for something to focus upon, the molecular structure of caffeine, the half-life of bacteria in morning blend.

She didn't hear der Root's phone ring. When she looked back up, he was listening, his skin turning ashen before her eyes. He looked at her and there was fear – there is no other word for it – fear in his gray eyes.

"You should have cleared it with me, dammit, Gus," he snapped into the phone. Whatever the person named Gus continued to say at the other end of the line had little effect on der Root's growing distraction. He nodded impatiently, listened, stared at the tabletop, rubbed his jaw, bit his lip. "Alright, Gus, I understand. They had badges. Write it all down, everything you saw and can remember. E-mail what you have to me. Right now, Gus. Now."

He hung up and settled his forearms on the table and looked at Lotte. der Root was blessed with youthful Dutch looks and a face that had never been lined by contemplation of failure. The unmistakable fear in his gaze aged him.

"Who was that?"

"Security at the lab. Gus," der Root shook his head in weary bemusement. "The one place in America that holds the keys to every plague, virus and biological threat to life on earth and they," he shook his head again, this time angrily, "and they put that idiot in charge of protecting mankind."

"Gus? That harmless guy at the front desk, you mean?" she asked.

"A janitorial crew – six of them – told him they were the new crew rotated in from the Arkstone lab."

"Arkstone?"

"There is no Arkstone. Six humorless white guys in blue overalls flash a badge on Sunday, snooker old Gus and clean my office and lab. Not any other rooms, it turns out, just mine."

"What'd they get?"

"Everything. Freezers, slides, sample vials, notes, computers, e-mails – yours – everything, including the lab animals. There isn't a trace of the earthstar, or you or Thunder Peak or anything else in my office," he said bitterly.

"What about the results files that went into this," she held up the three-page report.

"Gone."

"So this is all you have. All we have," she took stock, saying it for her own benefit as well as his, trying to catch up.

"That's right."

"What the hell's going on?" she asked.

"Your instincts were right about something up here," he said plainly.

"So now you believe me. Maybe you can explain why you haven't sent a team to investigate."

"That wouldn't be wise," he said cryptically.

"What does that mean?"

"Listen, I can control the situation."

"What situation? Doesn't the Fed always want to control 'situations,'" she gestured quotes around the word for emphasis.

"The Fed wants NOTHING to do with this. Neither do you."

They were at a stand off. Whatever the situation was, it had just escalated. der Root had cracked the door to his world and what Lotte glimpsed told her how unexpectedly deep and wide was the chasm that had grown between them.

"I need a sample for verification."

"Verification of what?"

"You don't want to know."

"Screw you, der Root," she stood to leave. "You haven't changed. Not really." She put a tip by her coffee cup and rose to leave. Whatever was happening was happening more quickly now. der Root wasn't here to help, despite the reports that he shared with her. He was competing with her.

"Where can I find you in an hour?" asked der Root.

She left without a word.

31

LONGWOOD

'You don't want to know,' thought Lotte as she set up the 200 power video microscope. What was that about? Of course she wanted to know. If he knew nothing else about her, he should realize that Lotte Keene needed to know. It was the strongest force in her life.

She decided to look more closely at this 'engineered' earthstar mushroom spore. Whatever had been done to it wasn't visible at the 40X magnification. That had been sufficient to reveal the zoospore, but not what made it so lethal. For that, she would need a full genetic profile, chemical analysis, and molecular map.

The chemical analysis would require time, equipment, and extensive supplies of solvents, enzymes, reactive agents, and cultures; none of which were readily available.

The genetic profiling couldn't be done here. None of the requisite technology existed within a 250-mile radius.

The molecular map. That could be accomplished in only two ways: painstaking chemical identification and quantification, and an electron microscope.

Lacking an electron microscope, she did the best she could with what she had: a Leica 200x video scope; a powerful, if finicky, hybrid. Finicky due to the video card interface with the digital sensors in the CCD. The optical quality of the lens was extraordinary. The video card – an adaptation of an iVidoptica gaming card – suffered from the turbulent pace of technical advances in chip speeds, heat dissipation and micro circuitry. Advances in each critical component of the circuitry were updated so rapidly that each card – which required up to four days to manufacture – featured slightly different combinations of technology.

By the time she had it properly calibrated, two hours had passed and half the afternoon was spent.

The inner world of the earthstar spore appeared dense and dark, much like the forest from which she had retrieved it.

Earthstar samples 1 and 2 revealed the expected molecular structures. Fused filaments and dikaryon formations. Cap, stem, and wedge-shaped gills lined with thousands of spores. The basidiospores – half with white nuclei, the other half with black nuclei – carried two sets of chromosomes, roughly analogous to male and female genes. The mushroom spore carried both sets of mating spores to evolve more rapidly and adapt to changing environmental conditions more readily. A very successful design, considering the widespread dispersal of mushrooms worldwide.

When she examined sample #3 she was surprised to see all black nuclei in the basidiospores. So, the killer earthstars would not be capable of propagation. That begged the question as to how the killer earthstar got into the Thunder Peak Wilderness if it didn't evolve there.

Looking closer at a spore cross-section, Lotte detected microscopic structures within each nucleus that didn't resemble anything that she had seen before. There were dozens of tiny, barely visible filaments. They looked to be small tubes, like pennette pasta, nanotubes many times thinner than human hair, scarcely large enough to detect under 200x magnification. More shadow than substance.

Lotte pulled away from the video monitor to rest her eyes. She would need to know what they were made of, precisely what molecules comprised of what atomic elements. She glanced back at the ghosting image of tiny tubular structures. What they were doing in functioning organic fungi was a puzzle.

She prepared another slide, taking pains to control the stain more carefully this time. When she looked at the new slide, she saw the same incredible structure within the cell. Lengths of tube formed by a web of as yet unidentified molecules.

Without the facilities of a full chemistry lab, she was limited in the tests she could perform to identify the nanotubes' composition. Traditional 'wet' methods wouldn't tell her enough of what she needed to know nor quickly enough. Neutralization, redox and complexometric titrations, titrimetric precipitations, and gravimetric analysis weren't going to help. UV absorption might tell her more quickly and she was prepared for that experiment. By scanning across a wide range of the UV spectrum, the molecular masses of the products in the sample could be calculated.

According to the mass spectrum, where there should have been three carbon atoms, there were sixty! The nanotubes were comprised of structures consisting of exactly 60 carbon atoms in the shape of spheres. A rarity in Nature.

Wait a minute, she tried to free her mind to recall, *what was it?* Carbon . . . a colleague at UC Boulder had told her about spherical molecules of 60 carbon atoms . . . what was it called? Molecules of pure carbon that formed geodesic sphere-shaped structures. Geodesic . . . Buckminster Fuller.

Buckminsterfullerene. Named for the architect and engineer who designed the geodesic dome. The carbon molecule always formed a geodesic sphere in a vacuum.

This spore was not a vacuum. Yet the only reference she had ever heard of nanotubes was by a colleague at UC Boulder who was excited about its relative strength and conductivity.

Buckminsterfullerene, the fourth known alletrope of carbon, was discovered accidentally by scientists Kroto and Smalley in 1985 in the course of their research into long chain carbon formation in the outer atmospheres of stars. The extremely rare carbon form is a super conductor, able to conduct minute electrical impulses with incredible efficiency, producing no measurable resistance, and therefore, no heat.

The soccer ball-shaped pure carbon molecule was the subject of extensive research by scientists in the pursuit of nanotechnology (ultra miniaturized nanoelectronic devices such as carbon-based single-electron transistors), widely considered to be the next leap forward in technology.

The details at last came together for Lotte. She had read about miniaturization research underway at IBM in which scientists used an atomic force microscope (AFM) to apply accurately measured force to atoms and molecules. They were devising means to create microscopic devices, circuits, transistors, and, eventually, machines so tiny they were nearly invisible to the naked eye. The research was preliminary but highly promising.

This spore was to toxicity what Ebola is to virus. Worse because it acted so rapidly. Yet it left so few clues behind. It was a super killer. But how did it destroy living organisms? All life is carbon-based, so far as we know. How could extra carbon be so deadly? She wanted a DNA analysis of the earthstar's organic foundation, but there was no time. Is it possible to 'grow' buckminsterfullerene in a mushroom, or any living matter? Or was it placed there by human intervention? She recalled the legend that monks placed the bubbles in Dom Perignon champagne one bubble at a time. It was absurd, of course. Or was it? The best she could do is plead with der Root to initiate a study. They could deconstruct the biochemistry and molecular chemistry later and devise an antidote.

Right now, she needed Ben to help her keep anyone from getting near the earthstars. There was no one else who understood how dire the situation had become. It was just Lotte and Ben against whoever created these mushrooms, the spores, the town, the protesters, and the coming storm.

The variable Pacific jet stream grew stronger out of the northwest and swept across the landscape carrying with it an amplified storm track. Roiling black clouds washed up against the two and a quarter mile high Sierras like a flood tide and spilled over into the Mojave Basin. Curtains of rain could be seen from miles away as they swept over forests and meadows.

No one seemed to notice. The roads were increasingly crowded with automobiles, recreational vehicles, pickups, media vans, SUVs, and more than a few German, Japanese and Swedish cars that Longwood was unaccustomed to seeing this far north. Even tour buses were winding their way toward the Thunder Peak Wilderness, chartered by well-meaning church, civic, and special interest groups determined to save the forest. Crowds of people flowed alongside the road, some carrying infants, others leaning forward under massive backpacks.

A bearded young man led one family making its way along the shoulder of the road with a blonde two-year-old on his shoulders and an infant in a large-wheeled stroller before him. He gestured to the children and his wife to the horizon, pointing out the razor sharp peaks and naming them. His family repeated the names in unison once or twice and then he pointed to the next natural marvel, said its name, told them a little about it and had them repeat the name back to him.

Soon a middle-aged couple in overalls, canvas jackets, and wide-brimmed hats chimed in with the young father's tutorial. A passing car of teenagers started to joke with them, but were so caught up in the atmosphere of purpose and good will that they too answered by repeating the name, picking up the game and continuing it down the road.

Despite the fury building in the approaching skies, benevolence calmed the air along Interstate 198 and 180 further north. Local ranchers stopped work in the fields and watched the influx of outsiders with a mixture of awe and concern. Many could be seen talking over the fence with neighbors, shaking their heads and trying to turn away but too fascinated by the spectacle to do anything but watch and try to understand.

Loggers formed in knots of resentment, hurling insults at the believers and demanding that the outsiders mind their own business.

There were monks from New Mexico, mystics who considered cathedral stands of old growth to be sacred and included them in their sacramental rites. There were nuns who came to Longwood to care for the unfortunate that were to be found at any large human movement. There were squint-eyed, leather-faced cowboys, and fresh-faced scholars from Pitzer and dozens of other colleges.

Local farmers set up makeshift vegetable and produce stands. There were hot dogs, hamburgers and chips distributed from food wagons; ices by roaming vendors; and gum, candy, Oreos, and lemonade sold by local children at roadside card tables. Several farmers and ranchers cleared out their attics of anything old and tried the market for antiques.

It seemed to the locals that the entire world had come to save the Thunder Peak Wilderness from Jasperson and his loggers. The northwestern entrance to the Thunder Peak Wilderness and the surrounding half-mile clear-cut stubble was rapidly being transformed into a frontier township comprised of tented neighborhoods, ersatz vehicle parking lots, open air encampments and enough campfire smoke to lend an ominous mood to the already foreboding afternoon. Groups congregated with like groups: church groups assembled near concentrations of spiritualists; *Earth Rebirth!* activists – there were over six hundred gathered so far - concentrated near Greenpeace, PETA, Earth First and a California contingent of the Sierra Club.

The more prosperous visitors tended to raise well-organized, even homey camps, complete with lanterns, gas stoves, plenty of bottled water and blaring news and music.

There were sit-ins near the entrance to the protected land, mostly by environmentalists who wanted to keep the loggers out. And everywhere one went, teach-ins could be heard. Biologists spoke about the rapidly vanishing wildlife and botanical diversity in this part of America due to logging.

Activist lawyers advised listeners about their rights in this volatile situation. "Do not resist the officer who comes to arrest you. Neither should you make his job any easier. Do not walk if they lift you to your feet; let them drag you to the paddy wagons. If any officer or guardsmen threatens you, beats you or uses excessive force – and that definitely includes pepper spray, people! – try to memorize their name, rank and appearance. We will be filing charges on your behalf!"

Most of the veteran activists came prepared with varied protective gear including gas masks, rebreathers, and goggles. Two out of every three had a camera: mini videocam, DSLR, or point and shoot. And all of the multitudes came with a growing certainty that this gathering was important, even historic.

Nate Stimson drove slowly through the camps to show the presence of law enforcement, for all the good he thought that would do. He and his pea shooter against the passionate, caring and concerned – if misguided, he thought as he adjusted his surgical mask – people who genuinely felt they had a stake in saving this piece of California. He didn't know whether to be relieved or scared to death when the announcement came over his radio that the Governor was sending in National Guardsmen to maintain order.

"Listen not to the pagan idolaters, for they are the voice of Satan!" A voice cut through the din like a bullhorn. Nate turned to see a tall, gaunt man in black raging into a microphone. "There are those who say the trees have rights. That they are sacred! What do we say to these unbelievers? I tell you to remind them of the First Commandment!"

His listeners recited with him: "Thou shalt not have other Gods besides me!"

Driving on, Nate slowed to hear the next evangelist on the opposite side of the road.

He was a barrel-chested working man with great calloused hands and a white mane swept back from his open expression. The stepladder on which he balanced above the heads of his listeners sagged and groaned with his passions, his roaring recriminations. "The Stroke is the sword of St. Peter, come to battle the traitors who would sacrifice the great trees on the Case-Kaiser's altar of greed!!"

Then Nate saw the group that most concerned him: the *Earth Rebirth!* group, or *tribe* as he had come to think of them. They were impressively organized. While hundreds sat in orderly lines two rows deep across the entrance gate to the Wilderness, there were a dozen on a raised stage, conducting non-stop seminars and rallies for their faithful and any others they could recruit. He recognized the speaker. It was articulate and fiery Spectacles.

"Clear-cutting is a crime against nature. An obscene gang rape, a kind of ethnic, or species cleansing." He paused to let that thought penetrate. He looked over the crowd and lifted his voice. "My friends, our opponents, the great old growth trees' opponents, want us to believe that mankind is meant to rule over all living things. I say that role is reserved for the Creator.

"They want us to believe that Nature is too great, too powerful to suffer long from their 'harvesting' of these two thousand year old trees. I say they should look to Central Africa, or the Amazon, or the Caucasus, or China's Jeng Shu province and reconsider their self-serving, shortsighted, and dangerous theories.

"They want us to believe that making a living at the expense of breathable air, a functioning watershed, a legacy for their grandchildren is an all right thing to do. 'Someone will figure out how to clean the air, desalinate ocean water; our grandchildren will have so much more technology than we do, they'll figure their problems out.' I say go try to breathe in Jeng Shu, go try to find water in Oklahoma, go walk a mile in your grandchildren's shoes."

"They say that we don't belong here, that these magnificent trees which have stood undisturbed since 1,000 years before Christ should fall to their whim. You know what I have to say about that. The same thing you and your loved ones have to say."

"Finally, they warn that they will destroy us if we get in their way." Murmurs coursed through the crowd as listeners related threats they had received from loggers. "I thank you for not rising to their bait, their malicious threats, and yes, in many cases, vandalizing your tents, your car tires. They say the disease that has killed five people up there is going to get us, too. Makes you wonder how much more they know, doesn't it?"

The crowd rose to its feet and shouted its agreement.

"I say the Thunder Peak Wilderness will not strike those who defend her. She will protect those who protect her."

The crowd – now more than a thousand strong – cheered.

"The time has come to show Case-Kaiser, California and the world that we are right about this," Spectacles shouted to be heard above the crowd.

Cheers climbed and the multitude pressed forward against the stage.

"We will penetrate the police line tomorrow. We will enter that magnificent old growth wilderness. And we will join the ancient trees as friends and defenders of the forest. As friends who come in peace and love. There is nothing in the universe more powerful than LOVE!"

Cheers shook the ground and electrified the air as everyone within earshot caught the fever that Spectacles offered.

As if in response, thunder rumbled over Thunder Peak. Distant lightning illuminated the high alpine peak in the waning afternoon light.

32

LONGWOOD

"Dammit, Lotte," Ben objected as he sat down in the kitchen, "I'm about to bury my mother."

"It's worse than I thought," Lotte kept a matter-of-fact tone as she laid out photographs on the table.

Ben scanned them, his expression neutral.

"In addition to the organic toxin, I discovered these," she pointed to faint shadows of the nanotubes, now glad she had packed the DSLR attachment for the Leica video microscope. Nothing like visual proof to move an investigation forward.

He leaned closer but didn't react. Then he stopped and he took a magnifying glass to the image of the dark nucleus "What- ?"

"It's a hollow filament," she explained. "Very strong structure for its size. There are at least four dozen in each nucleus."

Ben looked up at her, then back to the image.

"I remembered a colleague telling me about these things so I did some quick research. Turns out these are carbon nanotubes, super efficient conductors of minute electrical impulses. The geeks are making microscopic nanomachines with these. Most analysts say they'll be the next big thing. Computers so small you can barely

201

see them. Imagine the implications for medicine, business,--"

"Intelligence," Ben interjected.

"Sure," agreed Lotte. "Intelligence and its evil twin: warfare."

"Think about it. The human body is a bioelectrical organism. It functions on minute electrical synapses from cell to cell, delivering instructions from the brain to interpret what the senses collect, analyze the information, draw conclusions about how to react. Then the brain sends millions of instructions to muscles and nerves throughout the body to move, fight, or flee. And that's all in addition to the autonomic functions which are also governed by these minute electrical impulses."

"So what are you saying?" Ben sat upright. The way he was feeling, he didn't want to get into another theoretical exercise but she drew him in. "These carbon filaments short-circuit synaptic processes, overload the system?"

"Exactly." She waited for him to digest the implications, which were many.

He looked away and Lotte braced herself for the scolding she expected to follow. Ben was low on the usual reserves, irritable with grief, failure, and lack of sleep. She came into his ranch kitchen like a zealot tossing out conspiracy theories and threats from unseen bogeymen.

Then she saw that he was thinking, assembling her evidence, and holding it up to the light. She had seen the same expression thousands of times before. Scientists worked so intensely to solve theoretical puzzles in the mind that they lost track of everything else. Their facial expressions went slack while deductions and new theories assembled and dissembled in their brains.

"It's possible, I suppose," he came back. "Nerve impulses are electrochemical. The current is so weak that touching metal wires, or a car door handle does no harm." He straightened a paper clip, held it out between the thumb and forefinger of his right hand, and touched the tip of the wire to his left forefinger, completing the circuit, "too much resistance."

"Whereas in theory a filament this tiny could wreak havoc between cells—," added Lotte.

"In theory," cautioned Ben.

"So they short circuit every synapse in their path - like chaff."

"Forcing muscles to contract, tying nerves in knots—"

And whatever the nanotubes don't destroy by short circuiting

—"

"--the toxin kills," Lotte finished.

Ben saw where she was headed. He braced himself for her newest theory. "It's not natural," he allowed.

"No, this mutation of the earthstar genome is not natural. It didn't evolve here on Thunder Peak; it is intentional and comes from beyond these woods. It's engineered."

"Engineered," repeated Ben.

"Pure carbon, C60. Astronomers discovered it first in the atmosphere around stars, then replicated it in the lab. Forms into a sphere in a vacuum, a geodesic sphere. They named it *Buckminsterfullerene*."

"Cute."

"der Root said the earthstar is engineered. I didn't believe him before, I do now."

"Okay," Ben answered expectantly. "And your conclusion would be what: that men in black are getting ready to take over the planet with mushroom claymores," he suggested, referring to the claymore anti-personnel mine, another model of lethality.

Lotte didn't answer.

"der Root did the tests you requested?"

"Not that one, but enough." She rearranged the photos on the tabletop. "There's more."

"What?"

"I don't know, but there's something."

"Maybe he wants in on the next big outbreak. Could be professional jealousy."

"No. It's not that," she thought aloud as she mulled the possibilities. "It was the look on his face."

"You saw him? How?" asked Ben.

"He's in Longwood."

Ben waited.

"He finally returned my call; asked me to meet him at the Hut. That was one bizarre conversation, my friend," she laughed as she remembered. "That safari hat he wears makes him stick out like a kangaroo in Calgary. Vin der Root on safari in Longwood," she shook her head in bemusement.

Ben didn't laugh. "Tall guy? Bush jacket?"

"Yes."

"I saw him on my way out of town earlier," Ben leaned

forward. "He was into something heavy with Jasperson."

"Jasperson!?" Lotte froze. "Are you sure?"

Ben nodded ominously. "They were arguing, Jasperson pointing. The guy in the hat – der Root – was pointing right back. The hat caught my eye. The argument kept me watching."

"That son of a—"

"I don't know what they call it in Colorado, but up here when a sheep consorts with a wolf, we figure the sheep is either woefully naïve or it's not a sheep."

They stared at each other for several moments, Lotte futilely attempting to reign in her anger; Ben struggling with new doubts . . . about Lotte.

"We stop the spore, Ben, stop those *Earth Rebirth!* kids from getting themselves killed."

"We?"

"You and me."

"How do I know you're who you say you are, Doctor?" his voice was measured. "If you are a disease hunter who works for the government, why hasn't the government responded to your requests? If der Root's got dealings with Jasperson, does that mean you do, too?"

She was on the outside again. His calling her 'Doctor' stung. She cared more about Ben than she wanted to admit, and she knew she should be more careful, more objective. She was on his turf and had to respect his local perspective on this outbreak. He didn't trust the Government or any of its functionaries farther than he could throw a horse. Yet, she kept pushing him.

"I don't blame you for being suspicious. I bring it out in people. And I can't explain der Root's connection with Jasperson. But you've got to get over this wary Californian crap. There is a killer up there on Thunder Peak that so far only you and I can identify. This is a catastrophe in the making and, without you, I'm just not going to be able to do much to prevent it from killing more victims."

She held up a picture. "THIS means I need you and Longwood needs you. Mary Margaret needs you to get off your suspicious ass. Dammit, Ben . . . I know what it means to lose someone you love . . . Alice would want you to fight. If you don't help, she died for nothing!"

He tilted back on his chair and considered her for what seemed like a lifetime. After a moment, there was a shift behind his eyes. She saw the fence come down. He crossed over to her side and rejoined the fight.

"What do we have?" he said at last. "A mushroom with a lethal toxin as yet to be identified. And a cluster of super conductive threads which, being non-organic, could have gotten there just one way – by being manually injected."

"An engineered instrument of death," Lotte spat the words she was so angry now. "A weapon."

"Looks that way. And a Fed responsible for public health getting excitable with the one man who, if allowed to have his way with the Thunder Peak, can spread death over the Midwest and Northeast, killing millions," Ben reined in his own feelings for the sake of reaching some reliable conclusion.

Lotte paced to the sink and looked out the window. "Maybe it was Jasperson who was getting hot," she thought aloud, "and der Root was doing his job, threatening to bring the government down on him if he didn't back off." She couldn't believe der Root was as bad as the facts suggested.

Ben resisted. "You don't know Jasperson. He's the bully who does the threatening."

Afternoon light had climbed the wall. They were exhausted after the day's events. The unavoidable conclusion to be drawn so far made them feel worse.

The back door opened and Mary Margaret shuffled through without noticing her father or Lotte.

"M, how's Beauty doing," asked Ben, his voice brighter than he felt.

"Okay, I guess," M answered over her shoulder.

"M?"

She reappeared in the hallway arch.

"What do you mean, 'okay, I guess?'" he asked.

"I don't care. What's the use?" M looked at her shoes.

Ben glanced at Lotte, then went to his daughter. "You can't mean that, M."

"I do!"

"Why, Mary Margaret?" asked Lotte, also going to her.

M looked at her father and Lotte, then back to the floor. "She's just going to die, like everyone else." Her eyes welled up.

Ben wanted to argue with her, but no sound came. While he

was feeling sorry for himself, his daughter was losing faith in him, in medicine, in Nature, in God. It shouldn't have surprised him that she was reacting this way to overwhelming danger and her own fear, but it did. He was completely knocked down by M's murmured, 'I don't care.' The princess had cursed everything in her kingdom.

Ben wrapped her in his arms and held her tightly. "Beauty isn't going to die. Hear me?"

When she didn't respond, he took her face into his hands and repeated, "Hear me?"

She nodded and, after a moment of indecision, hugged him back.

"We're going to fight this thing and we're going to beat it."

M looked at Lotte as only a child can: openly trusting, surrendering everything to the need to believe her.

All of Lotte's unspent devotion to children she had never brought into the world overflowed its walls. She embraced both Mary Margaret and Ben.

"What's going on here?" asked Grace as she entered and took in the scene.

Ben looked up. "A father-daughter-doctor moment," he smiled.

"Daddy and Dr. Keene are going to save all of us!" M beamed through drying tears.

"Oh, are they?" answered Grace. The forced brightness in her voice did nothing to mask her concern.

"Go wash up, M," Ben turned his daughter to the hall and gave her a pat. Standing up, he faced Grace who had not moved from her place by the door.

"Grace, we have evidence of what's killing people. It's a mushroom spore—"

"Not just any spore," Lotte added.

"That's for sure," continued Ben. "It's some kind of bio-engineered plant—"

"Fungi," Lotte corrected him. "Not a plant, a fungi."

"Somebody planted it up there in the Thunder Peak Wilderness and it's going to kill again."

"If we don't stop them first," Lotte chimed in.

"We don't know how just yet, but we--," his voice trailed off as he noticed Grace's preoccupied expression. "What is it?" he asked.

The reason for Grace's disappointment was lost on Ben, but

Lotte read it as clearly as a book cover. Grace had mistaken their embrace and Ben's enthusiasm for something deeper. Her refusal to look at Lotte confirmed it.

"I'd better go and see if I can talk some sense into the Mayor," Lotte pushed through the door.

"What is it?" Ben asked again when Grace slammed her purse down on the table.

"You're pathetic, Ben. We talked about this before!"

Ben suddenly understood. He glanced out the door at Lotte getting into her van, then back at Grace. "No, Grace. It's not anything like that."

"Like what?"

"Like whatever you're thinking about Lotte and me. We now have evidence of criminal activity, and we can prove it. Lotte can't handle it alone. I have to help.

"Why her – why you! That woman has brought only misery to this family. She's turned Longwood against us. Mary Margaret is terrified. And she's got you--," she folded her arms and stopped herself from saying what she desperately wanted to say to Ben at that moment.

"Because, right now, crowds are threatening to enter the Wilderness to prove the Stroke won't hurt them. Storm clouds are gathering and may disperse the spore. Case-Kaiser is organizing crews to go in and cut. Because somebody murdered my mother! We're about to lose everything," he paused. "I have to do something."

33

LONGWOOD

At the Mayor's office in the vacated Five-and-Dime, Wilburn Spivey's part-time secretary, Flora Mendez, fielded calls from as far away as Stockholm. Forests in Sweden, Norway, Finland and Denmark are revered for their botanical, climatological, geological and spiritual powers. Beowulf grew in part from the deeply rooted Norse veneration for deep, dark forests.

Rumors of mounting tensions in the Thunder Peak Wilderness crowded the international grapevine that had connected environmentalists since John Muir's time. Now, the Internet accelerated the spread of information. The day began with a few messages left on the answering machine during the night and grew to an avalanche of inquiries, protests, threats, and requests for interviews to Longwood's City Hall and office of the Mayor.

The town's only municipal computer – a seven-year old IBM Pentium II 300 MHz castoff from the Case-Kaiser regional foreman's office – struggled mightily to cope with the tidal wave of e-mail. It had already crashed and been rebooted twenty times since midday. Mayor Spivey was thankful for Mrs. Mendez's dedicated efforts to keep a lid on official communications, but she was no more equipped for an international crisis than the computer. She'd been juggling two phone lines for five hours and she had aged ten years since arriving this morning to assist him.

The fax machine, which sat on a folding chair just out of reach, had run out of paper hours earlier and cried impotently like a neglected infant. Its persistent ringing added to the chaos.

"Governor, there is nothing more I can do here," Wilburn Spivey stood like a prize fighter at the Main Street window, holding the receiver to his red and swollen ear, and glared at the burned out hulk of Larson Black Kettle's Ford. It remained where the loggers had torched it. Spivey liked Longwood and the people who lived here, and that kind of violence brought them all down. This wasn't L.A. Not yet. Not by a long shot.

He had removed his jacket, revealing a shirt soaked through with perspiration. Flushed scarlet from the neck up, his face darkened as he endured the Governor's harangue. After five hours and more frustrating conversations with government, corporate and citizen callers than he could count, his capacity for reasonable dialogue had reached its end.

"Unlike you, Governor, I have no staff, no state shield of authority, no emergency powers, and no budget. I don't even have a desk! So don't tell me what I have to do." He glanced over at Flora and tried to wink, but his tortured nerves failed his bravado. He faltered and twitched epileptically. She worried he was in the grip of a seizure.

Turning back to the window, he noted that Main Street was now peaceful. Longwood was so peaceful in fact it was eerie. Bart Fielding was boarding up the A & P's windows. In expectation of more unrest or the approaching storm, wondered Spivey? That was the only activity he saw. The rabble had moved out to the Peak where all the action was. Then a vehicle pulled up directly in front of him. It was that Keene woman's micro van. He groaned as she got out and walked his way looking very determined.

Damn. Not *her*, not *now*.

He tried not to look her way when the bell above the front door announced her arrival, but his skills were worn thin. It was a little like watching an accident happen, he just couldn't discipline himself to look away.

The ringing phones and cacophonous voices – was it only the

209

two of them? – matched Lotte's urgent mood. She had proof that something of unprecedented lethality was loose in the Thunder Peak Wilderness and now that she knew it was man-made and not Mother Nature's defense she had more reason to be frightened than ever. Although the Mayor didn't know it yet, he was about to be scared, too. She saw him in the window shouting into his phone.

Without waiting for an invitation, she approached and interrupted. "Mayor, what the hell are you going to do about that circus out at the Thunder Peak? There's a killer—"

He gestured for her to wait.

"Dammit, Spivey! Unless you start doing your job, a whole lot of people, animals and who knows what else are going to DIE!"

She easily overpowered the Governor's voice. Spivey was suddenly caught between two powerful forces and ceased to function. All he could was watch helplessly as she wound up.

Outside the window, Ben's truck braked at the curb and he also moved quickly for the door.

"Listen to me," continued Lotte, loudly enough that Flora Mendez forgot who was on the other end of the phone in her right hand and watched, "the Stroke is REAL. It's not some New Age concept, or a product of some mass psychosis. It's as real as Nelson Hatch, Lars Broder and Alice McCandle." The bell over the door rang, as if tolling for Alice and the others.

The Mayor put down the phone, resigned to have to deal with this woman he considered to be a massive pain in the bu—

"Ben, tell the Mayor just how toxic the Thunder Peak Wilderness is right now."

"I don't know what Lotte's told you, but this is bigger than you can imagine. You have to hold off Jasperson's crews, those *Earth Rebirth!* kids and everybody else from getting anywhere near that mountain."

"Now you know I can't do that, Ben," Spivey spoke at last, bolstered by another male presence. "Those crews and heavy equipment have rolled in already. That's a hundred thousand dollar nut a day for Case-Kaiser. Those are *real* numbers. Every bit as real as your victims, lady," he pointedly added.

"They're not my victims, Mayor. They're yours, and they are just a preview of what's about befall your constituency!"

Spivey looked at Ben for support, or at least the voice of

reason. Ben wasn't playing. The Mayor looked across the room to Flora, although he didn't know why. The whole day was screwed. The town was out of control, out on some frontier rage bender. Jasperson and Case-Kaiser walked all over him like he was just so much red California dirt. His commission on the 'survey' of logging was probably no more likely to come through than his hopes for reelection. This maniac scientist from Boulder had no respect for anybody and wasn't going to work with him one little bit. Even the sky was swirling menacingly. What is an ambitious 50-year-old man stuck in the badlands supposed to do for his retirement, anyway?

"How bad is it?" he asked, exhaustion getting the better of him.

"As bad as anything I've ever seen, Mayor," Lotte said, allowing a touch of calm back into her voice. "It's a stage four biological agent that, while localized inside the Thunder Peak Wilderness to the best of my knowledge, is highly unstable. Anything disturbs it, it becomes airborne and carries as far as the wind. Anything that breathes it dies -- quickly."

"How do you know this?" asked the Mayor.

"I've seen for myself," Ben confirmed.

That was enough for Spivey, apparently. He didn't press her on it. "The surgical masks won't protect the loggers?"

"Can't guarantee it."

"It's contagious?"

"No, I don't believe it is. But it is transportable. That's how I was able to identify it and confirm its lethality, by collecting samples and bringing them back here to test."

The Mayor stepped back. It was an involuntary reaction to what she'd said.

Lotte smiled and calmed him. "I had a bio suit and the last active samples were sent to the CDC in Atlanta."

Rolling thunder sounded from miles away to the northwest. "The storm?!"

"It's hard to know, but . . ." she didn't need to finish.

"The pooch is screwed," the Mayor growled to himself.

"But, there's a lot we don't know," Lotte continued.

"Like what?"

"How much of this agent has been placed up there. There may not be much. This could be some kind of warning."

"That's right," Ben interjected. "We just don't know how bad this thing is. That's why you've got to help."

"What do you want?" Spivey asked plainly.

"Call off Case-Kaiser. Come up with some excuse," demanded Lotte.

Spivey looked at her in partial disbelief. "You don't know Case-Kaiser, do you, Doctor?" he asked rhetorically. "I could have an accident if they decided it would smooth things for them."

She saw he was deadly serious and looked at Ben.

"Wilburn," Ben said, "I don't know anything about what you have got going with Jasperson, but I do know how much worse than any of us can possibly imagine this so-called bio-Stroke is. It kills fast and ugly." Another thunderhead crashed in the darkening sky. Ben paced to the window to look and pounded the window frame with his right fist. His voice rose above the thunder. "It's killed five so far and it's about to kill hundreds more. And this damn thing is no *accident*. Somebody planted it up there!"

He turned to see Spivey, Lotte, and Flora all watching him and waiting.

"Stop Case-Kaiser. Declare Eminent Domain, say the President called you personally to offer his assistance and the situation has changed. Tell him you found Jesus, but stop him!"

Spivey nervously rubbed his jaw twice and looked at them both. "I don't know how, but I'll slow 'em down. Twenty-four hours." He looked tired, but Lotte noticed he stood a little taller.

"One more thing, Mayor," asked Lotte, "Where is Jasperson?"

"At his foreman's on-site office," the Mayor guessed.

"Have you seen Doctor der Root in town?"

"Left here half an hour ago."

"Here? Where was he going," asked Lotte?

"Out to that mess at the Peak entrance, I'd guess."

"What did he want?"

"Same as you two," the Mayor answered tiredly. "Keep everyone out of the Wilderness."

"Really?" Lotte and Ben asked in unison.

"What'd you expect? He is a public health official," answered the Mayor. Then as an afterthought, he added, "Isn't he?"

34

LONGWOOD

"Hurry, Ben!" Lotte urged him over the roar of his Wagoneer's V8.

No, don't hurry. I have to think.

der Root's working both sides of this thing threw her off balance. Not enough to slow her down, but enough to blunt the edge of her rage.

Ben had seen him meeting with the prince of darkness . . . Spivey said he had defended the Thunder Peak Wilderness, Jasperson's latest intended victim. Or, more accurately, the loggers and protestors who were about to enter the forest. What was she missing?

"There has to be a better use of our time, Lotte," Ben said over the roar as they sped up Route 212 into the sun.

"I have to talk to der Root."

"Can we come up with an antidote?"

"To THIS? To an as yet unknown genetic mutation, wrapped in carbon filaments hidden inside the cells of a spore we need a microscope to see? Inside earthstar mushrooms that are smaller than a golf ball scattered in an old growth forest that covers hundreds of square miles and came from God-knows-where!?" She chuckled bitterly.

"Lotte, I'm just saying—"

"NO! I," she stopped herself, then continued, "WE have to know what he's up to!"

Ben looked sideways at her. "What is it with you two?"

Lotte waved him off and stared ahead, willing the car to go faster.

How could she tell Ben how mistaken she'd been about der Root. Worse yet, that he could still reach her, hurt her.

"There he is," Ben interrupted, pointing to a knot of people gathered near the front gate.

She looked across the shifting sea of humanity that now inundated the small valley meadow outside the Wilderness entrance. The narrow road on which they were driving led up to the gate and turned to dirt and gravel on the other side. It looked like Heaven itself as it serpentined into the shaded woods.

"With Nate. See the truck?"

She saw the safari hat. She wanted to rip it off his head and stomp it into the mud.

The mood of the crowd was noticeably benevolent as the throng parted for Ben to edge his Jeep closer. Not festive, exactly, but buoyed by the sense of common purpose that brought them to Thunder Peak. Two rain squalls had already swept through this valley, but had done little to dampen the spirit of determination that bound so many diverse groups and agendas together.

Lotte opened the door and dove into the mass of bodies before Ben could find a place to park.

"Lotte, wait!"

She wasn't listening. He watched her push through the mob against its meandering current. He tried to turn left, but stopped short when he saw he was about to run over a sleeping infant in a car seat while hundreds of feet and now a Jeep coursed around it.

He struggled with the steering wheel to go right, but without power-assisted steering and forward motion, he had no leverage. He started to back up, but the mob had closed off the way behind him.

He turned off the ignition, wedged open the door, and joined the throng. As an afterthought, he put the key back in the ignition and left the truck unlocked in case anyone needed to move it.

He shouldered his way between the bodies in the general

direction of where he had seen Nate and der Root, occasionally glimpsing Lotte's wild hair bob in the currents ahead.

Her shouting cut through the buzz of the crowd from twenty yards away. Lotte's voice commanded attention and she was getting it from der Root, Nate, and at least two hundred people in the immediate vicinity.

"der Root! What are you doing!?!"

He didn't respond for a couple of moments.

"---with JASPERSON!!!" . . .

"Are you going to tell me just what you're up to or do I have to guess?!"

"Calm down, Lotte, I was going to find you after I talked to the Sheriff here."

"AFTER the Sheriff!! After the Mayor! After Jasperson!! Have I left anyone out there, Vinnie?"

"Lotte," der Root tried a calm voice.

She glared at him, seeing what he was doing and deciding she would have none of it. She snatched his hat and hurled it over the heads of the crowd like a Frisbee.

Nate glanced at Ben, who settled in to wait these two out.

"Lotte!" der Root snapped. "Cool down! Yes, I tracked down Jasperson to get a better handle on the chronology of events so far and what his plans are. I figured he could describe what his crews plan to do, when and what the expected effects will be."

Lotte folded her arms and forced herself to listen. He was right. That was so irritating. That and the way he sounded so reasonable, so rational, and caring.

"No one knows this rugged country better than the men who destroy it." He waited for her to respond, which wasn't going to be happening anytime soon. She was biting her tongue. She could taste the salty warmth spreading in her mouth.

"Right?" asked der Root reasonably.

"Am I right?" he repeated, this time looking at all three of them in turn.

35

WASHINGTON, D.C.

Stars glimmered over the Potomac River as Dr. Russell Clayton turned his Volvo Cross Country wagon east onto Arlington Memorial Drive. The District's natural beauty was at its peak as he headed into Washington. A dry, chilly breeze rattled bright foliage; the boisterous Potomac flashed whitecaps as it caroused its banks in a headlong rush to the ocean. He opened the moon roof and lowered his window to allow in the fresh air. The moon roof had been his wife's compromise. She never used it and didn't understand why he ever would. It messed the hair and was so noisy. He didn't have any hair and to him Nature made music, not noise.

Because it was Sunday evening, there was little traffic to compete with the wind and water. If you closed your eyes, you could imagine what it must have been like here four hundred years ago, before colonial settlement, before Jamestown and Virginia, before America.

Checking his watch, he saw he had time to spare so he turned north on the Rock Creek & Potomac Parkway and settled back into his seat, almost relaxed. Checking the rear and side view mirrors, he reminded himself not to get too relaxed. Altering his way into D.C. was a standard precaution. A different route every trip. That's what the others told him each time they spoke, which wasn't often. When he complained about it, they said it again, as if he were a child rather than the Nobel Laureate in molecular genetics he was. They were military men, seemingly incapable of understanding that he was just as aware as they of the threats lurking everywhere here. Every waiter had supernatural hearing and an insatiable appetite for non-reportable cash tips. The military couldn't trust the academics and the academics couldn't trust the military. Stasis, that was the term for it, he thought with satisfaction. Their equal and opposite tendencies actually maintained a paradoxical balance. Stasis. He was just as respectful of protocol as they were.

He turned south on Virginia, north on 20th, west on Pennsylvania, away from the White House, then east again on 'I' Street. He found a parking spot on the west side of Lafayette Park to his amazement, closed the moon roof, locked the car and walked north to 'I' again, where he strolled comfortably to 16th Street, occasionally pausing to take in the view. When he saw the doorman of the Carlton Hotel step inside the front door, he glanced quickly around once more and, confident that he wasn't being observed, slipped down the narrow walkway beside the Hotel.

The grand old hotel of America's capital city was the choice of visiting dignitaries, heads of state and business moguls. It offered uncompromising luxury in close proximity to historic landmarks, galleries, the White House, and other halls of power. Precisely the kind of place one would least expect to find anyone who was trying to vanish from sight for a meeting so important even the vaunted intelligence services would never know it occurred.

The black metal door set into the stone wall looked as if it hadn't been used for decades. He pulled the handle and it opened easily. He ducked inside and closed it with a whisper behind him.

Inside, he stood on a tiled landing from which a heavy door marked: 'Employees only - Alarm will sound' led into the hotel. To the right, a narrow stairway led down three flights, with similar security doors at each landing. At the bottom, a well-lit hallway led north underneath the hotel. Laundry carts, stacked chairs, and a floor polishing machine lined the hallway, which seemed to go on without end. In the opposite direction was an unlit alcove lined by a series of electrical utility panels festooned with aging DANGER -

HIGH VOLTAGE decals. It was a singularly uninviting place.

Dr. Clayton listened for activity on the stairs. Hearing nothing, he pulled open the center panel cover and pushed one of the lethal-looking circuit breakers. The panel gave under his hand and he stepped into darkness, closing the door behind him. As the panel latched behind him, lights came on illuminating a short hallway that turned right. That hall ended at a narrow elevator door. He entered and continued his descent below Washington D.C. for what he was told was 85 feet. How it was possible to build a structure 85 feet deep into the Chesapeake's alluvial muck and have it remain watertight was beyond him. But he didn't claim to understand geological and structural physics. Some things one had to simply trust. The door opened after several moments and he stepped into a small anteroom leading to an austere conference room.

The subterranean bunker humorously referred to as the *penthouse* by the nine individuals who knew of its existence was as 'black' as the projects they conceived and supervised. More classified than top secret, 'black' projects simply did not exist. According to protocol, Dr. Clayton met in this deep earth complex monthly or whenever a crisis required a face-to-face consultation. Today's meeting was a response to an NSA code *Blackbird* message.

His two colleagues were already reviewing multiple classified photographs and reports.

"Interior rates it as essential to the economy out there," said Stephen Small, Director of the NSA. "But I suspect if we looked, at least half their files on forestlands would be rated Essential."

"It's the last stand of old growth in the state, says here," Marine Colonel and special liaison to the Joint Chiefs, Michael Easta, read aloud. "That'd make it essential to a lot of people, I imagine. The environmentalists, Case-Kaiser, California tourism officials, Foresters. How about petroleum and mining? Have I left anybody out?"

"Besides being close enough to be considered within Sequoia National Park, Thunder Peak Wilderness is on sacred Ahwahnee land, stewarded in perpetuity by the Ahwahnee Nation," added Dr. Clayton as he poured himself a coffee and joined the others at the table.

"You've been doing your homework, Doctor," Small noted without looking up.

"It's what I'm good at," Clayton answered good-naturedly.

"It's also a hazard of your profession, Doctor," Director Small said plainly.

"How so?"

"Lotte Keene, Ph.D., has stumbled onto something she shouldn't have," explained Small.

Clayton leaned forward. "*That's* what's going on up there?"

"The evidence so far suggests an atypical cause of multiple deaths in the area. Colonel, would you mind?" Small gestured to the wall monitors.

Using a remote control, Colonel Easta rolled the BIOSAT-7 video. The three men watched it several times in silence.

"Looks like it. Nothing else kills that fast. But it's not possible," protested Clayton. "It's buried away someplace under Utah, isn't it?"

"As of 30 minutes ago, all known stocks were accounted for. Wasn't difficult. There's only one vial the size of a pen cap, frozen, sealed in tons of nonpermeable concrete and submerged in a radioactive pool," Colonel Easta reported, then added, "I don't even know where it is."

"So, if –" Clayton began to argue.

"If the only known strain is safely tucked away," Small interjected, "either that," he pointed to the BIOSAT-7 image of a dying man on the monitor, "is caused by something new, or we don't control the world's supply."

The three men looked at one another.

"Besides Dr. Keene, who in our opinion is in the clear, we're focusing on the usual suspects," Small continued. "We've all but eliminated every foreign element. Attacking a few disgruntled loggers in the back of beyond doesn't accomplish anything for anyone. We're still looking, but the source has to be either natural or domestic."

"Natural?" asked Clayton. He knew all about Nature's biological, chemical, and molecular physics. There was nothing in Nature that could kill that quickly.

"Just keeping an open mind, Doctor. Being thorough."

"It's not natural," Clayton said dismissively.

"Alright, it's not natural," Small didn't miss a beat. "So it's almost certainly domestic. Topping the list would be our friend, Gabriel, of course."

"Can't FBI detain him for a day or so, take his temperature?" asked Easta. It had been a long day already and his usual discipline was screwed down tight.

"If they could find him," answered Small.

"This is turning into a rumble up there. He's got to be in the thick of it," argued Easta.

"So we should arrest all those gathered up there?" It was a rhetorical question, Small double-checked his notes.

Easta sat back, clenching his jaw.

"If it's what we think it is," Clayton started to speak, but when he couldn't come up with a sufficiently descriptive term for apocalypse, he went silent.

"Gentlemen, we have to assume worst case here," Small took command of the room. "The cause of the Thunder Peak fatalities must not be learned. Not by the media, of course. Not by Dr. Lotte Keene. Not even by POTUS. National security is at stake," said Small with added emphasis.

"What are you saying, exactly," asked Dr. Clayton.

"I'm saying that anyone who knows how this has happened is to be silenced and the evidence be made to disappear," Small explained without a trace of emotion in his voice.

"Understood, Mr. Director," Easta agreed. "But you understand that is not in my charter."

"Of course. We must concur, however, before we leave this room."

All three nodded.

"You realize, gentleman," said Doctor Clayton, "that if this is what we believe it is, there will be no way to counter it or explain it away. If that storm stirs it up, winds will carry death to Europe."

"We can't control the wind yet," said Small, "but by god we can get the irresponsible fool who can point the finger!"

"What happens if the enemy gets it and uses it first?" worried Easta.

"It appears, Colonel, that he already has it . . ." Doctor Clayton suggested.

Director Small looked over. "Gabriel?"

Clayton weighed the implications for a moment and nodded stonily.

36

THUNDER PEAK

"Another fine day in the High Sierras, eh, Chief?!" shouted a lean kid from his truck's picket rail. A sun-boiled California cowboy, he was happy to be anywhere in open country. He looked comical with his head swimming inside a Kevlar helmet, totally out of place in crisp new camouflage fatigues.

Nate directed the troop truck forward and to the right. "Cover up, son!" Nate shouted and gestured for him to put on his surgical mask.

Forty-one, counted Nate as he waved another truck forward across the 'Four D' ranch's fallow northwest forty acres. The 500-horsepower truck made loud and quick work of the slight rise, clawing its way upslope for the assembly area half a mile away.

In the back, troops twisted around on their bench seats, pointing, exclaiming to their buddies, impressed by the still-growing crowds. Their youthful faces gave no sign of the tension associated with a military action. At least not yet. It would have looked like any weekend training exercise, except that they each wore protective surgical masks.

The ground trembled under Nate's boots. Five-ton troop

carriers rumbled past with monotonous regularity, one every twenty seconds, their massive six-by-six rugged terrain tires chewing up the road in much the same way the logging trucks masticated the government-built access roads.

The National Guardsmen would require scores of trucks, figured Nate. At the rate they flowed into the valley from the south and northeast, he estimated the population of the Thunder Peak Wilderness was about to double. The huge three-axle, six-wheeled, olive drab trucks looked like vertebrae in a great camouflage-painted snake serpentining toward a high country rendezvous, the part-time soldiers individual scales on the great military beast.

It was a well-equipped snake. There were cranes, oilers, trenchers, and razor-wire stretchers. It didn't take a veteran to recognize the hardware of a military action vs. a simple crowd control operation. The Guard was prepared for more than patrolling the Thunder Peak entrance. With what they were carrying with them, it looked like they could construct two or three concentration camp-style enclosures.

The next section of the convoy passing Nate included half a dozen prime movers, each with 16 troops in its back bed, and towing a Bradley Fighting Vehicle on a low boy trailer.

What were *they* for, he wondered. Did the planners in Sacramento know something the locals didn't yet know?

Nate tried not to dwell on how much trouble mixing thousands of committed believers with weekend warriors could stir up.

A Humvee pulled out of line and stopped beside him in the road. The Army lieutenant riding shotgun was a career man, not from California. Nate noticed his paratrooper's pins and airborne shoulder patch right away.

"Good day, Sheriff. I'm Colonel Walker, here to supervise this operation."

"Airborne. You slumming, Colonel? Or is there something about this operation that I need to know?"

Walker flashed his best West Point smile. "Nothing special, Sheriff. Routine police action. We'll keep folks outside the woods and have ourselves a good training exercise is the way I see it."

"You normally carry cranes, trenchers and all these occupation type vehicles on a training exercise?" asked Nate, trying to sound casual.

The colonel eyed the Sheriff more closely, tempered his smile and offered as much civility to this country tin badge as he was willing to give for the moment. As far as he was concerned, he controlled Longwood and the Thunder Peak Wilderness already. Any pleasantries were gifts from the superior occupying force. "That would fall under the heading of 'need to know.' You understand," he leaned forward and squinted at Nate's nametag, "Deputy Stimson."

A squad of four sergeants, all paratroopers, pulled up. The driver saluted the Colonel. "Standard picket, rotated four by four, Colonel?"

"Double it, sergeant."

The Sergeant's eyebrows lifted and waited for more of an explanation.

"That's all," Walker said firmly.

One of the sergeants in back exited the Hummer, began directing traffic in crisp confident movements, peeling every other transport off to the left behind the airborne sergeants.

"We've got it from here, Sheriff," said Walker. "I'm sure you've got plenty to do." With that, his vehicle sped off to the assembly point.

Nate stood dumbfounded for a few moments as trucks roared past him to the left and to the right.

"Clear, sir!" shouted the sergeant who had taken his place.

Nate weaved his way between the green giants back to his truck. The road was so packed with military traffic he couldn't get through. He cut across a shelf of grazing land and down a twenty-foot slope to a one lane back road that took him along the Thunder Peak Wilderness perimeter. Stopping every fifty feet, he stapled a fresh 'WARNING – DO NOT TRESPASS by order of Tulare County Sheriff' sign to a fence post or tree trunk.

The squall blew through just in time to clear the skies for Officer John Michaels' shift with his partner Chase Ingram. By the time they arrived at Sylvan Pass above Twin Lakes on Route 180, the worst of the morning's foul weather had moved east and the next front wasn't due until later in the afternoon. The waters on the lake below were still choppy and confused, but weren't boiling white like they had earlier in the morning and would again before the day was over.

While driving through Piute Pass, Michaels glimpsed three separate storm cells leaving the area, blowing east like great lumbering eighteenth century warships, canvas flying, plundering the sparsely settled Plains and leaving a mess in their wake.

A few power lines were down, but they'd be up again in a couple of hours. In the meantime, Michaels' and Ingram's job was to monitor every vehicle into the Thunder Peak Wilderness area from the southwest, warn individuals about the possible dangers in the area, check plates, cite drivers under the influence of alcohol or drugs, maybe snare a fugitive from justice, and otherwise show the shield early. It was important that the flood of protesters, camp followers and the curious understand that they were in California – the Golden State - and were expected to behave themselves.

They didn't anticipate much business today given the weather and the traffic stop's location. Sylvan Pass was a long drive from anywhere. It was also the choke point for traffic filtering northwest, but there was so little of anything for hundreds of miles east and south that Michaels and Ingram didn't expect much more than local ranchers, hermits, and truckers partial to long stretches of solitude.

So when they crested the pass and slowed at the turnaround, they were surprised to see summer-level traffic stretching as far as the horizon.

"This the right place, John?" asked Ingram irritably.

"This is it, all right."

"W'shoot, partner, I was hoping for some quiet time out here in the back of beyond. There must be, what, twenty, twenty-five vehicles a mile on that road."

Hardly a significant traffic load, but in this place it might as well have been rush hour on Manhattan's Roosevelt Drive.

"What's going on? Have they got rock bands playing up there? Some kinda California Woodstock or somethin'?"

"Call it," said Michaels.

"Tails," said Ingram.

Michaels flipped the coin and showed heads. "I'm up first," he announced, claiming the first shift. He would talk with drivers while Chase checked licenses against the watch sheet.

He swerved and parked the car across the northbound lane, leaving room for vehicles to pass on the shoulder after coming to a full stop. They retrieved the safety cones from the trunk, which

Ingram positioned in the north lane with flares to alert drivers.

Michaels let the first trucker through after saying howdy. He was a former teammate from high school football. The next car was a rental sedan, the driver a power tool salesman on his way to Pinehurst with a trunk full of sample boxes and promotional drill giveaways. Michaels compared the salesman's face and profile against the watch sheet attached to his clipboard. Eleven fugitives were identified by photos and descriptions provided by the FBI. Another three were identified by sketches and two of California's own special cases completed the page of people for whom the California State Police were looking. No other faces came close to the salesman's, decided Michaels.

No, he wasn't going anywhere farther north than Squaw Valley and then south to Orange Cove, Reedley and Visalia. He offered the officers free drill samples, but they declined. Ingram gave Michaels the nod that his license plate number was clean and Michaels directed the man to move along, politely wishing him a good afternoon.

The next vehicle to approach was a sports utility truck, a 1993 Ford Explorer that looked twice its age. Michaels guessed that it had one more California winter left in it, assuming the owner nursed it through with a gallon of Bondo, fresh tires and shocks. The gravel the Highway Department used on winter roads left its windshield and one headlight cracked.

When the Explorer slowed, Michaels saw it was occupied by five college-age kids - three males, two females - probably from the University of California downstate. Yep, he saw the parking decal on the windshield. They said they were on their way to Longwood to see what the commotion was all about. Michaels gave the driver's license and registration a perfunctory review, then bent down to look over the truck interior. There was no smell of alcohol or pot, although there were two cases of Bud longnecks in the back, still shrink-wrapped.

"How long do you plan to be in the Sequoia/Thunder Peak Wilderness area?" asked Michaels as he discreetly checked their faces against his watch sheet.

"Two, maybe three days," the driver said.

"Classes start again Monday," added the young man in the front passenger seat.

"We'd prefer you not add to the problems up there," Michaels tried to discourage them.

"Nothing like this ever happens in California, officer. Stockton Rodeo Days is the biggest rodeo I've ever seen and it doesn't compare with this," offered the driver. "We've got to see it, you know?"

"There's some concern about air quality up there. You'll need protective facemasks."

A young woman in the back seat displayed a package of surgical facemasks. "Saw it on the news. We're ready," she assured him.

Michaels glanced over at the cruiser and saw his partner with the radio microphone in his left hand nod. The license number checked out. There were no outstanding tickets or reports of the truck being stolen.

"Alrighty then, kids. You have a good time up there and obey the speed limits, y'hear," he waved them on. The Explorer pulled away loudly. Michaels added *new muffler* to the list of repairs the truck needed.

A few moments passed without another vehicle. The officers saw a pickup and a compact behind that approaching from a mile away. Just enough time to radio in the all clear status at the quarter hour and warm his toes by the cruiser's heater.

The truck was a rancher hauling a steer to a ranch in Pahaska. He'd be back this way before mid afternoon if the buyer's check had the right amount of zeroes.

Behind him was a three-year old gray Toyota, okay condition like the other 10,000 economy cars in this part of the state. They weren't flashy, but they were affordable and reliable. Nothing remarkable about this one, either; black vinyl interior, four on the floor, worn winter tires, the usual dings. The driver was a redheaded male about thirty years old, slight build, eyeglasses.

"Anything wrong, Officer?"

"License and registration?"

"Where are you headed today, Mr. Brach?"

"Longwood," the driver answered pleasantly.

"Not a good time to be in that area," Michaels said as he jotted down the driver's license number on his pad and scanned the watch sheet. None of the photos matched. One of the sketched suspects looked to be about the right age, give or take five years. There was no name, just an alias: 'Gabriel the Fox.' The drawing showed an intense, alert individual that reminded Michaels of a fox.

He compared it with the driver of the Toyota, who was bookish and introverted, lacking any of the intensity of the sketched suspect.

"May I ask what brings you to Longwood," Michaels asked in his most casual, lonesome-cop-stuck-out-in-the-middle-of-nowhere way.

"I'm interning with Case-Kaiser – the forest management company?"

"You're a graduate student then?"

Brach nodded, "Forestry, U of W," and adjusted his eyeglasses. "Go Grizzlies!" he smiled.

Michaels looked over to Ingram, got the nod and returned Brach's license and registration. "Good luck to you, Mr. Brach. Have a good day and watch your speed," Michaels waved him on.

Brach drove around the cruiser and accelerated north. He waited until he was a mile from the checkpoint before removing the eyeglasses and tossing them onto the passenger seat. His dark eyes focused intently on the road ahead.

37

LONGWOOD

"Whoever goes in there – woodcutter, *Earth Rebirther* or one of us – will disturb the spore," repeated Lotte to the small group gathered in Ben's great room at the ranch.

"And once airborne, there's a danger that the wind will carry it all the way to Chicago," added Nate Stimson.

"And the Ohio Valley and the entire Atlantic Seaboard," Ben said quietly. "Millions could die."

"What do we know?" asked Lotte, picking up some chalk and writing on Mary Margaret's old Playskool chalkboard. "Hypothesis: earthstar mushroom spore kills anyone who inhales it."

Everyone nodded.

"Conclusion:" she continued, "kill the mushroom,--"

"How?" asked Ben.

"It's probably impossible to find every killer mushroom, so those areas of the woods where we do find them will need to be destroyed," stated Lotte sadly.

"Can't we just go up there and pick them?"

"They may have dispersed. They could be spread throughout the entire Wilderness by now, waiting underground to sprout."

Everyone fell silent. The stark, hopeless facts descended over the room like a heavy blanket.

"No, there has to be a way," Ben thought aloud. "What kills mushrooms?" he persisted.

"The mushroom cap you see above ground is just the visible part of an organism that grows underground until the time comes for sexual development and reproduction. It's an erection. The main body of the fungi is in the mycelium underground. So even if you kill the mushroom above ground, you don't get the fungi underneath. It might grow back," Lotte's voice climbed in frustration.

"Can we spray the Peak with fungicide?"

"We could talk to the National Guard about spraying from one of their helicopters," suggested Nate.

"It won't make any difference," Vin der Root entered and stood in the doorway.

"It might," Lotte reasoned.

"NO!" shouted Vin, now red-faced and perspiring.

"What is it?" asked Ben, trying to understand.

"It won't work," der Root spat out the words one at a time, struggling for control.

"Why not, Vin?" demanded Lotte.

der Root stared at a terrible knowledge only he could see. "How soon until the first freeze?" he asked.

"What?"

"Dammit, when is the first freeze up on the Peak?"

"Couple weeks," responded Nate.

"A freeze will hold the mushroom's spore disbursal mechanism in suspension."

"How do you know?"

der Root didn't answer.

"Will a freeze kill it?"

He looked at Lotte, nodded no, and spoke slowly, "I completed the work we started at Chembotan. I engineered a biogenetic weapon . . ."

Lotte stared at him, struggling to grasp the full impact of her friend's confession. "The Earthstar? The mushroom?"

"For the DOD," he added and looked at the floor.

"DOD?!" wailed Lotte, now on her feet. "What do you mean 'work *we* started'? I didn't design a toxic fungi!"

229

"You researched how it was possible and that some would find it valuable."

Lotte paled as she gazed at him in utter horror.

"Chembotan's silent partner was the DOD," he continued in a monotone.

"Department of Defense," asked Ben?

"They saw merit in Lotte's theory: different categories of biological warfare agents – incapacitators as well as killers. With next to no incubation period, FX could be an ideal killer: neutralizing an enemy force before battle, and eliminate the risk of friendly casualties or the wartime atrocities associated with modern ethnic conflict. The Army thought it could win wars without having to send in troops."

"But you knew what they would do with it! You knew how much I feared what could happen!" Lotte threw up her hands. "Why, Vin? Why!?"

"You were always brilliant," he looked at her, suddenly older. "I had to work ten times as hard as you just to keep up. You abandoned that line of research. It was an opportunity . . . I combined two heretofore-unidentified genes in the *earthstar* genome, incorporated a trigger to emphasize its clotting properties by a factor of 1,200."

Ben and Nate observed in amazement. Lotte and der Root were talking about manipulating Nature itself like rational Frankensteins.

"The Army also commissioned another iteration of the FX bacteria injected with carbon nanotubes as a kind of—"

"Chaff," Lotte finished for him.

"Research showed that carbon nanofilaments or nanotubes confused minor electrochemical impulses in the body in the same way that chaff had been used at short circuiting power grids in Baghdad and Belgrade. It was designated FXX." der Root seemed to unfold as he confessed, telling them everything he knew, freeing himself.

"Wouldn't that create a permanent dead zone?" asks Ben.

"No," said Lotte, realizing that her worst fear – her genetic doomsday theory – had come to life. "Mushrooms have a short cycle that doesn't survive summer heat or winter freezes." She looked back to der Root, "Can they reproduce?"

"Doubtful," he answered.

"It's the perfect weapon: lethal yet quickly self-disarming,"

Lotte explained to the others.

"What happens to the carbon," asked Nate. "Does it remain in the area like unexploded land mines?"

"With death of the organism and subsequent decay, it breaks down naturally and adapts to the native local chemistry," he explained.

There was silence for several moments. Inexplicably, all eyes in the room turned to Lotte for some sign of what to do next.

"Is that all?" she asked.

"Itamarati—" der Root choked on the words and swallowed hard.

"No," Lotte mumbled involuntarily.

"It was a secret test against rebel paramilitaries."

"What paramilitaries?" roared Lotte. "There was no rebellion in Brazil!"

"They told me-" but he couldn't finish. "It went all wrong and instead killed peasant farmers, and . . ."

"And CHARLEY, you bastard!" screamed Lotte. She held her head and stammered as the full impact of Itamarati crashed in on her. He had completed her theoretical research and killed with it! Her mind raced, looking for holes in his version of events. "But the deaths stopped when the cutting stopped."

"Coincidence. A heat wave that killed the mushrooms coincided with our visit. We were lucky."

"'Lucky,' you sonofabitch!"

"The winds. They could have carried the spore hundreds of miles and killed every living thing in its path."

"It did," der Root said wearily. "There was a plume of death extending from Itamarati, carried by the westerly tropical winds across the Andes all the way to the Galapagos Islands. The mysterious deaths aboard the cruise ship *Nieuw Ryndam*? The die-off in the Galapagos? It all traced back to the hybrid earthstars released in Itamarati," his voice hollow with self-loathing.

A wail rose from Lotte's shattered heart. She lunged across the room at der Root, catching him squarely under the jaw. He levitated and flew backwards. Her fury couldn't be contained. All of the grief and self-doubt and longing that were her loss infused her with terrible power. "While I'm on the cross for my theories, you stood by and let them crucify me. YOU were *promoted*." She began to cry, "you let Charley die!"

"I loved her too, Lotte. Before Brazil, we were -- I thought she and I --"

Lotte turned and covered her ears, not wanting to know his last terrible secret.

"I had no choice," he turned to Ben. "The people I dealt with were not like other departments. Once in, you couldn't quit the club. Eventually the DOD withdrew funding, a California biotech conglomerate named CoGen bought Chembotan and the FXX strain was stored away somewhere in Hell.

"After Itamarati, I tried to find a way to undo the damage I had done. There was no way. They're too powerful. Eventually, I smuggled the FXX strain to *Earth Rebirth!* who promised to expose it to the media."

"Why didn't YOU expose what you'd done?!" Lotte demanded. She knew the answer but needed to hear her betrayer say it aloud.

He looked at her, struggling with his last ounce of self-respect and admitted the worst of it. "I wanted to keep my position at the CDC."

Silence again descended over the group.

"Why are you telling me now?" asked Lotte wearily.

He told them about the mushroom pizza and the note warning him to stay out of the Thunder Peak Wilderness. It was a threat: 'keep FXX to yourself or die.'

"Who threatened you?" asked Nate.

der Root pulled the note from his pocket and held it up.

"Fox," Nate said. "So it *is* Gabriel."

"I couldn't let any more die." der Root looked to Lotte, Ben, Nate and back to Lotte for recognition that he was still human, but no one gave him what he sought from them.

Earth Rebirth! had seeded the Thunder Peak Wilderness with the FXX strain. In their radical attempt to save the old growth trees, they were willing to kill. Yet, even they couldn't comprehend the scale of death that threatened the Midwest and Northeast states.

"I have to stop them," der Root mumbled, getting to his feet.

Nate stood, put on his hat. "I have to get out the word to the Mayor, the Governor, the National Guard. Can't let those kids go in there against this thing."

"You're right," agreed Ben. "Call me if I can help. I'll try to figure something out with Lotte. She'll know what to do next." He walked Nate to his truck.

"Lotte, I'm sorry," der Root stood before her with no more secrets. "If I could take it back--"

"You can't. I can't either." She turned to the window and looked out at the gnarled oak, the forlorn carriage. "She never told me."

"She didn't want you to know. She didn't think you would understand. It just didn't mean anything to her. It was you she loved."

You're wise beyond your years when it comes to science, Lotte Keene, she remembered Charley telling her the night before she died, *but you know nothing about what moves people.*

She pictured Charley with him and something deep inside her broke again. He turned to leave.

"What are you going to do," she asked, staring out the window.

"What's right." He walked to his rental car and steered toward Thunder Peak.

38

THUNDER PEAK

High on Thunder Peak's forested shoulders, the storm's winds gained force. Branches cracked and flew like shrapnel above 6,500 feet elevation. Dense stands of Fir and Spruce that had stood together against the elements, genes combining and recombining over millennia to accentuate their strengths and mask their weaknesses, and accustomed to the rip of 50 mph and higher winds, stoically endured the punishment. They had adapted by sinking deeper roots and, with the help of the arid climate, grew denser and more potent than any other stand in the lower forty-eight. This storm was shaping up to be a clash of forces unseen in Longwood since the 1947 Blow in which more than a thousand cattle and 22 Californians lost their lives.

While the contest of earth and wind approached its climax on the mountain, the crowd gathered below squatted in the purgatory between frequently torrential rain and foul muddy misery. Pilgrims were encamped under every available tree, truck and tarpaulin. Children sought protection under their mother's watchful arms. Pet dogs endured in the lee of tents. Men planted themselves under brims pulled low and stoically waited for some signal, some clear order.

For Vin der Root the realization that the order might never come came behind the wheel of his car on the rush to Thunder Peak. There was no epiphany, no sudden shift of the feeling in his bones. If his moment was to come, then he must give the order himself, he realized. The glimpse of sudden comprehension in Lotte's eyes was the trigger; now he was the bullet on a just trajectory. He would do right without placing himself in the equation, the usual risk/benefit calculation. He would save life. That was his mission. What followed didn't matter. Life was his single purpose.

Rounding a bend, he braked to avoid hitting a knot of horses fraying and grouping on the macadam. The rain had stopped but the road was still wet. The sound of the horses hooves rolled back nervously to him in the dry warm lap of his rental car. He could feel their crackling power transmitted from iron-shoes into the road where it vibrated through the brake pedal and up his leg. A young boy in a poncho and a wide black Stetson waved a stick with a red handkerchief tied to it to catch drivers' attention: horses have right of way in California. He glanced over his shoulder at der Root's car, jiggered his rein and called out to his charges' alert ears. The horses responded by shouldering off the road and into the shelter of a pine-lined arroyo.

der Root stomped on the accelerator. The rear tires spun uselessly and the car's rear end spasmed off the road. He forced himself to calm down, took a deep breath and tried easing the power to his now gravel-bound rear wheels. They bit through the gravel; found solid ground and pushed the car back onto the two-lane. He pushed down and was back up to speed in time to see a break in the sky over the Peak.

He saw the sign for the Thunder Peak Wilderness and felt his pulse jump. Just one mile farther. He had no idea what he would do when he got there. He had to get past the mobs, somehow break through the National Guard patrolling the perimeter and stop those *Earth Rebirth!* kids. That was enough for now.

The road ahead suddenly lifted and disappeared to the right. He braked but the tires wouldn't bite. The car began to slide sideways. He steered into the skid and the car righted itself but he was still hurtling toward the chasm. Pumping the brakes, the car started to slow, giving him time to see that a flash flood had filled an arroyo, overwhelmed the drainage pipe, and taken forty feet of the road down slope.

The car finally shuddered to a stop with two feet to spare. Turbulent flash flood waters climbed ten feet as he watched and were headed directly for him. He leaped out the door and sprinted back the way he had come for fifty yards before turning to look. When he did, the car and another 100 feet of the road were gone.

He climbed higher up the mountain where the runoff was limited to scores of fordable rushing streams. The next mile's trek over dense undergrowth and scree slowed but could not stall his progress. He willingly absorbed the sharp edges, thorn punctures, and inhospitable terrain as the beginning of his penance.

Before long, he was soaked through, scuffed, and bleeding. When he crested the rise that led into the shallow valley outside the Wilderness entrance, a land-locked sea of mud-bound humanity greeted him. What yesterday had been a raucous encampment was now a new mud city sprung overnight like mushrooms in storm-scrubbed air. He skidded down the slope and waded into its waters, pushing and shoving his way across the valley in the direction of the entrance. That was where the *Earth Rebirth!* leaders were encamped despite that location's vulnerability to harassment by loggers, locals and the National Guard.

He had to hand it to them. They lived their beliefs; conflict and real bodily danger be damned.

The first pair of Guardsmen he encountered were posted between the neatly organized *Earth Rebirth!* compound and an angry logger's bivouac of lean-tos, wood smoke and testosterone.

The guardsmen were kids with guns caught between two enemies ready to spring at each other and eyed der Root warily as he approached. His torn clothes and bleeding scratches told them what they thought they needed to know and they stopped him before he could get inside the *Earth Rebirth!* encampment.

"I'm a doctor," he explained patiently and flashed his CDC ID, which they read with interest. Up close, he saw their leather brown necks, premature wrinkles at the corners of their eyes and white teeth. These were California-raised young bucks, as out of place in green camouflage fatigues as the *Earth Rebirth!* activists in the remotest Sierra's no nonsense terrain.

"You'll need this, Doctor," the shorter one said as he handed him a thin package emblazoned with a Red Cross. He opened it and shook out an emergency poncho. It wasn't much, but it would keep him from getting any wetter than he was already. "A cold can kill a man up here, sir," explained the other one.

der Root thanked them and slipped it over his head.

"Doctor, the Colonel may have use of your services before long," said the tall one.

"Some of them radicals got past us and are up there," the other glanced over his shoulder at the Peak.

"Which way did they go?" asked der Root.

"Straight that-a-way," the tall one pointed to the right of the road. "Their friends created a diversion by picking a fight with the woodcutters over there. By the time we got it under control, they were over the fence—"

"Three of them. Saw their back is all. They were fast."

"I see," der Root studied the route they took in. "How long ago?"

"Forty-five minutes."

"Thanks, fellas," he said, now sure what to do.

"You'll be in the area, just in case we find 'em?"

"Sure." He entered the *Earth Rebirth!* camp and blended into the crowds.

The tents were four season rated and obviously well used. How many exotic places had that yellow expedition tent seen in its career of sheltering faithful environmentalists from snow, wind and cold - the North Slope during protests to save reindeer from oilmen? Patagonia while protecting the right whale from Japanese harpoons? The California Headwaters Forest to shield the mighty redwoods from Case-Kaiser's saws?

Activists were gathered in groups of three and four, studying topos, re-checking rappelling lines, carabiners, pitons, and packing dehydrated rations with impressive proficiency. Clearly these were veterans of campaigns he had only read about.

He wanted to find someone who could tell him more, give him a clue as to the trespassers' destination in the Wilderness. He asked every huddled group and got a dozen variations on the same theme: 'high as they can climb,' 'deep as they can penetrate,' 'far as the cause will take them.'

He wasn't getting anywhere. These were true believers. He climbed up on the hood of a pickup truck and shouted down to the *Earth Rebirth!* activists. "Listen to me! You have to stop what you're doing! You can't let any more of your people into the woods."

A few looked up to see who he was yelling at. When they got the gist of what he had to say, they dismissed him and returned to their preparations. There were people haranguing the crowd from truck hoods and roofs, fence posts and stepladders all over the place. He was one more evangelist trying to change minds that were already made up.

der Root spun around to address the woodcutters, too. "I'm an epidemiologist from the CDC in Atlanta. A virus hunter. There's a deadly virus in those woods that kills anyone who gets near it. If the wind turns and blows from the south, then the spores carrying the virus may blow through here. Get out! Go home! And if you can't do that, then at least cover your faces!"

The loggers, the soldiers, and scores of other passersby glanced up at him, decided he was just another radical, and went back to what they were doing.

A slim young man emerged from one of the tents and paused when he saw der Root. He stood straight in his foul weather gear, a curious blend of academic, aesthete and, oddly enough, military. He smiled openly at der Root when he caught his eye. Thinking he knew more than the others, der Root went to him and asked again, "the three who got inside, do you know where they're going exactly?"

The man didn't answer right off. He just kept smiling at der Root, comfortable with his own pace of things. "To the heart of the Thunder Peak old growth," he finally said. "To glory."

"We've got to stop them! They have no idea what's up there!"

"No, we've got to stop--" he pointed to the loggers and beyond to Longwood, "THEM."

He pulled back the hood of his parka and revealed waves of red hair. Looking directly at der Root, his dark eyes flashed. "Rejoice, Doctor, you made this glorious day possible." With that, he turned, padded into the throng, and vanished like a fox ...

der Root tried to follow, but it was useless. He was ill suited to the demands of a chase in the wild. The Fox was fleet, secretive, and intimately knowledgeable about his world, almost magical in his power of escape.

As der Root tested the perimeter either side of the entrance, he remained hopeful of seeing Gabriel again. He didn't realistically expect to, and he couldn't delay going after the three who were already inside, but hope still burned. A loud explosion sounded from the crowds below, followed by a thunderous cheer. He looked over to see a plume of black smoke – a petroleum-based fire – curl into the sky. Someone set a car alight and its gas tank had exploded. Responsible people in the crowd moved to dowse the fire and care for the injured. This included the two National Guardsmen der Root met earlier. He watched them charge the center of the crowd – this was his chance!

He took one look to make sure they were preoccupied and hurdled the gate to the road on the other side. He ran as fast as his tired, aching legs would carry him off to the right of the road, through elephant grass and into the woods. Only when he was more than fifty yards inside did he stop, duck behind a tree and look to see if he'd been observed.

He had. The *Earth Rebirthers* and loggers alike were on their feet and cheering him on though he was sure they could no longer see him. The guardsmen were nowhere to be seen yet. He pivoted and continued running up the mountain.

His lungs burned and his head swam, but he didn't permit himself to rest. The three had a forty-five minute head start. Fortunately for him, their tracks were clearly visible in the wet earth. This encouraged him beyond pain and he pushed himself harder still. After ten minutes, he was spent, but wouldn't rest, he slowed to a brisk walk, and kept going in what he hoped was a straight line.

The wind seemed blunter in wet air as he climbed, more like Georgia than what he had experienced so far in California. The woods smelled good between the rains. Clean, strong, fertile. Not like death at all.

He felt a vague and distant vertigo of the challenge of righting so many wrongs. Here among the long suffering matriarchs he felt lonelier than ever before. He wished for a partner – for Lotte and Charley as before - someone with whom he could bluff strength, pose the kind of character he admired in others but couldn't locate within himself.

After an hour more, he was above 7,000 feet, he guessed. He arrived in a dense stand of cathedral giant firs. The trail led directly into the cool darkness. He paused to listen for them and heard voices carry faintly from inside the stand. It was hard to tell how far.

Approaching silently, he followed the sound of the voices and came upon them in a small clearing. They were marveling at the great trees around and over them, alternately laughing, exclaiming, and even dancing. He felt like he was spying on woodland nymphs.

When he stepped into the open, they welcomed him.

"You see?" the middle one said to him with an ecstatic smile, "the trees and the woods are protecting us." She was a nymph, utterly innocent, observed der Root.

"You don't understand, it's not the trees that are dangerous," he said, trying to remain calm, "it's those." He pointed at a ring of ping-pong ball sized earthstar mushrooms circling the great trees.

One of the young men brightened and bent down to examine the mushrooms.

"Don't touch it!" warned der Root. "Don't disturb it in any way. It's poisonous."

"Earthstar?" Are you kidding?" the other man was incredulous. "Granted they don't taste very good, but they're not poisonous. No way!"

"Those aren't earthstars, not the kind you're familiar with anyway," der Root tried to explain.

"I think they're pretty, like little lights, like miniature luminari!" marveled the woman. "Let's dance, Jeff!" She wrapped herself in his arms and they flew off around the tree, weaving between the earthstars as they spun and twirled.

"NO!" shouted der Root from outside the ring, but they ignored him, surrendering themselves to what could only be described as pure joy. Around and around they danced, their toes just missing the earthstars.

Then der Root and the third man saw it simultaneously: Jeff's toe slipped on a wet patch and slid sideways. He recovered and flew on, but it was enough. They were downwind of the disturbed earthstar when the spores reached them. They missed a turn and tumbled to the ground frozen in each others' arms.

The third man gasped, "Jeff? Karen?" He looked at der Root, turned, and ran out of the stand.

"My God," screamed der Root as he looked at the beautiful young couple in their death embrace. Two more sacrifices to his hubris. Then at the dozens of earthstars glowing white in the darkness. He had committed the worst possible crime: he challenged God. He created a killer without a soul.

He walked deeper into the stand of giants, sat down against the largest, most majestic tree, and imagined what would happen. He imagined he heard chain saws buzzing in the distance, their gas engines sputtering down as one logger after another stepped back to observe his tree turn to lumber, fall to the ground where steel jaws would drag it away for dismemberment in the Case-Kaiser abattoir.

der Root said a prayer for Charley, then another for Lotte, and finally, one for his own soul.

The puffball looked so innocent, its eggshell white flesh pure against the forest's dark green shadows. The product of a billion years of evolution, refined, optimized and . . . now corrupted by his genetic tinkering. It was life and death itself.

The weight of his betrayal crashed in on him. He couldn't abide being in his own skin.

39

THUNDER PEAK

As the threat from the spore grew, the civilian and military infrastructure's independence waned. The sense of impending crisis was palpable. Distinctions between state and federal governments disintegrated under the overwhelming instinct to herd, unify and follow. Unwilling to delay, Federal authorities authorized Phase One.

The command came through secure e-mail on the CINC CHADOW system. The Office of Strategic Services at the Pentagon instructed the 390th Tactical Fighter Squadron of the Air National Guard's 366th Wing based in Idaho to immediately target Thunder Peak in the Sequoia National Forest with napalm-B. Expect precise coordinates by telemetry enroute.

The Navy's program to recycle Vietnam-era bomb grade napalm was nearing completion, but limited stocks remained at several air bases. California forces were not ordered to destroy their own precious old-growth. The 390th, along with units from Nevada, were to drop what they had on a quarter-mile square area of the forest in a cross-hatch pattern to assure comprehensive coverage. The operation was code-named: THUNDERBOLT.

Colonel Easta wondered if his bosses, the Joint Chiefs, understood that they may have been used by *Blackbird.* He had made sure that the crisis in California appeared to be one more call for help from overwhelmed state and federal authorities, another blurring of the line between military and civilian responsibility. He coded the order Urgent for immediate action. The Joint Chiefs balked at first, but they approved when it became clear that there was no alternative. The local fire department didn't have the skills or equipment. The CDC was involved, so it was clearly a serious matter. Once again, that left the military to step in and perform a domestic mission. It ran against everything they had ever been trained as American soldiers to do, but what could they do? They approved the mission.

Four F-15C two-seat strike jets from the 390th Fighter Squadron – the Wild Boars - scrambled out of Mountain Home Air Force Base in Idaho, formed up north of Sequoia Falls, and set a course for Thunder Peak. The Wild Boars with the blue and orange tail colors would be the first strike in Operation Thunderbolt.

At the same time, eight F-16 Fighting Falcon superjets of Arizona's 162nd Fighter Squadron formed up south of Kingman and sped northwest for the short flight to Thunder Peak. Each was loaded with six 700-pound napalm-filled canisters hanging from its wings. The weight was hardly noticeable to the young pilots who reveled in the 25,000-lb thrust Pratt & Whitney F100 engines. Each man was in combat mode, not inclined to think much about the implications of what they were ordered to do: torch an American landmark. They were the leading edge of Phase One. Three more flights were scrambling behind them at two-minute intervals. Sixteen strike jets and more than 67,000 pounds of jellified fire in four waves, once, twice, three times, and, if necessary, a fourth.

If they questioned why they were about to destroy the magnificent Thunder Peak Wilderness, they kept their questions to themselves. It was part training and part curiosity. Thirty-year-old National Guard pilots flying twenty-year-old fighter jets didn't have many opportunities to apply their training in live fire exercises. By temperament, they were ready to first do the job and ask questions later. Right now, there was a job to do.

"Target is twelve miles out," Lt. Paul Rodriguez's husky voice sounded in the other crews' helmets. "I'm going in low with Bird

Dog on my wing. We'll release and take a left to get out of the way. Fisher and Rainman, you hang back for two minutes, just in case there's dry timber in there that goes hot. Then go in, drop tight and we'll go home."

"Roger that," came back three acknowledgements.

Rodriquez and Bird Dog began their descent, leveled out at five hundred feet over the forest, and armed their loads.

Below, Vin der Root heard multiple crashes in the forest canopy over his head. Then the roar of the escaping fighter jets reached him and he understood. Bombs crashed and splintered through high branches from several hundred yards on his left to within 100 yards of where he was standing. Birds squawked and cackled in panic, flying in every direction at once.

One of the bombs flashed and the air filled with pungent jelly. Der Root's nose stung from the harsh gasoline odor. One of the objects caught fire and jelly ignited wherever the flame found it, on tree trunks, on birds, and in mid-air.

Breaking into a run in the opposite direction, he strained to recall a cave or a hollow where he could evade the fire, but nothing came to him. Flame erupted everywhere the napalm found dry fuel, but there was more smoke than fire.

Suddenly, the canopy overhead splintered and thundered. The bombs were falling in an arc directly at him. He pivoted left and kept running. The powerful stench hurt his throat, his lungs, his skin. He dodged and weaved through patches of blazing forest floor. Then he saw it, a small cave in the side of a bank just ahead. He pounded toward it and dropped to all fours as the canopy exploded directly overhead.

It was a small cave with solid rock walls, large enough for a bear. der Root pulled his shirt up to cover his nose and mouth. The sticky brownish jelly caught fire and sputtered out in the damp undergrowth. Thunder Peak's storm induced wet microclimate was defeating the U.S. Air National Guard's incendiaries. All they accomplished was to foul the forest floor with napalm-B and fill the air with countless plumes of white smoke that lifted small amounts of ash, smoke and, he realized, spores high into the warming air.

Ben and Lotte were still arguing over which of them would risk their lives to obtain more samples of the killer earthstar when they arrived back at the clinic. Neither was winning.

It started when Lotte delivered her condolences to Ben and Mary Margaret as she left Alice's funeral. When Ben asked why she was rushing off, Lotte told him she needed to go back into the Thunder Peak Wilderness. Her game plan called for her to gather more samples for three important reasons:

One: verify the molecular and genetic composition of the mushroom,

Two: test possible antidotes against it, and

Three: prove the weapon's existence in the likely event that the people behind it would attempt to cover up their crime.

Ben insisted that he be the one to go instead; he had a personal stake in defeating the earthstar.

Neither questioned the need to pursue a way to fight the mushroom and the monsters behind it.

A quantity of the killer puffball mushrooms would be required for all of this. Three or four would do, but because the killer earthstars were indistinguishable from the non-toxic ones, five times that many in a rigorous sampling would have to be collected in the hopes of finding five-to-ten percent that were killers. She thought enough questions remained unanswered to warrant remaining quiet about her plan. That meant keeping the grunt work to herself. He disagreed. And so they had debated it all the way into town.

He was right; the threat was so great and she was the only qualified scientist on site. If she were lost, injured or struck down by the mushroom, then Longwood and the United States east of the Sierras wouldn't stand a chance.

And she was right; she was the one qualified to identify the earthstar, to execute a scientific sampling, and she didn't have a child for whom she was responsible.

"Whoever is behind this is dangerous. They kill for a living, so they'll have no qualms eliminating one more problem," Lotte argued forcefully.

"But that's my point. YOU'RE the single person with the skills, the facts, the names who can nail these assholes. Stay out of sight. Fight this invisible monster as only you are qualified to do. In the big picture, I'm expendable. Let me make a difference."

"You have Mary Margaret to think about," she reiterated.

"I *am* thinking about her," he answered passionately.

"Don't you see? I'm responsible for all of this."

"No."

"Yes. If not for me, Vin der Root would never have engineered the earthstar."

"That's it, *he* engineered it! He's the one responsible for Sara Hart, Lars Broder, my mother, all of them!"

"From *my* concept, *my* founding research. It's *my* fault and *my* responsibility," she pounded her chest. Tears welled and she lost her voice. After a minute, she finally managed to speak. "Ben, enough. Don't fight me on this."

"Dammit Lotte. We're both right. I can't go, and you can't go." Without waiting for her to agree or disagree, he pulled a coin from his jeans pocket and flipped it end over end into the air. "Call it, Doctor."

Caught off guard, Lotte reflexively called, "heads."

He took away the hand covering the coin. America's proud eagle gleamed from the quarter.

"This is an emergency announcement from Governor Wade Prentice and the United States National Guard," a crisp authoritative voice on Ben's truck radio broke through his thoughts. "You are instructed to evacuate the area surrounding Thunder Peak including a twenty mile-radius from Longwood to Roaring Fork. There is no reason for alarm. This is a precautionary measure only. However, under the Emergency Powers Act, if you are found in violation of this order, you are subject to arrest, confinement and fines up to $100,000. Thank you for your cooperation."

Three flights of four jets soared at low altitude over the Wilderness from different directions as if to reinforce the government's message as Ben drove up the mountain. Smoke started to rise. The military was overreacting. They didn't have a clue about what was at stake up there. Smoke. "Dammit," he spat at the departing jets. "The spore may be in that smoke, morons!"

He disciplined himself to walk steadily when he entered the shaded stand in the TyChem 10,000 Level A suit. It took all his willpower. The urge to run was nearly overwhelming, but he understood how precarious his layer of thin yellow impermeable plastic composite was. Although woven of tough rip-stop material, there were sharp rocks and pointed branches everywhere, ready to puncture the only protection he had from certain death if the spore were airborne in the disturbed air.

The sound of the stiff fabric wrinkling as Ben moved combined with the staccato beat of rain on his hood made it impossible to hear anything outside his protective cocoon. If that bear or any other animal wanted to attack him, he wouldn't know until he was on the ground, too late to fight back.

The droplets on his suit were not rain. He recognized the brown jelly as it spotted his face shield, sleeves and legs: napalm-B. That's what the jets had been doing. He tried to brush off the gook. It only spread in greasy smears.

He walked steadily, stopping and surveying every ten paces. Visibility was marginal as the face screen fogged over in the cool forest air. He had taped over the suit's one-way vents. His respiration formed rain on the inside of the protective face screen. It was impossible to wipe away the mist, all he could do was jump up and down to help gravity clear the screen. By the time he entered the old growth stand, his clothes were soaked through, his boots filling with condensation.

The eighteen-pound sample case that seemed to get heavier as he climbed now felt like it weighed a hundred pounds. Every instinct for self-preservation protested the extra weight hanging from his shoulder.

His heart was thundering in his chest when he saw the two bodies entwined on the ground beneath the great conifer. He wanted to run to them, help them, but he had seen the bizarre symptoms before. It was too late. From where he stood, he peered at the bodies, the tree, the adjoining trees, and the scant low growth. There were no dead animals in view. A small shape darted past his head, soared to a branch above the dead couple and watched him with interest. Then he saw them. It was the pattern that drew his attention. Small white puffballs regularly spaced around the trunk of the tree.

He pivoted and saw the same pattern around the next largest tree. And the next.

Scrutinizing the ground ahead, he stepped carefully over the ring of earthstars and examined the couple. They gazed at one another, struck dead at the happiest moment of their lives. It was another sight that would haunt him for the rest of his days, he was certain.

Taking out a note pad, he sketched the scene from a bird's eye view, the tree at the center, the bodies nearby, the mushrooms in a great circle. Setting down the sample case, he flipped the latches, pulled out the top tray of vials and jars and took the largest specimens first. Cutting each off at the base of the stem, he carefully placed it whole in the jar, tightened the lid, and noted the order in which it was collected, its location, condition, and the time. He moved quickly to the next specimen, carefully looked at the ground around it, and planned his approach. Cutting, gingerly placing it in the jar, and tightening, he found an effective rhythm. In thirty minutes, he filled and labeled sixteen jars. He then moved to the second largest tree and repeated the sequence twelve times – every other specimen; half that number from around the third largest tree.

Huffing from the exertion and tension, he took a moment to breathe. Even the sound of his breathing suddenly repelled him. It was a sound of life in the presence of horrifying death. It was also the mechanism of their death. Suddenly, his panicking senses became certain that his suit could not protect him. Nothing was stronger than the sight of absolute, super-unatural death before him.

Pushing down harder on the fear that wanted to dominate him, he placed what he decided would be the last specimen jar in the sample case and latched it. Taking the roll of chemically treated sterile tape from the case's shoulder strap, he sealed the case in a neat web, covering every seam in the case. Then he wrapped more tape around the box, obsessed with locking the demon in the box without any possibility for escape.

He shouldered the sample case and started to leave, then remembered that three *Earth Rebirth!* activists had entered the Thunder Peak Wilderness. While every fiber of his being commanded him to leave *now*, he pushed himself to look around for the third.

Walking in the otherwise inspirational cathedral of old growth trees was like tiptoeing through a minefield, every step potentially life-ending. He moved slowly, scanning the ground ahead and to the sides as he walked. Moving in this way for forty yards, he saw more great trees, each girdled by innocuous-looking puffball mushrooms. The trees got larger and larger, the trunks now forty feet around. There was no sign of the third activist but scuffed footprints of someone running out of the old growth stand and to the south. He followed the footprints until they disappeared on an immense stone outcrop.

Ben turned around and headed back, intent now on his own escape. He was almost back to the sample case, it was just fifty yards up ahead, when he saw der Root on the next ridge staggering, obviously stunned. "You crazy bastard," Ben said, his voice unnaturally loud inside his suit.

There was nothing more he could do. der Root was as good as dead. Ben was too if he didn't get out of the woods FAST and down the mountain.

He looked up in some instinctive notion that God might be watching. Instead, he saw swept-wing B-1 bombers pulling away. Four guided bombs fell in a wide circle around them and burst, forming large mushroom cap-shaped clouds . . . Fuel Air Explosives!

Ben turned to see der Root coming to the same realization and staring in disbelief back at him. der Root cupped his hands to his mouth and shouted, but the distance was too great. He pointed wildly. Ben turned and saw the small lake below and to his right. He dropped the sample case and ran toward the water as fast as the suit permitted. The stench of the fuel was overwhelming. He imagined it dissolving his Tyvek suit.

Fuel air explosives were more powerful than conventional high-explosive munitions. Anyone who watched the evening news coverage of the Chechnya or Afghanistan wars knew that. They were capable of destroying vegetation, structures, and humans caught in their impact zone. They produced a shockwave that burst ear drums, crushed internal organs, ruptured lungs and other injuries too gruesome to contemplate.

He was above the lake and closing fast.

The small blast of the second-event detonators sounded as he jumped off the ridge.

When his feet hit the water, the blast roared in his suit with bone-jarring, concussive force. As he sank below the surface, the water above his head flew sideways as if cupped by an alien hand

and he became utterly disoriented in the maelstrom.

Vin der Root was half a heartbeat behind Ben, not yet completely submerged when the blast propelled him across the small lake and under the surface. When he came to, he was lying face up in the shallows of the opposite shore, every nerve ending screaming out in pain, but he was alive.

When Ben surfaced, he saw huge clouds of debris over clearings in the timber stands. The fuel air explosives had done only localized damage to the trees and, he was sure, catalyzed millions more spores into the sky.

He dogpaddled to shore and sat dumbfounded in the shallows. His body had absorbed some of the shock, but fortunately he was sufficiently far from the impact and the water dissipated much of the shockwave's energy. He felt like he had been tackled by the entire defensive line of the Chicago Bears, but he was intact.

He retrieved the sample case and started back, careful not to move too fast. He was just leaving the stand's coolest glade when he heard a groan and then a whine. He froze, spun around, and seeing nothing, decided it was his imagination, yet moved more quickly. He had done what he needed to do and had the samples. All he wanted now was to get back down the mountain out of this damn stifling suit and into his daughter's arms.

The trail got easier as he descended. About half way back down to the truck he heard the whine again. He spun, saw nothing, and continued forward. As he came around to the front, again he saw it - a large bear standing in the trail twenty yards ahead. It was drooling, wavering back and forth on its hind legs for balance. Its claws were as terrifying as any weapon Ben had ever imagined. The mental image of what they were about to do to his flesh under the suit was all he could think about.

He started to run and remembered that running from a bear often resulted in death. He froze again. *Make noise.* He shouted and clapped his hands. It was pathetic, his gloved hands made no sound. He was screaming wildly, incoherently. The last burst of life from a condemned man.

And then he was running again through scrub, over a boulder, between tree trunks and down the only possible escape route he could see. He didn't have a chance.

The Bear growled and watched the yellow suit bound wildly towards him. He stood wild-eyed.

Ben lunged down the slope faster and faster. Something caught his foot and he was flying through space. He crashed headlong onto the forest floor, skidded forward, uprooting small scrub, and crashed into a tree trunk. The world fell silent.

How was it that he could now smell earth and plants?

He opened his eyes. His face screen was ripped away. He swallowed, unsure whether to lie still or continue running.

And then he saw it. A mushroom less than four inches from his face. A puffball with a star pattern at its base. He scrambled and tiny spores rose into the air in an exquisite plume.

He was suddenly on his feet again and stumbling down the mountainside. His foot caught on an exposed root, and he fell over an outcrop. It wasn't an outcrop, it was a cliff...

40

WASHINGTON, D.C.

"The bottom line," Col. Easta asked Air National Guard General Brenton on the secure video link with Copper Mountain command, "is that conventional tactics failed to suppress the spore. Have we got that right, Sir?"

"That's affirmative," the General answered with a hint of personal disappointment. He was one hundred percent career military, which usually manifested itself in total personal control, yet a subtle change tightened General Brenton's demeanor. His eyes narrowed, he flexed his shoulders. If he felt uncomfortable being interrogated by a Colonel, he didn't let it show. Talking to the elusive *Blackbird* panel was enough to rattle any soldier, even a decorated 20-year veteran of three wars.

"It had to happen someday," NSA Director Small said tightly.

"Sorry it happened at all, but I'm ticked off that it happened on our watch," Dr. Russ Clayton looked at his colleagues.

"We have no choice," said Colonel Easta. "We have to sterilize that mountain."

They each nodded.

"General?"

"Yes."

"You will prepare for the unthinkable."

There was a pause. Then, "Colonel?"

"Yessir?"

"We have something else that just might work."

"Explain."

"It's a tactic we've been practicing for our next round with a desert dictator who burrows entire palaces deep underground. It entails a coordinated attack with multiple bunker busters laid down in a precise geometrical formation around the target. Their yield is in the hundreds of kilotons. Sets up what the eggheads call concussive dissonance that they think can turn the earth itself against the target."

"How does it do that?" Small leaned forward.

"Computer modeling indicates that it sets up such powerful opposing shock waves that it can turn stone to sand, burying whatever you're after. The boys down there in Santa Fe swear it can work."

"Against a mountain?"

"They say it'll just blow the shit out of pure granite. They tell me that, in theory, it could turn Mt. Rushmore into a cairn, a rock pile. If it works, they say it's like a dozen earthquakes concentrated in a controlled area."

"If it works."

"Yes, sir."

"What are the odds, General? We don't have any time for practice. There are no second chances here. The target contains a Category A Agent with potential to cause high mortality, public panic and social disruption. It HAS to work."

"I give it a seven percent chance of working the first time," the General estimated skeptically.

The *Blackbird* members waited for the General to offer more encouragement, but he had said all he had to say. They looked at one another and the consensus built invisibly between them.

"You have one hour, General," said Stephen Small.

Two B-2 Spirit stealth bombers from Missouri's Whiteman AFB's 325th Bomber Squadron were on station over Sequoia Park just west of Thunder Peak, circling like buzzards, waiting for the order to attack. Each carried eight 5,000-lb B61-11 new-generation bunker buster bombs packed with high explosives.

"What're the odds of something this crazy actually working, skipper?" asked the co-pilot.

The pilot, Captain Terrence Biggs, a thirty-two year old Tennessean from Nashville, glanced over at the man in the second seat. "7%, I'm told."

"The odds suck, but hell, we're the best there is, right? Besides, I wouldn't miss seeing this for anything."

A green light flashed on the console. The co-pilot turned a series of three dials to three pre-arranged settings, pushed another button and they both waited. The green light flashed three times, and then glowed steadily.

"The best there is, eh, Booney?" grinned Biggs. "We'll see about that." He depressed the talk switch on the yoke and spoke to the other B-2 crew. "We're authorized to go where American bombers have never gone before, fellas. Sixteen Busters in a perfect circle below around our own mountain. The targets are laser illuminated by our friends from the 390th. Now it's up to us."

"Good to go here, sir."

"Roger. Keep your airspeed steady at 500 knots, exactly.

"Five-zero-zero knots" the other pilot confirmed his airspeed. "Check."

"On my count: three... two ... one ..."

41

THUNDER PEAK

Lotte threaded her way through the flood of media vehicles surging toward the front line in the U.S. Air Force's military campaign against the FXX earthstar spore. National Guard troops seemed to be everywhere, but had their hands full maintaining order. Attempting to corral so many protestors, activists, and stubborn Californians who were resisting the command to evacuate the area was like herding cats. Despite this, the radio kept broadcasting stern warnings to everyone to get out of the area.

She was making the wide turn toward town when she felt the road lift several inches as if by the hand of God. Then it crashed back down. She tried to slow the van and keep from careening over the shoulder, but it took all her strength and concentration. A speeding jeep ahead wobbled, then rolled over the shoulder and into a field. The VW sounded like it was popping its seams. She held on with every ounce of strength she had. Eventually, she regained control and came to a stop across the road.

Reluctant to loosen her grip on the steering wheel, she reminded herself to breathe. The van was whole, except for the shattered rear window that lay on the road, and a hubcap that rolled down the centerline and wobbled noisily to rest.

The sky darkened as thousands of tons of debris lifted into California's blue skies. The roar beneath the earth's surface rumbled away to the west and under the valley floor.

Twin downbeats sounded, followed by an electronic flourish, and the familiar NEWS ALERT 3-D graphic splashed across television screens nationwide.

"This is a CNN News Alert. I am Bill Michaels with Daryn Yeager and this just in: A series of powerful explosions has rocked the area around Thunder Peak, California. We have unconfirmed reports of bombing, including napalm and fuel air explosives. Reporter Steve Carlton is on the scene. Steve, what can you tell us?"

A man wearing a tight fitting, sweat-stained safari shirt and an expensive haircut appeared on screen. He was in a helicopter high over what appeared to be a mountain wilderness. Behind him, smoke plumes rose from a portion of the forest.

"Since arriving on scene, Bill, I have witnessed two strikes by what appeared to be U.S. Air Force B-2 Spirit stealth bombers--"

"B-2 Spirit Bombers, Steve?" the anchor in Atlanta interrupted.

Carlton put a finger to his earpiece to better hear over the helicopter's propwash, "That's what we think, Bill and Daryn. They were circling at very high altitude so I can't be certain of their identity. Several large munitions were dropped; laser-guided, so-called 'bunker buster' bombs, my pilot Ron Kiesner, a former Gulf War pilot, informs us. As you can see behind me, there is smoke from several hot spots near the summit of that mountain right there, Thunder Peak." The camera zoomed in on the distant smoke amid the dense forest as Carlton continued his report. "The bunker buster bombs - massive 5,000-pound ground penetrating explosives, detonated in a necklace of death and now the debris from those explosions is beginning to cloud the sky." The camera tilted up and widened to show the spreading smoke. Suddenly a dark shape flashed by the helicopter at high speed, rocking the helicopter in its wake. "Bill and Daryn, that is our none too subtle invitation to leave the area. From over the Thunder Peak Wilderness near Longwood, California, this is Steve Carlton."

The co-anchors reappeared. "Is it war on America? More on

this developing story in a moment."

Broken glass jars, test tubes and beakers littered the floor of Ben's basement laboratory. The air was sharp with formaldehyde and alcohol, so Lotte first opened the windows. Nothing irreplaceable was lost; the spore sample slides remained safe secure in their impact cases. The cross ventilation helped clear the confined space and Lotte could begin to think clearly about what to do next.

She jumped when the telephone rang. Her already strained nerves were brittle after the events on the road.

"Dr. Keene?" an unfamiliar voice inquired.

"Yes."

"Dr. Lotte Keene?"

"Who is this?"

"Dr. Keene, my name is unimportant. You have stumbled into the middle of something very, very dangerous. As you no doubt know by now, we are working to fight that danger. We think you can help."

"We? Who is we?"

"There is no time, Dr. Keene. Believe me when I say that I know more about you, your research at Johns Hopkins, Dr. der Root, and the spore than you do."

"Listen, I don't care if you know what color underwear I'm wearing, I'm not talking until I know who the hell you are."

There was a brief silence on the line. "Alright, my name is Clayton. Dr. Russell Clayton. I'm a molecular—"

"--geneticist, Nobel laureate, America's brilliant and little published pioneer in molecular genetics."

"Oh, I am published, but not in the journals you read," he defended himself, a tinge of regret in his voice. "I find your Nature's Defense Theory intriguing, no, compelling is a better word. Your early work altered my way of thinking about genetics and their place in our world."

This time it was Lotte's turn to pause. She couldn't believe her ears. After more than two decades of rejections, humiliation in academia, and utter neglect from the leading minds in her field, Nobel laureate Russell Clayton was calling out of the blue to validate her life's work.

"I'll cut to my reason for calling. The FX biological agent is loose in the Thunder Peak Wilderness."

"And the FXX," Lotte added.

"We're not certain of how or why, but we will find out. Our highest priority at the moment is to defeat this tragedy before it becomes a catastrophe. I am hoping that your particular expertise, your perspective may illuminate something our best strategists have yet to devise. You have a unique approach to nature, both earth's and man's."

"You know that low temperature can slow it down?"

"Sounds logical. But slow it down is all; wouldn't neutralize it. No way to freeze a mountain that I know of, not in the next hour," Clayton thought aloud.

"Right. Extreme heat, on the other hand—"

"—could incinerate the organic mushroom matter, but—

"Right," interrupted Lotte, "you would need to apply extreme high heat to alter the molecular structure of the carbon nanotubes."

"-and return them to a low entropy state."

"Harmless."

"Ash."

There was another pause. Lotte had forgotten how good dabbling in pure theoretical physics could be.

"So. . ."

"So, your precision munitions couldn't destroy it," she peered out the window at the dusky sky, "they just created a greenhouse over California and we're all going to die. What the hell did you drop up there?"

"Napalm-B, fuel air explosives--"

"Dr. McCandle is up there collecting samples. He's tough and he's smart, but I've heard what those fuel air explosives can do."

"We had no choice."

"And we had no choice." She was worried about Ben. She pictured him dazed, deaf, disoriented and alone on the battlefield that Thunder Peak had become. "What was that last attack? I've been in earthquakes that were tamer."

"A new theory suggested that precise applications of subsonic dissonance could liquefy the geology, bury the spore. Sixteen bunker buster bombs."

"That didn't work, either. It looks like Armageddon out there, and Thunder Peak is <u>still</u> standing." *Nature always wins.* "You'd have to use something a thousand times hotter than anything I know about. A nuclear weapon perhaps, but that's impossible."

Another silence.

"I said that is crazy!"

Silence.

"No, you're not thinking of detonating a nuke are you?!"

"We can't rule out anything, Doctor. What would you do?"

"I wouldn't set off a nuclear bomb!"

"Thank you for your time, Doctor. I've enjoyed our discussion."

"Wait!"

The connection was dead.

42

THE WHITE HOUSE

President Thomas Stone was physically removed from his private office and whisked away as his Chief of Staff rushed alongside, assuring him that the Secret Service were merely doing their job. The President, his detail and aides rushed across the White House lawn to the waiting helicopter and were aboard by the time the White House press corps realized something unusual was happening. Marine One rotated and was flying past the Washington monument before one determined cameraman rolled tape and could record the abrupt departure.

Aboard Air Force One, President Stone began making phone calls. First the British Prime Minister, then, in carefully preplanned order, the Russian President, the Chinese Chairman, The French Premier, right on down the list of America's allies and enemies.

At the same time, the U.S. State Department invited most of the foreign ambassadors who happened to be in Washington to the State Department Situation Room on E. Street and provided confidential briefings. Those who were not present were contacted via secure satellite phone.

British Prime Minister Windsor listened quietly, then offered any and all assistance that may be required in the coming hours.

Russian President Nabokov agreed to stand down his forces, but insisted that the President remain in close contact with him. He did not know long his generals could be expected to trust the Americans.

The French premier bitterly resented the American screw-up. What was about to happen would strain American-French relations to the breaking point for the third time since World War II.

The Chinese Chairman asked his translator to repeat what the American President had told him five times and then hung up in a fit of rage. When President Stone called back, the Chairman sullenly refused to offer any indication of how his nation would react.

All American and NATO forces went on DEFCON One status worldwide.

At Whiteman AFB in Missouri, Captain Terrence Biggs and his co-pilot, signed the Flight Chief's receipt for one 2400-pound B88 tactical nuclear weapon, serial number B88o47, delivered, and strapped in to his B-2.

The Flight Chief gave him the ballpoint pen in honor of the occasion and suggested it might be worth something someday on e-Bay.

Biggs tried to smile as he slid the souvenir into his flight suit pen pocket. He could scarcely believe his orders or what was happening around him. Fortunately, he had trained years for this moment. His mind overruled every other physical reaction to the prospect of dropping more destructive power on his own people than the world had ever witnessed. He was just the unlucky guy to draw the ticket.

"Let's get it over with, Booney," he said humorlessly and climbed into the cockpit. Avionics on the plane were warmed up. They made quick work of the pre-flight check and were airborne within six minutes.

Three flights of four F-15s flew interference on the flight back up to California. Due to strict radio silence, there was no chatter.

43

THUNDER PEAK WILDERNESS

Lotte tried to reach Ben on his cell phone but there was no answer. She called Grace and reached her at Adrian Stimson's place. They were packing up and evacuating. Mary Margaret was frightened for her father, but otherwise she was alright, Grace assured her.

"Ben is on the Peak."

"I suspected as much since we didn't hear from him. I don't know what to tell M."

"He is tough. I'm on my way up there."

"Find him."

Driving up the mountain was like driving into hell. The air was filled with smoke, spores and lord knows what else. Pockets of burning undergrowth appeared unexpectedly as she inched her way up the narrow trail road.

Her phone rang. "Ben!"

"Dr. Keene, it's Rensberger, from Boulder?"

"What do you want Lieutenant? I'm busy."

"Something very, very big is about to happen on Thunder Peak. Get out of there NOW."

The hair on her neck stood on end. Just when she didn't think anything could surprise her, the clean scrubbed kid from Boulder reached out and touched her. *Jesus. Is he in on it with Clayton?*

"It's going to be an accidental detonation of one of our ICBMs. It going to go off course and detonate in your neck of the woods." His voice was rock steady. It was chilling.

"That's their line, is it?"

"Yes. Get as far away as you can. Drive west, against the wind, hear?"

Lotte didn't answer. My God, *Ben*. She weighed her options: try to find Ben and risk the samples, or turn west and hope the van had enough left to climb over the ridge. Ben would insist that he was expendable, but the spore samples were irreplaceable. They were the only proof of the conspiracy. If she didn't find an antidote, the entire human race and every living thing on the planet would be threatened.

What would Charley do? The same, Lotte was sure. She would insist on nailing the bastards with their own evidence.

Ben half staggered, half crawled down the mountain with the sample case. His suit was a shambles. His hair and eyebrows were singed off. He was deaf and seeing double, sometimes triple. The wilderness was a kaleidoscope of terror to him. Somehow, through the stench, the pain, the disorientation, fire, and smoke, he managed to navigate down the way he came.

Eventually, he came to the rise above where he parked the truck. It wasn't there. He looked around him to verify that this was the way he had approached. He recognized the boulder, the stand of ancients. But there was no truck. He stood unsteadily, trying feebly to regain his bearings.

Then he saw the rear wheels behind some scrub further down slope. The truck had evidently been upended and sent tumbling down the mountain by the blasts. Still, it was a touch of his world and he leaned forward to run to it. No sooner had he started than he stumbled. He climbed to his feet, walked a few unsteady steps farther and . . . blacked out.

'Against the wind, hear?' Lotte recalled Rensberger's insistence.

He was one of them and even he saw a terrible end to this unfolding tragedy.

She desperately wanted to save Ben, but finding him in this smoke and fire-filled wilderness was an impossibly long shot. Yes, it was hopeless, but if she turned back now, it would be like failing Charley again. Maybe this was her last best chance to redeem herself.

The front tires ran up against a fallen branch and the van lurched to a sudden stop. She gunned the already overworked engine, which coughed and then wailed as it loyally responded to her foot on the accelerator. The van groaned and creaked as it shuddered over the obstacle. She yanked on the emergency brake, got out, pulled the branch out from between the front and rear wheels and threw it off to the side. When she turned around, the van was gone. It had vanished in the blowing smoke and sparks. "Ben!" she shouted into the haunting swirl, "Ben!" She fell to her knees and wept. Whether from sorrow for Charley, for Ben or her own pathetic powerlessness, she didn't know, but it all overwhelmed her. Vin's betrayal. Charley's senseless murder. Ben's unnecessary death on this forsaken mountain. Tears came like a flood and she pounded the ground with her fists. It was over. She was going to die here.

A gust of wind came up, cooled her tears, and swept away much of the smoke. It felt good. Her throat burned from the foul air, but the freshet reminded her of hope. She straightened and, looking around, saw the van, five feet behind her where she had left it, door open, and engine running.

The beauty of science, Vin der Root had found, is that everything in the universe can be organized into absolutes. Charley had known this at some level when she said that Nature always wins. There were exceptions to every rule, of course, such as in theoretical mathematics, but even the exceptions followed a certain logic. He had followed his nature. He had been greedy and avaricious, and it was his nature that defeated him in the end.

He was trapped beside the lake. The shock wave of the bunker busters had shifted a massive boulder, which now sat on his left foot and left arm. He was in shock, bleeding from multiple open wounds, his tibia had punctured the skin and pointed a bloody shard accusingly at him. He recognized the symptoms of approaching mortality.

He fished his cell phone out of his jacket pocket and dialed.

Mineral Hill Road westbound was free of traffic. Lotte had seen only two pickup trucks in the last ten minutes, and those only for as long as it took them to speed by in their flight from what was coming. The van was a shambles and, under any other circumstances, would have been pulled over by the Highway Patrol for a litany of safety and equipment infractions. The engine was hoarse with exertion in the thin air and the VW had steadily lost speed as it climbed higher. She was making scarcely fifteen miles per hour headway.

A quarter mile ahead, the road crossed through a notch carved by WW-II Civilian Conservation Corps crews.

When her phone rang, she grabbed it and answered hopefully, "Ben?"

"Lotte, it's Vin. Listen, I don't have much time."

"Where are you?"

"On Thunder Peak. In the woods."

"Get the hell out of there! NOW!"

"I can't. It's too late for me."

"Vin—"

"Shut up, Lotte. For once, just listen. I'm sorry, for what I did with your work, for not caring enough to save Charley, for destroying our friendship." He coughed up blood and cleared his throat.

"None of that matters," Lotte screamed. "They are going to drop a bomb."

"Nuclear?"

Lotte didn't answer. She didn't have to.

"Good. Lotte, do whatever it takes to stop Gabriel, and Starli---"

SCREE-E-E-E-E-TCH!!

The sky flashed blindingly white in the rear view mirror. She looked at the phone in her hand in disbelief. An image of der Root being transformed to carbon in the ether occurred to her. When the shock wave arrived, it slammed into the van and sent it hurtling over the ridge to safety on the western slope.

"This just in," Bill Michaels interrupted regularly scheduled coverage of Wall Street quarterly earnings analysis, "an extraordinarily large explosion has rocked portions of western California just minutes ago. Initial reports include a flash that brightened the sky and was witnessed as far away as Las Vegas and San Francisco. This is the same area where several recent bombings by American military forces have been reported in the last twenty-four hours. Steve Carlton joins us from the area. Steve, is the situation there spinning out of control?"

The scene cut to a split screen with reporter Steve Carlton beside his helicopter. Falling debris and ash make it appear as if winter has descended on California. "Perhaps, Bill. But it is too early to be sure. Here is what we think we know: an immense explosion, many suspect a nuclear explosion, detonated over the Thunder Peak Wilderness less than fifteen minutes ago. Putting this together with reports received from our overseas bureaus about warnings from America's President to numerous foreign leaders about an imminent major event, it looks like that this explosion qualifies as that major event."

"Steve, we are receiving other reports from passing commercial airliners that the lethal blast has flattened trees for as much as three miles in every direction. Yet, that is infamously varied terrain, some of America's most rugged territory. Surely there are pockets of survivors. Are emergency personnel able to get into the area?"

"Right now, it is still chaos here, Bill. No doubt, the National Guard knows what to do in a situation like this. We're counting on them. As for us, Ron and I plan to get in the air to see for ourselves as soon as possible-" The image deteriorated into electronic 'snow' and the video link was lost.

44

VISALIA

I'm not dead.

Light lanced his eyes in an excruciating burst of pain. He endured the intense discomfort, blinking quickly, allowing his pupils and brain to acclimate to wherever he was.

A disembodied voice called for Doctor Scrabblebucket . . . *no . . . Dankofivewidgley.* He inched his head to one side. *Good, it moves.*

A cloud of noises collapsed into muted voices, the rush of air, the pulse of electronic beeps.

Blurs of light and dark gradually settled into colors and contours: a ceiling, his raised right arm in a partial cast from his wrist to above the elbow.

He swallowed and was grateful that he could - no respirator tube. He swiveled his head to the right and a moan traveled up his throat at the sight of Mary Margaret curled up asleep in the reclining chair between the bed and the window. He studied her for several minutes to convince himself that she was real, that this was really happening. She was in her jeans and good sweatshirt. Not how she was dressed when he last saw her at . . . where . . . her grandmother's wake. She held Pooh Bear in the crook of her arm and was dreaming.

He was alive, M was all right and the world hadn't ended.

A discreet vibration shook the bed. He turned to see a nurse checking his IV drip. She smiled when she caught him observing her.

"It's about time, Doctor McCandle," she said quietly.

"Where am—"

"St. Francis' hospital in Visalia. You were airlifted here fourteen hours ago. You came in with multiple fractures of your left tibia and fibula, a clean break of your right ulna and a number of contusions and abrasion to your face, chest and abdomen," she delivered the news in an encouraging tone to let him know that he had a future.

"Is that all?" Ben winced as the stitches on his jaw and forehead stretched and bled.

"A little old for leaping off cliffs, aren't you?" she quipped. She glanced over the bed at M. "She's been right there since we brought you down and tucked you in," she whispered. "Hope you don't mind, but I've decided to adopt her."

"How did I get here again?"

"Helicopter rescue. A logging survey crew found you, brought you down the mountain."

"Is Grace here, too?"

"Her mom? She arrived with you and has been here the whole time. Just stepped out for a bit. Said she'd be back in thirty minutes."

Ben struggled to assemble everything she'd told him into a coherent order but unknowns still outnumbered facts.

"The samples?"

"Samples?"

"And Lotte? Lotte Keene?"

"Who?"

"She's not my wife."

"Lotte?"

"No, Grace. I like the sound of that, though."

"Daddy?" said Mary Margaret as she rubbed sleep from her eyes and reached out to hug him. He held her close with his good arm and inhaled the innocent and miraculous fragrance of her young hair.

"Daddy, I was so scared. Does it hurt?"

"I'm fine, sweetheart. In fact, never been better."

He had no idea why he was so blessed, but he vowed never to forget it. To demonstrate the overpowering love he had for this little girl, to show what his own father never did.

'Love her. Just love my granddaughter.' He heard the echo of Alice's words in the kitchen. Why hadn't he told her he loved her as she went out the door? That had been his last chance and he let it slip away. *Once in a while a girl likes to hear the words.* Ben held M closer. *Love her.* It was that simple.

"I love you, sweetheart." He held her, determined never to let her slip away.

45

BOULDER

CDC Global Disease Detection and Emergency Response (GDDER) Satellite Monitoring Station – University of CO, Boulder

Whoever it was either didn't read the sign posted on her door or ignored it.

> *Dr. Lotte Keene*
> *is on assignment & unavailable*
> *until further notice.*

They knocked on the glass and tried the handle again. She turned off her desk lamp and waited. Finally, the sound of heavy rubber-soled boots, one of which squeaked, on the tile floor faded down the hallway.

Lotte returned to scanning the last of the hi-resolution chromosome stain films onto a DVD. It was a catalogue of diabolical ambition. Forty-two films in total, each one more explosive the last. In the wrong hands, it was a blueprint for

270

genocide.

The DNA studies were extraordinary in both the matches with earthstar mushroom chromosomes and the differences they illuminated. There it was, clear as day at position 11 on chromosome 4, the unusual match of AGTT where it would normally have been AGGT. Another unusual match appeared on chromosome 2. They weren't random aberrations; she read the identical modification on every sample tested. Those alternate codes were the spanner in the biogenetic gearworks.

Next, she scanned in X-ray and electron microscopic evidence of the carbon nanotubes onto a fourth DVD. There was overwhelming evidence on the four disks to prove the existence of the killer earthstar. Each of the files was a death warrant. The people who had done this had contravened every legal and ethical standard in the rapidly evolving biogenetic research field.

Once she knew what she was looking for, her results proved conclusively that der Root had indeed advanced her work from theory to reality: an engineered toxic branch on the evolutionary tree. He took what they had learned about hematopoietic growth factors – protein hormones produced by the body to regulate production and maturation of various blood forming cells – at Chembotan and reverse engineered the life-saving process to create a life-halting process.

If the people behind der Root cared so little for commonly accepted standards of ethical conduct, and they held innocent life in such low regard, then they would care nothing about the life of anyone who tried to stop them. Lotte Keene was now their enemy. She knew they would be coming to stop her. That knock on the door may have been the scout, the first probe of her known workspace.

The computer finished writing the last file to DVD #4 and returned control of the program to Lotte. She quickly wrote 'X-rays and EM' on the DVD with an indelible marker, inserted it in the jewel case and labeled it '4/4.' She took one last look at the DVDs, verified all four were labeled. These went into a Priority Mail mailer. She scrawled a quick cover note to Ben and Grace, stuffed it into the small book-sized self-mailer with the discs and sealed the box. She began to handwrite the address and then decided against it - too easy to identify the sender. She pulled her old typewriter from the closet and typed the label to Ben at the ranch.

The glass in the door rattled again under a forceful knocking. She froze, afraid to breathe. Again the knock came. The phone's shrill ring shattered whatever sense of sanctuary the familiar laboratory offered her. She jumped. Stifling a scream with her hand, she forced herself to remain still. After two more impatient knocks, she heard the squeak of a boot sole on the tile, then watched as the corner of a credit card appeared through the gap in the doorjamb. There was a click and the door slowly opened. Moving quickly, silently, she scooped up her shoulder bag and slipped down the back stairway.

She skirted the quadrangle by using a shortcut through the vacant chapel and darted into Marmion Hall. Again taking the back stairs, she managed to get to the NSF satellite monitoring studio without being noticed and let herself in through the utility door. From there, she followed the tunnel of wires behind the racks of monitors and controllers. She peered through a gap between two rack-mounted signal amplifiers and saw that Lieutenant Rensberger's cubicle was vacant. Good. He wasn't supposed to report for his shift for a half hour. *Just enough time.*

She slipped into his chair, dialed the number she had memorized in the 805 area code.

A crisp female voice answered, "ReCombinant Genetics, Mr. Lassen's office."

The executive secretary put Lotte through to Bernard Lassen, Ph.D., Chairman of America's largest independent biotechnology company.

"Dr. Keene, I'm pleased you called. Have you reconsidered my proposal?"

"You remember me, then?"

"It wasn't that long ago, Doctor," he said pleasantly. "Besides, like I told you in Washington when CoGen bought Chembotan, we could use your special talent. Tell me what you need," his voice was steady, confident, to the point. It brought him back to her: his clear blue eyes, the even tan of an active life, the intelligent high forehead, and not a hair out of place. Now, he had remembered her. A part of her was flattered.

The other part raised its guard a little higher. ReCombinant Genetics – known popularly as CoGen - owned the early work on the killer mushroom. And although she couldn't prove it yet, she was certain that Chembotan/CoGen had completed the project under der Root's supervision. The DOD would have preferred to keep the circle small. And Lassen didn't get where he was by pure luck. He had to have been intimately aware of, if not involved in, the earthstar project.

CoGen - heaviest of biotech heavies - learned long ago that vision and secrecy in genetic research were its keys to success. Vision of future market needs and secrecy in developing new products for those markets. CoGen made billions of dollars with its genetic therapies for blood cell production, autoimmunity, neurobiology and soft-tissue repair.

What most distinguished it was Chairman Bernard Lassen's knack for identifying vaccines BEFORE they were needed. It was uncanny. In fact it was untrue, Lotte was certain. Rather than dig for the difficult and often arcane scientific facts, however, the business media fell under the wizard's spell. His biotech coups made irresistible headlines and boosted circulation. They were in business, too.

The development process for researching, testing and manufacturing vaccines can take 7-12 years, but CoGen had consistently been first to market with advanced vaccines within 1-2 years of new viral outbreaks. Armed with gene sequence information before it was needed, CoGen identified biotech niche markets and exploited them before the competition could effectively address those same market niches. The competition was left flat-footed, requiring years to develop their own vaccines.

Lotte didn't want to make it to easy for Lassen. He was a serious strategist who placed value on tactics. She needed to keep him off balance.

"I've been working on the outbreak in central California," she began.

"The *Ahwahnee Stroke,* I believe they're calling it. Catchy."

"I've identified it."

"Excellent, Doctor. California and America will be in your debt. This is what I was saying about your talent. What is the source?"

He was very good. She was sure that he knew the source of the 'Stroke' and would give himself away with a hesitation, a more guarded response, at least. If he was behind the earthstar's creation, then she expected him to want to control qualified understanding

273

of the mushroom and its mechanism. He could come up with an antidote (which might already exist in some CoGen lab, waiting for the right time to announce its readiness to save lives) . . . for an exorbitant price. But he hadn't flinched. Either he didn't know anything, or he was testing her.

She thought for a moment. Maybe he didn't have it yet. Maybe he needed her help to develop it. She didn't have time to be cautious. She needed access to his resources and CoGen files now.

"It is a mushroom."

"A mushroom."

"Yes. I'm thinking CoGen is the only company with the scientific expertise necessary to create such a lethal mushroom."

"You think so."

"I do. And there's another interesting aspect to this outbreak."

"What's that?"

"The symptoms match a similar outbreak in Brazil," she said and stopped, hoping he would fill the silence with something, anything that would tell her what he knew.

"Itamarati," she eventually added.

"So are you going to join us, Doctor?"

"I'm interested."

"What can I do to promote your interest into a commitment?"

"I'd need protection from government interference in my work, including the DOD and NSA."

"I think we can manage that," he said, more seriously now.

"I'd need my own lab and access to all of the data . . ."

"Certainly."

"And enough to keep comfortable and safe for the rest of my years," she fought the urge to smile. She couldn't believe what she was saying.

"You know," he changed the subject, taking a casual tone as one would with a friend, "it's a shame about our profession."

"How so?"

"A control factor for a test in a remote area fails. People – innocent people -- are hurt."

He DID know! Now that she had taken his bait, he was trusting her a little.

"Those are the risks we take in the pursuit of the common good. If we are not willing to risk life itself, where is the dignity in life? Would you agree, Doctor?"

Lotte swallowed bile rising in her throat and struggled to remain calm. She saw Charley on the examination table in Itamarati. Alice. Vin.

"It's our calling, a noble one to be sure." She felt like she was going to vomit.

There was another silence, a few moments. "You can help us find an antidote," he said, his tone more serious yet.

She knew they had arrived at the bottom line: CoGen had created the killer earthstar mushroom, yet didn't have an antidote. The project had spun out of his control. Maybe the Pentagon or *Blackbird* or some other black operation had modified his reengineered mushroom. Maybe the carbon nanotubes were a top-secret freelance modification he didn't know about. It wasn't *Earth Rebirth's!* doing. No, she could count on one hand the scientists who were capable of an innovation like that. She and Vin were two of the five. More likely than not, the other three, probably less, were known only to *Blackbird.*

"I'm particularly intrigued with the potential for techniques to automate determination of post-translational modification (PTM) of proteins," he explained further.

He really did not have an antidote. He was pushing strategies for expediting the traditional development, testing and manufacturing processes. Somehow, he had lost his advantage on this project. Her suspicion that the killer mushroom was modified by some rogue force in the government was gaining credence by the second. Not that it wouldn't be nearly as effective without the carbon nanotubes, just not absolutely lethal.

Her mind began to work the problem. It was the firehouse dog response. PTM is the process by which gene products, the proteins, are altered after they have been expressed to produce the functional molecule. Modification of protein functions might include glycosylation or the addition of sugars and phosphorylation, which was often important in signaling events within or between cells.

"CDC, along with select advanced biogenetic research laboratories, have licensed our patents that allow routine, high throughput and sensitive analysis of protein glycosylation. You have certainly used our technology," he continued, now thoroughly immersed in the academic side of his job, talking to her as a professional colleague.

She was in. "Yes, of course. It's not my specialty, but I know it well."

"Good. How soon can you get to work? May I send a plane for you?"

"Look for me by the start of the week. I have some business first."

"Certainly, Doctor Keene. Welcome aboard."

"One more item, Mr. Lassen? My work for you is between you and me. And it ends when I deliver the antidote, understood?"

There was a long pause. It was unusual for a scientist to request anonymity in the biotech field. And it was unheard of for an employer to grant it. Like Silicon Valley, biotech had its own constellation of scientific celebrities. They were good for attracting investors, good for employee morale, and helped keep the press hungry when management needed them.

"Agreed," said Lassen after a several seconds of silence. "Your lab will be waiting for you. See you in a few days, Doctor. Good bye."

"Good bye," Lotte said and hung up. She took a deep breath, the first since she had sat down. Looking at her watch she saw that it was a minute after Rensberger's shift started.

She slipped out of his cubicle and behind the equipment rack just as he entered the suite. She made her way silently behind the equipment toward the utility door until she heard it. A familiar sound. She listened more closely. As he crossed to his cubicle, a distinctive squeak sounded from his right boot on the raised tile flooring.

46

MEEKER PARK, CO

After stopping at an Internet Café in Meeker Park and then dropping the discs in the mail to Ben at Grace's White Raven Studio, Lotte turned the van off Route 7 onto westbound 36, which took her through Rocky Mountain National Park and back over the Continental Divide toward Milner Pass. She had uploaded the files to herself under multiple aliases at six separate e-mail accounts in cyberspace. In the event that anything went wrong, she would be able to download the crucial biochemical data from anywhere in the world.

The outside temperature dropped as the van climbed above 10,000 feet. Despite the chill, she refused to roll up the window. She wanted to feel it and prepare herself for what was to come.

They'd find her eventually, she knew that. The only question was how long it would take them to task one of their birds to scan this part of Colorado, and then how good their analyst was at photo intel. Sooner or later, some sharp eye would spot the dated VW on the remote two lane. Based upon that certainty, she had no data with her in the van. If and when they caught up with her, she didn't want to give them the satisfaction of thinking they had their secret back safely in their possession. They should worry.

She straightened behind the wheel and took a deep breath. The road stretched out ahead with no other traffic in sight. She checked her rearview mirror again and was rewarded with empty road behind her as well.

The sky was afternoon blue and there were white clouds over the crowns of the trees. The speedometer needle vibrated at the 70 miles per hour mark.

Putting on her hands-free headset, she plugged it into the cell phone she'd taken from Dr. Wrigley's lab at the end of the hall. Emeritus professor of biochemistry, seventy-six years old, absent from his lab more than he was there, and increasingly forgetful, Dr. Wrigley provided her with a convenient way to confuse her pursuers. His departmental cell phone was where it always was, in the charger stand on his file cabinet. She didn't think of it as stealing, exactly.

She dialed the number Grace had given her for Ben's hospital room.

"Hello?" M answered.

"How is your Dad?" Lotte tried to keep her tone light.

"He's been asking about you."

"Oh, what does he want from me now!"

M giggled.

"Hi there," Ben said tiredly. "I'm alive. Fancy that."

"Bet you're a terrible patient," Lotte nudged.

"When are you coming back?"

"'Fraid I've got more important things to do than hold your hand."

"You got the—"

"Yes," she interrupted, hoping he understood that the NSA eavesdrops on telephone conversations, e-mail, faxes, and communications of all kinds. Their software listens for thousands of key words. No doubt 'mushroom' and 'samples' were now on the list. When they detected a conversation containing them, surveillance recording and location tracking would commence immediately.

"Solution?"

"No, not yet."

Ben sensed that she was in danger and trusted her lead. "I see, I guess."

After several moments, she apologized.

"For what?"

"Alice."

There was another pause. "She always said that she lived the way she did because when her time came she didn't want regrets. She didn't want to second-guess anything. I don't think she did."

"Like Charley," Lotte answered, grateful for his implicit absolution. "But Vin . . ."

Ben didn't speak. He gave her the space she needed.

"What will you do?"

"Disappear, work on my new theory."

"Another one?"

"It could fix everything. After that, a remote spot where I can sleep for a week, then decide what to do with the rest of my life. If you're smart, you'll get on with yours, too."

She remembered standing by the window at the ranch that last day looking up at Thunder Peak. Ben joined her, and she turned in such a way that her breasts pressed against his chest. She was grieving one kind of death and contemplating rebirth. She should have placed a hand on his hip, she thought. He should have turned her to him and . . .

"Good-bye, Ben."

"See you, Lotte," he said.

The line clicked off. Ben pushed the phone away. He was offended by the mournful tone yet lacked the will to end the connection.

Lotte put the phone on the passenger seat along with the headset and saw the turnout ahead. A single car – a VW Beetle - was parked near the lookout rail. No one was around it. The road ahead swept left in a wide mile-long arcing turn that would lead her to the highest point in this part of Colorado's Rocky Mountains. After the next crest, the road traversed a brief ridge to the next, slightly lower peak. The stretch between the peaks was the most dangerous eighty yards in the American West. Besides the two mile drop-off into impossibly deep crevasses on either side, the road itself jogged 28-degrees halfway across the narrow stretch. Easy enough for the careful driver who paid attention, but a challenge to anyone who came off the previous wide turn too fast.

New guardrail glinted halfway across the ridge, she noticed. Some poor soul lost it there recently. Glancing down at the road, she saw the tell tale skid marks. Whoever died here was just bone down there by now. There were limits to what the state trooper could do. Any vehicle lost over this particular stretch was surrendered to Nature. It was just too daunting a task to attempt to retrieve the remains.

A half-mile to go. She checked the rear view mirror, gripped the wheel firmly and, at the place where the skid marks began, gave a sudden twist and hit the brake pedal.

Ed Rensberger sat alone in the darkened monitoring room at GDDER in Boulder. The muted whoosh of air conditioning sounded from vents high in the darkened walls, out of view of the glow cast by the double rows of high-resolution monitors. His face looked darker, healthier in the dim, reflected light. He took a sip of tea, typed a brief command into the keyboard and the image on the 'LINE' monitor magnified.

The image was of mountainous terrain in northwestern Colorado. There was no activity in the image to attract the eye. Just treeless rocky peaks, inhospitable scree fields on the slopes and farther down the mountainsides, dense stands of trees. Pines according to the map on his desktop.

There was a line across the image that began straight on the left and then wandered as it bisected the image on the monitor.

Rensberger tapped the joystick on his control panel and watched as, two seconds later, the line moved toward the center of the image. Another few keystrokes and the image magnified again.

The satellite now faithfully tracked the line, keeping it in the center of the screen.

He noted the time, jotted an entry in his notebook and sat back in his chair with the tea.

It was times like this when nothing was happening that his mind tended to wander. Sometimes, when he was sleepy or really bored, he sought distraction with whatever sensory input was available. He would imagine seeing shapes in the jumble of lines and shades. Recognizing the symptoms, he stood up, stretched, performed some energetic windmills, took deep breaths and sat down again refreshed.

A small light rectangle moved onto the screen and followed the line west. It was a vehicle and it gave off a higher than ambient heat ignature.

He checked to make sure that the hard drive was recording, then magnified the image again.

It wasn't going terribly fast, he noted. He moved to another console and commenced a search of the databanks for this particular heat signature. The system came back with a diagram and picture of a VW Microvan, 1981-1987 vintage.

Pushing himself back to the primary console, he took manual control to make sure he kept the VW centered in the screen for as long as possible to give the analyst the best possible imagery.

Then something strange happened. The image of the van began to glow brighter. It drifted left, and then veered right and off the road, bursting into flames. The heat bloomed and flared out the frame.

Rensberger watched the glow drift and fall.

He realized what was happening and entered a rapid-fire series of commands that adjusted the satellite's camera aiming platform. The burning van slid off the bottom of the monitor screen as the satellite looked away, protecting its hypersensitive light and heat sensors.

After making sure that the satellite wasn't damaged, he typed a priority-encrypted e-mail describing what he had seen and addressed it: *Blackbird.*

47

LONGWOOD

As Colorado State Trooper Rick Bass rounded one of the mountain's innumerable ridges, his eyes swept the road ahead for anything out of place.

He took one look at the skid marks as they came into view and knew what his day was going to be like. They were darker than on his last patrol. He squinted to see them more clearly. Sure enough they were darker and wider. Then he saw the ruptured guardrail hanging like ribbon remnants in the morning sunlight. Slowing as he approached, the convergence of one skid mark into the old one confirmed his suspicion: another vehicle lost control here and its driver was now dead amid the wreckage more than a mile below.

He turned on his rooftop array, braked to a stop, then backed off the ridge and onto the narrow shoulder fifty yards back. "Dispatch, this is Bass, three-seven-five," he radioed in, "I'm a mile marker three-oh-two on Route three-six at Trail Ridge. I have new skid marks and heavily damaged guardrail. No vehicle in sight Investigating. Over."

"Roger three-seven-five. Investigating skid marks."

There was no smoke visible but he detected a pungent trace of petroleum-based fire. The signature in the usually pure evergreen-scented air was unmistakable.

He already knew where to look. He had investigated five single-vehicle accidents on this stretch in two years. As a Trooper, his responsibility was for traffic enforcement and accident investigation. If he found any hint of a crime, he'd turn the investigation over to the State Police.

There was a twisted section of rounded bumper caught in the guardrail. An import, he figured. American bumpers were more squared. As he got closer, he recognized the distinctive double-ridged shape of a VW van bumper. No mistaking it. Colorado had enough VW vans to qualify it as the state car.

There wasn't much shoulder beyond the rail, less than a yard. From there the slope steepened into a vertigo inducing 70-degree descent. Some scrub was pulled from the soil, hanging from the mountainside by a single slender root. Caught in that five feet beyond his reach was a Colorado license plate. Assuming it belonged to the van, that was a fortuitous piece of luck. Since there wasn't any chance of retrieving the vehicle, the plate could identify the registered owner. That would fill more blanks in the files than he had in any of the previous accident investigations. Those drivers simply vanished in the vast, impenetrable West.

He got the grappling hook and line from the trunk and practiced his aim on a bare section of slope. He would only have one chance to capture the precariously hanging plate. A single slender branch held it aloft. A stiff gust of wind might get it before he could.

His first toss overshot the spot at which he was aiming by three feet.

A second easy, underhanded toss landed the hook the correct distance from the ledge, but a foot to the right of his target.

Shit - The plate swung in the wind like a mobile. He held his breath. It swung back and forth and started to twirl, then came to rest in its original position.

He swung the hook in a shallow arc for one more practice. Once back. Twice and . . . he let gravity control the descent, feeling the line slide across his palm for a second and then his hand closed. One of the hook's three prongs glinted and bit into the scrabble exactly where he wanted it.

He stepped over to the place on the ledge directly above the plate, which was starting to swing again.

The plate fidgeted.

He swung once, twice and . . .

The hook flew on its irreversible trajectory. Bass watched in disbelief as the plate caught a gust broadside and lurched off the branch. There was nothing he could do except hope he'd given the hook enough momentum and trust to luck that it could bat his target back to the slope and give him another shot.

But it wasn't to be. The gust strengthened and lifted the license plate higher.

A clink sounded. A gleam reflected off pointed tips and both hook and plate fell to the earth and paused at the end of his line. One of the hook's prongs had threaded the needle. It had found one of the plate's mounting holes. Bass carefully pulled in the line hand over hand.

When it arrived on the shoulder at his feet, Bass looked down and whistled softly. He picked it up and started for his car radio. The computer could ID a Colorado plate in seconds.

Grace waved to Hank Guffman as they passed one another on the approach to her White Raven studio. It was surreal, thought Ben in the back seat, that life went on here while, in the Thunder Peak Wilderness, a nuclear blast had erased life in an area the size of a small town. He pushed down his rising anger and frustration and forced himself to focus.

Hank had just made his morning delivery and was driving left handed from the passenger side in his old Ford Escort with the cracked windows and 'Official Mail Carrier' decal on the door. Ben wondered why Hank didn't slide back behind the wheel for the two-mile drive to the next mailbox.

The studio looked like a Hollywood set when Grace pulled into the drive. Frost decorated the windowpanes, icicles hung from the eaves, and first snow blanketed the roof, trees and fence.

M burst from the truck and bolted towards the barn to check on Beauty, where they had relocated her.

"M! Your mask!" Grace called out. It was too late, M was halfway to the barn. Grace turned to Ben, who was stretched out in the back, his leg resting in its cast on the bench seat. "I hope Nate found time to get out here this morning, freshen Beauty's hay."

"He was just here. New truck tracks," observed Ben.

"Good. Now wait, I'll get your crutches," Grace directed him as he climbed out.

"No more crutches, darlin'," he bellowed. "Three days in the city was enough."

"City!" Grace laughed.

Ben pushed himself out into the cold air, shifted for balance and took in the sight of home after hours on the road.

"Think we still need the masks?" Grace asked as she brought the crutches anyway and escorted him inside.

"der Root said the frost would 'deactivate it.' Turn on the news and I'll check in with Nate, see what's going on," he said as made offee.

"Beauty is getting better. She's eating," announced M as she ntered.

The sound of the television came on in the other room.

"Two important stories lead the news at this hour."

"Ben," Grace called from the great room.

"I hear it."

She turned it louder.

"Despite ongoing protests, Case-Kaiser crews entered the Thunder Peak Wilderness by order of the Secretary of the Interior to harvest deadwood and elected live trees. Highly placed sources in the company say that it was difficult o find sufficient manpower because skilled loggers have been frightened away by he outbreak in that area. Eight deaths are known to have occurred in the last wo weeks.

"And yesterday - the first day of cutting - two loggers were mauled and illed by a bear. Although shot multiple times, the bear escaped and remains at arge. Citing rising costs, Case-Kaiser announced this morning that it has shut lown operations and is leaving the area. Dangerous days in the Thunder Peak ld growth wilderness."

"Yea for Thunder Peak!" Grace applauded.

"And this just in: in a related story from Boulder, Colorado," the iewsreader continued, "Epidemiologist Lotte Keene, who had been investigating he Thunder Peak Wilderness outbreak is presumed dead after her van lummeted 6,200 feet from Milner Pass into an inaccessible ravine. Details are ketchy due to the remote location of the mishap. Cause of the accident is under nvestigation..."

Ben moved as quickly as he was able to the great room, but the iewscaster had already proceeded to another story.

"That's *IT*?" Grace objected. "An important scientist dies and they don't even have a reporter out there? A helicopter Something!"

Ben clenched his jaw, unable to speak. There were no words.

He lumbered out the door and stood on the snow-covered porch. *It couldn't be*. Lotte had sounded so alive on the phone. She was going to make everything right.

Above the studio, Thunder Peak shined like a granite broadsword in the clearing air. He visualized Lotte as Diana, Rome's goddess of the hunt, sword upraised, confident of her place in the universe, equal to any challenge in the natural world.

But the mushroom was not of the natural world.

Quiet moments with her in the last week returned to him. Their professional connection had grown into friendship. She was one of those rare people who came into your life like a tornado, turned everything upside down and forced you to reevaluate what was important. Then she was gone.

She was too focused, too smart to die. *Or be killed*, suspicion darted like a cat between his thoughts. He shook his head to toss it off, but the cat lingered and began to yowl at him.

'Freud said it best, *there are no accidents*,' she had argued when he had dismissed her theory for the third time.

'In her blind rush for life, Nature expands to fill every cranny with creation. Her need for equilibrium is absolute in the long term. Yet in the short term, her exuberance creates imbalances. Man, who has climbed the million-year ladder to the top of the food chain, exalts in his powers and gets carried away. He has godlike power over so many aspects of creation that he comes to believe he *is* god.'

Now, her fundamental concern over man's potential for evil and her wariness of authority had gotten to him. He had adopted her credo of doubt.

He needed to move, to do something. He limped awkwardly across the drive to the mailbox. The thought occurred to him that he might slip and break his other leg. He chuckled bitterly. So be it. He'd still be alive, and Lotte would still be dead.

There wasn't much of anything in the mail: a bill for propane, another for feed, a mass mailed flyer from Senator Prentice's office in Washington D.C. And a small priority mail box. He checked the label. There was nothing there to tell him who it was from. The ostmark said 'Meeker Park, CO.'

Meeker Park. He didn't know anybody there. He pulled on the ardboard tab, reached inside and found four discs and a note.

He took a deep breath. The cold air burned going down. He ooked up at the Thunder Peak again and, suddenly bone weary, mped back towards the house but stopped when he saw Grace nd M at the front door watching him.

"Dear Ben,

Not much time - These contain everything I've been able to learn about the arthstar. Hide them somewhere safe. You've seen how bad it can be. Make it ood.

Just when I lost everything and needed a place to fall apart, you made me hole. I'm one lucky firedog.

Life is short, hold Grace and M close. Don't miss me too much . . .

Love, Lotte"

48

MOSCOW – THOUSAND OAKS - WASHINGTON

<u>Third Directorate, Kremlin - Moscow, Russia</u>

General Vatutin despised this arrogant Chinese bastard haranguin him. Here he was at the peak of his game in a top floor corne office of the Third Directorate overlooking Lenin's tomb and Re Square. Twenty-three years in uniform, seven of those dodgin mudjaheddin bullets, grenades, mines, and stinger missiles; th years since dodging the tentacles of interfering power seekers wh rotated through the Kremlin like drunken apparatchiks on holiday stealing the silver, embezzling what they could before being ouste to make room for the next thief.

He hated the way his thoughts turned bitter every time he ha to sit through one of these official so-called *consultations* with high ranking members of the People's Army. He loved Russia. He wa proud of his people for having taken control of their fate. The were grasping the future and making it their own. If it weren't fo those isolated old men in Beijing who sent this soldier here, toda would have been a rather pleasant workday.

But no, General Zedong felt duty-bound to lecture him on how the Russian military had lost its vision; how the People's Army was the result of uncountable centuries of vision, purpose and discipline in service to the people; how his wise leaders kept corrosive Western influences far from China's heartland; and how China would rule the entire world soon, certainly in his lifetime. "Our glorious new silent cities, for example," he beamed. "Our dedicated planners are developing entire new master planned cities the size of some nations in my homeland's rich western forestland," he bragged unabashedly.

"Silent?" asked Vatutin, as much to play the interested host as out of professional curiosity.

"While Russia takes on the high profile western style of media in which nothing is secret, our leadership guides my people quietly, patiently to build a civilization that will shame the so-called Seven Wonders of the World!"

Vatutin pretended to appear impressed by this. He knew all about the rapid pace of development of China's significant natural resources, of course. If the General hadn't gotten carried away with his particularly off-putting jingoism, he, too, would have recognized this and not behaved so amateurishly.

Vatutin toyed with the notion of dropping a hint about the Americans' research into biogenetic weapons. But why give him anything? Like every other Russian, Vatutin had a healthy fear of invasion by China. They weren't ready yet, but he could see the day coming. One thing Zedong had right was that China would indeed dominate the world, and soon. When that day came, he wanted every advantage he could use against the invaders. Sooner or later, he would get his hands on the American researcher and he could hold off this arrogant tiger before he could destroy Russia's magnificent forestlands to the southeast.

CoGen Biotech Campus - Thousand Oaks, CA

The campus in the foothills of the Santa Monica Mountains north of Malibu was darkened for the night. Construction cranes perched in the moonlight among the dozens of buildings, looking down on the collegial campus like huge dozing storks. Although the surrounding hillsides were free of development, the future of

Ventura County was foretold in the wide new roads rolled ou across open land and into the foothills where they ended, for now When CoGen's exuberant public relations executives calle Thousand Oaks paradise in recruiting literature, biotech's best an brightest came from all over the world to see for themselves an stayed.

Near the center of the campus, building No. 403 squatte behind double fencing and roving guard dog teams. The sign at th single access gate to the compound said:

AUTHORIZED PERSONNEL ONLY
Level Four
Precautions Strictly Enforced

Inside the second fence, another sign stated more clearly:

GOVERNMENT PROPERTY
U.S. DEPARTMENT OF DEFENSE
Special Biotechnology Applications Research
DOD 32(NSA)119

Interior lights glowed dimly through the tinted second floo windows. Inside, a vast laboratory with rows of benches with rack of chemical containers, beakers, dispensing and wash bottles, glas burets, cabinets and booths. The machinery of biochemistry.

In glass-walled rooms running the length of the north wall o the laboratory were biohazard isolation booths.

Biohazard decals posted every three feet warned of the extrem danger within the closed cell air-locked rooms. Another sig reminded the lab workers to have someone observe them fron outside in the event of an accidental leak or other mishap.

Within the booths were scores of planter beds in racks. In th first room were a variety of annual and perennial flowers.

The second held tree saplings: evergreen and selecte deciduous.

The third was filled with mosses, ferns, and lichens.

The last two rooms were dedicated exclusively to puffbal mushrooms ranging in dimensions from golf ball-sized to eighteen inch diameter giants.

A solitary figure in a white lab coat stood before a large light box studying chromosome stain films.

In the room next to the lab, planter beds of mushrooms grew aside glass-walled laminar flow booths.

Lotte nodded approvingly as she read the chromosome stain films. She had learned more about mushrooms and genetic recombination in one week than she would have believed possible before her time on Thunder Peak. She had plenty of help: der Root's files and the ghosts of Charley and the others haunting her in the laboratory. She couldn't escape them. They wouldn't let her rest until she defeated the earthstar mushroom. She couldn't sleep for more than an hour or two a night anyway, so she worked at a superhuman pace.

Armed with the data from Boulder, Lotte discovered that recombining the very same genes der Root had modified enabled her to not only reverse his programming of the earthstar but also to make it resistant to subsequent recombination! She couldn't do anything about the killer mushroom already out in the wrong hands. Logic told her that there couldn't be many. The carbon nanotubes-enhanced FXX strain was extraordinarily difficult to create, transport, and distribute. But the FX - the 'platform' for the FXX - she could definitely do plenty to neutralize. The ease with which she had been able to get inside the mindset of the biochemical and biogenetic weapon-makers made her question whether her original intentions had been so pure and benevolent. If she had the ability to predict twenty years earlier that biogenetic weapons were not only possible, but also inevitable, then maybe she was destined to create them.

She paled at the thought, but pushed ahead. She was on the brink of proving that she was a creator and defender, NOT a destroyer.

Rushing to the high-powered microscope, she peered intensely at proof that she was right about Gene 12. And herself.

After inoculating herself with a colorless fluid from a vial marked 'F Ant 34-a,' Lotte stepped into biohazard containment room No. 4, then into the booth filled with mature earthstars.

She held her breath and offered a silent prayer. "Please." Finally, she inhaled deeply. Nothing happened. She checked the clock through the glass wall as she exhaled slowly and waited a few moments longer. Nothing.

She took another deep breath.

Nothing.

She tapped a plump, overripe earthstar mushroom and watched a plume of fine amber dust rise into the air. Then another. And another.

She was immune. Yes!

She stripped and put her lab coat, scrubs, underwear, even the barrette holding her hair into the sterilizer furnace and made sure they were burned to ashes before stepping through a plain-looking door in the back of the room into a bright white airlock. There was a latching sound behind her and a muted hiss as the airlock pressurized. A small sign on the door behind her said: "Return to Level Four containment NOT possible through this door."

A small EXIT sign over the opposite door illuminated and she passed through it into a narrow tiled room about six feet long. When the door sealed behind her, dense steam billowed from a dozen jets and filled the room with an odorless white mist. The room temperature climbed and she felt her pores opening. She inhaled the mist and visualized the cleansing effects of the potent antibiotics infiltrating her bloodstream. After ten minutes in the room, the mist was blown out through narrow vents and another door opened.

The next chamber was a shower. After that a circular room with lamps in the walls and ceiling, and six stainless steel chaises arrayed in a circle. She pulled a package from a wall dispenser, unwrapped a pair of sterile, black plastic eye guards, laid down on one of the chaises and put on the eye guards.

"Ready," she said in a normal voice.

"UV decontamination cycle will last three minutes, commencing 3, 2, 1 . . . Intense purple light filled the room and bathed Lotte in its glow. After :90 seconds, the voice stated: "Turn over, please." She turned as instructed. The warmth of the UV lamps would have lulled her to sleep if it weren't for the excitement making her restless to finish up at CoGen and disappear again.

The lights clicked off and she exited into another tiled room lined with paper-covered benches.

"Enhanced oxygen will accelerate your body's recovery from the previous cycles. Present cycle time: thirty minutes commencing now."

She dressed in a disposable paper jumpsuit and laid down on one of the benches, but couldn't stop her mind. She needed to go. She wanted to move to the next phase of her plan and get away as quickly as possible.

Showered and changed into her own jeans, turtleneck sweater and sandals, she dialed Bernard Lassen. "I've done it, Doctor Lassen. It works," she said proudly.

"A deposit has been made to your account per your instruction. You can confirm that, if you like," responded Bernard Lassen.

"I have. Now I expect you to honor our agreement: CoGen gets my antidote, Nature gets a break, and I get my life back . . ."

Hanging up, she inserted a flash drive and uploaded her custom computer virus utility, *Datastar*. CoGen's intranet server accepted the uploaded utility in forty seconds. *Datastar* then spread its tentacles throughout the network, each operating autonomously. Instantly, *Datastar* commenced scanning files, identifying destructive recombinant genes in development. When it did, the files' data froze on screen - like victims of the modified earthstar mushroom - then deteriorated before her eyes.

The flash drive ejected automatically. She placed it and a vial of the earthstar antidote in her briefcase and locked it. Finally, she turned off the lights and left.

Her new pale blue VW EuroVan was packed for a long trip. It started eagerly. She eased it across campus without calling attention to herself or the car, accelerating only when she found the ramp to the southbound 101.

Inside the building and throughout the worldwide CoGen intranet, the *Datastar* virus spread, silently killing all new genetic virus development research files. It wouldn't touch any of the beneficial research files. Its algorithm sought out and infected CoGen's toxic combinations only, destroying them. Eventually they would defeat *Datastar*, but it would distract them from creating sinister new ones for a month or two at least, she hoped.

She couldn't undo the damage done by viruses already released into the world, but she had thrown a wrench into the machinery that was creating new killers.

Congressional Hearing Room - Washington, D.C.

"Doctor McCandle, we thank you for your fascinating tale," th
familiar voice of actor-turned-politician, Richard Reston, broke th
solemn silence of the hearing room. All eyes turned to the secor
man on the right side of the panel as he was recognized by th
chair. "Frankly, I still do not understand why it is you appearir
here in Dr. Keene's place. Are you an epidemiologist?"

"You know I am a medical doctor, Congressman Retson."

"Do you have some unique forestry credentials that I missed i
your background?"

"Congressman, I am here in Dr. Keene's place because she ha
disappeared under mysterious circumstances, which has prevente
her appearance before you today. I was her partner in th
identification of the earthstar mushroom as the source of th
Thunder Peak outbreak; I am an eyewitness to multiple deatl
caused by this biochemically-engineered mushroom; I can veri
the source, authenticity and accuracy of the documents before you

"And, as an American who up until a few days ago trusted th
basic integrity and honesty of my government, I have an obligatic
to tell you what I know and why I believe it warrants, at minimur
the restriction of clear-cutting in Oregon's Willamette Nation
Forest, or at most, a cessation of all domestic logging.

"Whatever you decide to do, I demand an immedia
investigation into the participation of this government in th
Thunder Peak deaths as well as those in Itamarati, Brazil."

The Congressmen from Texas, Oregon and Montar
immediately made motions to dismiss the witness. Committe
Chairman Buellton gaveled them down.

"You demand?" repeated the Chairman.

"I urgently request . . . sir," Ben glared.

The cable news networks were by now carrying the C-SPAI
live feed from the Hearing Room to a nationwide audience. At th
Hut Café, Longwood's citizens cheered one of their own. Na
Stimson noticed how Ben seemed dwarfed by the architecture an
outnumbered by the hundreds of opponents to his appearance i
the room. Lobbyists for every major oil, lumber and miner
company filled the gallery and jeered him despite the usually stri
prohibition against partisan displays of any kind by the chair.

"Dr. Keene was a highly experienced epidemiologist and sh
was instrumental in saving uncounted lives on every continent," h

ised his voice, determined to be heard. "Her idealism and
edication to saving life was exceeded only by the heinous nature
f her betrayal by this government, and corporations who place
rofits before people. And when she was about to expose the
errible truth, she disappeared."

"The Colorado State Trooper's report says nothing about foul
lay, Dr. McCandle," Representative Bauer of Texas reminded Ben
vith exaggerated sincerity.

"My point, precisely, Congressman," answered Ben.

Bauer made a show of surprise at Ben's answer and shook his
ead as if to say, 'I've tried to be reasonable. What am I to
onclude in the face of such blatantly irresponsible rhetoric?'

"Ask yourself who stands to gain from her death," continued
en, looking up and down the panel of faces, then ticking off the
ispects on his fingers: "Chembotan/CoGen, the DOD and . . .
ie United States Government."

Committee members, aides, lobbyists, and citizen observers
rupted at once, shouting to be heard. Buellton rapped his gavel
oudly. Leaning forward, he asked, "Are you accusing the Federal
overnment of conspiracy to cover up murder, Dr. McCandle?"

"Yes, Mr. Chairman," Ben answered plainly. "I am. I'm
ccusing you, me, and everyone who supports business as usual."

Buellton's face darkened with rage. He was losing control of his
ommittee, this hearing, and his hard-earned image of firm and fair
eadership. "DOCTOR McCandle," he roared, "I remind you that
ou are a guest of this committee--"

Unfazed, Ben responded, "The choice is yours whether to
elieve the evidence, Chairman Buellton. Resistance to change is
iatural. I lived that way. Sooner or later, however, what you refuse
o see will roll right over you," he looked directly at each of them.
Remember Darwin, Congressmen. Adapt or die."

The air suddenly filled with the pop of photographers'
lectronic flashes and the whine of motor drives. Committee
iembers watched dumbfounded as Ben stood and turned
wkwardly in his leg cast to leave. Grumbles and curses rippled
icross the assembled groups in the gallery.

Ben winked at Mary Margaret as she rushed to him. Grace slid
inder his arm and the three of them walked up the aisle for the
louble doors. The lobbyists in the gallery parted sullenly as they
iassed. The press in the back of the room formed a wall of light,

microphones and shouted questions. There was more media still i
the rotunda. As he waved them off, Ben was sure the world ha
gone completely mad.

Rainforest Research Encampment outside Itamarati, Brazil

It was late morning; the sun was at its zenith and peasant
stopped at Lotte's research station on their way home for th
midday siesta. The adults accepted their inoculations bravely an
held the younger children for theirs. Occasional crying by
frightened child stirred the other unseen creatures in the fores
The birdsong in the high branches reminded Lotte of anothe
remote forest in the United States.

Sister Paolo, a dark-skinned Portuguese woman in her thirtie
brought Lotte a bottled water and relieved Sister Theresa at th
table with the hypodermic syringes and viles labeled 'F Ant 34-a
Lotte wiped perspiration from her forehead and eyes and took
long drink from the plastic bottle.

"Graças, Irmã Paolo."

"De nada, Doutorra."

They worked in silence for a few moments. Sister Paolo'
demeanor suggested she had something to say, however, and
distracted Lotte. Finally, she asked the discreet nun what was o
her mind.

"Some *Ianquis* were seen in the village where they refueled the
Jeep and drove south. You are safe, for today at least."

Lotte continued inoculating the last of the midday patients, sa
back contentedly and looked plainly at the nun. "They will com
sooner or later, Sister. This time, you and your people will be saf
In the meantime," she nodded at the muddy but still new-lookin
EuroVan parked beside her hut, "I am packed and ready to g
anywhere there are victims and a biogenetic mystery to be solved."

"It is your calling, no?"

Lotte shrugged and smiled. "It is my nature."

Thunder Peak

In a deep ravine on the western face of Thunder Peak, sigh

ɔursed through the forest as ancient trees that had escaped the
last by virtue of their location combed the wind. To Thunder
eak's creatures after the nightmare events of the preceding week,
was the sound of life itself.

Deep in a remote alpine cave, the Bear lay on his side wearily
cking his shoulder and foreleg wounds. With a plaintive moan, he
ipped into a dream-filled sleep. His legs moved, walking even in
umber. Gradually, he slipped into a deep hibernative rest. He
ould be safe here with healing sleep his only activity until spring.

Nature would rule for one more season.

49

Officially, the evacuation of Jeng Shu, China's new industrial ci
located in the densely forested Kunlun Mountains, is attributed t
accidental contamination of the water supply. Official sources sa
that solvent from a petrochemical refinery was released when
section of pipe alongside the Nu Jiang River burst and release
toxic effluent into the region's primary watershed. An investigatio
is underway.

Chinese in the area as well as surveillance reports by th
Americans, Russians, French, Israelis, Germans, Japanese, Britis
and other nations with satellite surveillance assets believe it is
cover story.

At the United Nations and in the world press, calls for mor
openness in global environmental crises rise to a strident pitcl
China's official government news agency responds predictably:
refuses to issue visas to reporters and turns into itself as it has don
for millennia.

During a panel discussion at the 27th annual convention of th
International Forestry Management Association in Victoria, Britis
Columbia, a Chinese forestry biologist asserts the need for study c
old growth forests as integrated ecosystems rather than simpl

ploitable natural resources. New diseases – particularly in ggressively exploited areas – might be Nature's way of telling rest managers that their approach is misguided. The following change is excerpted from the seminar transcript:

Q: What diseases?

A: Sudden death, severe symptomologies. Look to the cent deaths in America's Sequoia National Forest.

Q: Are you seeing such deaths in China?

A: (PAUSE) Next question?

Q: Dr. Lee, are you aware of sudden deaths in China's gging industry?

A: The matter is under study. I cannot say.

Q: It's a simple question, Doctor.

A: (Pause) I see deaths higher than expected in aggressively gged areas. Certain areas have become toxic to animals and umans. Perhaps Nature is speaking to us.

Q: Dr. Lee, are you saying that forests are resisting logging . fighting back?

A: Are you saying they are not?

The United States Centers for Disease Control have offered gent biotechnological assistance in responding to the rising eaths in China's southwestern forests. China has refused any help d stated emphatically that the Jeng Shu situation is an internal atter. The Chinese regime insists that it will solve the crisis its wn way and without interference from the outside world.

ABOUT THE AUTHOR

MARK ROGER BAILEY is a novelist, screenwriter and director. He writes about pathfinders and the challenges that test them. An Emmy, Andy, Telly and Hermes award-winner, he has directed positioning, marketing and coverage of international events including the historic Stars & Stripes '87 America's Cup victory in Australia; major motion pictures including Jerry Maguire, Legends of the Fall, and Close Encounters; television specials such as Hollywood Gets MADD; and significant news events including the launch of the Robert Redford Conservancy for Southern California Sustainability. He and his wife live in California.

Made in the USA
Las Vegas, NV
18 October 2021